OUR LADY OF THE FLOWERS

Our Lady of the Flowers

JEAN GENET

Translated by Bernard Frechtman
Introduction by Jean-Paul Sartre

faber and faber

This edition first published in 2009
by Faber and Faber Ltd
Bloomsbury House, 74–77 Great Russell Street
London WC1B 3DA

The introduction by Jean-Paul Sartre is from the author's *Saint-Genet, comedien et
martyr*, copyright 1952 by *Librairie Gallimard*, and is published by permission of
Librairie Gallimard. The English edition of *Saint Genet* is published by Messrs. W. H.
Allen, whose permission for the use of this extract is gratefully acknowledged.

A CIP record for this book is available from the British Library

ISBN 978-0-571-25115-5

Were it not for Maurice Pilorge, whose death keeps plaguing my life, I would never have written this book. I dedicate it to his memory.

J. G.

TRANSLATOR'S NOTE

Our Lady of the Flowers (*Notre-Dame des Fleurs*) was published in a limited edition by L'Arbalète of Lyons in 1943. A trade edition, revised by the author, was issued by the Librairie Gallimard in 1951.

An English translation based on the Arbalète edition was published by the Editions Morihien of Paris in 1949. The present text, which follows the now standard Gallimard edition, has been revised and corrected for English and American publication. Like the former, it is unabridged and unexpurgated.

The translator is indebted to Richard Seaver of Grove Press for the exceptional care with which he read the translation, and takes this occasion to express gratitude for the number and diversity of his suggestions.

INTRODUCTION

by Jean-Paul Sartre

Our Lady of the Flowers, which is often considered to be Genet's masterpiece, was written entirely in the solitude of a prison cell. The exceptional value of the work lies in its ambiguity. It appears at first to have only one subject, Fatality: the characters are puppets of destiny. But we quickly discover that this pitiless Providence is really the counterpart of a sovereign—indeed divine—freedom, that of the author. *Our Lady of the Flowers* is the most pessimistic of books. With fiendish application it leads human creatures to downfall and death. And yet, in its strange language it presents this downfall as a triumph. The rogues and wretches of whom it speaks all seem to be heroes, to be of the elect. But what is far more astonishing, the book itself is an act of the rashest optimism.

French prison authorities, convinced that "work is freedom," give the inmates paper from which they are required to make bags. It was on this brown paper that Genet wrote, in pencil, *Our Lady of the Flowers*. One day, while the prisoners were marching in the yard, a turnkey entered the cell, noticed the manuscript, took it away, and burned it. Genet began again. Why? For whom? There was small chance of his keeping the work until his release, and even less of getting it printed. If, against all likelihood, he succeeded, the book was bound to be banned; it would be confiscated and scrapped. Yet he wrote on, he persisted in writing. Nothing in the world mattered to him except those sheets of brown paper which a match could reduce to ashes.

In a sense, *Our Lady* is the height of aloofness. We do not even find in it—or at least not at first—the attempt at communication (a hesitant and contradictory attempt, to be sure) that resulted in his first poem, "The Condemned Man." A convict lets himself sink like a rock to the depths of reverie. If the world of human beings, in its terrible absence, is still in some way present, it is solely because this solitude is a defiance of that world: "The whole world is dying of panicky fright. Five million young men of all tongues will die by the cannon that erects and discharges. . . . But where I am I can muse in comfort on the lovely dead of yesterday, today, and tomorrow."

The world has isolated him as if he were pestiferous, it has cooped him in. Very well, he will intensify the quarantine. He will sink to depths where no one will be able to reach him or understand him; amidst the turmoil of Europe, he will enjoy a ghastly tranquillity. He rejects reality and, in order to be even more certain that he will not be recaptured, logic itself. He is going to find his way back to the great laws of the participationist and autistic thinking of children and schizophrenics. In short, we are confronted with a regression toward infantilism, toward the childish narcissism of the onanist.

One is bored in a cell; boredom makes for amorousness. Genet masturbates: this is an act of defiance, a willful perversion of the sexual act; it is also, quite simply, an idiosyncrasy. The operation condenses the drifting reveries, which now congeal and disintegrate in the release of pleasure. No wonder *Our Lady* horrifies people: it is the epic of masturbation. The words which compose this book are those that a prisoner said to himself while panting with excitement, those with which he loaded himself, as with stones, in order to sink to the bottom of his reveries, those which were born of the dream itself and which are dream-words, dreams of words. The reader will open *Our Lady of the Flowers*, as one might open the cabinet of a fetishist, and find there, laid out on the shelves, like shoes that have been sniffed at and kissed and bitten hundreds of times, the damp and evil words that gleam with the excitement which they arouse in another person and which we cannot feel. In *The Counterfeiters*, little Boris inscribes on a piece of parchment the words: "Gas, Telephone. One hundred thousand rubles." "These six words were the open sesame of the shameful Paradise into which sensual pleasure plunged him. Boris called this parchment his *talisman*." In a certain sense, *Our Lady* is Genet's collection of erotic talismans, the thesaurus of all the "Gas, Telephone. One hundred thousand rubles" that have the power to excite him. There is only one subject: the pollutions of a prisoner in the darkness of his cell; only one hero: the masturbator; only one place: his "evil-smelling hole, beneath the coarse wool of the covers." From beginning to end we remain with him who buries himself under the covers and gathers in "my cupped hands my crushed farts, which I carry to my nose." No events other than his vile metamorphoses. At times, a secret gangrene detaches his head from his body: "With my head still under the covers, my fingers digging into my eyes and my mind off somewhere, there remains only the lower part of my body, detached, by my digging fingers, from my rotting head." At others, an abyss opens at the bottom of the hole and Genet falls into the fathomless pit. But we always come back in the end to the gesture of solitude, to the flying fingers: "a kind of unclean and supernatural transposition displaces the truth. Everything within me turns worshiper."

This work of the mind is an organic product. It smells of bowels and sperm and milk. If it emits at times an odor of violets, it does so in the manner of decaying meat that turns into a preserve; when we poke it, the blood runs and we find ourselves in a belly, amidst gas bubbles and lumps of entrails. No other book, not even *Ulysses*, brings us into such close physical contact with an author. Through the prisoner's nostrils we inhale his own odor. The "double sensation" of flesh touching itself, of two fingers of the same hand pressing against each other, gives us a phantom otherness-in-unity. This self-intimacy is traversed by an ideal separating surface, the page on which Genet writes *Our Lady of the Flowers*.

But, at the same time, this work is, without the author's suspecting it, the journal of a detoxication, of a conversion. In it Genet detoxicates himself of himself and turns to the outside world. In fact, this book *is* the detoxication itself. It is not content with bearing witness to the cure, but concretizes it. Born of a nightmare, it effects—line by line, page by page, from death to life, from the state of dream to that of waking, from madness to sanity—a passageway that is marked with relapses. Before *Our Lady*, Genet was an esthete; *after* it, an artist. But at no moment was a decision *made* to achieve this conversion. The decision *is Our Lady*. Throughout *Our Lady* it both makes and rejects itself, observes and knows itself, is unaware of itself, plays tricks on itself and encumbers itself everywhere, even in the relapses. On every page it is born of its opposite, and at the very moment it leads Genet to the borderline of awakening, it leaves on the paper the sticky traces of the most monstrous dream. At times the art of the tale aims only at bringing the narrator's excitement to its climax, and at times the artist makes the excitement he feels the pretext of his art. In any case, it is the artist who will win. Seeking excitement and pleasure, Genet starts by enveloping himself in his images, as the polecat envelops itself in its odor. These images call forth by themselves words that reinforce them; often they even remain incomplete; words are needed to finish the job; these words require that they be uttered and, finally, written down; writing calls forth and creates its audience; the onanistic narcissism ends by being staunched in words. Genet writes in a state of dream and, in order to consolidate his dreams, dreams that he writes, then writes that he dreams, and the act of writing awakens him. The consciousness of the word is a local awakening within the fantasy; he awakes without ceasing to dream. Let us follow him in these various phases of his metamorphosis.

I — THE CREATURES

Under his lice-ridden coverings, this recumbent figure ejects, like a starfish, a visceral and glandular world, then draws it back and dissolves it within itself. In this world, creatures wriggle about for a moment, are resorbed, reappear, and disappear again: Darling, Our Lady, Gorgui, Gabriel, Divine. Genet relates their story, describes their features, shows their gestures. He is guided by only one factor, his state of excitement. These figures of fantasy must provoke erection and orgasm; if they do not, he rejects them. Their truth, their density, are measured solely by the effect they produce upon him.

Here is Divine. Divine is Genet himself, is "a thousand shapes, charming in their grace, [that] emerge from my eyes, mouth, elbows, knees, from all parts of me. They say to me, 'Jean, how glad I am to be living as Divine and to be living with Darling.'" Genet objectifies himself, as we all do in our dreams. As a sovereign creator, he cannot *believe* in the real existence of Darling; he believes in him through Divine. As Divine, he projects all his masochism, his vainglorious desire for martyrdom. As Divine, he has the disturbing and voluptuous expeiience of aging; he "realizes" his dreadful fear of growing old. She is the only one of his creatures whom he does not desire; he makes her be desired by the others. She excites him through Darling or Gorgui. Divine is an ambiguous character who serves both to bring his entire life into focus in the lucidity of his gaze and to let him plunge more deeply into sleep, to sink to the depths of a cosy horror, to drown in his opera.

The others—all the others, except the girl-queens—are the creatures and objects of his feminine desires. The whole graceful procession of Pimps, those lovely vacant-eyed does, are the means he chooses for being petted, pawed, tumbled, and entered.

Here is how Darling was born: "Very little of this Corsican remains in my memory: a hand with too massive a thumb . . . and the faint image of a blond boy. . . . The memory of his memory made way for other men. For the past two days, in my daydreams, I have again been mingling his (made-up) life with mine. . . . For two successive days I have fed with his image a dream which is usually sated after four or five hours. . . . I am worn out with the invented trips, thefts, rapes, burglaries . . . in which we were involved. . . . I am exhausted; I have a cramp in my wrist. The pleasure of the last drops is dry. . . . I have given up the daydream. . . . I have quit, the way a contestant in a six-day bicycle race quits; yet the memory of [him] refuses to disappear as the memory of my dream-friends usually does. It floats about. It is less sharp than when the adventures were taking place, but it lives in me nevertheless. Certain details persist more obstinately in remaining. . . . If I continue, he will rise up, become erect.

. . . I can't bear it any longer. I am turning him into a character whom I shall be able to torment in my own way, namely, Darling Daintyfoot."

Our Lady "was born of my love for Pilorge."

Here is Gorgui: "Clément Village filled the cell with an odor stronger than death. . . . I have tried to recapture in the cell where I am now writing the odor of carrion spread by the proud-scented Negro, and thanks to him I am better able to give life to Seck Gorgui. . . . You know from *Paris-Soir* that he was killed during the jailbreak at Cayenne. But he was handsome. He was perhaps the handsomest Negro I have ever seen. How lovingly I shall caress, with the memory of him, the image I shall compose, thanks to it, of Seck Gorgui. I want him too to be handsome, nervous, and vulgar."

Sometimes a gesture alone remains, or an odor, or a simple relic whose erotic potency, which has been experienced again and again, is inexhaustible. A few schematic features can be sufficient: what remains of Roger the Corsican? A nebulous, "faint image of a blond boy," and a few solid elements: a hand, a gait, a chain, a key. Around these sacred remains Genet drapes another flesh. He "fits" them with other memories richer and less sacred: the color of a skin or a look which excited him elsewhere, on another occasion. Darling's eyes will be weary after love-making; Genet will "cull" this fatigue and the circles under the eyes from the face of another youngster whom he saw leaving a brothel. This mask of flesh is becoming to the archaic skeleton. Whereupon Genet gets an erection. This erection is not merely the index of his achievement, but its goal—as if Flaubert had described the poisoning of Emma Bovary only to fill his own mouth with ink. The character has no need to be judged according to other criteria. There is no concern with his mental or even physical verisimilitude: Darling remains the same age all his life. To us who are not sexually excited, these creatures should be insipid. And yet they are not. Genet's desire gives them heat and light. If they were conceived in accordance with verisimilitude, they would perhaps have a more general truth, but they would lose that absurd and singular "presence" that comes from their being born of a desire. Precisely because *we* do not desire them, because they do not cease, in our eyes, to belong to another person's dream, they take on a strange and fleeting charm, like homely girls who we know are passionately loved and whom we look at hesitantly, vaguely tempted, while wondering: "But what does he see in her?" Darling and Divine will always baffle the "normal" reader, and the more they elude him, the more true we think them. In short, we are fascinated by someone else's loves.

As soon as the character is modeled, baked, and trimmed, Genet launches him in situations which he evaluates according to the same rules. He is telling *himself* stories in order to please *himself*. Do the situation and the character harmonize? Yes and no. The author is the only one to decide. Or rather, it is not he who decides, but the capricious and blasé little fellow he carries between his thighs. Depending on Genet's mood of the moment, Darling will be victim or tyrant. The same male who cleaves the queens like a knife will stand naked and dirty before the guards who manhandle him. Does he lack coherence? Not at all. Amidst his metamorphoses he retains, without effort, a vital, ingrained identity that is more convincing than the studied unity of many fictional characters because it simply reflects the permanence of the desire it arouses. At times Genet submits to the Pimps, at times he betrays them in secret, dreaming that they are being whipped. But in order for his pleasure to have style and taste, those whom he adores and those who are whipped must be the *same*. The truth about Darling is that he is both the glamorous pimp and the humiliated little faggot. That is his coherence. Although his other features are only dream images, they have, nevertheless, the gratuitousness, mystery, and stubbornness of life. Each time Darling is arrested, he is proud of dazzling the jail-birds by the elegance of his attire. The prospect delights him in advance. This is the "kind of detail one doesn't invent." And indeed, Genet did not invent it. But he did not observe it either. He simply has his hero experience in glory what he himself experienced in shame. Humiliated at having to appear for questioning in a prisoner's outfit, he takes his revenge in fantasy, in the guise of Darling.

We can be sure that our "dreamer" never leaves reality; he *arranges* it. That is why this introvert, who is incapable of true relations with others, can create such vivid figures as Darling, Divine, and Mimosa. He weaves a dream around his experiences, and that means, most of the time, that he simply changes their sign. Out of his hatred for women, his resentment against his guilty mother, his desire for femininity, his realism, his taste for ceremonies, he will create Ernestine. She will try to murder her son because Genet's mother abandoned him and because the author dreams of killing a young man. She will shoot wide of the mark because Genet knows that he is not of the "elect," that he will never be a murderer. She will march in Divine's funeral procession as the servant girl will march in that of her child[1] because Genet, when he was a child, followed (or dreamed of following) that of a little girl with whom he was in love. All these traits will finally compose a fleeting and inimitable figure that will have the contingency and truth of life and that will be the obverse of the fake coin of which Genet himself is the reverse. He plays, he alters a situation, a character, sure of never making an error since he is obeying his desires, since he

[1] In *Funeral Rites.*

checks on his invention by his state of excitement. At
times he stops and consults himself; he hesitates playfully:
"So Divine is alone in the world. Whom shall I give her
for a lover? The gypsy I am seeking? . . . He accompanies
her for a while in the passing crowd . . . lifts her from the
ground, carries her in front of him without touching her
with his hands, then, upon reaching a big melodious house,
he puts her down . . . picks up from the mud of the gutter
a violin . . . [and] disappears." The scenery is put up as he
goes along, as in dreams: Genet brings out the props when
they are needed, for example, the gypsy, a leitmotif of his
solitary pleasures. We are told he plays the guitar. The
reason is that Genet was once in love with a guitarist. Besides, for this fetishist the guitar is an erotic object because it has a round, low-slung rump. We read in his
poem "The Galley:" "Their guitar-like rumps burst into
melody"; the low-pitched sounds of the plucked strings
are the farts that "stream from downy behinds." Later, in
Funeral Rites, Jean Decarnin will be metamorphosed into
a guitar. In this autistic thinking, the guitarist *is* his own
guitar. When Genet brings Divine and the gypsy together, immediately "he lifts her from the ground without
touching her with his hands." On his penis, of course. Our
lonely prisoner dreams of straddling a huge, powerful
member that rises slowly and lifts him from the ground.
Later, it will be the mast that Genet climbs in *Miracle of
the Rose* and the cannon in *Funeral Rites.* But this pattern
is linked more particularly—I do not know why—with his
desire for gypsies. In *The Thief's Journal,* he will spring
into the air on a gypsy's prick. The scene is merely outlined in *Our Lady,*[1] for the reason that other forces and
desires prevented it from being filled in. This triumphal
cavalcade was not meant for poor Divine. It does not suc-

[1] In fact, Genet dropped the entire passage from the revised edition. (Translator's note.)

ceed in exciting Genet; he immediately loses interest in it. From the gypsy is born a melody, which floats for a moment, then suddenly condenses and becomes a "melodious house," just a bare detail, the minimum required for the gypsy to be able to push open a door and disappear, dissolved in his own music.

Genet shows everything. Since his only aim is to please himself, he sets down everything. He informs us of his erections that come to nothing just as he does of those that come off successfully. Thus, his characters have, like *real* men, a life *in action,* a life involving a range of possibilities. Life in action may be defined as the succession of images that have led Genet to orgasm. He will be able to repeat the "effective" scenes indefinitely, at will, without modifying them, or to vary them around a few fixed elements. (Here too a selection takes place. There are some whose erotic power is quickly exhausted: the "dreams are usually sated after four or five hours." Others, which have deeper roots, remain at times in a state of virulence, at times inert and floating, awaiting a new embodiment.) The possibilities, on the other hand, are all the images that he has caressed without attaining orgasm. Thus, unlike *our* possibilities, which are the acts that we can and, quite often, do perform, these fictional possibilities represent simply the missed opportunities, the permission that Genet pitilessly refuses his creatures. He once said to me: "My books are not novels because none of my characters make decisions on their own." This is particularly true of *Our Lady* and accounts for the book's desolate, desert-like aspect. Hope can cling only to free and active characters. Genet, however, is concerned only with satisfying his cruelty. All his characters are inert, are knocked about by fate. The author is a barbaric god who revels in human sacrifice. This is what Genet himself calls the "Cruelty of the Creator." He kicks Divine toward saintliness. The unhappy girl-queen undergoes her ascesis in an agony. Genet diverts himself by imposing upon her the progressive austerity he wishes to achieve freely himself. It is the breath of Genet that blights the soft flesh of Divine; it is the hand of Genet that pulls out her teeth; it is the will of Genet that makes her hair fall out; it is the whim of Genet that takes her lovers from her. And it is Genet who amuses himself by driving Our Lady to crime and then drawing from him the confession that condemns him to death. But cannot the same be said of every novelist? Who, if not Stendhal, caused Julien Sorel to die on the scaffold? The difference is that the novelist kills his hero or reduces him to despair in the name of truth, or experience, so that the book may be more beautiful or because he cannot work out his story otherwise. If Julien Sorel is executed, it is because the young tutor on whom he was modeled lost his head. The psychoanalyst has, of course, the right to seek a deeper, a criminal intention behind the author's conscious motives, but, except for the Marquis de Sade and two or three others, very few novelists take out their passions on their characters out of sheer cussedness. But listen to Genet: "Marchetti will remain between four white walls to the end of ends. . . . It will be the death of Hope. . . . I am very glad of it. Let this arrogant and handsome pimp in turn know the torments reserved for the weakly." Moreover, the author himself, that owl who says "I" in the heart of his darkness, hardly comes off any better. Later, he will reserve certain active roles for himself. We shall see him strike and dominate Bulkaen, or slowly get over the death of Jean Decarnin. Later, Jean Genet will become "the wiliest hoodlum," Ulysses. For the time being, he is lying on his back, paralyzed. He is passively waiting for a judge to decide his fate. He too is in danger of being sent to a penal colony for life. Yes, *Our Lady of the Flowers* is a dream. Only in dreams do we find this dreadful passivity. In dreams the characters wait for their night to end. In dreams, stranglers pass through walls, the fugitive has leaden soles, and his revolver is loaded with blanks.

II — THE WORDS

Yet, by the same movement that chains him in his work to these drifting, rudderless creatures, he frees himself, shakes off his reverie and transforms himself into a creator. *Our Lady* is a dream that contains its own awakening.

The reason is that the imagination depends on words. Words complete our fantasies, fill in their gaps, support their inconsistency, prolong them, enrich them with what cannot be seen or touched. It was long ago pointed out that no image can render so simple a sentence as "I'm going to the country tomorrow." This is perhaps not entirely so, but it is true that abstract connections are expressed more frequently by our inner monologues than by the play of our imagination. "Marchetti will remain between four white walls to the end of ends." We can be fairly sure that this sentence occurred to Genet spontaneously and that it replaced images which were too vague or schematic. The reason is that there are abstract relationships which can be erotic. The *idea* that Marchetti will remain a prisoner *forever* is certainly even more exciting to this resentful sadist than the *image* of his being humiliated by the guards. There is something final and inexorable about it that only words can render. Images are fleeting, blurred, individual; they reflect our particularity. But words are social, they universalize. No doubt Genet's language suffers from deep lesions; it is stolen, faked, poeticized. No matter: with words, the Other reappears.

We observed earlier that Genet's two contradictory

components (quietism-passivity-masochism; activism-fe-
rocity-existence) united for a moment in masturbation
only to disunite after pleasure. Genet the onanist at-
tempted to make himself an object for a subject which,
disguised as Darling or Gorgui, was no other than himself,
or, as subject, he hounded Divine, an imaginary object
and also himself. But the Word expresses the relationship
of Narcissus to himself; he is *with* the subject *and* with
the object. It is no accident that the Word frequently accompanies the act of masturbation, that Gide shows Boris
uttering his incantatory formula as an "open sesame." The
onanist wants to take hold of the word *as an object*. When
it is repeated aloud or in a whisper, it immediately ac-
quires an objectivity and presence that are lacking in the
object. The image remains something absent; I do not
really *see* it, nor do I hear it. It is I who exhaust myself
trying to hold it up. But if I utter the word, I can hear it.
And if I succeed in taking my mind off myself when the
word comes out of my mouth, if I succeed in forgetting
that it is I who say it, I can listen to it as if it *emanated from
someone else*, and indeed even as if it were sounding all
by itself. Here is a phrase that still vibrates in Genet's ears.
What does he say? "To the end of ends." To the end of
ends Marchetti will remain in jail. It seems that an absolute sentence has been delivered in the cell and that the
images have taken on flesh. To the end of ends: is it therefore true? But this *object* which has surged up in the real
world has a shape, a face. Genet can pluck from its visual
physiognomy or sound structure the erotic object which
he lacks. When he speaks of Darling's "downy behind" we
can be sure that he does not couple these words for the
truth or beauty of the assemblage, but for its power of
suggestion. He is enchanted with the feminine ending of
the masculine noun *derrière* (behind). Fake femininity?
Fake masculinity? The rump is the secret femininity of

males, their passivity. And what about *douillet* (downy)?
Where does its *meaning* begin? Where does its significance end? The fleshy blossoming of the diphthong suggests a kind of big, heavy, wet, silky flower; the trim,
dainty flectional ending evokes the coy grace of a fop.
Darling drapes himself in his behind as in a quilted wrap
(*douillette*). The word conveys the thing; it is the thing
itself. Are we so far from poetry? Can it be that poetry is
only the reverse side of masturbation?

Genet would not be true to himself if he were not fascinated by the sacrilege to be committed. We saw a while
ago that he *listened* to words. He is now going to direct his
attention to the verbal act, to perceive himself in the
process of talking. The naming of forbidden pleasures is
blasphemous. The man who masturbates humbly, without
saying a word or being too preoccupied with what his
hand is doing, is half forgiven; his gesture fades out in
the darkness. If it is named, it becomes *the* Gesture of the
masturbator, a threat to everyone's memory. In order to
increase his pleasure, Genet names it. To whom? To nobody and to God. For him, as for primitives, the Word has
metaphysical virtues. It is evil, it is delightful that an obscene word resound in the semi-darkness of his cell, that
it emerge from the dark hole of his covers. The order of
the universe is thereby upset. A word uttered is word as
subject; heard, it is *object.* If you read *Our Lady of the
Flowers,* you will see the sentence manifest one or the
other of these verbal functions, depending on the poet's
mood. Read the description of the love-making of Darling
and Divine, or of the first night that Divine spent with
Gabriel, or of Gorgui's sexual play with Divine and Our
Lady. Read them, for I dare not transcribe them or comment upon them too closely. You will be struck, in most
cases, by the incantatory use of the present tense, which is
intended to draw the scene into the cell, on to Genet's

body, to make it contemporary with the caresses he lavishes on himself. It is also a finical, slightly breathless precision, expressing an eagerness to find the detail that excites. Here the word is a quasi-object. But this hoarse, hasty, scrupulously careful voice that is panting with incipient pleasure, suddenly breaks. Genet's hand puts down the pen; one of the scenes is hastily finished off: "and so on"; another ends with a series of dots. The next moment, Genet, still in a swoon, moans with gratitude: "Oh, I so love to talk about them! . . . The whole world is dying of panicky fright. Five million young men . . . will die. . . . But where I am I can muse in comfort on the lovely dead of yesterday, today, and tomorrow. I dream of the lovers' garret." This time the word is subject; Genet wants to be heard, to create a scandal. This abandoned "where I am I can muse in comfort" is the giggle of a woman who is being tickled. It is a challenge.

At the beginning, Genet *utters* the words or dreams them; he does not write them down. But before long these murmurs cease to satisfy him. When he listens to himself, he cannot ignore the fact that it is he who is speaking. It is in the eagerness for pleasure that he speaks, and he does so in order to excite himself further. And as soon as he surprises himself in the act of speaking, his sacrilegious joy vanishes. He is aware that he alone hears himself and that a moan of pleasure will not keep the earth from turning. Therein lies the trap: he will write. *Scripta manent:* tomorrow, in three days, when he finds the inert little sketch that confronts him with all its inertia, he will regard the phrase as an erotic and scandalous object. A drifting, authorless sentence will float toward him. He will read it for the first time. A sentence? Why not a whole story? Why not perpetuate the memory of his latest pleasures? Tomorrow a dead voice will relate them to him. He writes obscene and passionate words as he wrote his poems, in order to reread himself.

This is only an expedient. Even when he reads the sentence, Genet still knows who set it down. He is therefore going to turn, once again, to the Other, for it is the Other who confers upon the word a veritable objectivity—*by listening to it*. Thus do toilet-poets engrave their dreams upon walls; others will read them, for example that gentleman with a mustache who is hurrying to the street urinal. Whereupon the words become huge, they scream out, swollen with the other's indignation. Unable to *read* what he writes, Genet empowers the Others to carry on for him. How could it be otherwise? They were already present in the heart of the word, hearers and speakers, awaiting their turn. It was Another who spoke those words which were uttered in the absolute; it was to Others that Genet dedicated these blasphemies which were addressed to the absolute. What Others? Certainly not the prisoners in the neighboring cells who are singing and dreaming and fondling themselves in their melancholy solitude? How could he hope for a moment to scandalize these brothers-in-misery? But, long before, he had been taken by surprise and singled out by men. Later, when he became a thief, he danced before invisible eyes in empty apartments. Is it not to this same omnipresent and fictive public that he is going to dedicate his solitary pleasures? The Just—*they* are his public. It is they whom he is taunting and by whom he wants to be condemned. He provokes outraged voyeurs in order to take his pleasure in a state of shame and defiance.

Thus far, there is no art. Writing is an erotic device. The imaginary gaze of the gentle reader has no function other than to give the word a new and strange consistency. The reader is not an end; he is a means, an instrument that doubles the pleasure, in short a voyeur despite himself.

Genet is not yet speaking to *us*; he is talking to himself, though wanting to be heard. Intent on his pleasure, he does not so much as glance at us, and though his monologue is secretly meant for us, it is for us as witnesses, not as participants. We shall have the strange feeling that we are intruders and that nevertheless our *expected* gaze will, in running over the words on the page, be caressing Genet physically. He has just discovered his public, and we shall see that he will be faithful to it. A real public? An imaginary public? Does Genet write without expecting to be read? Is he already thinking of publishing? I imagine that he himself does not know. As a thief, he streamed with light, wanted to be caught, to end in a blaze of glory, and at the same time, frightened to death, did all he could to elude the cops. It is in the same state of mind that he starts to write.

A dream public, dream orgies, dream speeches. But when the dream word is written down, it becomes a true word. Divine, writes Genet, "sat down . . . and asked for tea." This is all that is needed to generate an event in the world. And this event is not the materialization of Divine, who remains where she is, in Genet's head or around his body, but quite simply the appearance of letters on paper, a general and objective result of an activity. Genet wanted to give his dream characters a kind of presence. He failed, but the dream itself, as signification, is present on the sheet "in person"; the sentence is impregnated with an event of the mind and reflects it. Whereupon Genet ceases to feel; he knows that he *did* feel. Let us recall little Culafroy's reverie that was condensed into the single word "suns," which he uttered in the presence of a real listener. Genet immediately observes: "It was the word-poem that fell from the vision and began to petrify it." He has also said of Divine that "it was necessary that [she] never formulate her thoughts aloud, for herself. Doubtless there had been times, when she had said to herself aloud 'I'm just a foolish girl,' but having felt this, she felt it no longer, and, in saying it, she no longer thought it." When confronted with the words that were uttered, she thinks that she thought it. She reflects upon herself, and she who reflects is no longer she who experienced: a pure Divine gazes at herself in the mirror of language. Similarly with Genet: while writing, he has eyes only for Divine, but as soon as the ink is dry he ceases to see her, he sees his own thought. He wanted to *see* Divine sitting down and asking for tea. A metamorphosis takes place beneath his pen and he sees himself thinking that Divine is sitting down. This mystifying transformation is the exact counterpart of that which led him to his semi-madness. Formerly, he wanted to act, and all his acts changed into gestures. Now, he wants to make a gesture, to brave an imaginary public, and an act is reflected in the signs he has traced: "I wrote that." Has he thus awakened at last? In one sense, he has, but in another, he is still dreaming, steeped in his excitement, tangled up in his images. A curious kind of thinking indeed, a thinking that becomes hallucinated, reflects upon its hallucinations, recognizes them as such and frees itself from them only to fall again into the trap of a delirium that extends to its reflection. It envelops its madness in a lucid gaze that disarms it, and its lucidity is in turn enveloped and disarmed by madness. The dream is at the core of the awakening, and the awakening is snugly embedded in the dream. Let us read a passage taken at random from *Our Lady:* "Darling loves Divine more and more deeply, that is, more and more without realizing it. Word by word, he grows attached. But more and more neglects her. She stays in the garret alone. . . . Divine is consumed with fire. I might, just as she admitted to me, confide that if I take contempt with a smile or a burst of laughter, it is not yet—and will it some day be?—out of contempt for contempt, but rather in order not to be ridiculous, not to be reviled, by anything or anyone, that I have placed myself lower than dirt. I could not do otherwise. If I declare that I am an old whore, no one can better that, I discourage insult. People can't even spit in my face any more. And Darling Daintyfoot is like the rest of you; all he can do is despise me. . . . To be sure, a great earthly love would destroy this wretchedness, but Darling is not yet the Chosen One. Later on, there will come a soldier, so that Divine may have some respite in the course of that calamity which is her life. Darling is merely a fraud ('an adorable fraud,' Divine calls him), and he must remain one in order to preserve *that appearance of a rock walking blindly through* my tale (*I left out the d in blindly, I wrote 'blinly'*).[1] It is only on this condition that I can like him. I say of him, as of all my lovers, against whom I butt and crumble: 'Let him be steeped in indifference, let him be petrified with blind indifference.' Divine will take up this phrase and apply it to Our Lady of the Flowers." A story at first, up to "Divine is consumed with fire." Genet lets himself be taken in by it, grows excited; this is the dream. Suddenly, the awakening: jealous of the emotion that Divine's misfortunes have aroused in him and that they may arouse in an imaginary reader, he cries out in annoyance: "I too could make myself interesting if I wanted to." Implying: "But I have too much pride." This time, he speaks about *himself*, not about an invented hero. Is this a *true* awakening? No, since he continues to affirm the real existence of Divine: "I might, just as she admitted to me . . ." But the very next moment Divine is himself: "All [Darling] can do is despise me." An awakening this time? Yes and no. Genet has resorbed Divine into himself, but Darling continues to live his independent life. Here

[1] The words in italics do not appear in the revised edition. (Translator's note.)

and there we come upon sentences which seem to have
been written without a pause and which give the impression that Genet, completely taken up with lulling his
dream, has not reread what he has set down. Certain
sentences limp because they have not been looked after;
they are children that have been made to walk too soon:
"I might, just as she admitted to me, confide that if I take
contempt with a smile or a burst of laughter, it is not yet—
and will it some day be?—out of contempt for contempt,
but rather in order not to be ridiculous, not to be reviled, by anything or anyone, that I have placed myself
lower than dirt." Two propositions have collided: this contempt that I take "with a smile or a burst of laughter is not
out of contempt for contempt, but rather in order not to
be ridiculous [infer: that I like it]" and "it is not out
of contempt for contempt but rather in order not to be ridiculous that I have placed myself lower than dirt." In
short, at this level the words are inductors with relation to
each other; they attract and engender one another, in accordance with grammatical habits, within an unheeding
consciousness that wants only to weep tears over itself.
The sentence takes shape all by itself; it is the dream. But
immediately afterward, Genet writes, parenthetically: "I
left out the d in blindly, I wrote 'blinly.'" This time he reflects *on the sentence*, hence on his activity as a writer. It
is no longer the love of Divine and Darling that is the object of his reflection, but the slip of his sentence and of his
hand. This error in spelling draws his attention to the
meaning of the sentence. He contemplates it, discovers it,
and decides: "Divine will take up this phrase and apply it
to Our Lady of the Flowers." This time we feel we are
reading a passage from *The Journal of Crime and Punishment* or *The Journal of The Counterfeiters*. A perfectly
lucid writer is informing us of his projects, goes into detail
about his creative activities. Genet awakens; Darling in

turn becomes a pure and imaginary object. Will Darling be the Chosen One? No, "Darling is merely a fraud . . . and he must remain one, etc." But *who is it* who has just awakened? The writer or the onanist? Both. For we are given two reasons explaining why Darling must not change: "in order to preserve my tale," and "it is only on this condition that I can like him." Now, the former is that of the creator who wants his work to keep its severity of line, but the latter is that of the masturbator who wants to prolong his excitement. In the end he seems to merge with himself as the pure will that keeps the fantasies well in hand, for he writes, with sudden tranquillity: "It is Darling whom I cherish most, for you realize that, in the final analysis, it is my own destiny, be it true or false, that I am draping (at times a rag, at times a court robe) on Divine's shoulders. Slowly but surely I want to strip her of every vestige of happiness so as to make a saint of her. . . . A morality is being born, which is certainly not the usual morality. . . . And I, more gentle than a wicked angel, lead her by the hand." But this very detachment seems suspect. Why plume oneself on it, why bring it to our attention? Is it that he wants to shock us? Where does the truth lie? Nowhere. This lucid dreamer, this "evil angel," retains within himself, in a kind of undifferentiated state, the masturbator, the creator, the masochist who tortures himself by proxy, the serene and pitiless god who plots the fate of his creatures and the sadist who has turned writer in order to be able to torture them more and whose detachment is merely a sham. *Our Lady* is what certain psychiatrists call a "controlled waking dream," one which is in constant danger of breaking up or diverging under the pressure of emotional needs and which an artist's reflective intelligence constantly pulls back into line, governing and directing it in accordance with principles of logic and standards of beauty. By itself, the story becomes plodding, tends toward stereotypes, breaks up as soon as it ceases to excite its author, contradicts itself time and again, is enriched with odd details, meanders off, drifts, bogs down, suddenly reappears, lingers over trivial scenes, skips essential ones, drops back to the past, rushes years ahead, spreads an hour over a hundred pages, condenses a month into ten lines, and then suddenly there is a burst of activity that pulls things together, brings them into line and explains the symbols. Just when we think we are under the covers, pressed against the warm body of the masturbator, we find ourselves outside again, participating in the stony power of the demiurge. This development of onanistic themes gradually becomes an introspective exploration. The emotional pattern begets the image, and in the image Genet, like an analyst, discovers the emotional pattern. His thought crystallizes before his eyes; he reads it, then completes and clarifies it. Whereupon reflection is achieved, in its translucent purity, as *knowledge* and as *activity*.

A rapid study of the "free play" of his imagination will enable us to understand this better. We are going to see Genet inflate his dream to the breaking point, to the point of his becoming God, and then, when the bubble bursts, to discover he is an author.

III — THE IMAGES

He amuses himself. His comparisons and metaphors seem to obey only his fancy. The sole rule of this sinister playfulness is that he be pleased. But this is the sternest of rules. Nothing is so constraining as to have to flatter the quirks and fancies of a single master. The master requires of his fictions that they show him things as they are—that is his realism—but with the slight displacement that will enable him to see them as he would like them to be. Behind each image is, to use the words of Kant, a pattern "in unison with the principle and the phenomenon, which makes possible the application of the former to the latter." In the case of Genet the poet, the principles are his basic desires, the rules of his sensibility, which govern a very particular approach to the world. The patterns come afterward. They organize the images in such a way that the latter reflect back to him, through the real, his own plan of being. Their structure and "style," their very matter, express Genet and Genet only. The stones, plants, and men of which he speaks are his masks. His imagination has a certain homosexual and criminal twist.[1]

*
*   *

There are two types of unification in modern poetry, one expansive, the other retractile. The aim of both is to enable us to perceive an esthetic order behind the freaks of chance. But the first tendency—which is that of Rimbaud —forcibly compels natural diversity to symbolize an *explosive unity*. We are gradually made to see in a miscellaneous collection the breaking up of a prior totality whose elements, set in motion by centrifugal force, break away from each other and fly off into space, colonizing it and there reconstituting a new unity. To see the dawn as a "people of doves" is to blow up the morning as if it were a powder keg. Far from denying plurality, one discovers it everywhere, one exaggerates it, but only to present it as a moment in a progression; it is the abstract instant that

[1] It must be understood that to *prove* is also a function of the imagination. The imagination *represents* objects to us in such a way as to incline our judgment in the direction we wish. The drawings of a madman do not simply *express* his terrors; they aim at maintaining them and confining him within them.

congeals it into an exploding but static beauty. Impenetrability, which is an inert resistance of space, the sagging of a dead weight, is transformed into a conquering force, and infinite divisibility into a glorious burst of continuity; persons are refulgent sprays whose dynamic unity is combustion. If this violence congeals, the flare falls in a rain of ashes. We shall *then* have discontinuity and number, those two names of death. But as long as the explosion lasts, juxtaposition signifies progress. *Beside* means *beyond.* For each object, scattered everywhere, in all directions, launched with all the others upon an infinite course, to *be* is to participate in the raging tide whereby the universe at every moment wins new areas of being from nothingness. This Dionysian imagery gladdens our hearts, fills us with a sense of power. It derives its force from an imperial pride, from a generosity that gushes forth and spends itself utterly. Its aim is to force the externality of Nature to reflect to man his own transcendence. For those who want "to change life," "to reinvent love," God is nothing but a hindrance. If the unity is not dynamic, if it manifests itself in the form of restrictive contours, it reflects the image of their chains. Revolutionaries break the shells of being; the yolk flows everywhere.

Compared to them, how *miserly* Genet seems (as does Mallarmé). His patient will-to-unify is constricting, confining; it is always marking out limits and grouping things together. His aim is not to present externality as an expansive power, but to make of it a nothingness, a shadow, the pure, perceptible appearance of secret unities.[1] In or-

---

[1] If I were not afraid of opening the way to excessive simplification and of being misunderstood, I would say that there is a "leftist" turn of imagination and a "rightist" one. The former aims at representing the unity that human labor forcibly imposes upon the disparate; the latter, at depicting the entire world in accordance with the type of a hierarchical society.

der to do so, he reverses the natural movement of things; he transforms centrifugal into centripetal forces. "A cherry branch, supported by the full flight of the pink flowers, surges stiff and black from a vase." As we read this sentence from *Our Lady,* we actually feel a transformation taking place in our very vision. The image does, to be sure, begin with a movement; in Genet's pan-sexualism, the erection of the penis plays a very special role. But the erectile movement—stiffening, hardening, swelling—is not at all explosive. It accords very well with the poet's essentialism. The penis proceeds from potentiality to the act, *regains* its favored form, that is, its natural limits, from which it will depart only to collapse. The cherry branch is thus a penis. But in the very same sentence its expansive force disappears. It *surged* stiff and black from a vase; it is now borne up by flowers. It is passive, indolently supported by angels. A flowering branch normally suggests the image of a blossoming, of an expansion, in short, of a centrifugal explosion. The poetic movement parallels the natural movement and goes from the tree to the bud, from the bud to the flower. But Genet's image, instead of bringing the flowers *out* of the branch, brings them *back* to it, glues them to the wood. The movement of the image is from without inward, from the wings to the axis.[1] In general, his poetic patterns present closed and stable units. When Divine enters Graff's Café at about two A.M., "the customers were a muddy, still shapeless clay." The creator's power agglutinates the customers, presses the discrete particles against each other and gives them the unity of a paste. The next moment, "as the wind turns leaves, so she turned heads, heads which all at once became light." The allusion to the wind creates circularity. The whirl of faces that are turned inward reflects Di-

[1] See also, at the end of the book: "The swan, borne up by its mass of white feathers, *cannot* go to the bottom of the water," etc.

vine, at the center. The movement closes in on itself; a form has just been born, a form which has the calm cohesion of geometric figures. In the same way, a few astringent words are enough to transform the courtroom audience into a single being: "The courtroom crowd . . . is sparkling with a thousand poetic gestures. It is as shuddering as taffeta. . . . The crowd is not gay; its soul is sad unto death. It huddled together on the benches, drew its knees and buttocks together, wiped its collective nose, and attended to the hundred needs of a courtroom crowd." And further on: "The judge was twisting his beautiful hands. The crowd was twisting its faces." The moments of a succession are united by a dynamic form: "A clerk called the witnesses. They were waiting in a little side room. . . . The door opened, each time, just enough to let them edge through sideways, and one by one, drop by drop, they were infused into the trial." The words "drop by drop," though stressing the fact that each witness is a *singular object,* refer to a unity without parts, to the undifferentiated continuity of a liquid mass filling the "little side room" and pressing against the door as against the inner surface of a vase. Divine is sitting in a bar. Customers enter, men who have perhaps never seen each other. They come from diverse places and have diverse destinies. In order to unify them, Genet makes use of the revolving door: "When the revolving door turned, at each turn, like the mechanism of a Venetian belfry, it presented a sturdy archer, a supple page, an exemplar of High Faggotry." The word "presented" agglutinates these individuals, changes them, by analogy, into fashion models *presenting* gowns, subjects their comings and goings to a providential design, makes of each angle of the revolving door a niche, a little cell, a loggia. This time the privileged witness—Divine, Genet's substitute—is external to the system, and the painted wooden figures turn their faces outward. But the word "mechanism" recaptures them, assembles them about their axis of rotation, and sets the merry-go-round in motion, thus re-establishing the reign of circularity.

This passage and others in the same vein warrant our comparing this kind of arch fancy to the humor of Proust. Proust, too, has a tendency to tighten the bonds of the real world, which are always a little loose, to give an additional turn of the screw, to assume that there is an order among objects that actually have none. The author of *Cities of the Plains*, also a homosexual and a recluse, likewise practiced "a selection among things which rids [him] of their usual appearance and enables [him] to perceive analogies." One need only recall the description of the restaurant at Rivebelle: "I looked at the round tables whose innumerable assemblage filled the restaurant like so many planets as planets are represented in old allegorical pictures. Moreover, there seemed to be some irresistibly attractive force at work among these divers stars, and at each table the diners had eyes only for the tables at which they were not sitting. . . . The harmony of these astral tables did not prevent the incessant revolution of the countless servants who, because, instead of being seated like the diners, they were on their feet, performed their evolutions in a more exalted sphere. No doubt they were running, one to fetch the hors d'oeuvres, another to change the wine or with clean glasses. But despite these special reasons, their perpetual course among the round tables yielded, after a time, to the observer the law of its dizzy but ordered circulation. . . . People began to rise from table; and if each party while their dinner lasted . . . had been held in perfect cohesion about their own, the attractive force that had kept them gravitating round their host of the evening lost its power at the moment when, for coffee, they repaired to the same corridor that had been used for the tea parties; it often happened that

in its passage from place to place some party on the
march dropped one or more of its human corpuscles who,
having come under the irresistible attraction of the rival
party, detached themselves for a moment from their
own."[1] The same circular, planetary units; the same homosexual archness, which, in the case of one, metamorphoses
men into wooden effigies and, in that of the other, into
stellar masses; the same fundamental resentment; the
same contemplative quietism; the same Platonism. But in
the case of Proust, who is more positive, the whimsical
humor is counteracted by the will to give his comparisons
a scientific basis. Genet, who rejects modern culture, bases
his on magic, on craftsmanship. He pushes the "organization" of his universe to the point of identifying persons
with their symbolic properties and attributes.[2] Here is Divine's fan: ". . . she would pull the fan from her sleeve . . . ,
unfurl it, and suddenly one would see the fluttering
wing in which the lower part of her face was hidden. Divine's fan will beat lightly about her face all her life." At
times, an entire human body, an entire person, extends
through others and serves as their link, their entelechy,
their unity. "He was waiting for Alberto, who did not
come. Yet all the peasant boys and girls who came in had
something of the snake fisher about them. They were like
his harbingers, his ambassadors, his precursors, bearing
some of his gifts before him, preparing his coming by
smoothing the way for him. . . . One had his walk, another
his gestures, or the color of his trousers, or his corduroy, or

[1] *Within a Budding Grove*, translated by C. K. Scott Moncrieff.
[2] For Mallarmé, the element of chance and the externality of the
Real are expressed by the word "outspread" (*éployé*): "all the futile abyss outspread." And the unifying act of the poet is expressed
by its opposite: "to fold" (*reployer*): "to fold its division." It is thus
a matter of compressing multiplicity until the elements interpene-
trate and form an indivisible totality.

Alberto's voice; and Culafroy, like someone waiting, never doubted that all these scattered elements would eventually fuse and enable a reconstructed Alberto to make [a] solemn, appointed, and surprising entrance." Of course, this is merely a way of saying that, while waiting for Alberto, Culafroy thinks he recognizes him in every passerby. But Genet takes this pretext for kneading the matter of the world and pursuing his act of unification. Here, too, the movement is retractile. It is not a matter of Alberto's exploding in all directions and spattering on all the figures, but rather of a condensation of scattered elements which suddenly spring together to effect the synthetic reconstitution of the snake charmer. Even when Genet says of Our Lady that he *is* a wedding feast, his aim is not to disseminate Our Lady over all the wedding guests, but to bring them all together in Our Lady,[1] just as he brought all the country people together in Alberto. He effects a recomposition.

In short, one might contrast the humanistic universe of Rimbaud or Nietzsche,[2] in which the powers of the negative shatter the limits of things, with the stable and theological universe of Baudelaire or Mallarmé, in which a divine crosier shepherds things together in a flock, imposing unity upon discontinuity itself. That Genet chose the latter is only to be expected. In order to do evil, this outcast needs to affirm the pre-existence of good, that is, of order. At the very source of his images is a will to compel reality to manifest the great social hierarchy from which he is excluded. There is a manly generosity in the explosive

---

[1] The fact is that the content suggests an incipient outburst, for the image is meant to signify the joyous blossoming of the murderer. But this burst is immediately checked and organized, just as the stiff, black surging is checked and fixed forever by its contours.

[2] Nietzsche used to call himself an explosion, an infernal machine.

images of Rimbaud. They are ejaculations; they manifest the unity of the *undertaking*. An entire man plunges forward. It is his freedom in action which will unite the diverse elements. He *maps out* the lines, and they exist through the movement that maps them out. The quiet feminine passivity of Genet thrusts him into a ready-made world in which the lines and curves struggle against the dispersion and splintering *ad infinitum* by means of an objective power of cohesion intermediary between activity and passivity.[1] When the prisoner *wants to please himself*, he does not imagine that he is acting, that he himself is imposing unity upon diversity, but he pleases himself in being, *as creator*, at the source of the magical cohesion that produces the objective unity of the things. In short, incapable of *carving out* a place in the universe for himself, he *imagines* in order to convince himself that he has created the world which excludes him.[2]

When he was free, he roamed over Europe, convinced that the events of his life had been planned by Providence, of which he was the sole concern. Rejecting even the idea of chance, his mind acted upon his perception so that it could discern everywhere the signs of an external and providential order. When he thought he had discovered beneath the disordered multiplicity of human beings an

[1] This perhaps parallels a distinction between the "feminine" imagination (which reinforces in the woman—when she is her master's accomplice—the illusion of being at the center of a beautiful order) and the "manly," explosive imagination (which contains and transcends anguish by means of the images it forms).

[2] In Mallarmé, the act is not the unification of the diverse by a progressive operation, but a *form in action* which, if it exists, appears all at once and which is dispersed by the diversity of the real: "the place a lapping below, sufficient for dispersing the empty act." It goes without saying that between Mallarmé and Rimbaud, the two pure and opposite types of imagination, there exists a series of mixed, transitional types.

esthetic form that insured their cohesion, he allowed his
intense satisfaction to substitute for actual fact. ". . . populous streets on whose throng my gaze happens to fall: a
sweetness, a tenderness, situates them outside the moment; I am charmed and—I can't tell why—that mob of
people is balm to my eyes. I turn away; then I look again,
but I no longer find either sweetness or tenderness. The
street becomes dismal, like a morning of insomnia." The
reason is that he had succeeded in discovering an order
in this concourse of chance elements. And if he found it
there, he did so because he had put it there. His questing
eyes roamed over nature as if it were a picture puzzle in
which he had to discover the hunter's rifle between the
branches or in the grass. Later, during his period of im-
prisonment, he again made use of these patterns, but instead of using them to decipher, he transformed them into
rules for building. In reconstructing the universe in his
book, he satisfies his desire since he makes himself both
the Providence that governs things and the man who discovers the designs of Providence. As we have already
seen, in most of his descriptions a circular movement is
organized and the objects, which are drawn into this
round, turn their faces to the motionless center. In general, this motionless mover is Genet himself or one of his
substitutes. But even when the center is merely a figure-
head, this planetary attraction which makes things gravi-
tate about a central mass is to him a symbol of Providence.
He reconstructs the real on every page of his book in such
a way as to produce for himself proof of the existence of
God, that is, of his own existence.

This hierarchical conception of a world in which forms
dovetail has a name: essentialism. Genet's imagination is
essentialist, as is his homosexuality. In real life, he seeks
the Seaman in every sailor, the Eternal in every pimp. In
his reverie he bends his mind to justifying his quest. He

generates each of his characters out of a higher Essence; he reduces the episode to being merely the manifest illustration of an eternal truth.

The chief characters in *Our Lady,* those whose function is to embody Genet's destiny, can be viewed as examples of Platonic idealism: "to Divine, Darling is only . . . the physical expression, in short, the symbol of a being (perhaps God), of an idea that remains in heaven." Most of the time, however, his essentialism takes on the features of Aristotelian alchemy, because he forces his fictions to furnish him with proof of the powers of language. He wants to convince himself by means of his own tale that naming changes being. When he was named a *thief* he was transformed; since then, as we have seen, the verb *to be* has been enchanted. "His head is a singing copse. He himself *is* a beribboned wedding feast skipping . . . down a sunken April road." "The policemen held me up. . . . They *were* the Holy Women wiping my face." The verb in these sentences expresses an inert and instantaneous metamorphosis intermediary between the state and the flux, as the cohesion of forms, which we mentioned above, is intermediary between activity and passivity. Genet says "Gabriel is a soldier." This sentence does not have the same taste in his mouth as in ours. He immediately adds: "The army is the red blood that flows from the artilleryman's ears; it is the little lightfoot soldier of the snows crucified on skis, a spahi on his horse of cloud that has pulled up at the edge of Eternity; it is masked princes and brotherly murderers in the Foreign Legion"; etc. To us, "to be a soldier" means to exercise a function for a limited time, to become a subject who has been given abstract rights and duties. To Genet it means to share suddenly and magically in the virtues, mysteries, and legendary history of a huge, multicolored beast; to be a soldier is to be the entire army, just as the latest bearer of a noble name is

both his entire family and his entire House. This is so because Genet, an exile from our bourgeois, industrial de-
mocracy, was cast into an artificial medieval world. He
was thrust into a grim feudal system; he belongs to the
military society of "strong" and "weak." For him, *to be* is
to be identified with a group that confers the honors of
the name. The progression from one caste to another is a
new birth which occurs by formal *naming*, and the new
member of the caste possesses, within himself, the entire
caste: a sailor is the entire fleet, a murderer is all of crime.
Names are titles, and "titles are sacred." In the twelfth
century this conception of society was justified by an essentialism that extended to all of nature. In order for a
knight to be defined by his membership in the order of
knighthood, God had to have created the world in such a
way that the rose was defined by its belonging to the order
of florality. The social hierarchy is legitimate if God willed
it, and the manifest proof of this will is to be found in the
hierarchy of things. Inversely, the thinking of an agricul-
tural community is naturally essentialist; wheat, cattle, all
the goods of this world, reproduce by birth, and these
births, which are sacred, symbolically manifest initiation,
just as initiation symbolizes birth.

This philosophy of concept was destroyed by science
and industrial practice which substituted for it a philosophy of judgment. Inactive, parasite of an industrious society, convinced of his predestination, Genet must liken
his thinking to the idle and parasitic thinking of the medieval clerk. The logical framework of the social world
which he invents for his ethical needs is the military
hierarchy of concepts. Does he *believe* in it? Of course
not. He is far too intelligent. He cannot entirely overlook
the discoveries of science nor the working world that terri-
fies and disgusts but also fascinates him. But *precisely because he does not believe in it*, he must convince himself.

One of the major demands he imposes upon his imagination is that it present to him the everyday world—our world—in such a light as to *verify* his *conceptualism*. From the universe that he recreates with the purpose of offering it to himself as an object of imaginary experience one could derive the principles of a scholastic philosphy: *the concept is the form that is imposed upon all matter* (in other words, it is initiation or birth that creates the person); *in changing form, the same matter changes being* (in other words, one moves from one caste to another as a result of naming); *any reality that, in any aspect of its nature, pertains to a concept immediately becomes the singular expression of the entire concept*—thus, every object can *simultaneously* or *successively* express immutable and conflicting Ideas, and these Ideas are concrete totalities, actual principles of individuation (in other words, since the group is eminently present in each of its members and confers upon each his sacred reality, an individual who belongs to several groups at the same time is simultaneously and entirely each of these groups). Is this a kind of Aristotelianism? One would think so at times, for it seems—this is the theory of gesture which we set forth above—that men and things are visited by essences that settle upon them for a moment and disappear: if they make a movement or strike another attitude or if there is simply a change in the surrounding environment, they immediately receive a new name, a new being. Policemen have only to be attentive to Divine and they immediately become Holy Women. And in order for Divine to be an infanta all that is needed is a four-wheeled carriage and an iron gate. The animating force of all these metamorphoses is, as for the medieval clerk, *analogy;* every apparent analogy is a sign of deep identity. Resting against the cushions of a carriage, Divine is in a position analogous to that of an infanta; therefore she *is* an infanta. The weight of the word "infanta" crushes the details of the image that might check the metamorphosis and does away with Divine's masculinity and poverty. In the realm of the imaginary, the operation succeeds every time: "the royal idea is of this world." Take the word *royal* as in the old expression "royal art": this is conceptualism. The aim of this masturbator is very like that of the alchemists. He wants to give lead the form of gold. For Genet this means to place, in imagination, a piece of lead in a system of relations that ordinarily refer to gold, and then imperceptibly to speak of lead as if it were gold.

Time—opaque, irrational, nullifying time, the time of chance and of ignorance, the time through which we grope our way—disappears in this perspective. An event is nothing other than a transubstantiation, in short a naming. A being receives a new essence and a new name. When Genet describes a scene minutely, he does so because it excites him. Moreover, these favored—and, in general, erotic—scenes are *frequentative*. That is, he gathers together in a single narration a hundred events that recurred in the course of time in an identical way. And, in that case, the tale is not, as one might think, a later "digest" of a hundred experiences whose fundamental identity is gradually isolated. On the contrary, the identity is posited at the very beginning; it is the concept that is temporalized, the sacred essence that is projected into and developed in duration. Thereupon, the event becomes a ceremony, and the tale changes into a ritual. At times the characters exchange words, but these words reach us in the flow of the sacred discourse that announces the rites. Most often the words are the rites themselves: "She meets him in the evening on the promenade of the boulevard, where he tells her very sweetly the story of his life, for he knows nothing else. And Divine says: 'It's not your life story you're telling me, Archangel, but an underground passage of my own, which I was unaware of.' Divine also says: 'I love you as if you were in my belly,' and also: 'You're not my sweetheart, you're myself. My heart or my sex. A branch of me.' And Gabriel, thrilled, though smiling with pride, replies: 'Oh, you little hussy!' His smile whipped up at the corner of his mouth a few delicate balls of white foam." Note the sudden change to the past tense; the *words* are in the present because they are *carmina sacra*.

As for the events which he reports, they are of only secondary interest to him. We know that he loathes history and historicity. In the case of a unique and dated fact that cannot be passed over in silence, Genet limits himself to a summary account of the experience. He describes a petty agitation which has no interest other than that of preparing for the formal appearance of the *essence*. For example, Divine *meets* Gabriel. The onanist hesitates for a long time: in what form will this event give him the most pleasure? Will Gabriel appear in a baron̄presented" by the revolving door? Will he be walking down a steep street? Or will he emerge from a grocery shop? Genet finally does not choose. The circumstances matter little to him, provided they comply with requirements whose origin is his own choice of himself. All that is necessary is that they magnify the meeting without failing to satisfy Genet's deep resentment against all handsome men. In short, it is a matter of inventing the overwhelming advent of an archangel with the soul of a doll. The revolving door will *present* the handsome soldier in the magnificence of a crystal setting. Immediately Genet compares its incessant rotation to the "mechanism of a Venetian belfry," the effect of which is to transform all who enter, and Gabriel himself, into painted wooden figures. If the soldier goes down "an almost vertical street," he is changed by his movement into an angel who swoops down upon Divine from the sky.

Genet immediately re-establishes equilibrium by comparing him, in parentheses, to a bewitched dog. The ringing of the grocery bell preludes the meeting majestically,
like a theater orchestra announcing the coming of the
emperor. But the soldier who comes out of the shop is
holding in his hand a very childish object: a surprise package. Wooden beauty, dog-archangel, emperor with the
soul of a doll. Slyly and discreetly the tale is composed in
such a way as to suggest in the order of the succession the
major qualities that constitute the essence of the "boy-
queens": a staggering beauty, a soul that is a "looming
emptiness, sensitive and proud." The story is a projection of
the concept into the temporal flow. But time itself is suddenly effaced. All these details have been given only to prepare for the meeting. Now, the meeting is intemporal: "I
should have liked to talk to you about encounters. I have a
notion that the moment that provoked—or provokes—them
is located outside time, that the shock spatters the surrounding time and space." This is so because the meeting is not
to be confused with the clash of two atoms that happen to
be projected against each other and that cling to each
other. It is the appearance of a celestial form which "of
two makes but one," a conceptual and intemporal unit that
is imposed upon the soldier and the old queen. From that
moment on, the characters themselves are transformed.
Gabriel becomes *the* soldier; Divine is no longer Divine,
the vicious "camp" who will kill a child and destroy Our
Lady: "Aging Divine sweats with anxiety. She *is* a poor
woman who wonders, 'Will he love me?'" And the tran-
sition from duration to timelessness is marked by the sub-
stitution of the present for the past tense. "The revolving
door present*ed* . . . Gabriel appear*ed* . . . he *had* just
bought a surprise package . . . he *was* a soldier." And
then suddenly: "Divine, of course, *calls* him Archangel.
. . . He lets himself be worshiped without batting an eye-

lash. He *doesn't* mind. . . ." etc. We are on the inner side
of the meeting, in the eternal present of love.

Genet has systematically neglected the particulars. We
shall never know what Divine and Gabriel said to each
other, which of the two took the initiative in approaching
the other, etc. Nevertheless, Genet, like all great writers,
is a storyteller, and we shall find in *Our Lady* several accounts of specific and dated events, for example the murder of old Ragon or the trial of Our Lady of the Flowers.
But even then the fictional or pseudo-fictional episodes
offer a surprising mixture of the temporal and the eternal.
Genet, who is both a realist and an idealist, shows himself
in his accounts to be both an empiricist and a Platonist.
These accounts offer at first the resistance and irrational
opacity of the event only to be metamorphosed all at once
into classifications and descriptions of essence. In Plato,
the hierarchy of ideas represents the immutable truth; the
myth introduces time, space, and movement into this calm
sphere. In Genet, the relations are reversed, but in any case
it is art and art alone which, in both writers, links truth to
the myth. Art alone enables *Our Lady of the Flowers* to be
both the "golden legend" and the botany of the "under-
world." It is art that gives this tear-soaked manuscript the
air of being a "Mirror of the World." G. K. Chesterton said
that the modern world is full of Christian ideas run wild.
Our Lady of the Flowers would surely have confirmed him
in his view. It is an "Itinerary of the Soul toward God,"
the author of which, run wild, takes himself for the
Creator of the universe. Every object in it speaks to us of
Genet as every being in the cosmos of Saint Bonaventura
speaks to us of God. Sabunde, following Lully, declares
that the Creation "is a book," that God "has given us two
books," that of Holy Scriptures and that of Nature. Genet
reverses the terms. For him, the Book is the Creation of
the World; Nature and the Holy Scriptures are one and

the same. This is not surprising since, in his view, words contain within themselves the substantial reality of things. The being of the thief is contained in the name "thief." Hence, the being of trees and flowers, of animals and men, is contained in the words that designate them. For the medieval philosophers, "life is only a pilgrimage to God: the physical world is the road that leads us to Him. The beings along the way are signs, signs that may at first seem puzzling to us, but if we examine them carefully, faith, with the aid of reason, will decipher, under characters that are always different, a single word, a call that is always the same: God."[1] Replace God by Genet and you have the universe of *Our Lady of the Flowers,* whose only reason for being is to express Genet—who has written only in order to be read by Genet—and to recall him constantly to love of Genet.[2]

Each creature is the word incarnate. As in Bonaventura, none of them is in itself the sufficient reason for its existence; each of them opens out in order to reveal, in its depths, its creator. In each of them, multiple forms are graded hierarchically so as to constitute a unit. Each is a microcosm that symbolizes the whole universe and, through it, God the creator of the universe. Note how the following few lines recall medieval poetry, the attraction of like by like, the participations, the magical action of analogy: "Children ran about in the glades and pressed their naked bellies, though sheltered from the moon, against the trunks of beeches and oaks that were as sturdy as adult mountaineers whose short thighs bulged beneath their buckskin breeches, at a spot stripped of its bark, in such a way as to receive on the tender skin of their little white bellies the discharge of sap in the spring." Whiteness of the little bel-

[1] Gilson, *La Philosophie au Moyen Age.*

[2] "Creatura mundi est quasi quidam liber in quo legitur Trinitas fabricatrix."

lies, whiteness of the moon. At the contact of the children's flesh, the trees became flesh and their sap sperm. The tree symbolizes the man. In the following passage, the man symbolizes an entire forest: "Under his rough blue bark he wore a white silk shirt, which blends with the blue linen of the pajamas, and their slowly wafted entanglement is the oriflamme of Joan of Arc which floats very blandly at the end of a banner, sole pillar of a basilica."[1] And finally he symbolizes everything, he is a little world that concentrates the great world within itself: "What is a malefactor? A tie dancing in the moonlight, an epileptic rug, a stairway going up flat on its belly, a dagger on the march since the beginning of the world, a panicky phial of poison, gloved hands in the darkness, a sailor's blue collar, an open succession, a series of benign and simple gestures, a silent hasp." And: "Swallows nest under his arms. They have masoned a nest there of dry earth. Snuff-colored velvet caterpillars mingle with the curls of his hair. Beneath his feet, a hive of bees, and broods of asps behind his eyes."[2] Genet's reveries about words ("the poetry . . . contained in the word *esclave* (slave), in which are found . . . the word *clé* (key), and the word *genou* (knee)" recall those of Vincent de Beauvais and Honorius of Autun (mulier-mollis aer; cadaver-caro data vermibus); his bestiary evokes that of Alexander Neckham. When he writes, for example: "Certain animals, by their gaze, make us possess at one swoop their absolute being: snakes, dogs," he brings to mind the definitions in *The Book of the Treasure:* "The cock is a domestic bird that

[1] This passage was dropped from the revised edition. (Translator's note.)

[2] Cf. *Elucidarium:* "The flesh of man is the earth, his breath is the air, his blood the water, the fire is his vital heat, his eyes are the sun and the moon, his bosom receives the humours of the body as the sea the waves," etc.

dwells among men and by its voice tells the hours of the day and night and the changes of the weather . . . when the crocodile conquers men, it weeps as it eats them." Our industrial twentieth century has witnessed the birth of three medieval edifices, of unequal value: the work of Giraudoux, *Ulysses*, and *Our Lady of the Flowers*.

Thus, Genet is God. When he was free, he wished to be only the *object* of providential solicitude, and if he identified himself with Providence, he did so chiefly to be sure of being well treated. In short, he was still *of the world*. In prison, he lets go, he drifts out of the universe. In the isolation of the cell, the captive's imagination takes a cosmic turn. He gives his characters the All for setting. "Darling is a giant whose curved feet cover half the globe as he stands with his legs apart in baggy, sky-blue silk underpants." "Your face, like a lone nocturnal garden in Worlds where Suns spin about!" And again: "Snow was falling. About the courtroom, all was silence. The Criminal Court was abandoned in infinite space, all alone. It had already ceased to obey the laws of the earth. Swiftly it flew across stars and planets." In a later work too, Genet will revert to this strange longing of a soul that wants to be all because it is nothing: "A blazing or casual meditation on the planetary systems, the suns, the nebulae, the galaxies, will never console me for not containing the world. When confronted with the Universe, I feel lost." In fact, even when the universe is not mentioned, it is present; it slips into Divine's garret, into the dormitories of the reform school. The silence of the young inmates is "the silence of the jungle, full of its pestilence, of its stone monsters . . ."; "the hand of the man condemned to death . . . which I see when he puts it through the grating of his cell . . . is the Space-Time amalgam of the anteroom of death." Time and again Genet says of his heroes that they are "alone in the world." And when he refuses Divine the happiness of

loving and being loved so as to doom her more surely to
the heaven of his black mystique, he apologizes for not
saving her by "a great *earthly* love." The adjective stresses
Divine's relationship with the entire globe. In short, his
characters are not first defined by the relations they maintain with their fellows but by the place they occupy in
Creation. Before being human and social, the persons and
events have a religious dimension: they have dealings
with the All. If Divine and Darling suddenly became conscious of themselves and their solitude, they could say,
with the mystics, "God, the world, and I." And God, of
course, is the great barbaric goddess, Genet, the Mother,
Genemesis, who probes them with her finger tip. And as if
that were still not enough, this savage demiurge takes
pleasure in the universalizations, the morbid generaliza-
tions that are found particularly in schizophrenics. Every
event refers to the entire world because it makes the individual think of all the events of the same type that are
taking place on earth at the same moment: "The corpse of
the old man, of *one of those thousands of old men whose
lot is to die that way,* is lying on the blue rug." In the outhouse, the child Genet finds "a reassuring and soothing
peace . . . [feels] mysteriously moved, because it was there
that *the most secret part of human beings* came to reveal
itself." At other times, he starts from the universal, then,
on a sudden impulse, stops short at a particular exemplar,
just as Napoleon would suddenly swoop down on one of
the soldiers of his Old Guard and pinch his ear: "Recently
[the guards] have been wearing a dark blue uniform. . . .
They are aviators fallen from the sky. . . . They are guardians of tombs." And so on for two pages. Then, suddenly,
laterally, at the turn of a sentence, Genet introduces *a*
guard, who seems the embodiment of all jailers. "Not a
flower bespatters their uniform, not a crease of dubious
elegance, and if I could say of one of them that he walked

on velvet feet, it was because a few days later he was to betray, to go over to the opposite camp, which is the thieving camp. . . . I had noticed him at mass, in the chapel. At the moment of communion, the chaplain left the altar. . . ." It is as if a movie camera, as in King Vidor's *The Street*, were first fixed on the city, ranged slowly over the panorama, stopped at *a* house, approached *a* window, slid along ideal rails, entered *a* room and there, from among a thousand characters, all of them more or less alike, suddenly focused upon *an* individual who thereupon woke up and started living. This is the sport of a god.

Apart from the very particular case of philosophical intuition, one is rarely able to perceive creatures against the background of the universe, for the reason that they are all involved in the world and are equally part of it. If a given clerk, a given magistrate, wanted to view the earth in perspective, he would have to cut himself off from his function, his family, would have to break the bonds of his social relationships and, from his self-enclosed solitude, consider men as if they were painted objects. The novelist himself often has difficulty in establishing this distance between himself and his creation. No sooner are his characters conceived than they enter into various relationships with other characters, and the latter with others, and so on. The author exhausts himself in the effort to follow these relations in detail; he sees things and people through the eyes of his heroes, who are threatened by specific dangers and thrust into particular situations; he never has the leisure to raise his head and take a commanding view of the whole. In fact, if he has any fellow feeling for the human beings about whom he is writing, he will plant his feet on the ground with them. Only a god can take a lofty view of his work and of the living creatures that people it, and he can do so because he has never been in the world and has no relation with it other than that of having

created it. A god, or a pariah whom the world has re-
jected. Society excluded Genet and locked him out; it
drove him from nature. He was forced from the very beginning into the solitude that the mystic and the meta-
physician have such difficulty in attaining: "The whole
world that mounts guard around the Santé Prison knows
nothing, wishes to know nothing of the distress of a little
cell, lost amidst others." For this captive, the universe is
everything that is denied him, everything from which the
walls of his prison separate him. He, in turn, rejects what
is denied him; his resentment finishes the job: "The world
of the living is never too remote from me. I remove it as far
as I can with all the means at my disposal. The world withdraws until it is only a golden point in [a] somber . . . sky."
When he creates an imaginary universe on paper, he produces it at a respectful distance. It is the same universe
from which he was excluded, as far away and inaccessible
as the other, and it discloses totality because of its remote-
ness. This absence of connection with external reality is
transfigured and becomes the sign of the demiurge's independence of his creation. He works at arm's length, he
stands clear of the object he is sculpting. In the realm of
the imaginary, absolute impotence changes sign and becomes omnipotence Genet plays at inventing the world in
order to stand before it in a state of supreme indifference.
The "golden point in a somber sky" ends by becoming the
sole object of the creator's efforts, just as it is the object of
all the captive's thoughts. He molds his characters—even
those who have no function other than that of exciting him
—out of common clay, at a distance, and they appear to
him at once in their relation to the All. Divine and Darling
are inhabitants of Montmartre and Montmartre is a prov-
ince of the Universe. They met on the street to which
Genet will perhaps never go back; they frequent bars to
which he cannot return. They are *beings of the outside,*

and their *involvement in all Being* is not meant to mani
fest to Genet *his* own presence but to let him see his absence from All in the most favorable light, to convince him
that this absence is deliberate. If he is not in the midst of
men, it is because he has drawn them from the clay and
fashioned them in his own way, it is because he governs
their destinies. Since the pariah and God are alike external
to nature, it will suffice for the pariah, in his cell, to dare
invent being: he will be God. Genet creates in order to enjoy his infinite power. However, his too-human finiteness
makes it impossible for him to conjure up the celestial
sphere and the globe in the detailed distinctness of their
parts; he sees the world as a big, dark mass, as a dim jumble of stars, in short, *as a background*. Genet fakes; unable to follow the royal progression of Creation, he creates
his heroes *first* so as to introduce *afterward* into each of
them a primordial and constituent relation to the universe.
No matter—it suffices to look at Divine or Darling in order
for this unseen, unnamed universe which they imply to
spread its dark velvet about them.

To us, this overweening pride and reckless unhappiness
often seem exquisitely naïve. The just man, immersed in
his community, determines each individual's importance,
including his own, by means of an infinite system of refer-
ences in which each man serves as a measure for all and
each. Whatever the object he considers, he knows that its
dimensions vary with the perspective, distance, or unit of
comparison; that what appears to him to be a mountain
will be a molehill to someone else and that the other's
point of view is neither more nor less true than his. But
Genet, who is shut in, has no point of comparison. If he
serves a two-year sentence, he is equidistant from Brazil
and the Place Pigalle, that is, two years away. He does
not touch the earth; he soars above it. Since he is equally
absent from everything, his imagination is omnipresent;

he is not in space. Every object therefore takes on for him the dimensions his fancy confers upon it, and these dimensions are *absolute*, that is, they are not given as a relationship of the object with other objects but as the immediate relationship of the thing to its creator. They can increase or diminish without those of the other varying, and since Genet wishes to ignore the severe and disagreeable laws of perspective—which are all right for the free citizens of French society—a hoodlum in Montmartre and a star in the sky seem to him equally close. Often he amuses himself by enlarging or shrinking a victim (all things remaining equal, moreover), in order to punish or test or glorify him. This ghastly book has at times the naïve poetry of the early astrolabes and maps of the world. Against a background of oceans, mountains or fields of stars appear animals and persons—the Scorpion, the Ram, Gemini—all of the same size, all equally alone. But this strange freshness is only an appearance. We sense behind it the maniacal will—which has become exacerbated in prison—to regard the Nay as the symbol of the Yea and the Nought as the symbol of the All. Precisely because he feels lost "when confronted with the universe," he wants to delude himself into thinking that he is creating the universe. If his characters are cosmic, it is because he is confined in "the obscene (which is the off-scene, not of this world)." The God of the Middle Ages wrote "the book of creatures" to reveal his existence to man, his only reader. Similarly with Genet: his "book of creatures" is *Our Lady of the Flowers*, and he intends it for only one reader, only one man, himself. By their suffering and purity, Our Lady and Darling, saints and martyrs, bear witness before this wonderstruck man to his Divine existence.

So Genet has become God in reverie. He creates the world and man in his image; he manipulates the elements, space, light-years; he has gone quite mad. But the awaken-

ing is contained in the dream, for in the depths of his delirium this imaginary creator of Reality connects with himself as a real Creator of an imaginary world. His feeling of
omnipotence leaves him with a taste of bitterness and
ashes. His characters are too docile; the objects he describes are both blinding and too pallid. Everything collapses, everything ends; only the words remain. To be
frightened, at the height of one's power, by silence and
the void, to elect to be God, to produce beings by decree
and to find onself a man and a captive, to feel a sudden
need of others in the lofty pride of solitude, to count on
others to confer upon one's creatures the flesh, density,
and rebelliousness that one is incapable of giving them—
such is the lot of the creator of images. The artist is a God
who has need of human beings. It is not through their
self-sufficiency that the creatures escape their creator, but
through their nullity. Genet and Jouhandeau, ambushed
in Nothingness, hoped to avoid the gazé of God, who sees
only Being. Their fictions play the same trick on them.
Owing to the modicum of reality that Genet communi-
cates to her, Divine *is Genet*. She merges with him; she
dissolves into a kind of turbidity, into moistness and
swoons. She can *be Divine* only insofar as she is not Genet,
that is, in so far as she is *absolutely nothing*.

Thus, the characters in *Our Lady of the Flowers*, born,
for the most part, of Genet's fancy, change into quiet
exigencies; they will live only if he believes in them. Genet
the Creator therefore calls Genet the reader to the rescue,
wants him to read and be taken in by the phantasmagoria.
But Genet cannot read his work; he is too aware that he
has put into it what he wanted to find in it, and he can find
nothing in it precisely because he cannot forget what he has
put into it. So long as he fondled them in reverie, the figures seemed domesticated and familiar; when they are set
down on paper, they are reproaches, shadows that can

neither take on flesh and blood nor vanish, and that beg *to be:* "Forget what you know, forget yourself, prefer us, imagine that you're meeting us, believe in us." And since Genet is powerless to animate them, to confer *objectivity* upon them, they beg to exist for all, that is, through all. If the "book of creatures" was composed in order to tell men about God, there had to be a God to write it and men to read it, and Genet cannot be God and man at the same time. Now that his dreams are written down, he is no longer either God or man, and he has no other way of regaining his lost divinity than to manifest himself to men. These fictions will assume a new objectivity for him if he obliges others to believe in them. And at the core of all his characters is the same categorical imperative: "Since you don't have faith enough to believe in us, you must at least make others adopt us and must convince them that we exist." In writing out, for his own pleasure, the incommunicable dreams of his particularity, Genet has transformed them into exigencies of communication. There was no invocation, no call. Nor was there that aching need for self-expression that writers have invented for the needs of personal publicity. You will not find in Genet the "fateful gift" and "imperiousness of talent" about which the highminded are in the habit of sounding off. To cultivated young men who go in for literature, the craft of writing appears first as a means of communication. But Genet began to write in order to affirm his solitude, to be self-sufficient, and it was the writing itself that, by its problems, gradually led him to seek readers. As a result of the virtues —and inadequacies—of words, this onanist transformed himself into a writer. But his art will always smack of its origins, and the "communication" at which he aims will be of a very singular kind.

Our Lady of the Flowers

Weidmann appeared before you in a five o'clock edition, his head swathed in white bands, a nun and yet a wounded pilot fallen into the rye one September day like the day when the world came to know the name of Our Lady of the Flowers. His handsome face, multiplied by the presses, swept down upon Paris and all of France, to the depths of the most out-of-the-way villages, in castles and cabins, revealing to the mirthless bourgeois that their daily lives are grazed by enchanting murderers, cunningly elevated to their sleep, which they will cross by some back stairway that has abetted them by not creaking. Beneath his picture burst the dawn of his crimes: murder one, murder two, murder three, up to six, bespeaking his secret glory and preparing his future glory.

A little earlier, the Negro Angel Sun had killed his mistress.

A little later, the soldier Maurice Pilorge killed his lover, Escudero, to rob him of something under a thousand francs, then, for his twentieth birthday, they cut off his head while, you will recall, he thumbed his nose at the enraged executioner.

Finally, a young ensign, still a child, committed treason for treason's sake: he was shot. And it is in honor of their crimes that I am writing my book.

I learned only in bits and pieces of that wonderful blossoming of dark and lovely flowers: one was revealed to me by a scrap of newspaper; another was casually alluded to by my lawyer; another was mentioned, almost sung, by the prisoners—their song became fantastic and funereal (a *De Profundis*), as much so as the plaints which they sing in the evening, as the voice which crosses the cells and reaches me blurred, hopeless, inflected. At the end of the phrases it breaks, and that break makes it so sweet that it seems borne by the music of angels, which horrifies me, for angels fill me with horror, being, I imagine, neither mind nor matter, white, filmy, and frightening, like the transluscent bodies of ghosts.

These murderers, now dead, have nevertheless reached me, and whenever one of these luminaries of affliction falls into my cell, my heart beats fast, my heart beats a loud tattoo, if the tattoo is the drum-call announcing the capitulation of a city. And there follows a fervor comparable to that which wrung me and left me for some minutes grotesquely contorted, when I heard the German plane passing over the prison and the burst of the bomb which it dropped nearby. In the twinkling of an eye, I saw a lone child, borne by his iron bird, laughingly strewing death. For him alone were unleashed the sirens, the bells, the hundred-and-one cannon shots reserved for the Dauphin, the cries of hatred and fear. All the cells were atremble, shivering, mad with terror; the prisoners pounded the doors, rolled on the floor, shrieked, screamed blasphemies, and prayed to God. I saw, as I say, or thought I saw, an eighteen-year-old child in the plane, and from the depths of my 426 I smiled at him lovingly.

I do not know whether it is their faces, the real ones, which spatter the wall of my cell with a sparkling mud, but it cannot be by chance that I cut those handsome, vacant-eyed heads out of the magazines. I say vacant, for all the eyes are clear and must be sky-blue, like the razor's edge to which clings a star of transparent light, blue and vacant like the windows of buildings under construction, through which you can see the sky from the windows of the opposite wall. Like those barracks which in the morning are open to all the winds, which you think are empty and pure when they are swarming with dangerous males, sprawled promiscuously on their beds. I say empty, but if they close their eyes, they become more disturbing to me than are huge prisons to the nubile maiden who passes by the high barred windows, prisons behind which sleeps, dreams, swears, and spits a race of murderers, which makes of each cell the hissing nest of a tangle of snakes, but also a kind of confessional with a curtain of dusty serge. These eyes, seemingly without mystery, are like certain closed cities—Lyons, Zurich—and they hypnotize me as much as do empty theaters, deserted prisons, machinery at rest, deserts, for deserts are closed and do not communicate with the infinite. Men with such faces terrify me, whenever I have to cross their paths warily, but what a dazzling surprise when, in their landscape, at the turning of a deserted lane, I approach, my heart racing wildly, and discover nothing, nothing but looming emptiness, sensitive and proud like a tall foxglove!

I do not know, as I have said, whether the heads there are really those of my guillotined friends, but I have recognized by certain signs that they—those on the wall—are thoroughly supple, like the lashes of whips, and rigid as glass knives, precocious as child pundits and fresh as forget-me-nots, bodies chosen because they are possessed by terrible souls.

The newspapers are tattered by the time they reach my cell, and the finest pages have been looted of their finest flowers, those pimps, like gardens in May. The big, inflexible, strict pimps, their members in full bloom—I no

longer know whether they are lilies or whether lilies and
members are not totally they, so much so that in the evening, on my knees, in thought, I encircle their legs with
my arms—all that rigidity floors me and makes me confuse them, and the memory which I gladly give as food for
my nights is of yours, which, as I caressed it, remained
inert, stretched out; only your rod, unsheathed and
brandished, went through my mouth with the suddenly
cruel sharpness of a steeple puncturing a cloud of ink, a
hatpin a breast. You did not move, you were not asleep,
you were not dreaming, you were in flight, motionless and
pale, frozen, straight, stretched out stiff on the flat bed,
like a coffin on the sea, and I know that we were chaste,
while I, all attention, felt you flow into me, warm and
white, in continuous little jerks. Perhaps you were playing
at coming. At the climax, you were lit up with a quiet
ecstasy, which enveloped your blessed body in a supernatural nimbus, like a cloak that you pierced with your
head and feet.

Still, I managed to get about twenty photographs, and
with bits of chewed bread I pasted them on the back of
the cardboard sheet of regulations that hangs on the wall.
Some are pinned up with bits of brass wire which the foreman brings me and on which I have to string colored glass
beads.

Using the same beads with which the prisoners next
door make funeral wreaths, I have made star-shaped
frames for the most purely criminal. In the evening, as you
open your window to the street, I turn the back of the
regulations sheet toward me. Smiles and sneers, alike inexorable, enter me by all the holes I offer, their vigor penetrates me and erects me. I live among these pits. They
watch over my little routines, which, along with them,
are all the family I have and my only friends.

Perhaps some lad who did nothing to deserve prison—

a champion, an athlete—slipped in among the twenty by mistake. But if I have nailed him to my wall, it was because, as I see it, he had the sacred sign of the monster at the corner of his mouth or the angle of the eyelids. The flaw on the face or in the set gesture indicates to me that they may very possibly love me, for they love me only if they are monsters—and it may therefore be said that it is this stray himself who has chosen to be here. To provide them with a court and retinue, I have culled here and there, from the illustrated covers of a few adventure novels, a young Mexican half-breed, a gaucho, a Caucasian horseman, and, from the pages of these novels that are passed from hand to hand when we take our walk, clumsy drawings: profiles of pimps and apaches with a smoking butt, or the outline of a tough with a hard-on.

At night I love them, and my love endows them with life. During the day I go about my petty concerns. I am the housekeeper, watchful lest a bread crumb or a speck of ash fall on the floor. But at night! Fear of the guard who may suddenly flick on the light and stick his head through the grating compels me to take sordid precautions lest the rustling of the sheets draw attention to my pleasure; but though my gesture may be less noble, by becoming secret it heightens my pleasure. I dawdle. Beneath the sheet, my right hand stops to caress the absent face, and then the whole body, of the outlaw I have chosen for that evening's delight. The left hand closes, then arranges its fingers in the form of a hollow organ which tries to resist, then offers itself, opens up, and a vigorous body, a wardrobe, emerges from the wall, advances, and falls upon me, crushes me against my straw mattress, which has already been stained by more than a hundred prisoners, while I think of the happiness into which I sink at a time when God and His angels exist.

No one can tell whether I shall get out of here, or, if I do, when it will be.

So, with the help of my unknown lovers, I am going to write a story. My heroes are they, pasted on the wall, they and I who am here, locked up. As you read on, the characters, and Divine too, and Culafroy, will fall from the wall onto my pages like dead leaves, to fertilize my tale. As for their death, need I tell you about it? For all of them it will be the death of him who, when he learned of his from the jury, merely mumbled in a Rhenish accent: "I'm already beyond that" (Weidmann).

This story may not always seem artificial, and in spite of me you may recognize in it the call of the blood: the reason is that within my night I shall have happened to strike my forehead at some door, freeing an anguished memory that had been haunting me since the world began. Forgive me for it. This book aims to be only a small fragment of my inner life.

Sometimes the cat-footed guard tosses me a hello through the grate. He talks to me and, without meaning to, tells me a good deal about my forger neighbors, about arsonists, counterfeiters, murderers, swaggering adolescents who roll on the floor screaming: "Mama, help!" He slams the grate shut and delivers me to a tête-à-tête with all those fine gentlemen whom he has just let slip in and who twist and squirm in the warmth of the sheets and the drowsiness of the morning to seek the end of the thread which will unravel the motives, the system of complicity, a whole fierce and subtle mechanism which, among other neat tricks, changed a few pink little girls into white corpses. I want to mingle them too, with their heads and legs, among my friends on the wall, and to compose with them this children's tale. And to refashion in my own way, and for the enchantment of my cell (I mean that thanks to her my cell will be enchanted), the story of Divine, whom

I knew only slightly, the story of Our Lady of the Flowers, and, never fear, my own story.

Description of Our Lady of the Flowers: height, 5 ft. 7 in., weight, 156 lbs., oval face, blond hair, blue eyes, mat complexion, perfect teeth, straight nose.

Divine died yesterday in a pool of her vomited blood which was so red that, as she expired, she had the supreme illusion that this blood was the visible equivalent of the black hole which a gutted violin, seen in a judge's office in the midst of a hodge-podge of pieces of evidence, revealed with dramatic insistence, as does a Jesus the gilded chancre where gleams His flaming Sacred Heart. So much for the divine aspect of her death. The other aspect, ours, because of those streams of blood that had been shed on her nightshirt and sheets (for the sun, poignant on the bloody sheets, had set, not nastily, in her bed), makes her death tantamount to a murder.

Divine died holy and murdered—by consumption.

It is January, and in the prison too, where this morning, during the walk, slyly, among prisoners, we wished each other a happy New Year, as humbly as servants must do among themselves in the pantry. The chief guard gave us each a little half-ounce packet of coarse salt as a New Year's gift. Three hours after noon. It has been raining behind the bars since yesterday, and it's windy. I let myself drift, as to the depth of an ocean, to the depths of a dismal neighborhood of hard and opaque but rather light houses, to the inner gaze of memory, for the matter of memory is porous. The garret in which Divine lived for such a long time is at the top of one of these houses. Its large window propels the eyes (and delights them) toward the little Montmartre Cemetery. The stairway leading up to it plays an important role today. It is the antechamber, sinuous as the hallways of the Pyramids, of

Divine's temporary tomb. This cavernous hypogeum looms up, pure as the bare marble arm in the darkness which is devouring the queen to whom it belongs. Coming from the street, the stairway mounts to death. It ushers one to the final resting place. It smells of decaying flowers and already of the odor of candles and incense. It rises into the shadow. From floor to floor it dwindles and darkens until, at the top, it is no more than an illusion blending with the azure. This is Divine's landing. While in the street, beneath the black haloes of the tiny flat unbrellas which they are holding in one hand like bouquets, Mimosa I, Mimosa II, Mimosa the half-IV, First Communion, Angela, Milord, Castagnette, Régine—in short, a host, a still long litany of creatures who are glittering names—are waiting, and in the other hand are carrying, like umbrellas, little bouquets of violets which make one of them lose herself, for example, in a reverie from which she will emerge bewildered and quite dumbfounded with nobility, for she (let us say First Communion) remembers the article, thrilling as a song from the other world, from our world too, in which an evening paper, thereby embalmed, stated:

"The black velvet rug of the Hotel Crillon, where lay the silver and ebony coffin containing the embalmed body of the Princess of Monaco, was strewn with Parma violets."

First Communion was chilly. She thrust her chin forward as great ladies do. Then she drew it in and wrapped herself in the folds of a story (born of her desires and taking into account, so as to magnify them, all the mishaps of her drab existence) in which she was dead and a princess.

The rain favored her flight.

Girl-queens were carrying wreaths of glass beads, the very kind I make in my cell, to which they bring the odor of wet moss and the memory of the trail of slime left on the white stones of my village cemetery by snails and slugs.

And all of them, the girl-queens and boy-queens, the aunties, fags, and nellies of whom I am speaking, are assembled at the foot of the stairway. The girl-queens are huddled together, chattering and chirping around the boy-queens, who are straight, motionless, and vertiginous, as motionless and silent as branches. All are dressed in black: trousers, jacket, and overcoat, but their faces, young or old, smooth or crinkly, are divided into quarters of color like a coat of arms. It is raining. With the patter of the rain is mingled:

"Poor Divine!"

"Would you believe it, my dear! But at her age it was fatal."

"It was falling apart. She was losing her bottom."

"Hasn't Darling come?"

"Hi there!"

"Dig *her!*"

Divine, who disliked anyone's walking over her head, lived on the top floor of a middle-class apartment house in a sober neighborhood. It was at the foot of this house that the crowd belonging to this backstage conversation shuffled about.

Any minute now the hearse, drawn perhaps by a black horse, will come to take away Divine's remains and carry them to the church, then here, close by, to the little Montmartre Cemetery, which the procession will enter by the Avenue Rachel.

The Eternal passed by in the form of a pimp. The prattle ceased. Bareheaded and very elegant, simple and smiling, simple and supple, Darling Daintyfoot arrived. There was in his supple bearing the weighty magnificence of the barbarian who tramples choice furs beneath his muddy boots. The torso on his hips was a king on a throne. Merely to have mentioned him is enough for my left hand in my torn pocket to. . . . And the memory of Darling will not leave me until I have completed my gesture. One day the door of my cell opened and framed him. I thought I saw him, in the twinkling of an eye, as solemn as a walking corpse, set in the thickness—which you can only imagine —of the prison walls. He appeared standing before me with the same graciousness that might have been his lying naked in a field of pinks. I was his at once, as if (who said that?) he had discharged through my mouth straight to my heart. Entering me until there was no room left for myself, so that now I am one with gangsters, burglars, and pimps, and the police arrest me by mistake. For three months he regaled himself with my body, beating me for all he was worth. I dragged at his feet, more trampled on than a dust mop. Ever since he has gone off free to his robberies, I keep remembering his gestures, so vivid they revealed him cut out of a faceted crystal, gestures so vivid that you suspected they were all involuntary, for it seems utterly impossible that they were born of ponderous reflection and decision. Of the tangible him there remains, sad to say, only the plaster cast that Divine herself made of his cock, which was gigantic when erect. The most impressive thing about it is the vigor, hence the beauty, of that part which goes from the anus to the tip of the penis.

I shall say that he had lace fingers, that, each time he awoke, his outstretched arms, open to receive the World, made him look like the Christ Child in his manger—with the heel of one foot on the instep of the other—that his eager face offered itself, as it bent backward facing heaven, that, when standing, he would tend to make the basket movement we see Nijinsky making in the old photos where he is dressed in shredded roses. His wrist, fluid as a violinist's, hangs down, graceful and loose-jointed. And at

times, in broad daylight, he strangles himself with his
lithe arm, the arm of a tragedienne.

This is almost an exact portrait of Darling, for—we shall
see him again—he had a talent for the gesture that thrills
me, and, if I think about him, I can't stop praising him
until my hand is smeared with my liberated pleasure.

A Greek, he entered the house of death walking on air.
A Greek, that is, a crook as well. As he passed—the motion
was revealed by an imperceptible movement of the torso
—within themselves, secretly, Milord, the Mimosas,
Castagnette, in short, all the queens, imparted a tendril-
like movement to their bodies and fancied they were enlacing this handsome man, were twining about him. Indifferent and bright as a slaughterhouse knife, he passed
by, cleaving them all into two slices which came noiselessly together again, though emitting a slight scent of
hopelessness which no one divulged. Darling went up the
stairs two at a time, an ample and forthright ascension,
which may lead, after the roof, on steps of blue air, up to
heaven. In the garret, less mysterious since death had con-
verted it into a vault (it was losing its equivocal meaning,
was again assuming, in all its purity, that air of incoherent
gratuity that these funereal and mysterious objects, these
mortuary objects lent it: white gloves, a lampion, an artilleryman's jacket, in short, an inventory that we shall list
later on), the only one to sigh in her mourning veils was
Divine's mother, Ernestine. She is old. But now at last the
wonderful, long-awaited opportunity does not escape her.
Divine's death enables her to free herself, by an external
despair, by a visible mourning consisting of tears, flowers,
and crape, from the hundred great roles which possessed
her. The opportunity slipped between her fingers at the time
of an illness which I shall tell about, when Divine the Gay-
time Girl was still just a village youngster named Louis
Culafroy. From his sick bed, he looked at the room where

an angel (once again this word disturbs me, attracts me, and
sickens me. If they have wings, do they have teeth? Do
they fly with such heavy wings, feathered wings, "those
mysterious wings?" And scented with that wonder: their
angel's name, which they change if they fall?), an angel,
a soldier dressed in light blue, and a Negro (for will my
books ever be anything but a pretext for showing a soldier
dressed in sky blue, and a brotherly Negro and angel playing dice or knuckle bones in a dark or light prison?) were
engaged in a confabulation from which he himself was excluded. The angel, the Negro, and the soldier kept assuming the faces of various schoolmates and peasants, but
never that of Alberto the snake fisher. He was the one
Culafroy was waiting for in his desert, to calm his torrid
thirst with that mouth of starry flesh. To console himself,
he tried, despite his age, to conceive a kind of happiness
in which nothing would be winsome, a pure, deserted,
desolate field, a field of azure or sand, a dumb, dry, mag-
netic field, where nothing sweet, no color or sound, would
remain. Quite some time before, the appearance on the
village road of a bride wearing a black dress, though
wrapped in a veil of white tulle, lovely and sparkling, like
a young shepherd beneath the hoar frost, like a powdered
blond miller, or like Our Lady of the Flowers whom he
will meet later on and whom I saw with my own eyes here
in my cell one morning, near the latrines—his sleepy face
pink and bristly beneath the soapsuds, which blurred his
vision—revealed to Culafroy that poetry is something
other than a melody of curves on sweetness, for the tulle
snapped apart into abrupt, clear, rigorous, icy facets. It
was a warning.

He was waiting for Alberto, who did not come. Yet all the
peasant boys and girls who came in had something of the
snake fisher about them. They were like his harbingers,
his ambassadors, his precursors, bearing some of his gifts

before him, preparing his coming by smoothing the way for him. They shouted hallelujah. One had his walk, another his gestures, or the color of his trousers, or his corduroy, or Alberto's voice; and Culafroy, like someone waiting, never doubted that all these scattered elements would eventually fuse and enable a reconstructed Alberto to make the solemn, appointed, and surprising entrance into his room that a dead and alive Darling Daintyfoot made into my cell.

When the village abbé, hearing the news, said to Ernestine: "Madame, it's a blessing to die young," she replied: "Yes, your Lordship," and made a curtsey.

The priest looked at her.

She was smiling in the shiny floor at her antipodal reflection which made her the Queen of Spades, the ill-omened widow.

"Don't shrug your shoulders, my friend. I'm not crazy."

And she wasn't crazy.

"Lou Culafroy is going to die shortly. I feel it. He's going to die, I can tell."

"He's going to die, I can tell," was the expression torn alive—and helping her to fly—from a book, and bleeding, like a wing from a sparrow (or from an angel, if it can bleed crimson), and murmured with horror by the heroine of that cheap novel printed in tiny type in newsprint—which, so they say, is as spongy as the consciences of those nasty gentlemen who debauch children.

"So, I'm dancing the dirge."

He therefore had to die. And in order for the pathos of the act to be more virulent, she herself would have to be the cause of his death. Here, to be sure, morality is not involved, nor the fear of prison, or of hell. With remarkable precision, the whole mechanism of the drama presented itself to Ernestine's mind, and thereby to mine. She would simulate a suicide. "I'll say he killed himself." Ernestine's logic, which is a stage logic, has no relationship with what is called verisimilitude, verisimilitude being the disavowal of unavowable reasons. Let us not be surprised, we shall be all the more astonished.

The presence of a huge army revolver at the back of a drawer was enough to dictate her attitude. This is not the first time that things have been the instigators of an act and must alone bear the fearful, though light, responsibility for a crime. This revolver became—or so it seemed—the indispensable accessory of her gesture. It was a continuation of her heroine's outstretched arm, in fact it haunted her, since there's no denying it, with a brutality that burned her cheeks, just as the girls of the village were haunted by the brutal swelling of Alberto's thick hands in his pockets. But—just as I myself would be willing to kill only a lithe adolescent in order to bring forth a corpse from his death, though a corpse still warm and a shade sweet to hug, so Ernestine agreed to kill only on condition that she avoid the horror that the here below would not fail to inspire in her (convulsions, squirting blood and brain, reproaches in the child's dismayed eyes), and the horror of an angelic beyond, or perhaps to make the moment more stately—she put on her jewels. So in the past I would inject my cocaine with a cut-glass syringe shaped like the stopper of a decanter and put a huge diamond on my index finger. She was not aware that by going about it in this way she was aggravating her gesture, changing it into an exceptional gesture, the singularity of which threatened to upset everything. Which is what happened. With a kind of smooth sliding, the room descended till it blended with a luxurious apartment, adorned with gold, the walls hung with garnet-red velvet, the furniture heavy but toned down with red faille curtains; here and there were large beveled mirrors, adorned with candelabra and their crystal pendants. From the ceiling—an important detail—hung a huge chandelier. The floor was covered with thick blue and violet carpets.

One evening, during her honeymoon in Paris, Ernestine had glimpsed from the street, through the curtains, one of those elegant, well-heated apartments, and as she walked demurely with her arm in her husband's—demurely still— she longed to die there of love (phenobarbital and flowers) for a Teutonic knight. Then, as she had already died four or five times, the apartment had remained available for a drama more serious than her own death.

I'm complicating things, getting involved, and you're talking of childishness. It *is* childishness. All prisoners are children, and only children are underhanded, wily, open, and confused. "What would top it all," thought Ernestine, "would be for him to die in a fashionable city, in Cannes or Venice, so that I could make pilgrimages to it."

To stop at a Ritz, bathed by the Adriatic, wife or mistress of a Doge; then, her arms full of flowers, to climb a path to the cemetery, to sit down on a simple flagstone, a white, slightly curved stone, and, all curled up in fragrant grief, to brood!

Without bringing her back to reality, for she never left reality, the arrangement of the setting obliged her to shake off the dream. She went to get the revolver, which had long since been loaded by a most considerate Providence, and when she held it in her hand, weighty as a phallus in action, she realized she was big with murder, pregnant with a corpse.

You, you have no idea of the superhuman or extra-lucid state of mind of the blind murderer who holds the knife, the gun, or the phial, or who has already released the movement that propels to the precipice.

Ernestine's gesture might have been performed quickly, but, like Culafroy in fact, she is serving a text she knows nothing about, a text I am composing whose *dénouement* will occur when the time is ripe. Ernestine is perfectly aware of how ridiculously literary her act is, but that she has to submit to cheap literature makes her even more touching in her own eyes and ours. In drama, as in all of life, she escapes vainglorious beauty.

Every premeditated murder is always governed by a preparatory ceremonial and is always followed by a propitiatory ceremonial. The meaning of both eludes the murderer's mind. Everything is in order. Ernestine has just time to appear before a Star Chamber. She fired. The bullet shattered the glass of a frame containing an honorary diploma of her late husband. The noise was frightful. Drugged by sleeping pills, the child heard nothing. Nor did Ernestine. She had fired in the apartment with the garnet-red velvet, and the bullet, shattering the beveled mirrors, the pendants, the crystals, the stucco, the stars, tearing the hangings—in short, destroying the structure which collapsed—brought down not sparkling powder and blood, but the crystal of the chandelier and the pendants, a gray ash on the head of Ernestine, who swooned.

She came back to her senses amidst the debris of her drama. Her hands, freed from the revolver, which disappeared beneath the bed like an ax at the bottom of a pond, like a prowler into a wall, her hands, lighter than thoughts, fluttered about her. Since then, she has been waiting.

That was how Darling saw her, intoxicated with the tragic. He was intimidated by her, for she was beautiful and seemed mad, but especially because she was beautiful. Did he, who himself was handsome, have to fear her? I'm sorry to say I know too little (nothing) about the secret relations between people who are handsome and know it, and nothing about the seemingly friendly but perhaps hostile contacts between handsome boys. If they smile at each other over a trifle, is there, unknown to them, some tenderness in their smile, and do they feel its influence in some obscure way? Darling made a clumsy sign of the cross over the coffin. His constraint gave the impression that he was deep in thought; and his constraint was all his grace.

Death had placed its mark, which weighs like a lead seal at the bottom of a parchment, on the curtains, the walls, the rugs. Particularly on the curtains. They are sensitive. They sense death and echo it like dogs. They bark at death through the folds that open, dark as the mouth and eyes of the masks of Sophocles, or which bulge like the eyelids of Christian ascetics. The blinds were drawn and the candles lighted. Darling, no longer recognizing the attic where he had lived with Divine, behaved like a young man on a visit.

His emotion beside the coffin? None. He no longer remembered Divine.

The undertaker's assistants arrived almost immediately and saved him from further embarrassment.

In the rain, this black cortege, bespangled with multi-colored faces and blended with the scent of flowers and rouge, followed the hearse. The flat round umbrellas, undulating above the ambulating procession, held it suspended between heaven and earth. The passersby did not even see it, for it was so light that it was already floating ten yards from the ground; only the maids and butlers might have noticed it, but at ten o'clock the former were bringing the morning chocolate to their mistresses and the latter were opening the door to early visitors. Besides, the cortege was almost invisible because of its speed. The hearse had wings on its axle. The abbé emerged first into the rain singing the *dies irae*. He tucked up his cassock and cope, as he had been taught to do at the seminary when the weather was bad. His gesture, though automatic, released within him, with a placenta of nobility, a series of sad and secret creatures. With one of the flaps of

the black velvet cope, the velvet from which are made
Fantômas' masks and those of the Doges' wives, he tried
to slip away, but it was the ground that gave way under
him, and we shall see the trap into which he fell. Just in
time, he prevented the cloth from hiding the lower part of
his face. Bear in mind that the abbé was young. You could
tell that under his funereal vestments he had the lithe
body of a passionate athlete. Which means, in short, that
he was in travesty. In the church—the whole funeral service having been merely the "do this in memory of me"—
approaching the altar on tiptoe, in silence, he had picked
the lock of the tabernacle, parted the veil like someone
who at midnight parts the double curtains of an alcove,
held his breath, seized the ciborium with the caution of
an ungloved burglar, and finally, having broken it, swallowed a questionable host.

From the church to the cemetery, the road was long and
the text of the breviary too familiar. Only the dirge and
the black, silver-embroidered cope exuded charms. The
abbé plodded through the mud as he would have done in
the heart of the woods. "Of what woods?" he asked himself. In a foreign country, a forest of Bohemia. Or rather of
Hungary. In choosing this country, he was no doubt
guided by the precious suspicion that Hungarians are the
only Asiates in Europe. Huns. The Hunis. Attila burning
the grass, and his soldiers warming between their brutal
and colossal thighs (like those, and perhaps even larger
than those, of Alberto, Darling, and Gorgui) and their
horses' flanks the raw meat that they will eat. It is autumn.
It is raining in the Hungarian forest.

Every branch that he has to push aside wets the priest's
forehead. The only sound is the patter of the drops on the
wet leaves. Since it is evening, the woods become more
and more alarming. The priest draws the gray coat more

tightly about his splendid loins, the great cape, like his cope of today, which envelops him over there.

In the forest is a sawmill; two young men work it and hunt. They are unknown in the region. They have (the abbé knows this as one knows things in dreams without having learned them) been around the world. And so here the abbé was chanting the dirge as he would have sung it there when he met one of the strangers, the younger, who had the face of the butcher of my village. He was on his way back from hunting. In the corner of his mouth, an unlit butt. The word "butt" and the taste of the sucked tobacco made the abbé's spine stiffen and draw back with three short jerks, the vibrations of which reverberated through all his muscles and on to infinity, which shuddered and ejaculated a seed of constellations.

The woodcutter's lips came down on the abbé's mouth, where, with a thrust of the tongue more imperious than a royal order, they drove in the butt. The priest was knocked down, bitten, and he expired with love on the soggy moss. After having almost disrobed him, the stranger caressed him, gratefully, almost fondly, thought the abbé. With a heave, he shouldered his game bag, which was weighted down with a wildcat, picked up his gun, and went off whistling a raffish tune.

The abbé was winding his way among mausoleums; the queens were stumbling over the stones, getting their feet wet in the grass, and among the graves were being angelicized. The choir boy, a puny lad with ringworm, who hadn't the slightest suspicion of the adventure the abbé had just had, asked him whether he might keep his skullcap on. The abbé said yes. As he walked, his leg made the movement peculiar to dancers (with one hand in their pocket) as they finish a tango. He bent forward on his leg, which was slightly advanced on the tip of the toe; he slapped his knee against the cloth of the cassock, which flapped back and forth like the bell-bottomed trousers of a swaying sailor or a gaucho. Then he began a psalm.

When the procession arrived at the hole which had already been dug, perhaps by the gravedigger Divine used to see from her window, they lowered the coffin in which Divine lay wrapped in a white lace sheet. The abbé blessed the grave and handed his sprinkler to Darling, who blushed to feel it so heavy (for he had to some degree returned, after and beyond Divine, to his race, which was akin to that of young gypsies, who are willing to jerk you off, but only with their feet), then to the queens, who turned the whole area into a squealing of pretty cries and high giggles. Divine departed as she would have desired, in a mixture of fantasy and sordidness.

Divine is dead, is dead and buried . . .
. . . is dead and buried.

Since Divine is dead, the poet may sing her, may tell her legend, the Saga, the annals of Divine. The Divine Saga should be danced, mimed, with subtle directions. Since it is impossible to make a ballet of it, I am forced to use words that are weighed down with precise ideas, but I shall try to lighten them with expressions that are trivial, empty, hollow, and invisible.

What is involved for me who is making up this story? In reviewing my life, in tracing its course, I fill my cell with the pleasure of being what for want of a trifle I failed to be, recapturing, so that I may hurl myself into them as into dark pits, those moments when I strayed through the trap-ridden compartments of a subterranean sky. Slowly displacing volumes of fetid air, cutting threads from which hang bouquets of feelings, seeing the gypsy for whom I am looking emerge perhaps from some starry river, wet, with mossy hair, playing the fiddle, diabolically whisked away by the scarlet velvet portiere of a cabaret.

I shall speak to you about Divine, mixing masculine and feminine as my mood dictates, and if, in the course of the tale, I shall have to refer to a woman, I shall manage, I shall find an expedient, a good device, to avoid any confusion.

Divine appeared in Paris to lead her public life about twenty years before her death. She was then thin and vivacious and will remain so until the end of her life, though growing angular. At about two A.M. she entered Graff's Café in Montmartre. The customers were a muddy, still shapeless clay. Divine was limpid water. In the big café with the closed windows and the curtains drawn on their hollow rods, overcrowded and foundering in smoke, she wafted the coolness of scandal, which is the coolness of a morning breeze, the astonishing sweetness of a breath of scandal on the stone of the temple, and just as the wind turns leaves, so she turned heads, heads which all at once became light (giddy heads), heads of bankers, shopkeepers, gigolos for ladies, waiters, manager, colonels, scarecrows.

She sat down alone at a table and asked for tea.

"Specially fine China tea, my good man," she said to the waiter.

With a smile. For the customers she had an irritatingly jaunty smile. Hence, the "you-know-what" in the wagging of the heads. For the poet and the reader, her smile will be enigmatic.

That evening she was wearing a champagne silk short-sleeved blouse, a pair of blue trousers stolen from a sailor, and leather sandals. On one of her fingers, though preferably on the pinkie, an ulcer-like stone gangrened her. When the tea was brought, she drank it as if she were at home, in tiny little sips (a pigeon), putting down and lifting the cup with her pinkie in the air. Here is a portrait of her: her hair is brown and curly; with the curls spilling over her eyes and down her cheeks, she looks as if she were wearing a cat-o'-nine-tails on her head. Her forehead is somewhat round and smooth. Her eyes sing, despite their despair, and their melody moves from her eyes to her teeth, to which she gives life, and from her teeth to all her movements, to her slightest acts, and this charm, which emerges from her eyes, unfurls in wave upon wave, down to her bare feet. Her body is fine as amber. Her limbs can be agile when she flees from ghosts. At her heels, the wings of terror bear her along. She is quick, for in order to elude the ghosts, to throw them off her track, she must speed ahead faster than her thought thinks. She drank her tea before thirty pairs of eyes which belied what the contemptuous, spiteful, sorrowful, wilting mouths were saying.

Divine was full of grace, and yet was like all those prowlers at country fairs on the lookout for rare sights and artistic visions, good sports who trail behind them all the inevitable hodge-podge of side shows. At the slightest movement—if they knot their tie, if they flick the ash of their cigarette—they set slot machines in motion. Divine knotted, garroted arteries. Her seductiveness will be implacable. If it were only up to me, I would make her the kind of fatal hero I like. Fatal, that is, determining the fate of those who gaze at them, spellbound. I would make her with hips of stone, flat and polished cheeks, heavy eyelids, pagan knees so lovely that they reflected the desperate intelligence of the faces of mystics. I would strip her of all sentimental trappings. Let her consent to be the frozen statue. But I know that the poor Demiurge is forced to make his creature in his own image and that he did not invent Lucifer. In my cell, little by little, I shall have to give my thrills to the granite. I shall remain alone with it for a long time, and I shall make it live with my breath and the smell of my farts, both the solemn and the mild ones. It will take me an entire book to draw her from her petrifaction and gradually impart my suffering to her, gradually deliver her from evil, and, holding her by the hand, lead her to saintliness.

The waiter who served her felt very much like snickering, but out of decency he did not dare in front of her. As for the manager, he approached her table and decided that as soon as she finished her tea, he would ask her to leave, to make sure she would not turn up again some other evening.

Finally, she patted her snowy forehead with a flowered handkerchief. Then she crossed her legs; on her ankle could be seen a chain fastened by a locket which *we* know contained a few hairs. She smiled all around, and each one answered only by turning away, but that was a way of answering. The whole café thought that the smile of (for the colonel: the invert; for the shopkeepers: the fairy; for the banker and the waiters: the fag; for the gigolos: "*that one*"; etc.) was despicable. Divine did not press the point. From a tiny black satin purse she took a few coins which she laid noiselessly on the marble table. The café disappeared, and Divine was metamorphosed into one of those monsters that are painted on walls—chimeras or griffins— for a customer, in spite of himself, murmured a magic word as he thought of her:

"Homoseckshual."

That evening, her first in Montmartre, she was cruising. But she got nowhere. She came upon us without warning. The habitués of the café had neither the time nor, above all, the composure to handle properly their reputations or their females. Having drunk her tea, Divine, with indifference (so it appeared, seeing her), wriggling in a spray of flowers and strewing swishes and spangles with an invisible furbelow, made off. So here she is, having decided to return, lifted by a column of smoke, to her garret, on the door of which is nailed a huge discolored muslin rose.

Her perfume is violent and vulgar. From it we can already tell that she is fond of vulgarity. Divine has sure taste, good taste, and it is most upsetting that life always puts someone so delicate into vulgar positions, into contact with all kinds of filth. She cherishes vulgarity because her greatest love was for a dark-skinned gypsy. On him, under him, when, with his mouth pressed to hers, he sang to her gypsy songs that pierced her body, she learned to submit to the charm of such vulgar cloths as silk and gold braid, which are becoming to immodest persons. Montmartre was aflame. Divine passed through its multi-colored fires, then, intact, entered the darkness of the promenade of the Boulevard de Clichy, a darkness that preserves old and ugly faces. It was three A.M. She walked for a while toward Pigalle. She smiled and stared at every man who strolled by alone. They didn't dare, or else it was that she still knew nothing about the customary routine: the client's qualms, his hesitations, his lack of assurance as soon as he approaches the coveted youngster. She was weary; she sat down on a bench and, despite her fatigue, was conquered, transported by the warmth of the night; she let herself go for the length of a heartbeat and expressed her excitement as follows: "The nights are mad about me! Oh the sultanas! My God, they're making eyes at me! Ah, they're curling my hair around their fingers (the fingers of the nights, men's cocks!). They're patting my cheek, stroking my butt." That was what she thought, though without rising to, or sinking into, a poetry cut off from the terrestrial world. Poetic expression will never change her state of mind. She will always be the tart concerned with gain.

There are mornings when all men experience with fatigue a flush of tenderness that makes them horny. One day at dawn I found myself placing my lips lovingly, though for no reason at all, on the icy banister of the Rue

Berthe; another time, kissing my hand; still another time,
bursting with emotion, I wanted to swallow myself by
opening my mouth very wide and turning it over my head
so that it would take in my whole body, and then the
Universe, until all that would remain of me would be a
ball of eaten thing which little by little would be annihilated: that is how I see the end of the world. Divine
offered herself to the night in order to be devoured by it
tenderly and never again spewed forth. She is hungry.
And there is nothing around. The pissoirs are empty; the
promenade is just about deserted. Merely some bands of
young workmen—whose whole disorderly adolescence is
manifest in their carelessly tied shoelaces which hop about
on their insteps—returning home in forced marches from
an evening of pleasure. Their tight-fitting jackets are like
fragile breastplates or shells protecting the naïveté of their
bodies. But by the grace of their virility, which is still as
light as a hope, they are inviolable by Divine.

She will do nothing tonight. The possible customers
were so taken by surprise that they were unable to collect their wits. She will have to go back to her attic with
hunger in her belly and her heart. She stood up to go. A
man came staggering toward her. He bumped her with his
elbow.

"Oh! sorry," he said, "terribly sorry!"

His breath reeked of wine.

"Quite all right," said the queen.

It was Darling Daintyfoot going by.

Description of Darling: height, 5 ft. 9 in., weight 165
lbs., oval face, blond hair, blue-green eyes, mat complexion, perfect teeth, straight nose.

He was young too, almost as young as Divine, and I
would like him to remain so to the end of the book. Every
day the guards open my door so I can leave my cell and

go out into the yard for some fresh air. For a few seconds, in the corridors and on the stairs, I pass thieves and hoodlums whose faces enter my face and whose bodies, from afar, hurl mine to the ground. I long to have them within reach. Yet not one of them makes me evoke Darling Daintyfoot.

When I met Divine in Fresnes Prison, she spoke to me about him a great deal, seeking his memory and the traces of his steps throughout the prison, but I never quite knew his face, and this is a tempting opportunity for me to blend him in my mind with the face and physique of Roger.

Very little of this Corsican remains in my memory: a hand with too massive a thumb that plays with a tiny hollow key, and the faint image of a blond boy walking up La Canebière in Marseilles, with a small chain, probably gold, stretched across his fly, which it seems to be buckling. He belongs to a group of males who are advancing upon me with the pitiless gravity of forests on the march. That was the starting point of the daydream in which I imagined myself calling him Roger, a "little boy's" name, though firm and upright. Roger was upright. I had just got out of the Chave prison, and I was amazed not to have met him there. What could I commit to be worthy of his beauty? I needed boldness in order to admire him. For lack of money, I slept at night in the shadowy corners of coal piles, on the docks, and every evening I carried him off with me. The memory of his memory made way for other men. For the past two days, in my daydreams, I have again been mingling his (made-up) life with mine. I wanted him to love me, and of course he did, with the candor that required only perversity for him to be able to love me. For two successive days I have fed with his image a dream which is usually sated after four or five hours when I have given it a boy to feed upon, however

handsome he may be. Now I am exhausted with inventing
circumstances in which he loves me more and more. I am
worn out with the invented trips, thefts, rapes, burglaries,
imprisonments, and treachery in which we were involved,
each acting by and for the other and never by or for himself, in which the adventure was ourselves and only ourselves. I am exhausted; I have a cramp in my wrist. The
pleasure of the last drops is dry. For a period of two days,
between my four bare walls, I experienced with him and
through him every possibility of an existence that had to
be repeated twenty times and got so mixed up it became
more real than a real one. I have given up the daydream.
I was loved. I have quit, the way a contestant in a six-day
bicycle race quits; yet the memory of his eyes and their fatigue, which I have to cull from the face of another youngster whom I saw coming out of a brothel, a boy with firm
legs and ruthless cock, so solid that I might almost say it
was knotted, and his face (it alone, seen without its veil),
which asks for shelter like a knight-errant—this memory
refuses to disappear as the memory of my dream-friends
usually does. It floats about. It is less sharp than when the
adventures were taking place, but it lives in me nevertheless. Certain details persist more obstinately in remaining:
the little hollow key with which, if he wants to, he can
whistle; his thumb; his sweater; his blue eyes. . . . If I continue, he will rise up, become erect, and penetrate me so
deeply that I shall be marked with stigmata. I can't bear
it any longer. I am turning him into a character whom I
shall be able to torment in my own way, namely, Darling
Daintyfoot. He will still be twenty, although his destiny
is to become the father and lover of Our Lady of the
Flowers.

To Divine he said:
"Terribly sorry!"

In his cups, Darling did not notice the strangeness of this passerby with his aggressive niceness:

"What about it, pal?"

Divine stopped. A bantering and dangerous conversation ensued, and then everything happened as was to be desired. Divine took him home with her to the Rue Caulaincourt. It was in this garret that she died, the garret from which one sees below, like the sea beneath the watchman in the crow's nest, a cemetery and graves. Cypresses singing. Ghosts dozing. Every morning, Divine will shake her dustrag from the window and bid the ghosts farewell. One day, with the help of field glasses, she will discover a young gravedigger. "God forgive me!" she will exclaim, "there's a bottle of wine on the vault!" This gravedigger will grow old along with her and will bury her without knowing anything about her.

So she went upstairs with Darling. Then, in the attic, after closing the door, she undressed him. With his jacket, trousers, and shirt off, he looked as white and sunken as an avalanche. By evening they found themselves tangled in the damp and rumpled sheets.

"What a mess! Man! I was pretty groggy yesterday, wasn't I, doll?"

He laughed feebly and looked around the garret. It is a room with a sloping ceiling. On the floor, Divine has put some threadbare rugs and nailed to the wall the murderers on the walls of my cell and the extraordinary photographs of good-looking kids, which she has stolen from photographers' display windows, all of whom bear the signs of the power of darkness.

"Display window!"

On the mantelpiece, a tube of phenobarbital lying on a small painted wooden frigate is enough to detach the room from the stone block of the building, to suspend it like a cage between heaven and earth.

From the way he talks, the way he lights and smokes his cigarette, Divine has gathered that Darling is a pimp. At first she had certain fears: of being beaten up, robbed, insulted. Then she felt the proud satisfaction of having made a pimp come. Without quite seeing where the adventure would lead, but rather as a bird is said to go into a serpent's mouth, she said, not quite voluntarily and in a kind of trance: "Stay," and added hesitantly, "if you want to."

"No kidding, you feel that way about me?"

Darling stayed.

In that big Montmartre attic, where, through the skylight, between the pink muslin puffs which she has made herself, Divine sees white cradles sailing by on a calm blue sea, so close that she can make out their flowers from which emerges the arched foot of a dancer. Darling will soon bring the midnight-blue overalls that he wears on the job, his ring of skeleton keys and his tools, and on the little pile which they make on the floor he will place his white rubber gloves, which are like gloves for formal occasions. Thus began their life together in that room through which ran the electric wires of the stolen radiator, the stolen radio, and the stolen lamps.

They eat breakfast in the afternoon. During the day they sleep and listen to the radio. Toward evening, they primp and go out. At night, as is the practice, Divine hustles on the Place Blanche and Darling goes to the movies. For a long time, things will go well with Divine. With Darling to advise and protect her, she will know whom to rob, which judge to blackmail. The vaporish cocaine loosens the contours of their lives and sets their bodies adrift, and so they are untouchable.

Though a hoodlum, Darling had a face of light. He was the handsome male, gentle and violent, born to be a pimp, and of so noble a bearing that he seemed always to be

naked, save for one ridiculous and, to me, touching movement: the way he arched his back, standing first on one
foot, then on the other, in order to take off his trousers and
shorts. Before his birth, Darling was baptized privately,
that is, beatified too, practically canonized, in the warm
belly of his mother. He was given the kind of emblematic
baptism which, upon his death, was to send him to limbo;
in short, one of those brief ceremonies, mysterious and
highly dramatic in their compactness, sumptuous too, to
which the Angels were convoked and in which the vota-
ries of the Divinity were mobilized, as was the Divinity Itself. Darling is aware of this, though only slightly, that is,
throughout his life, rather than anyone's telling him such
secrets aloud and intelligibly, it seems that someone whispers them to him. And this private baptism, with which
his life began, gilds his life as it unfolds, envelops it in a
warm, weak, slightly luminous aureole, raises for this
pimp's life a pedestal garlanded with flowers, as a maiden's
coffin is bedecked with woven ivy, a pedestal massive
though light, from the top of which, since the age of
fifteen, Darling has been pissing in the following position:
his legs spread, knees slightly bent, and in more rigid
jets since the age of eighteen. For we should like to stress
the point that a very gentle nimbus always isolates him
from too rough a contact with his own sharp angles. If he
says, "I'm dropping a pearl," or "A pearl slipped," he
means that he has farted in a certain way, very softly, that
the fart has flowed out very quietly. Let us wonder at the
fact that it does suggest a pearl of dull sheen: the flowing, the muted leak, seems to us as milky as the paleness
of a pearl, that is, slightly cloudy. It makes Darling seem
to us a kind of precious gigolo, a Hindu, a princess, a
drinker of pearls. The odor he has silently spread in the
prison has the dullness of the pearl, coils about him, haloes
him from head to foot, isolates him, but isolates him much

less than does the remark that his beauty does not fear to utter. "I'm dropping a pearl" means that the fart is noiseless. If it rumbles, then it is coarse, and if it's some jerk who drops it, Darling says, "My cock's house is falling down!"

Wondrously, through the magic of his high blond beauty, Darling calls forth a savanna and plunges us more deeply and imperiously into the heart of the black continents than the Negro murderer will plunge me. Darling adds further:

"Sure stinks. I can't even stay near me. . . ."

In short, he bore his infamy like a red-hot brand on raw flesh, but this precious brand is as ennobling as was the fleur-de-lis on the shoulders of hoodlums of old. Eyes blackened by fists are the pimp's shame, but Darling says:

"My two bouquets of violets." He also says, regarding a desire to shit:

"I've got a cigar at the tip of my lips."

He has very few friends. As Divine loses hers, he sells them to the cops. Divine does not yet know about this; he keeps his traitor's face for himself alone, for he loves to betray. When Divine met him, he had just got out of jail, that same morning, having served a minimum sentence for robbery and receiving stolen goods, after having coldly ratted on his accomplices, and on some other friends who were not accomplices.

One evening, as they were about to release him from the police station to which he had been taken after a raid, when the inspector said to him, in that gruff tone that makes one think they won't go any further: "You wouldn't happen to know who's going to pull a job? All you have to do is stooge for us, we can come to some arrangement," he felt, as *you* would say, a base caress, but it was all the sweeter because he himself regarded it as base. He tried to seem nonchalant and said:

"It's a risky business."

However, he noticed that he had lowered his voice.

"You don't have to worry about that with me," continued the inspector. "You'll get a hundred francs each time."

Darling accepted. He liked selling out on people, for this dehumanized him. Dehumanizing myself is my own most fundamental tendency. On the first page of an evening paper he again saw the photograph of the ensign I mentioned earlier, the one who was shot for treason. And Darling said to himself:

"Old pal! Buddy!"

He was thrilled by a prankishness that was born from within: "I'm a double crosser." As he walked down the Rue Dancourt, drunk with the hidden splendor (as of a treasure) of his abjection (for it really must intoxicate us if we are not to be killed by its intensity), he glanced at the mirror in a shop window where he saw a Darling luminous with extinguished pride, bursting with this pride. He saw this Darling wearing a glen plaid suit, a felt hat over one eye, his shoulders stiff, and when he walks he holds them like that so as to resemble Sebastopol Pete, and Pete holds them like that so as to resemble Pauley the Rat, and Pauley to resemble Teewee, and so on; a procession of pure, irreproachable pimps leads to Darling Daintyfoot, the double crosser, and it seems that as a result of having rubbed against them and stolen their bearing, he has, you might say, soiled them with his own abjection; that's how I want him to be, for my delight, with a chain on his wrist, a tie as fluid as a tongue of flame, and those extraordinary shoes which are meant only for pimps—very light tan, narrow and pointed. For, thanks to Divine, Darling has gradually exchanged his clothes, which were shabby from months in a cell, for some elegant worsted suits and scented linen. The transformation has delighted him. For he is still the child-pimp. The soul of the ill-tempered hoodlum has remained in the cast offs. Now he feels in his pocket, and strokes with his hand, better than he used to feel his knife near his penis, a .38 caliber gun. But we do not dress for ourselves alone, and Darling dressed for prison. With each new purchase, he imagines the effect on his possible prison mates at Fresnes or the Santé. Who, in your opinion, might they be? Two or three hoods who, never having seen him, could recognize him as their peer, a few wooden-faced men who might offer him their hand or, from a distance, during the medical examination or while returning from the daily walk, would rap out from the corner of their mouth, with a wink: " 'lo, Darling." But most of his friends would be jerks who were easily dazzled. Prison is a kind of God, as barbaric as a god, to whom he offers gold watches, fountain pens, rings, handkerchiefs, scarves, and shoes. He dreams less of showing himself in the splendor of his new outfits to a woman or to the people he meets casually in daily life than of walking into a cell with his hat tilted over one eye, his white silk shirt open at the collar (for his tie was stolen during the search), and his English raglan unbuttoned. And the poor prisoners already gaze at him with respect. On the basis of his appearance, he dominates them. "I'd like to see the look on their mugs!" he would think, if he could think his desires.

Two stays in prison have so molded him that he will live the rest of his life for it. It has shaped his destiny, and he is very dimly aware that he is ineluctably consecrated to it, perhaps ever since the time he read the following words that someone had scribbled on the page of a library book:

Beware:
First: Jean Clément, known as the Queen,
Second: Robert Martin, known as the Faggot,

Third: Roger Falgue, known as Nelly.
The Queen has a crush on Li'l Meadow (society sis),
The Faggot on Ferrière and Grandot,
Nelly on Malvoisin.

The only way to avoid the horror of horror is to give in to it. He therefore wished, with a kind of voluptuous desire, that one of the names were his. Besides, I know that you finally tire of that tense, heroic attitude of the outlaw and that you decide to play along with the police in order to reassume your sloughed-off humanity. Divine knew nothing about this aspect of Darling. Had she known it, she would have loved him all the more, for to her love was equivalent to despair. So they are drinking tea, and Divine is quite aware she is swallowing it the way a pigeon swallows clear water. As it would be drunk, if he drank it, by the Holy Ghost in the form of a dove. Darling dances the java with his hands in his pockets. If he lies down, Divine sucks him.

When she talks to herself about Darling, Divine says, clasping her hands in thought:

"I worship him. When I see him lying naked, I feel like saying mass on his chest."

It took Darling some time to get used to talking about her and to her in the feminine. He finally succeeded, but he still did not tolerate her talking to him as to a girl friend. Then little by little he let her do it. Divine dared say to him:

"You're pretty," adding: "like a prick."

Darling takes what comes his way in the course of his nocturnal and diurnal expeditions, and bottles of liquor, silk scarves, perfumes, and fake jewels accumulate in the garret. Each object brings into the room the fascination of a petty theft that is as brief as an appeal to the eyes. Darling steals from the display counters of department stores, from parked cars; he robs his few friends; he steals wherever he can.

On Sunday, Divine and he go to mass. Divine carries a gold-clasped missal in her right hand. With her left, she keeps the collar of her overcoat closed. They walk without seeing. They arrive at the Madeleine and take their seats among the fashionable worshipers. They believe in the bishops with gold ornaments. The mass fills Divine with wonder. Everything that goes on there is perfectly natural. Each of the priest's gestures is clear, has its precise meaning, and might be performed by anyone. When the officiating priest joins the two pieces of the divided host for the consecration, the edges do not fit together, and when he raises it with his two hands, he does not try to make you believe in the miracle. It makes Divine shudder.

Darling prays, saying:

"Our Mother Which art in heaven . . ."

They sometimes take communion from a mean-looking priest who maliciously crams the host into their mouths.

Darling still goes to mass because of its luxuriousness.

When they get back to the garret, they fondle each other.

Divine loves her man. She bakes pies for him and butters his roasts. She even dreams of him if he is in the toilet. She worships him in any and all positions.

A silent key is opening the door, and the wall bursts open just as a sky tears apart to reveal The Man, like the one Michelangelo painted nude in *The Last Judgment*. When the door has been closed, as gently as if it were made of glass, Darling tosses his hat on the couch and his cigarette butt any old place, though preferably to the ceiling. Divine leaps to the assault, clings to her man, licks him, and envelops him; he stands there solid and motionless, as if he were Andromeda's monster changed to a rock in the sea.

Since his friends keep away from him, Darling sometimes takes Divine to the Roxy Bar. They play poker-dice.
Darling likes the elegant movement of shaking the dice.
He also likes the graceful way in which fingers roll a cigarette or remove the cap of a fountain pen. He gives no
thought to either his seconds or his minutes or his hours.
His life is an underground heaven thronged with barmen,
pimps, queers, ladies of the night, and Queens of Spades,
but his life is a Heaven. He is a voluptuary. He knows all
the cafés in Paris where the toilets have seats.

"To do a good job," he says, "I've got to be sitting
down."

He walks for miles, preciously carrying in his bowels
the desire to shit, which he will gravely deposit in the
mauve tiled toilets of the Café Terminus at the Saint-
Lazare Station.

I don't know much about his background. Divine once
told me his name; it was supposed to be Paul Garcia. He
was probably born in one of those neighborhoods that
smell of the excrement which people wrap in newspapers
and drop from their windows, at each of which hangs a
heart of lilacs.

Darling!

If he shakes his curly head, you can see the earrings
swinging at the cheeks of his predecessors, the prowlers of
the boulevards, who used to wear them in the old days.
His way of kicking forward to swing the bottoms of his
trousers is the counterpart of the way women used to
kick aside the flounces of their gowns with their heels when
they waltzed.

So the couple lived undisturbed. From the bottom of
the stairs, the concierge watches over their happiness. And
toward evening the angels sweep the room and tidy up.
To Divine, angels are gestures that are made without her.

Oh, I so love to talk about them! Legions of soldiers

wearing coarse sky-blue or river-colored denim are hammering the azure of the heavens with their hobnailed
boots. The planes are weeping. The whole world is dying
of panicky fright. Five million young men of all tongues
will die by the cannon that erects and discharges. Their
flesh is already embalming the humans who drop like flies.
As the flesh perishes, solemnity issues forth from it. But
where I am I can muse in comfort on the lovely dead of
yesterday, today, and tomorrow. I dream of the lovers'
garret. The first serious quarrel has taken place, which
ends in a gesture of love. Divine has told me the following
about Darling: when he awoke one evening, too weary to
open his eyes, he heard her fussing about in the garret.

"What are you doing?" he asked.

Divine's mother (Ernestine), who called the wash the
wash basin, used to do the wash basin every Saturday. So
Divine answers:

"I'm doing the wash basin."

Now, as there was no bathtub in Darling's home, he used
to be dipped into a wash basin. Today, or some other day,
though it seems to me today, while he was sleeping, he
dreamed that he was entering a wash basin. He isn't, of
course, able to analyze himself, nor would he dream of
trying to, but he is sensitive to the tricks of fate, and to
the tricks of the theater of fear. When Divine answers,
"I'm doing the wash basin," he thinks she is saying it to
mean "I'm playing at being the wash basin," as if she were
"doing" a role. (She might have said: "I'm doing a loco-
motive.") He suddenly gets an erection from the feeling
that he has penetrated Divine in a dream. In his dream he
penetrates the Divine of the dream of Divine, and he possesses her, as it were, in a spiritual debauch. And the following phrases come into his mind: "To the heart, to the
hilt, right to the balls, right in the throat."

Darling has "fallen" in love.

I should like to play at inventing the ways love has of surprising people. It enters like Jesus into the heart of the impetuous; it also comes slyly, like a thief.

A gangster, here in prison, related to me a kind of counterpart of the famous comparison in which the two rivals come to know Eros:

"How I started getting a crush on him? We were in the jug. At night we had to undress, even take off our shirts in front of the guard to show him we weren't hiding anything (ropes, files, or blades). So the little guy and me were both naked. So I took a squint at him to see if he had muscles like he said. I didn't have time to get a good look because it was freezing. He got dressed again quick. I just had time to see he was pretty great. Man, did I get an eyeful (a shower of roses!). I was hooked. I swear! I got mine (here one expects inescapably: I knocked myself out). It lasted a while, four or five days. . . ."

The rest is of no further interest to us. Love makes use of the worst traps. The least noble. The rarest. It exploits coincidence. Was it not enough for a kid to stick his two fingers in his mouth and loose a strident whistle just when my soul was stretched to the limit, needing only this stridency to be torn from top to bottom? Was that the right moment, the moment that made two creatures love each other to the very blood? "Thou art a sun unto my night. My night is a sun unto thine!" We beat our brows. Standing, and from afar, my body passes through thine, and thine, from afar, through mine. We create the world. Everything changes . . . and to know that it does!

Loving each other like two young boxers who, before separating, tear off each other's shirt, and, when they are naked, astounded by their beauty, think they are seeing themselves in a mirror, stand there for a second open-mouthed, shake—with rage at being caught—their tangled hair, smile a damp smile, and embrace each other

like two wrestlers (in Greco-Roman wrestling), interlock
their muscles in the precise connections offered by the
muscles of the other, and drop to the mat until their warm
sperm, spurting high, maps out on the sky a milky way
where other constellations which I can read take shape: the
constellations of the Sailor, the Boxer, the Cyclist, the Fiddle, the Spahi, the Dagger. Thus a new map of the heavens
is outlined on the wall of Divine's garret.

Divine returns home from a walk to Monceau Park.
A cherry branch, supported by the full flight of the pink
flowers, surges stiff and black from a vase. Divine is hurt.
In the country, the peasants taught her to respect fruit
trees and not to regard them as ornaments; she will never
again be able to admire them. The broken branch shocks
her as you would be shocked by the murder of a nubile
maiden. She tells Darling how sad it makes her, and he gives
a horselaugh. He, the big-city child, makes fun of her
peasant scruples. Divine, in order to complete, to consum-
mate the sacrilege, and, in a way, to surmount it by willing it, perhaps also out of exasperation, tears the flowers to
shreds. Slaps. Shrieks. In short, a love riot, for let her touch
a male and all her gestures of defense modulate into caresses. A fist, that began as a blow, opens, alights, and
slides into gentleness. The big male is much too strong for
these weak queens. All Seck Gorgui had to do was to rub
lightly, without seeming to touch it, the lump his enormous tool made beneath his trousers, and none of them
were henceforth able to tear themselves away from him
who, in spite of himself, drew them straight home as a
magnet attracts iron filings. Divine would be fairly strong
physically, but she fears the movements of the riposte,
because they are virile, and her modesty makes her shy
away from the facial and bodily grimaces that effort requires. She did have this sense of modesty, and also a
modesty about masculine epithets as they applied to her.

As for slang, Divine did not use it, any more than did her
cronies, the other Nellys. It would have upset her as much
as whistling with her tongue and teeth like some cheap
hood or putting her hands in her trousers pockets and
keeping them there (especially by pushing back the flaps
of her unbuttoned jacket), or taking hold of her belt and
hitching up her trousers with a jerk of the hips.

The queens on high had their own special language.
Slang was for men. It was the male tongue. Like the language of men among the Caribees, it became a secondary
sexual attribute. It was like the colored plumage of male
birds, like the multicolored silk garments which are the
prerogative of the warriors of the tribe. It was a crest and
spurs. Everyone could understand it, but the only ones
who could speak it were the men who at birth received as
a gift the gestures, the carriage of the hips, legs and arms,
the eyes, the chest, with which one can speak it. One day,
at one of our bars, when Mimosa ventured the following
words in the course of a sentence: ". . . his screwy stories
. . . ," the men frowned. Someone said, with a threat in his
voice:

"Broad acting tough."

Slang in the mouths of their men disturbed the queens,
although they were less disturbed by the made-up words
peculiar to that language than by expressions from the ordinary world that were violated by the pimps, adapted
by them to their mysterious needs, expressions perverted,
deformed, and tossed into the gutter and their beds. For
example, they would say: "Easy does it," or, "Go, thou art
healed." This last phrase, plucked from the Gospel, would
emerge from lips at the corner of which was always stuck
a crumb of tobacco. It was said with a drawl. It would
conclude the account of a venture which had turned out
well for them. "Go . . . ," the pimps would say.

They would also say curtly:

"Cut it."

And also: "To lie low." But for Darling the expression did not have the same meaning as for Gabriel (the soldier who is to come, who is already being announced by an expression which delights me and seems suitable only to him: "I'm running the show."). Darling took it to mean: you've got to keep your eyes open. Gabriel thought: better clear out. A while ago, in my cell, the two pimps said: "We're making the pages." They meant they were going to make the beds, but a kind of luminous idea transformed me there, with my legs spread apart, into a husky guard or a palace groom who "makes" a palace page just as a young man makes a chick.

To hear this boasting made Divine swoon with pleasure, as when she disentangled—it seemed to her that she was unbuttoning a fly, that her hand, already inside, was pulling up the shirt—certain pig-latin words from their extra syllables: edbay, allbay.

This slang had insidiously dispatched its emissaries to the villages of France, and Ernestine had already yielded to its charm.

She would say to herself: "A Gauloise, a butt, a drag." She would sprawl in her chair and murmur these words as she inhaled the thick smoke of her cigarette. The better to conceal her fantasy, she would lock herself up in her room and smoke. One evening, as she opened the door, she saw the glow of a cigarette at the far end of the darkness. She was terrified by it, as if she were being threatened by a gun, but the fright was short-lived and blended into hope. Vanquished by the hidden presence of the male, she took a few steps and collapsed in an easy chair, but at the same time the glow disappeared. No sooner had she entered than she realized that she was seeing in the mirror of the wardrobe opposite the door, isolated by the darkness from the rest of the image, the glow of the cigarette she had lit, and she was glad that she had struck the match in the dark hallway. Her true honeymoon might be said to have taken place that evening. Her husband was a synthesis of all men: "A butt."

A cigarette was later to play her a shabby trick. As she walked down the main street of the village, she passed a young tough, one of those twenty faces I have cut out of magazines. He was whistling; a cigarette was stuck in the corner of his little mug. When he came abreast of Ernestine, he lowered his head, and the nodding gesture made him look as if he were ogling her tenderly. Ernestine thought that he was looking at her with "impertinent interest," but the fact is he was going against the wind, which blew the smoke into his eyes and made them smart, thus causing him to make this gesture. He screwed up his eyes and twisted his mouth, and the expression passed for a smile. Ernestine drew herself up with a sudden movement, which she quickly repressed and sheathed, and that was the end of the adventure, for at that very moment the village hood, who had not even seen Ernestine, felt the corner of his mouth smiling and his eye winking. With a tough-guy gesture, he hitched up his pants, thereby showing what the position of his true head made of him.

Still other expressions excited her, just as you would be moved and disturbed by the odd coupling of certain words, such as "bell and candle," or better still, "a Tartar ball-hold," which she would have liked to whistle and dance to the air of a java. Thinking of her pocket, she would say to herself: "My pouch."

While visiting a friend: "Get a load of that." "She got the works." About a good-looking passerby: "I gave him a hard-on."

Don't think that Divine took after her in being thrilled by slang, for Ernestine was never caught using it. "To get damned sore," coming from the cute mouth of an urchin, was enough to make both mother and son regard the one who said it as a sulking little mug, slightly husky, with the crushed face of a bulldog (that of the young English boxer Crane, who is one of my twenty on the wall).

Darling was growing pale. He knocked out a pink-cheeked Dutchman to rob him. At the moment, his pocket is full of florins. The garret knows the sober joy that comes from security. Divine and Darling sleep at night. During the day, they sit around naked and eat snacks, they squabble, forget to make love, turn on the radio, which drools on and on, and smoke. Darling says shit, and Divine, in order to be neighborly, even more neighborly than Saint Catherine of Siena, who passed the night in the cell of a man condemned to death, on whose prick her head rested, reads *Detective Magazine*. Outside the wind is blowing. The garret is cosily heated by a system of electric radiators, and I should like to give a short respite, even a bit of happiness, to the ideal couple.

The window is open on the cemetery.

Five A.M.

Divine hears church bells ringing (for she is awake). Instead of notes, which fly away, the chimes are strokes, five strokes, which drop to the pavement, and, on that wet pavement, bear Divine with them, Divine who three years before, or perhaps four, at the same hour, in the streets of a small town, was rummaging through a garbage can for bread. She had spent the night wandering through the streets in the drizzling rain, hugging the walls so as to get less wet, waiting for the angelus (the bells are now ringing low mass, and Divine relives the anguish of the days without shelter, the days of the bells) which announces that the churches are open to old maids, real sinners, and tramps. In the scented attic, the morning angelus violently

changes her back into the poor wretch in damp tatters who
has just heard mass and taken communion in order to rest
her feet and be less cold. Darling's sleeping body is warm
and next to hers. Divine closes her eyes; when the lids
join and separate her from the world which is emerging
from the dawn, the rain begins to fall, releasing within her
a sudden happiness so perfect that she says aloud, with a
deep sigh: "I'm happy." She was about to go back to sleep,
but the better to attest her marital happiness she recalled
without bitterness the memories of the time when she was
Culafroy, when, having run away from the slate house, she
landed in a small town, where, on golden, pink, or dreary
mornings, tramps with souls—which, to look at them, one
would call naïve—of dolls, accost each other with gestures one would also call fraternal. They have just got up
from park benches on which they have been sleeping,
from benches on the main square, or have just been born
from a lawn in the public park. They exchange secrets
dealing with Asylums, Prisons, Pilfering, and State Troop-
ers. The milkman hardly disturbs them. He is one of them.
For a few days Culafroy was also one of them. He fed on
crusts, covered with hair, that he found in garbage cans.
One night, the night he was most hungry, he even wanted
to kill himself. Suicide was his great preoccupation: the
song of phenobarbital! Certain attacks brought him so
close to death that I wonder how he escaped it, what imperceptible shock—coming from whom?—pushed him
back from the brink. But one day there would be, within
arm's reach, a phial of poison, and I would have only to
put it to my mouth; and then to wait. To wait, with un-
bearable anguish, for the effect of the incredible act, and
marvel at the wondrousness of an act so madly irremediable, that brings in its wake the end of the world which
follows from so casual a gesture. I had never been struck by
the fact that the slightest carelessness—sometimes even less

than a gesture, an unfinished gesture, one you would like
to take back, to undo by reversing time, a gesture so mild
and close, still in the present moment, that you think you
can efface it—Impossible!—can lead, for example, to the
guillotine, until the day when I myself—through one of
those little gestures that escape you involuntarily, that it is
impossible to abolish—saw my soul in anguish and immediately felt the anguish of the unfortunate creatures
who have no other way out than to confess. And to wait.
To wait and grow calm, because anguish and despair are
possible only if there is a visible or secret way out, and to
trust to death, as Culafroy once trusted the inaccessible
snakes.

Up to that time, the presence of a phial of poison or a
high-tension wire had never coincided with periods of dizziness, but Culafroy, and later Divine, will dread that
moment, and they expect to encounter it very soon, a moment chosen by Fate, so that death may issue irremedia-
bly from their decision or their lassitude.

There were random walks through the town, along dark
streets on sleepless nights. He would stop to look through
windows at gilded interiors, through lacework illustrated
with elaborate designs: flowers, acanthus leaves, cupids
with bows and arrows, lace deer; and the interiors, hollowed out in massive and shadowy altars, seemed to him
veiled tabernacles. In front of and beside the windows,
taper-like candelabra mounted a guard of honor in still
leafy trees which spread out in bouquets of enamel, metal,
or cloth lilies on the steps of a basilica altar. In short, they
were the surprise packages of vagrant children for whom
the world is imprisoned in a magic lattice, which they
themselves weave about the globe with toes as hard and
agile as Pavlova's. Children of this kind are invisible. Con-
ductors do not notice them on trains, nor do policemen
on docks; even in prison they seem to have been smuggled

in, like tobacco, tattooing ink, moonbeams, sunbeams, and the music of a phonograph. Their slightest gesture proves to them that a crystal mirror, which their fist sometimes bespangles with a slivery spider, encages the universe of houses, lamps, cradles, and baptisms, the universe of humans. The child we are concerned with was so far removed from this that later on all he remembered of his escapade was: "In town, women in mourning are very smartly dressed." But his solitude made it possible for him to be moved by petty miseries: a squatting old woman who, when the child suddenly appeared, pissed on her black cotton stockings; in front of restaurant windows bursting with lights and crystals and silverware, but still empty of diners, he witnessed, spellbound, the tragedies being performed by waiters in full dress who were dialoguing with a great flourish and debating questions of precedence until the arrival of the first elegant couple which dashed the drama to the floor and shattered it; homosexuals who would give him only fifty centimes and run off, full of happiness for a week; in stations at major junctions he would observe at night, from the waiting rooms, male shadows carrying mournful lanterns along multitudes of tracks. His feet and shoulders ached; he was cold.

Divine muses on the moments which are most painful for the vagabond: at night, when a car on the road suddenly spotlights his poor rags.

Darling's body is burning. Divine is lying in its hollow. I do not know whether she is already dreaming or merely reminiscing: "One morning (it was at the crack of dawn), I knocked at your door. I was weary of wandering through the streets, bumping into ragpickers, stumbling over garbage. I was seeking your bed, which was hidden in the lace, the lace, the ocean of lace, the universe of lace. From the far end of the world, a boxer's fist sent me sprawling into a tiny sewer." Just then, the angelus tolled. Now she is asleep in the lace, and their married bodies are afloat.

Here am I this morning, after a long night of caressing my beloved couple, torn from my sleep by the noise of the bolt being drawn by the guard who comes to collect the garbage. I get up and stagger to the latrine, still entangled in my strange dream, in which I succeeded in *getting my victim to pardon me*. Thus, I was plunged to the mouth in horror. The horror entered me. I chewed it. I was full of it. My young victim was sitting near me, and his bare leg, instead of crossing his right, went through the thigh. He said nothing, but I knew without the slightest doubt what he was thinking: "I've told the judge everything, you're pardoned. Besides, it's me sitting on the bench. You can confess. And you don't have to worry. You're pardoned." Then, with the immediacy of dreams, he was a little corpse no bigger than a figurine in an Epiphany pie, than a pulled tooth, lying in a glass of champagne in the middle of a Greek landscape with truncated ringed columns, around which long white tapeworms were twisting and streaming like coils, all this in a light seen only in dreams. I no longer quite remember my attitude, but I do know that I believed what he told me. Upon waking, I still had the feeling of baptism. But there is no question of resuming contact with the precise and tangible world of the cell. I lie down again until it's time for bread. The atmosphere of the night, the smell rising from the blocked latrines, overflowing with shit and yellow water, stir childhood memories which rise up like a black soil mined by moles. One leads to another and makes it surge up; a whole life which I thought subterranean and forever buried rises to the surface, to the air, to the sad sun, which give it a smell of decay, in which I delight. The reminiscence that really tugs at my heart is that of the toilet of the slate house. It was my refuge. Life, which I saw far off and blurred through its darkness and smell—an odor that filled me with compassion, in which the scent of the elders and the loamy earth was dominant, for the outhouse was at the far end of the garden, near the hedge—life, as it reached me, was singularly sweet, caressing, light, or rather lightened, delivered from heaviness. I am speaking of the life which was things outside the toilet, whatever in the world was not my little retreat with its worm-eaten boards. It seemed to me as if it were somewhat in the manner of floating, painted dreams, whereas I in my hole, like a larva, went on with a restful nocturnal existence, and at times I had the feeling I was sinking slowly, as into sleep or a lake or a maternal breast or even a state of incest, to the spiritual center of the earth. My periods of happiness were never luminously happy, my peace never what men of letters and theologians call a "celestial peace." That's as it should be, for I would be horrified if I were pointed at by God, singled out by Him; I know very well that if I were sick, and were cured by a miracle, I would not survive it. Miracles are unclean; the peace I used to seek in the outhouse, the one I am going to seek in the memory of it, is a reassuring and soothing peace.

At times it would rain. I would hear the patter of the drops on the zinc roofing. Then my sad well-being, my morose delectation, would be aggravated by a further sorrow. I would open the door a crack, and the sight of the wet garden and the pelted vegetables would grieve me. I would remain for hours squatting in my cell, roosting on my wooden seat, my body and soul prey to the odor and darkness; I would feel mysteriously moved, because it was there that the most secret part of human beings came to reveal itself, as in a confessional. Empty confessionals had the same sweetness for me. Back issues of fashion magazines lay about there, illustrated with engravings in which the women of 1910 always had a muff, a parasol, and a dress with a bustle.

It took me a long time to learn to exploit the spell of these nether powers, who drew me to them by the feet, who flapped their black wings about me, fluttering them like the eyelashes of a vamp, and dug their branchlike fingers into my eyes.

Someone has flushed the toilet in the next cell. Since our two latrines are adjoining, the water stirs in mine, and a whiff of odor heightens my intoxication. My stiff penis is caught in my underpants; it is freed by the touch of my hand, strikes against the sheet, and forms a little mound. Darling! Divine! And I am alone here.

It is Darling whom I cherish most, for you realize that, in the final analysis, it is my own destiny, be it true or false, that I am draping (at times a rag, at times a court robe) on Divine's shoulders.

Slowly but surely I want to strip her of every vestige of happiness so as to make a saint of her. The fire that is searing her has already burned away heavy bonds; new ones are shackling her: Love. A morality is being born, which is certainly not the usual morality (it is consonant with Divine), though it is a morality all the same, with its Good and Evil. Divine is not beyond good and evil, there where the saint must live. And I, more gentle than a wicked angel, lead her by the hand.

Here are some "Divinariana" gathered expressly for you. Since I wish to show the reader a few candid shots of her, it is up to him to provide the sense of duration, of passing time, and to assume that during this first chapter she will be between twenty and thirty years of age.

DIVINARIANA

Divine to Darling: "You're my Maddening Baby!"

—Divine is humble. She is aware of luxury only through a certain mystery which it secretes and which she fears. Luxury hotels, like the dens of witches, hold in thrall aggressive charms which a gesture of ours can free from marble, carpets, velvet, ebony, and crystal. As soon as she accumulated a little money, thanks to an Argentine, Divine trained herself in luxury. She bought leather and steel luggage saturated with musk. Seven or eight times a day, she would take the train, enter the Pullman car, have her bags stacked in the baggage racks, settle down on the cushions until it was time for the train to leave, and, a few seconds before the whistle blew, would call two or three porters, have her things removed, take a cab and have herself driven to a fine hotel, where she would remain long enough to install herself discreetly and luxuriously. She played this game of being a star for a whole week, and now she knows how to walk on carpets and talk to flunkeys, who are luxury furnishings. She has domesticated the charms and brought luxury down to earth. The sober contours and scrolls of Louis XV furniture and frames and woodwork sustain her life—which seems to unroll more nobly, a double stairway—in an infinitely elegant air. But it is particularly when her hired car passes a wrought-iron gate or makes a delicious swerve that she is an Infanta.

—Death is no trivial matter. Divine already fears being caught short for the solemnity. She wants to die with dignity. Just as that air-force lieutenant went into combat in his dress uniform so that, if the death that flies overtook him in the plane, it would find and transfix him as an officer and not a mechanic, so Divine always carries in her pocket her oily gray diploma for advanced study.

—He's as dumb as a button, as a button on ... (Mimosa is about to say: your boot).

Divine, blandly: on your fly.

—She always had with her, up her sleeve, a small fan made of muslin and pale ivory. Whenever she said some-thing that disconcerted her, she would pull the fan from her sleeve with the speed of a magician, unfurl it, and sud-denly one would see the fluttering wing in which the lower part of her face was hidden. Divine's fan will beat lightly about her face all her life. She inaugurated it in a poultry shop on the Rue Lepic. Divine had gone down with a sister to buy a chicken. They were in the shop when the butcher's son entered. She looked at him and clucked, called the sister and, putting her index finger into the rump of the trussed chicken that lay on the stall, she cried out: "Oh, look! Beauty of Beauties!" and her fan quickly fluttered to her blushing cheeks. She looked again with moist eyes at the butcher's son.

—On the boulevard, policemen have stopped Divine, who is tipsy. She is singing the *Veni Creator* in a shrill voice. In all the passersby are born little married couples veiled in white tulle who kneel on tapestried prayer stools; each of the two policemen remembers the time he was best man at a cousin's wedding. In spite of this, they take Divine to the station. Along the way she rubs against them, and they each get a hard-on, squeeze her more tightly, and stumble on purpose in order to tangle their thighs with hers. Their huge cocks are alive and rap sharply or push with desperate, sobbing thrusts against the door of their blue woolen pants. They bid them open,

like the clergy at the closed church door on Palm Sunday.
The little queens, both young and old, scattered along the
boulevard, who see Divine going off, borne away to the
music of the grave nuptial hymn, the *Veni Creator,* cry
out:

"They're going to put her in irons!"

"Like a sailor!"

"Like a convict!"

"Like a woman in childbirth!"

The solid citizens going by form a crowd and see nothing, know nothing. They are scarcely, imperceptibly, dis-
lodged from their calm state of confidence by the trivial
event: Divine being led away by the arm, and her sisters
bewailing her.

Having been released, the next evening she is again at
her post on the boulevard. Her blue eyelid is swollen:

"My God, Beauties, I almost passed out. The policemen
held me up. They were all standing around me fanning
me with their checked handkerchiefs. They were the Holy
Women wiping my face. My Divine Face. 'Snap out of it,
Divine! Snap out of it,' they shouted, 'snap out of it, snap
out of it!' They were singing to me.

"They took me to a dark cell. Someone (Oh! that SOME-
ONE who must have drawn them! I shall seek him throughout the fine print on the heavy pages of adventure novels
which throng with miraculously handsome and raffish
page boys. I untie and unlace the doublet and hip boots
of one of them, who follows Black-Stripe John; I leave
him, a cruel knife in one hand and his stiff prick clutched
in the other, standing with his face to the white wall, and
here he is, a young, fiercely virgin convict. He puts his
cheek to the wall. With a kiss, he licks the vertical surface,
and the greedy plaster sucks in his saliva. Then a shower
of kisses. All his movements outline an invisible horseman
who embraces him and whom the inhuman wall confines.

At length, bored to tears, overtaxed with love, the page draws. . . .) had drawn, dear ladies, a whirligig of ah! yes yes, my Beauties, dream and play the Boozer so you can fly there—I refuse to tell you what—but they were winged and puffy and big, sober as cherubs, splendid cocks, made of barley sugar. Ladies, around some of them that were more upright and solid than the others, were twined clematis and convolvulus and nasturtium, and winding little pimps too. Oh! those columns! The cell was flying at top speed! It drove me simply mad, mad, mad!"

The sweet prison cells! After the foul monstrousness of my arrest, of my various arrests, each of which is always the first, which appeared to me in all its irremediable aspects in an inner vision of blazing and fatal speed and brilliance the moment my hands were imprisoned in the steel handcuffs, gleaming as a jewel or a theorem, the prison cell, which now I love as one loves a vice, consoled me, by its being, for my own being.

The odor of prison is an odor of urine, formaldehyde, and paint. I have recognized it in all the prisons of Europe, and I recognized that this odor would finally be the odor of my destiny. Every time I backslide, I examine the walls for the traces of my earlier captivities, that is, of my earlier despairs, regrets, and desires that some other convict has carved out for me. I explore the surface of the walls, in quest of the fraternal trace of a friend. For though I have never known what friendship could actually be, what vibrations the friendship of two men sets up in their hearts and perhaps on their skin, in prison I sometimes long for a brotherly friendship, but always with a man—of my own age—who is handsome, who would have complete confidence in me and be the accomplice of my loves, my thefts, my criminal desires, though this does not enlighten me about such friendship, about the odor, in both friends, of its secret intimacy, because for the occasion I make myself a male who knows that he really isn't one. I await the revelation on the wall of some terrible secret: especially murder, murder of men, or betrayal of friendship, or profanation of the dead, a secret of which I shall be the resplendent tomb. But all I have ever found has been an occasional phrase scratched on the plaster with a pin, formulas of love or revolt, more often of resignation: "Jojo of the Bastille loves his girl for life." "My heart to my mother, my cock to the whores, my head to the hangman." These rupestral inscriptions are almost always a gallant homage to womanhood, or a smattering of those bad stanzas that are known to bad boys all over France:

> *When coal turns white,*
> *And soot's not black,*
> *I'll forget the prison*
> *That's at my back.*

And those pipes of Pan that mark the days gone by!

And then the following surprising inscription carved in the marble under the main entrance: "Inauguration of the prison, March 17, 1900," which makes me see a procession of official gentlemen solemnly bringing in the first prisoner to be incarcerated.

—Divine: "My heart's in my hand, and my hand is pierced, and my hand's in the bag, and the bag is shut, and my heart is caught."

—Divine's kindness. She had complete and invincible confidence in men with tough, regular faces, with thick hair, a lock of which falls over the forehead, and this confidence seemed to be inspired by the glamor these faces had for Divine. She had often been taken in, she whose critical spirit is so keen. She realized this suddenly, or gradually, tried to counteract this attitude, and finally intellectual scepticism, struggling with emotional consent, won out and took root in her. But in that way she is still in error, because she now takes it out on the very young men to whom she feels attracted. She receives their declarations with a smile or ironic remark that ill conceals her weakness (weakness of the faggots in the presence of the lump in Gorgui's pants), and her efforts not to yield to their carnal beauty (to make them dance to her tune), while they, on the other hand, immediately return the smile, which is now more cruel, as if, shot forth from Divine's teeth, it rebounded from theirs, which were sharper, colder, more glacial, because in her presence their teeth were more coldly beautiful.

But, to punish herself for being mean to the mean, Divine goes back on her decisions and humiliates herself in the presence of the pimps, who fail to understand what's going on. Nevertheless, she is scrupulously kind. One day, in the police wagon, on the way back from court, for she often slipped, particularly for peddling dope, she asks an old man:

"How many?"

He answers:

"They slapped me with three years. What about you?"

She's down for only two, but answers:

"Three years."

—July Fourteenth: red, white, and blue everywhere. Divine dresses up in all the other colors, out of consideration for them, because they are disdained.

Divine and Darling. To my mind, they are the ideal pair of lovers. From my evil-smelling hole, beneath the coarse wool of the covers, with my nose in the sweat and my eyes wide open, alone with them, I see them.

Darling is a giant whose curved feet cover half the

globe as he stands with his legs apart in baggy, sky-blue silk underpants. He rams it in. So hard and calmly that anuses and vaginas slip onto his member like rings on a finger. He rams it in. So hard and calmly that his virility, observed by the heavens, has the penetrating force of the battalions of blond warriors who on June 14, 1940, buggered us soberly and seriously, though their eyes were elsewhere as they marched in the dust and sun. But they are the image of only the tensed, buttressed Darling. Their granite prevents them from being slithering pimps.

I close my eyes. Divine: a thousand shapes, charming in their grace, emerge from my eyes, mouth, elbows, knees, from all parts of me. They say to me: "Jean, how glad I am to be living as Divine and to be living with Darling."

I close my eyes. Divine and Darling. To Darling, Divine is barely a pretext, an occasion. If he thought of her, he would shrug his shoulders to shake off the thought, as if the thought were a dragon's claws clinging to his back. But to Divine, Darling is everything. She takes care of his penis. She caresses it with the most profuse tenderness and calls it by the kind of pet names used by ordinary folk when they feel horny. Such expressions as Little Dicky, the Babe in the Cradle, Jesus in His Manger, the Hot Little Chap, your Baby Brother, without her formulating them, take on full meaning. Her feeling accepts them literally. Darling's penis is in itself all of Darling: the object of her pure luxury, an object of pure luxury. If Divine is willing to see in her man anything other than a hot, purplish member, it is because she can follow its stiffness, which extends to the anus, and can sense that it goes farther into his body, that it is this very body of Darling erect and terminating in a pale, tired face, a face of eyes, nose, mouth, flat cheeks, curly hair, beads of sweat.

I close my eyes beneath the lice-infested blankets. Divine has opened the fly and arranged this mysterious **area** of her man. Has beribboned the bush and penis, stuck flowers into the buttonholes of the fly. (Darling goes out with her that way in the evening.) The result is that to Divine, Darling is only the magnificent delegation on earth, the physical expression, in short, the symbol of a being (perhaps God), of an idea that remains in heaven. They do not commune. Divine may be compared to Marie-Antoinette, who, according to my history of France, had to learn to express herself in prison, willy-nilly, in the slang current in the eighteenth century. Poor dear Queen!

If Divine says in a shrill voice: "They dragged me into court," the words conjure up for me an old Countess Solange, in a very ancient gown with a train of lace, whom soldiers are dragging on her knees, by her bound wrists, over the cobblestones of a law court.

"I'm swooning with love," she said.
Her life stopped, but around her life continued to flow. She felt as if she were going backward in time, and wild with fright at the idea of—the rapidity of it—reaching the beginning, the Cause, she finally released a gesture that very quickly set her heart beating again.

Once again the kindness of this giddy creature. She asks a young murderer whom we shall eventually meet (Our Lady of the Flowers) a question. This casual question so wounds the murderer that Divine sees his face decomposing visibly. Then, immediately, running after the pain she has caused in order to overtake it and stop it, stumbling over the syllables, getting all tangled up in her saliva, which is like tears of emotion, she cries out:
"No, no, it's me."

The friend of the family is the giddiest thing I know in the neighborhood. Mimosa II. Mimosa the Great, the One, is now being kept by an old man. She has her villa in Saint-Cloud. As she was in love with Mimosa II who was then a milkman, she left her her name. The II isn't pretty, but what can be done about it? Divine has invited her to high tea. She came to the garret at about five o'clock. They kissed each other on the cheek, being very careful to make sure their bodies did not touch. She greeted Darling with a male handshake, and there she is sitting on the couch where Divine sleeps. Darling was preparing the ladies' tea; he had his little coquetries.

"It's nice of you to have come, Mimo. We see you so seldom."

"That's the least I could do, my dear. Besides, I simply adore your little nook. It has quite a vicarage effect with the park in the distance. It must be awfully nice having the dead for neighbors!"

Indeed, the window was very lovely.

When the cemetery was beneath the moon, at night, from her bed, Divine would see it bright and deep in the moonlight. The light was such that one could clearly discern, beneath the grass of the graves and beneath the marble, the spectral unrest of the dead. Thus, the cemetery, through the fringed window, was like a limpid eye between two wide-open lids, or, better still, it was like a blue glass eye—those eyes of the fair-haired blind—in the hollow of a Negro's palm. It would dance, that is, the wind stirred the grass and the cypresses. It would dance, that is, it was melodic and its body moved like a jellyfish. Divine's relations with the cemetery: it had worked its way into her soul, somewhat as certain sentences work their way into a text, that is, a letter here, a letter there. The cemetery within her was present at cafés, on the boulevard, in jail, under the blankets, in the pissoirs. Or, if you prefer, the cemetery was present within her somewhat as that gentle, faithful, submissive dog was present in Darling, occasionally giving the pimp's face the sad, stupid look that dogs have.

Mimosa is leaning out the window, the bay window of the Departed, and is looking for a grave with her finger pointing. When she has found it, she yelps:

"Ah! you hussy, you harlot, so you finally kicked off! So now you're good and stiff beneath the icy marble. And I'm walking on your rugs, you bitch!"

"You're wackeroo," muttered Darling, who almost bawled her out in whore (a secret language).

"Darling, I may be wacky with love for you, you great big terrible Darling, but Charlotte's down there in the grave! Charlotte's right down there!"

We laughed, for we knew that Charlotte was her grandfather who was down in the cemetery, with a grant in perpetuity.

"And how's Louise (that was Mimosa's father)? And Lucie (her mother)?" asked Divine.

"Ah! Divine, don't talk to me about them. They're much too well. The dumb bitches'll never kick off. They're just a couple of filthy sluts."

Darling liked what the faggots talked about. He especially liked, provided it was done in private, the way they talked. While preparing the tea, he listened, with a gliding caravel on his lips. Darling's smile was never stagnant. It seemed forever twitching with a touch of anxiety. Today he is more anxious than usual, for tonight he is to leave Divine; in view of what is going to happen, Mimosa seems to him terrible, wolflike. Divine has no idea of what is in store. She will learn all at once of her desertion and of Mimosa's shabby behavior. For they have managed the affair without losing any time. Roger, Mimosa's man, has taken a powder.

"My Roger's off to the wars. She's gone to play Amazon."

Mimosa said that one day in front of Darling, who offered, in jest, to replace Roger. Well, she accepted.

Our domestic life and the law of our Homes do not resemble your Homes. We love each other without love. Our homes do not have the sacramental character. Fags are the great immoralists. In the twinkling of an eye, after six years of union, without considering himself attached, without thinking that he was causing pain or doing wrong, Darling decided to leave Divine. Without remorse, only a slight concern that perhaps Divine might refuse ever to see him again.

As for Mimosa, the fact of hurting a rival is enough to make her happy about the pain she is causing.

The two queens were chirping away. Their talk was dull compared to the play of their eyes. The eyelids did not flutter, nor did the temples crinkle. Their eyeballs flowed from right to left, left to right, rotated, and their glances were manipulated by a system of ball bearings. Let us listen now as they whisper so that Darling may draw near and, standing beside them, pachyderm that he is, make titanic efforts to understand. Mimosa whispers:

"My dear, it's when the Cuties still have their pants on that I like them. You just look at them and they get all stiff. It drives you mad, simply mad! It starts a crease that goes on and on and on, all the way down to their feet. When you touch it, you keep following the crease, without pressing on it, right to the toes. My love, you'd think that the Beaut was going straight down. For that, I recommend sailors especially."

Darling was smiling faintly. He knows. The Big Beaut of a man does not excite him, but he is no longer surprised that it excites Divine and Mimosa.

Mimosa says to Darling:

"You're playing hostess. To get away from us."

He answers:

"I'm making the tea."

As if realizing that his answer was too noncommittal, he added:

"No news from Rogerboy?"

"No," said Mimosa, "I'm the Quite-Alone."

She also meant: "I'm the Quite-Persecuted." When they had to express a feeling that risked involving an exuberance of gesture or voice, the queens contented themselves with saying: "I'm the Quite-Quite," in a confidential tone, almost a murmur, heightened by a slight movement of their ringed hand which calms an invisible storm. Old-timers who, in the days of the great Mimosa, had known the wild cries of freedom and the mad gestures of boldness brought on by feelings swollen with desires that contorted the mouth, made the eyes glow, and bared the teeth, wondered what mysterious mildness had now replaced the disheveled passions. Once Divine began her litany, she kept on until she was exhausted. The first time Darling heard it, he merely looked at her in bewilderment. It was in the room; he was amused; but when Divine began again in the street, he said:

"Shut up, chick. You're not gonna make me look like an ass in front of the boys."

His voice was so cold, so ready to give her the works, that Divine recognized her Master's Voice. She restrained herself. But you know that nothing is so dangerous as repression. One evening, at a pimp's bar on the Place Clichy (where, out of prudence, Darling usually went without her), Divine paid for the drinks and, in picking up the change, forgot to leave a tip on the counter for the waiter. When she realized it, she let out a shriek that rent the mirrors and the lights, a shriek that stripped the pimps:

"My God, I'm the Quite-Giddy!"

Right and left, with the merciless speed of misfortune, two slaps shut her up, shrank her like a greyhound, her head no longer even as high as the bar. Darling was in a rage. He was green beneath the neon. "Beat it," he said. He, however, went on sipping his cognac to the last drop.

These cries (Darling will say: "She's losing her yipes," as if he were thinking: "You're losing money," or, "You're putting on weight.") were one of the idiosyncrasies of Mimosa I that Divine had appropriated. When they and a few others were together in the street or a queer café, from their conversations (from their mouths and hands) would escape ripples of flowers, in the midst of which they simply stood or sat about as casually as could be, discussing ordinary household matters:

"I really am, sure sure sure, the Quite-Profligate."

"Oh, Ladies, I'm acting like such a harlot."

"You know (the *ou* was so drawn out that that was all one noticed), *yoouknow*, I'm the Consumed-with-Affliction."

"Here here, behold the Quite-Fluff-Fluff."

One of them, when questioned by a detective on the boulevard:

"Who are you?"

"I'm a Thrilling Thing."

Then, little by little, they understood each other by saying: "I'm the Quite-Quite," and finally: "I'm the Q'Q'."

It was the same for the gestures. Divine had a very great one: when she took her handkerchief from her pocket, it described an enormous arc before she put it to her lips. Anyone trying to read something into Divine's gesture would have been infallibly mistaken, for two gestures were here contained in one. There was the elaborated gesture, which was diverted from its initial goal, and the one that contained and completed it by grafting itself on just at the point where the first ceased. Thus, in taking her hand out of her pocket, Divine had meant to extend her arm and shake her unfurled lace handkerchief. To shake it for a farewell to nothing, or to let fall a powder which it did not contain, a perfume—no, it was a pretext. This tremendous gesture was needed to relate the following oppressive drama: "I am alone. Save me who can." But Darling, though unable to destroy it completely, had reduced the gesture, which, without, however, becoming trivial, had turned into something hybrid and thereby strange. He had, in overwhelming it, made it overwhelming. Speaking of these constraints, Mimosa had said:

"Our males have turned us into a garden of rheumatics."

When Mimosa left the garret, Darling tried to pick a quarrel with Divine so he could leave her. He found nothing to quarrel about. That made him furious with her. He called her a bitch and left.

So Divine is alone in the world. Whom shall I give her for a lover? The gypsy I am seeking? The one whose figure, because of the high heels of his Marseilles pumps, resembles a guitar? About his legs there coil and climb, the better to hug him coldly at the buttocks, the trousers of a sailor.

Divine is alone. With me. The whole world that stands guard around the Santé Prison knows nothing, has no desire to know anything, of the distress of a little cell, lost amidst others, which are all so much alike that I, who know it well, often mistake it. Time leaves me no respite; I feel it passing. What shall I do with Divine? If Darling comes back, it will not be long before he leaves again. He has tasted divorce. But Divine needs a few jolts which squeeze her, pull her apart, paste her back together, shatter her, till all I have left of her is a bit of essence which I am trying to track down. That is why M. Roquelaure (127, Rue de Douai, an employee of the Municipal Transport Company), when he went down at seven A.M. to get

the milk and the morning paper for himself and Mme.
Roquelaure, who was combing out her hair in the kitchen,
found in the narrow hallway of the house, on the floor, a
trampled fan. The plastic handle was encrusted with fake
emeralds. He kicked at the rubbish boyishly and kept
shoving it out onto the sidewalk and then into the gutter.
It was Divine's fan. That very evening Divine had met
Darling quite by chance and had gone with him, without
reproaching him for his flight. He listened to her, whistling
as he did, perhaps a bit contrite. They happened to run
into Mimosa. Divine bent to the ground in a deep bow,
but Mimosa, in a voice that sounded male to Divine for
the first time, screamed:

"Get the hell out of here, you dirty whore, you dirty
cocksucker!"

It was the milkman. . . . This is not an unfamiliar phenomenon, the case of the second nature that can no longer
resist and allows the first to break out in blind hatred.
We wouldn't mention it were it not a matter of showing
the duplicity of the sex of fags. We shall see the same
thing happen again in the case of Divine.

So it was quite serious. Here again, Darling, with magnificent cowardice (I maintain that cowardice is an active
quality, which, once it assumes this intensity, spreads like
a white dawn, a phantasm, about handsome young cow-
ards who move within it in the depths of a sea), did not
deign to take sides. His hands were in his pockets.

"Go on, kill each other," he said with a sneer.

The sneer, which still rings in my ears, was uttered one
evening in my presence by a sixteen-year-old child. This
should give you an idea of what satanism is. Divine and
Mimosa fought it out. Leaning against the wall of a house,
Divine gave little kicks and beat down on the air with her
fists. Mimosa was the stronger and hit hard. Divine managed to break away and run, but Mimosa caught her just

as she reached the half-open door of a house. The struggle continued in the hallway with hushed voices and pulled punches. The tenants were asleep; the concierge heard nothing. Divine thought: "The concierge can't hear anything because her name is Mme. Muller." The street was empty. Darling, standing on the sidewalk with his hands still in his pockets, was gazing thoughtfully at the garbage in the can that had been put outside. Finally, he made up his mind and left.

"They're both frigging idiots."

On the way, he thought: "If Divine's got a shiner, I'll spit in her dirty mug. Boy, fags are rough." But he came back to live with Divine.

So Divine found her pimp again, and her friend Mimosa. And resumed her life in the garret, which was to last another five years. The garret overlooking the dead. Montmartre by night. The Shame-on-Me-Crazy. We're approaching thirty. . . . With my head still under the covers, my fingers digging into my eyes and my mind off somewhere, there remains only the lower part of my body, detached, by my digging fingers, from my rotting head.

A guard who goes by; the chaplain who comes in and doesn't talk of God. I no more see them than I know that I'm in the Santé Prison. Poor Santé which goes to the trouble of keeping me.

Darling loves Divine more and more deeply, that is, more and more without realizing it. Word by word, he grows attached. But more and more neglects her. She stays in the garret alone; she offers up to God her love and sorrow. For God—as the Jesuits have said—chooses a myriad of ways to enter into souls: the golden powder, a swan, a bull, a dove, and countless others. For a gigolo who cruises the tearooms, perhaps He has a way that theology has not catalogued, perhaps He chooses to be a tearoom. We might also wonder, had Churches not existed, what form the sanctity (I am not saying her path to salvation) of Divine and of all the other Saints would have taken. We must realize that Divine does not live with gladness of heart. She accepts, unable to elude it, the life that God makes for her and that leads her to Him. But God is not gilt-edged. Before His mystic throne, useless to adopt artful poses, pleasing to the Greek eye. Divine is consumed with fire. I might, just as she admitted to me, confide that if I take contempt with a smile or a burst of laughter, it is not yet—and will it some day be?—out of contempt for contempt, but rather in order not to be ridiculous, not to be reviled, by anything or anyone, that I have placed myself lower than dirt. I could not do otherwise. If I declare that I am an old whore, no one can better that, I discourage insult. People can't even spit in my face any more. And Darling Daintyfoot is like the rest of you; all he can do is despise me. I have spent whole nights at the following game: working up sobs, bringing them to my eyes, and leaving them there without their bursting, so that in the morning my eyelids ache, they feel hard and stony, as painful as a sunburn. The sob at my eyes might have flowed into tears, but it remains there, weighing against my eyelids like a condemned man against the door of a cell. It is especially then that I realize how deeply I suffer. Then it's the turn for another sob to be born, then another. I swallow them all and spit them out in wisecracks. So my smile, which others may call my whistling in the dark, is merely the inordinate need to activate a muscle in order to release an emotion. We are, after all, familiar enough with the tragedy of a certain feeling which is obliged to borrow its expression from the opposite feeling so as to escape from the myrmidons of the law. It disguises itself in the trappings of its rival.

To be sure, a great earthly love would destroy this wretchedness, but Darling is not yet the Chosen One.

Later on, there will come a soldier, so that Divine may have some respite in the course of that calamity which is her life. Darling is merely a fraud ("an adorable fraud," Divine calls him), and he must remain one in order to preserve my tale. It is only on this condition that I can like him. I say of him, as of all my lovers, against whom I butt and crumble: "Let him be steeped in indifference, let him be petrified with blind indifference."

Divine will take up this phrase and apply it to Our Lady of the Flowers.

This movement makes Divine laugh with grief. Gabriel himself will tell us how an officer who loved him, unable to do better, used to punish him.

Our Lady of the Flowers here makes his solemn entrance through the door of crime, a secret door, that opens on to a dark but elegant stairway. Our Lady mounts the stairway, as many a murderer, any murderer, has mounted it. He is sixteen when he reaches the landing. He knocks at the door; then he waits. His heart is beating, for he is determined. He knows that his destiny is being fulfilled, and although he knows (Our Lady knows or seems to know it better than anyone) that his destiny is being fulfilled at every moment, he has the pure mystic feeling that this murder is going to turn him, by virtue of the baptism of blood, into Our Lady of the Flowers. He is excited as he stands in front of, or behind, the door, as if, like a fiancé in white gloves. . . . Behind the wood, a voice asks:

"What is it?"

"It's me," mutters the youngster.

Confidently, the door opens and closes behind him.

Killing is easy, since the heart is on the left side, just opposite the armed hand of the killer, and the neck fits so neatly into the two joined hands. The corpse of the old man, one of those thousands of old men whose lot it is to die that way, is lying on the blue rug. Our Lady has killed him. A murderer. He doesn't say the word to himself, but rather I listen with him in his head to the ringing of chimes that must be made up of all the bells of lily-of-the-valley, the bells of spring flowers, bells made of porcelain, glass, water, air. His head is a singing copse. He himself is a beribboned wedding feast skipping, with the violin in front and orange blossoms on the black of the jackets, down a sunken April road. He feels himself, youngster that he is, leaping from flowery vale to flowery vale, straight to the mattress where the old man has tucked away his little pile. He turns it over, turns it back, rips it open, pulls out the wool, but he finds nothing, for nothing is so hard to find as money after a premeditated murder.

"Where does the bastard keep his dough?" he says aloud.

These words are not articulated, but, since they are only felt, are rather spat out of his throat in a tangled mass. It is a croak.

He goes from one piece of furniture to the next. He loses his temper. His nails catch in the grooves. He rips fabrics. He tries to regain his composure, stops to catch his breath, and (in the silence), surrounded by objects that have lost all meaning now that their customary user has ceased to exist, he suddenly feels himself in a monstrous world made up of the soul of the furniture, of the objects; he is seized with panic. He swells up like a bladder, grows enormous, able to swallow the world and himself with it, and then subsides. He wants to get away. As slowly as he can. He is no longer thinking about the body of the murdered man, nor the lost money, nor the lost time, nor the lost act. The police are probably lurking somewhere. Got to beat it fast. His elbow strikes a vase standing on a commode. The vase falls down and twenty thousand francs scatter graciously at his feet.

He opened the door without anxiety, went out on the landing, leaned over, and looked down the silent stairwell, between the apartments, at the glittering ball of cut crystal. Then he walked down the nocturnal carpet and into the nocturnal air, through the silence which is that of eternal space, step by step, into Eternity.

The street. Life is no longer unclean. With a feeling of lightness, he runs off to a small hotel which turns out to be a dive, and rents a room. There, to assuage him, the true night, the night of the stars, comes little by little, and a touch of horror turns his stomach: it is that physical disgust of the first hour, of the murderer for the murdered, about which a number of men have spoken to me. It haunts you, doesn't it? The dead man is rigorous. Your dead man is inside you; mingled with your blood, he flows in your veins, oozes out through your pores, and your heart lives on him, as cemetery flowers sprout from corpses. . . . He emerges from you through your eyes, your ears, your mouth.

Our Lady of the Flowers would like to vomit out the carcass. The night, which has come on, does not bring terror. The room smells of whore. Stinks and smells fragrant.

"To escape from horror, as we have said, bury yourself in it."

All by itself the murderer's hand seeks his penis, which is erect. He strokes it through the sheet, gently at first, with the lightness of a fluttering bird, then grips it, squeezes it hard; finally he discharges into the toothless mouth of the strangled old man. He falls asleep.

To love a murderer. To love to commit a crime in cahoots with the young half-breed pictured on the cover of the torn book. I want to sing murder, for I love murderers. To sing it plainly. Without pretending, for example, that I want to be redeemed through it, though I do yearn for redemption. I would like to kill. As I have said above, rather than an old man, I would like to kill a handsome blond boy, so that, already united by the verbal link that joins the murderer and the murdered (each existing thanks to the other), I may be visited, during days and nights of hopeless melancholy, by a handsome ghost of which I would be the haunted castle. But may I be spared the horror of giving birth to a sixty-year-old corpse, or that of a woman, young or old. I am tired of satisfying my desire for murder stealthily by admiring the imperial pomp of sunsets. My eyes have bathed in them enough. Let's get to my hands. But to kill, to kill you, Jean. Wouldn't it be a question of knowing how I would behave as I watched you die by my hand?

More than of anyone else, I am thinking of Pilorge. His face, cut out of *Detective Magazine*, darkens the wall with its icy radiance, which is made up of his Mexican corpse, his will to death, his dead youth, and his death. He spatters the wall with a brilliance that can be expressed only by the confrontation of the two terms that cancel each other. Night emerges from his eyes and spreads over his face, which begins to look like pines on stormy nights, that face of his which is like the gardens where I used to spend the night: light trees, the opening in a wall, and iron railings, astounding railings, festooned railings. And light trees. O Pilorge! Your face, like a lone nocturnal garden in Worlds where Suns spin round! And on it that impalpable sadness, like the light trees in the garden. Your face is dark, as if in broad daylight a shadow had passed over your soul. It must have made you feel slightly cool, for your body shuddered with a shudder more subtle than the fall of a veil of the tulle known as "gossamer-fine tulle," for your face is veiled with thousands of fine, light, microscopic wrinkles, painted, rather than engraved, in criss-cross lines.

Already the murderer compels my respect. Not only because he has known a rare experience, but because he has suddenly set himself up as a god, on an altar, whether of shaky boards or azure air. I am speaking, to be sure, of the conscious, even cynical murderer, who dares take it upon himself to deal death without trying to refer his acts to some power of a given order, for the soldier who kills does not assume responsibility, nor does the lunatic, nor the jealous man, nor the one who knows he will be forgiven; but rather the man who is called an outcast, who, confronted only with himself, still hesitates to behold himself at the bottom of a pit into which, with his feet together, he has—curious prospector—hurled himself with a ludicrously bold leap. A lost man.

Pilorge, my little one, my friend, my liqueur, your lovely hypocritical head has got the ax. Twenty years old. You were twenty or twenty-two. And I am. . . . I envy you your glory. You would have done me in, as they say in jail, just as you did in the Mexican. During your months in the cell, you would have tenderly spat heavy oysters from your throat and nose on my memory. I would go to the guillotine very easily, since others have gone to it, particularly Pilorge, Weidmann, Angel Sun, and Soclay. Besides, I am not sure that I shall be spared it, for I have dreamed myself in many agreeable lives; my mind, which is eager to please me, has concocted glorious and charming adventures for me, made especially to order. The sad thing about it is, I sometimes think, that the greater part of these creations are utterly forgotten, though they constitute the whole of my past spiritual concert. I no longer even know that they existed, and if I happen now to dream one of these lives, I assume it is a new one, I embark upon my theme, I drift along, without remembering that I embarked upon it ten years earlier and that it sank down, exhausted, into the sea of oblivion. What monsters continue their lives in my depths? Perhaps their exhalations or their excrements or their decomposition hatch at my surface some horror or beauty that I feel is elicited by them. I recognize their influence, the charm of their melodrama. My mind continues to produce lovely chimeras, but so far none of them has taken on flesh. Never. Not once. If I now try to indulge in a daydream, my throat goes dry, despair burns my eyes, shame makes me bow my head, my reverie breaks up. I know that once again a possible happiness is escaping me and escapes me because I dreamed it.

The despondency that follows makes me feel somewhat like a shipwrecked man who spies a sail, sees himself saved, and suddenly remembers that the lens of his spyglass has a flaw, a blurred spot—the sail he has seen.

But since what I have never dreamed remains accessible, and as I have never dreamed misfortunes, there remains little for me to live but misfortunes. And misfortunes to die, for I have dreamed magnificent deaths for myself in war, as a hero, covered elsewhere with honors, and never by the gallows. So I still have something left.

And what must I do to get it? Almost nothing more.

Our Lady of the Flowers had nothing in common with the murderers of whom I have spoken. He was—one might say—an innocent murderer. To come back to Pilorge, whose face and death haunt me: at the age of twenty he killed Escudero, his lover, in order to rob him of a pittance. During the trial, he jeered at the court; awakened by the executioner, he jeered at him too; awakened by the spirit of the Mexican, sticky with hot, sweet-smelling blood, he would have laughed in its face; awakened by the shade of his mother, he would have flouted it tenderly. And so Our Lady was born of my love for Pilorge, with a smile in his heart and on his bluish white teeth, a smile that fear, which made his eyes start out of his head, will not tear away.

One day, while idling in the street, Darling met a woman of about forty who suddenly fell madly in love with him. I sufficiently hate the women who are in love with my lovers to admit that this one powders her fat red face with white face powder. And this light cloud makes her look like a family lamp shade with a transparent, pink muslin lining. She has the slick, familiar well-heeled charm of a lamp shade.

When he walked by, Darling was smoking, and a slit of abandon in the woman's hardness of soul chanced just then to be open, a slit that catches the hook cast by innocent looking objects. If one of your openings happens to be loosely fastened or a flap of your softness to be floating, you're done for. Instead of holding his cigarette between the first joint of the forefinger and middle finger, Darling was pinching it with his thumb and forefinger and covering it with the other fingers, the way men and even small boys usually hold their pricks when they piss at the foot of a tree or into the night. The woman (when he spoke to Divine about her, Darling referred to her as "the floozy" and Divine called her "that woman") was unaware of the virtue of that position and, as far as certain details are concerned, of the position itself. But its spell therefore acted upon her all the more promptly. She knew, though without quite knowing why, that Darling was a hard guy, because to her a hard guy was, above all, a male with a hard-on. She became mad about him. But she came too late. Her round curves and soft femininity no longer acted upon Darling, who was now used to the hard contact of a stiff penis. At the woman's side, he remained inert. The gulf frightened him. Still, he made an effort to overcome his distaste and keep the woman attached to him in order

to get money from her. He acted gallantly eager. But a
day came when, unable to bear it any longer, he admitted
that he loved a—earlier he might have said a boy, but now
he has to say a man, for Divine is a man—a man then. The
lady was outraged and uttered the word fairy. Darling
slapped her and left.

But he did not want his dessert to escape him (Divine
was his steak), and he went back to wait for her one day
at the Saint Lazare Station, where she got off, for she
came in every day from Versailles.

The Saint Lazare Station is the movie-stars' station.

Our Lady of the Flowers, still and already wearing the
light, baggy, youthful, preposterously thin and, in a word,
ghostlike gray-flannel suit that he was wearing the day of
the crime and that he will be wearing the day of his death,
came there to buy a ticket for Le Havre. Just as he got to
the platform, he dropped his wallet which was stuffed with
the twenty thousand franc notes. He felt it slip from his
pocket and turned around just in time to see it being
picked up by Darling. Calmly and fatally, Darling examined it, for though he was a genuine crook, nevertheless he did not know how to be at ease in original postures
and imitated the gangsters of Chicago and Marseilles.
This simple observation also enables us to indicate the importance of dreaming in the life of the hoodlum, but what
I want particularly to show you by means of it is that I
shall surround myself only with roughnecks of undis-
tinguished personality, with none of the nobility that
comes from heroism. My loved ones will be those whom
you would call "hoodlums of the worst sort."

Darling counted the bills. He took ten for himself, put
them into his pocket and handed the rest to Our Lady,
who stood there dumbfounded. They became friends.

I leave you free to imagine any dialogue you please.
Choose whatever may charm you. Have it, if you like, that

they hear the voice of the blood, or that they fall in love at first sight, or that Darling, by indisputable signs invisible to the vulgar eye, betrays the fact that he is a thief.... Conceive the wildest improbabilities. Have it that the depths of their being are thrilled at accosting each other in slang. Tangle them suddenly in a swift embrace or a brotherly kiss. Do whatever you like.

Darling was happy to find the money. However, with an extreme lack of appropriateness, all he could say, without unclenching his teeth, was: "Guy's no dope." Our Lady was boiling. But what could he do? He was too familiar with Pigalle-Blanche to know that you must not put on too bold a front with a real pimp. Darling bore, quite visibly, the external marks of the pimp. "Have to watch my step," Our Lady felt within him. So he lost his wallet, which Darling had noticed. Here is the sequel: Darling took Our Lady of the Flowers to a tailor, a shoe shop, and a hat shop. He ordered for both of them the bagatelles that make the strong and terribly charming man: a suede belt, a felt hat, a plaid tie, etc. Then they stopped at a hotel on the Avenue de Wagram. Wagram, battle won by boxers!

They· spent their time doing nothing. As they walked up and down the Champs-Elysées, they let intimacy fuse them. They made comments about the women's legs, but, as they were not witty, their remarks had no finesse. Since their emotion was not torn by any point, they quite naturally skidded along on a stagnant ground of poetry. They were child-roughnecks to whom chance had given gold, and I enjoy giving it to them, just as I enjoy hearing an American hood—it's amazing—say the word dollar and speak English. When they were tired, they went back to the hotel and sat for a long time in the big leather chairs in the lobby. Even there, intimacy evolved its alchemy. A solemn marble stairway led to corridors covered with red

carpets, upon which one moved noiselessly. During a high
mass at the Madeleine, when Darling saw the priests
walking on carpets, after the organ had stopped playing,
he began to feel uneasy at the mystery of the deaf and
the blind, the tread upon the carpets that he recognizes
in the grand hotel, and as he walks slowly over the moss,
he thinks, in his guttersnipe language: "Maybe there's
something." For low masses are said at the end of the halls
of big hotels, where the mahogany and marble light and
blow out candles. A mingled burial service and marriage
takes place there in secret from one end of the year to the
other. People move about like shadows. Does this mean
that my ecstatic crook's soul lets slip no opportunity for
falling into a trance? Oh to feel yourself flying on tiptoe
while the soles of humans move flat on the ground! Even
here, and at the Fresnes Prison, the long fragrant corridors
that bite their tails restore to me, despite the precise,
mathematical hardness of the wall, the soul of the hotel
thief I long to be.

The stylish clients moved about the lobby in front of
them. They took off their furs, gloves, and hats, drank
port, and smoked Craven cigarettes and Havana cigars. A
bellboy scurried about. They knew they were characters
in a movie. And so, mingling their gestures in this dream,
Darling and Our Lady of the Flowers quietly wove a
brotherly friendship. How hard it is for me not to mate the
two of them better, not to arrange it so that Darling, with
a thrust of the hips—rock of unconsciousness and inno-
cence, desperate with love—deeply sinks his smooth,
heavy prick, as polished and warm as a column in the sun,
into the waiting mouth of the adolescent murderer who is
pulverized with gratitude.

That too might be, but will not. Darling and Our Lady,
however rigorous the destiny I plot for you, it will never
cease to be—oh, in the very faintest way—tormented by

what it might also have been but will not be because
of me.

One day, Our Lady, quite naturally, confessed to the
murder. Darling confessed to his life with Divine. Our
Lady, that he was called Our Lady of the Flowers. Both
of them needed a rare flexibility to extricate themselves
without damage from the snares that threatened their
mutual esteem. On this occasion, Darling was all charm
and delicacy.

Our Lady of the Flowers was lying on a couch. Darling,
seated at his feet, watched him confess. It was over, as
far as the murder was concerned. Darling was the theater
of a muted drama. Confronting each other were the fear of
complicity, friendship for the child, and the taste, the desire for squealing. He still had to admit to the nickname.
Finally he got to it, little by little. As the mysterious name
emerged, it was so agonizing to watch the murderer's
great beauty writhing, the motionless and unclean coils
of the marble serpents of his drowsy face moving and
stirring, that Darling realized the gravity of such a confession, felt it so deeply that he wondered whether Our
Lady was going to puke pricks. He took one of the child's
hands, which was hanging down, and held it between his
own.

". . . You understand, there were guys that called
me . . ."

Darling held on to his hand. With his eyes, he was
drawing the confession toward him:

"It's coming, it's coming."

During the entire operation, he did not take his eyes
off the eyes of his friend. From beginning to end, he smiled
with a motionless smile that was fixed on his mouth, for
he felt that the slightest emotion on his part, the slightest
sign or breath, would destroy . . . It would have broken
Our Lady of the Flowers.

When the name was in the room, it came to pass that the murderer, abashed, opened up, and there sprang forth, like a Glory, from his pitiable fragments, an altar on which there lay, in the roses, a woman of light and flesh.

The altar undulated on a foul mud into which it sank: the murderer. Darling drew Our Lady toward him, and, the better to embrace him, struggled with him briefly. I would like to dream them both in many other positions if, when I closed my eyes, my dream still obeyed my will. But during the day it is disturbed by anxiety about my trial, and in the evening the preliminaries of sleep denude the environs of my self, destroy objects and episodes, leaving me at the edge of sleep as solitary as I was one night in the middle of a stormy and barren heath. Darling, Divine, and Our Lady flee from me at top speed, taking with them the consolation of their existence, which has its being only in me, for they are not content with fleeing; they do away with themselves, dilute themselves in the appalling insubstantiality of my dreams, or rather of my sleep, and become my sleep; they melt into the very stuff of my sleep and compose it. I call for help in silence; I make signals with the two arms of my soul, which are softer than algae, not, of course, to some friend firmly planted on the ground, but to a kind of crystallization of the tenderness whose seeming hardness makes me believe in its eternity.

I call out: "Hold me back! Fasten me!" I break away for a frightful dream which will go through the darkness of the cells, the darkness of the spirits of the damned, of the gulfs, through the mouths of the guards, the breasts of the judges, and will end by my being swallowed very very slowly by a giant crocodile formed by the whiffs of the foul prison air.

It is the fear of the trial.

Weighing upon my poor shoulders are the dreadful weight of legal justice and the weight of my fate.

How many policemen and detectives, with their teeth on edge, as is so aptly said, for days and nights, were making relentless efforts to unravel the puzzle I had set? And I thought the affair had been shelved, whereas they kept plugging away, busying themselves about me without my being aware of it, working on the Genet material, on the luminous traces of the Genet gestures, working away on me in the darkness.

It was a good thing that I raised egoistic masturbation to the dignity of a cult! I have only to begin the gesture and a kind of unclean and supernatural transposition displaces the truth. Everything within me turns worshiper. The external vision of the props of my desire isolates me, far from the world.

Pleasure of the solitary, gesture of solitude that makes you sufficient unto yourself, possessing intimately others who serve your pleasure without their suspecting it, a pleasure that gives to your most casual gestures, even when you are up and about, that air of supreme indifference toward everyone and also a certain awkward manner that, if you have gone to bed with a boy, makes you feel as if you have bumped your head against a granite slab.

I've got lots of time for making my fingers fly! Ten years to go! My good, my gentle friend, my cell! My sweet retreat, mine alone, I love you so! If I had to live in all freedom in another city, I would first go to prison to acknowledge my own, those of my race, and also to find you there.

Yesterday I was summoned by the examining magistrate. From the Santé to the Law Court, the jolting and the smell of the police van had nauseated me. I appeared before the judge as white as a sheet.

As soon as I entered his chambers, I was struck by the

gloom, despite the dusty, secret flowering of the criminal
files, caused by the presence of the smashed violin that
Divine also saw. And, because of that Christ, I was open
to pity. Because of it and of the dream in which my victim
came to forgive me. In fact, the judge smiled at me very
kindly. I recognized my victim's smile in my dream and
recalled, or realized again, that he himself was supposed
to have been both a judge on a bench, whom I confused
perhaps intentionally with the examining magistrate, and
an examining magistrate. Knowing that I had been pardoned by him, feeling tranquil and sure, not with a certainty resulting from logic, but out of a desire for peace, a
desire to return to the life of men (the desire that makes
Darling serve the police so as to return to his place among
human beings through having served order, and at the
same time to depart from the human through deliberate
baseness), sure that everything had been forgotten, hyp-
notized by the pardon, with a sense of confidence, I confessed.

The clerk recorded the confession, which I signed.

My lawyer was stupefied, staggered. What in the world
had I done? Who tricked me? Heaven? Heaven, dwelling
of God and his Court.

I went back through the underground corridors of the
Court and returned to my dark, icy little cell in the "Mousetrap." Ariadne in the labyrinth. The most alive of worlds,
human beings with the tenderest flesh, are made of marble. I strew devastation as I pass. I wander dead-eyed
through cities and petrified populations. But no way out.
Impossible to retract the confession, to annul it, to unravel
the thread of time that wove it, and to make it unwind and
destroy itself. Flee? What an idea! The labyrinth is more
tortuous than the summing-up of judges. What about the
guard leading me? A guard of massive bronze to whom I
am chained by the wrist. I quickly concoct a scheme of

seducing him, of kneeling before him, first laying my forehead on his thigh, devoutly opening his blue pants. . . .
What folly! I'm done for. Why didn't I steal a tube of strych-
nine from a pharmacy, as I had meant to? I could have
kept it on me and concealed it while I was being searched.
One day, utterly weary of the land of the Chimeras—the
only one worth inhabiting, "the nothingness of human
things being such that, save for the being who is by himself, nothing is beautiful, but that which is not" (Pope)[1]
—I would, without any vain ornamentation surrounding
the act, have poisoned myself. For, my good friends, I am
ripe for the Send-off.

There are times when we suddenly understand the
hitherto unperceived meaning of certain expressions. We
live them and mutter them. For example: "I felt the earth
giving way beneath me." This is a phrase that I have read
and said a thousand times without living it. But it was
enough, when I awoke, to linger over it for ten seconds as
I was being visited by the memory of my arrest (the remains of last night's nightmare), for the dream element
that created the expression to envelop me, or rather to
give me the sensation of internal, visceral emptiness that is
also caused by the precipices from which one falls at night
with a feeling of certainty. I felt that way last night. No
outstretched, merciful arm tries to catch me. A few rocks
might perhaps offer me a stony hand, but just far enough
away for me to be unable to grab it. I was falling. And in
order to delay the final shock—for the feeling of falling
caused me that intoxication of absolute despair, which is
akin to happiness during the fall, but it was also an intoxication fearful of awakening, of the return to things
that are—in order to delay the shock at the bottom of the

[1] These are not Pope's exact words, but a translation of the author's misquotation, from memory, of a French version. (Translator's note.)

gulf and the awakening in prison with my anguish at the thought of suicide or jail, I accumulated catastrophes, I provoked accidents along the verticality of the precipice, I summoned up frightful obstacles at the point of arrival. It was the very next day that the influence of this un-dissipated dream made me pile up details, all of them serious, in the confused hope that they were staving off the inevitable. I was slowly sinking.

Yet, back in my 426, the sweetness of my work entrances me. The first steps I take, with my hands on my hips, which seem to be pitching, make me feel as if Darling, who is walking behind, were passing through me. And here I am again in the soothing comfort of the elegant hotel which they will have to leave, for twenty thousand francs is not eternal.

During his stay at the hotel, Darling had not been to the garret. He had left Divine without any news. Our dearest was dying of anxiety. So, when Our Lady and he ran out of money, he thought about going back. Dressed like fake monarchs, they returned to the attic, where, with blankets stolen from cars, they arranged a bed for the murderer on the rug. He slept there, near Divine and Darling. When she saw them enter, Divine thought she had been for-gotten and replaced. Not at all. We shall see later the kind of incest that bound the two lads together.

Divine worked for two men, one of whom was her own.

Until then, she had loved only men who were stronger and just a little, a tiny bit older, and more muscular than herself. But then came Our Lady of the Flowers, who had the moral and physical character of a flower; she was smitten with him. Something different, a kind of feeling of power, sprang up (in the vegetal, germinative sense) in Divine. She thought she had been virilified. A wild hope made her strong and husky and vigorous. She felt muscles growing, and felt herself emerging from a rock carved by

Michelangelo in the form of a slave. Without moving a muscle, though straining within herself, she struggled internally just as Laocoön seizes the monster and twists it. Then, bolder still, she wanted to box, with her arms and legs of flesh, but she very quickly got knocked about on the boulevard, for she judged and willed her movements not in accordance with their combative efficiency but rather in accordance with an esthetic that would have made of her a hoodlum of a more or less gallant stripe. Her movements, particularly a hitching of the belt and her guard position, were meant, whatever the cost, at the cost of victory itself, to make of her not the boxer Divine, but a certain admired boxer, and at times several fine boxers rolled into one. She tried for male gestures, which are rarely the gestures of males. She whistled, put her hands into her pockets, and this whole performance was caried out so unskillfully that in the course of a single evening she seemed to be four or five characters at the same time. She thereby acquired the richness of a multiple personality. She ran from boy to girl, and the transitions from one to the other—because the attitude was a new one—were made stumblingly. She would hop after the boy on one foot. She would always begin her Big Scatterbrain gestures, then, suddenly remembering that she was supposed to show she was virile so as to captivate the murderer, she would end by burlesquing them, and this double formula enveloped her in strangeness, made her a timid clown in plain dress, a sort of embittered swish. Finally, to crown her metamorphosis from female into tough male, she imagined a man-to-man friendship which would link her with one of those faultless pimps whose gestures could not be regarded as ambiguous. And to be on the safe side, she invented Marchetti. It was a simple matter to choose a physique for him, for she possessed in her secret, lonely-girl's imagination, for her nights' pleasure, a stock of thighs, arms, torsoes, faces, hair, teeth, necks, and knees, and she knew how to assemble them so as to make of them a live man to whom she loaned a soul—which was always the same one for each of these constructions: the one she would have liked to have herself. The invented Marchetti had a few adventures with her, in secret. Then, one night, she told him that she was tired of Our Lady of the Flowers and that she was willing to let Marchetti have him. The agreement was sealed with a male handshake. The dream was as follows: Marchetti comes breezing into the place with his hands in his pockets.

"Hello, kid," he says to Divine.

He sits down and they have a man-to-man talk about the grind. Our Lady arrives. Shakes hands with Marchetti. Marchetti kids him a bit about his girl's puss. As for me (Divine is talking to herself in secret), I pretend not to see them. But I'm sure that now, thanks to me, Our Lady is going to tear off a quickie with Marchetti (he has too nice a name to need a given name). I busy myself for three minutes about the room. I manage it so that my back is turned to them. I turn around. I see them billing and cooing, and Marchetti's fly is open. The love-making begins.

Divine had not become virile; she had aged. An adolescent now excited her, and that was why she had the feeling of being old, and this certainty unfurled within her like the hangings formed by the wings of bats. That evening, undressed and alone in the garret, she saw with fresh eyes her white, hairless body, smooth and dry, and, in places, bony. She was ashamed of it and hastened to put out the lamp, for it was the ivory body of Jesus on an eighteenth-century crucifix, and relations with the divinity, even a resemblance to it, sickened her.

But along with this desolation, a new joy was being born within her.

The joy that precedes suicides. Divine was afraid of her daily life. Her flesh and soul were turning sour. There came for her the season of tears, as we speak of the season of rains. Once she has switched off the light and created darkness, for nothing in the world would she take a step out of bed, where she thinks she is safe, but in the same way that she thinks she is safe in her body. She feels rather protected by the fact of being in her body. Outside reigns terror. One night, however, she dared open the door of the garret and take a step out on the dark landing. The stairway was filled with the wails of sirens calling her to the bottom. They were not exactly wails or songs, nor exactly sirens either, but they were quite clearly an invitation to madness or to death by falling. Mad with fright, she went back to the garret. It was the moment before alarm clocks start ringing. If she was spared fears, during the day she knew another torture: she would blush. For the veriest trifle, she would become the Very Crimson, the Purplish One, Her Eminence. It must not be thought that she was ashamed of her profession. She had known too well and too early how to penetrate steadily to the depths of despair not to be, at her age, dead to all sense of shame. Calling herself an old whorish whore, Divine simply forestalled mockery and insults. But she blushed about little things which seemed trivial, which we think insignificant, until the moment when, observing more closely, she realized that the blush had spread just when someone was humiliating her unwittingly. A mere trifle humiliated Divine. The kind of humiliation which—she was again Culafroy—laid her lower than the ground, by the mere power of words. Words again took on for her the magic of boxes empty, when all is said and done, of everything that is not mystery. When closed words, sealed, hermetic words, open up, their meanings escape in leaps and bounds that assault and leave us panting. Brew, which is a word from sorcery, led me to the home of the old maid who grinds coffee, mixes in some chicory, and brews; through coffee grounds (this is a trick of hocus-pocus), it leads me back to sorcery. The word Mithridate: one morning Divine suddenly comes upon it again. It had once opened up and revealed to Culafroy its virtue, and the child, going back up the centuries to the fifteen hundreds, buried himself in the Rome of the Pontiffs. Let us take a look at this period in Divine's life. As aconite was the only poison he could procure, every night, in a long, stiff-pleated dressing gown, he would open the door of his room, which was on a level with the garden, would step over the railing—gesture of a lover, burglar, dancer, somnambulist, mountebank—and jump into the vegetable garden, which was bounded by a hedge of elders, mulberries, and black thorns, but where someone had laid out, between the vegetable beds, borders of reseda and marigolds. Culafroy would gather a bunch of Napel aconite leaves. He would measure them with a six-inch ruler, increase the dose each time, roll them up, and then swallow. But the poison had the double virtue of killing and raising from the dead those it killed, and presto! it would act. The Renaissance would take possession of the child through the mouth, just as the Man-God does of the little girl who, sticking out her tongue, though piously, swallows the host. The Borgias, Astrologers, Pornographers, Princes, Abbesses, and Condottieri would receive him naked on their knees, which were hard beneath the silk; he would tenderly place his cheek against an erect penis, stony beneath the silk, of stone as unyielding as the chests of Negro jazzmen must be beneath the shiny satin of their jackets.

It was in a green alcove, for feasts that end in death by

daggers, scented gloves, a treacherous wafer. Beneath the moon, Culafroy became this world of poisoners, pederasts, thieves, sorcerers, warriors, and courtesans, and the surrounding nature, the vegetable garden, remaining what they were, left him all alone, possessing and possessed by an epoch, in his barefoot walk, beneath the moon, about the cabbage and lettuce beds where lay an abandoned rake and spade, left him free to lift and draw trains of brocade with lofty gestures. No episode from history or a novel organized the dream mass; only the murmur of a few magic words thickened the darkness, from which there loomed a page or horseman, a handsome cocksman, disheveled by a broadcloth night. . . . *"Datura fastuosa, Datura stramonium,* Belladona. . . ."

As the coolness of the night that fell upon his white robe would make him feel chilly, he would walk to the wide-open window, slip under the railing, close the window, and lie down in a huge bed. When day came, he was again the shy, pale schoolboy stooping with the weight of his books. But one does not have enchanted nights without the days retaining some telltale signs, which are to the soul what circles are to the eyes. Ernestine used to dress him in very short blue serge pants, over which he wore a black schoolboy's smock that buttoned down the back with white glazed buttons; she also made him wear black wooden sabots and black cotton stockings that concealed his rather thin calves. He was not in mourning for anyone, and it was touching to see him all in black. He belonged to the race of harried children, early wrinkled, volcanic. Emotions ravage faces, root out peace, swell the lips, crease the brow, and make the eyebrows quiver with shudders and subtle convulsions. His schoolmates called him "Coolie," which name, uttered during their games, was a slap in the face. But children of this kind, like vagabonds, have in their bags charming or terrible tricks by means of which they open out warm and downy havens where they drink red wine that makes them drunk and where they are loved in secret. Culafroy would escape through the ceiling of the village school, like a hunted thief, and among the unsuspecting schoolboys, during the clandestine recreations (the child is the re-creator of heaven and earth), he would meet Jean the Black Terror. When school was over, he returned to the house nearest the school and thus avoided having to take part in the voodoo mysteries of the schoolboys who were freed at four o'clock from parents and teachers. His room was a little nook with mahogany furniture and was decorated with colored prints of autumn landscapes, which he did not look at because the only faces he could find there were those of three green nymphs. Childhood wearies of the conventional myths foisted upon a conventional childhood; it doesn't care a rap about picture-book fairies and decorative monsters, and my personal fairies were the slender butcher with the pointed mustache, the consumptive schoolmistress, the pharmacist; everyone was a fairy, that is, was isolated by the halo of an unapproachable, inviolable existence, through which all I could see was gestures whose continuity—hence whose logic and element of reassurance—escaped me, and every fragment of which raised a new question for me, word by word, and disturbed me.

Culafroy would enter his room. Immediately he is in his vatican, a sovereign pontiff. He lays his bag, which is crammed with books and pads, on a straw chair; from under the bed he pulls out a case. Old playthings pile up, torn and dog-eared picture albums, a shaggy teddybear, and from that bed of darkness, from that tomb of still fragrant and radiant glories, he pulls out a grayish violin which he himself has made. His hesitant gesture makes him blush. He feels the humiliation, stronger than the green shame of someone's spitting on your back, that he

had felt while putting it together—though not while con-
ceiving it—just about a week before, with the cardboard
binding of the picture album, the piece of broom handle
and four white threads, the strings. It was a flat gray violin,
a two-dimensional violin, with only the soundboard and
the neck, and four white strings, geometric and rigorous,
spanning the extravagance, a phantom violin. The bow
was a walnut twig, from which he had peeled the bark.
The first time Culafroy had asked his mother to buy him
a violin, she had winced. She had been salting the soup.
None of the following images had appeared before her
eyes with any precision: a river, flames, escutcheoned
oriflammes, a Louis XV heel, a page in blue tights, the
page's craft and slyness, but the disturbance that each of
them created within her, a plunge into an ink-black lake,
held her for a moment between life and death, and when,
two or three seconds later, she came to herself, a nervous
shudder ran through her which made the hand salting the
soup tremble. Culafroy did not know that a violin, because
of its tortured lines, could upset his sensitive mother, and
that violins moved about in her dreams in the company
of lithe cats, at corners of walls, under balconies where
thieves divide the night's loot, where other toughs slouch
around a lamppost, on stairways that squeak like violins
being skinned alive. Ernestine wept with rage at being
unable to kill her son, for Culafroy was not what one could
kill, or rather we can see that what one killed in him made
possible another birth: rods, straps, spankings, and slaps
lose their power, or rather change their virtues. The word
violin was never uttered again. In order to study music,
that is, to make the same gestures as some pretty youngster in a magazine, Culafroy made the instrument, but in
front of Ernestine never again would he utter the word
that begins with the same syllable as violate. The making
took place in the greatest secrecy, at night. During the

day, he buried it away at the bottom of the case of old toys. Every evening, he took it out. With humiliation, he learned by himself how to place his left fingers on the white threads, according to the instructions in an old manual that he found in the attic. Each silent session exhausted him. The disappointing squeak that the bow tore from the strings gave his soul gooseflesh. His heart was drawn out fine and unraveled into strained silences— ghosts of sounds. His frustration haunted him throughout the lesson, and he studied in a state of constant shame. He felt shifty and humiliated, as we do on New Year's Day. Our good wishes are furtive and whispered, as, among others, those of proud servants and lepers must be. Since these are gestures reserved for the masters, we often feel as if we were using their wardrobes to receive each other. They embarrass us, as the unlined dress-jacket must embarrass the apprentice butler who wears it. One evening, Culafroy made a broad, extravagant, tragedian's gesture. A gesture that went beyond the room, entered into the night, where it continued on to the stars, among the Bears, and even farther; then, like the snake that bites its tail, it returned to the shadow of the room, and into the child who drowned in it. He drew the bow from the point to the base, slowly, magnificently; this final laceration sawed his soul apart; the silence, the shadow, and the hope of separating these diverse elements, which fell away severally, thus dashed to the ground an attempt at construction. He let his arms drop, and the violin and the bow; he wept like a child. The tears ran down his flat little face. Once again he realized it was all hopeless. The magic net through which he had tried to gnaw tightened about him, isolating him. With a feeling of utter emptiness, he went to the little mirror of the dresser and looked at his face, for which he felt the tenderness one feels for a homely little dog when that dog is one's own. The shadow,

which had somehow slipped into the room, installed itself.
Culafroy let it be. All that interested him was the face in
the mirror and its changes, the globes of the luminous
eyes, the halo of shadow, the black spot of the mouth,
the illuminated forefinger that supported his bent head.
His head was bent so that he could see himself in the mirror, but he had to raise his eyes, and this made him observe himself in the sly way that actors do in films: "I
might be a great artist." He did not formulate this idea
clearly; nevertheless, the splendor involved in it made him
lower his head a little more. "The weight of destiny," he
thought. In the gleaming rosewood of the dresser, he saw
a fleeting scene, similar in essence to many others that
often visited him: a small boy was crouching beneath a
barred window, in a dark room, where he himself was
walking about with his hands in his pockets.

Capitals rose up from his sandy childhood. Capitals like
cactuses beneath the sky. Cactuses like green suns, radiat-
ing pointed rays and steeped in poison. His childhood, like
a sahara, quite tiny or immense—we don't know—a childhood sheltered by the light, the scent, and the flow of
personal charm of a huge flowering magnolia that rose
into a sky deep as a grotto above the invisible though
present sun. This childhood was withering on its broiling
sand, with—in moments swift as pencil strokes and as
thin, thin as the paradise one sees between the eyelids of
a Mongol—a glimpse of the invisible and present magnolia. These moments were at all points like those of
which the poet speaks:

> *I saw in the desert*
> *Your open sky . . .*

Ernestine and her son lived in the only house in the
village, except for the church, that had a slate roof. It was
a large, rectangular freestone building, divided into two

sections by a corridor that opened up like a heroic breach
between the rocks. Ernestine had a rather large income
that had been left her by her husband when he committed
suicide by leaping into the green moat of the local castle.
She could have lived in luxury, could have been waited on
by several servants and have moved about amidst huge
mirrors that rose from the carpets to the gilded ceiling.
She denied herself the luxury and beauty that kill reverie.
Love too. Once upon a time love had placed her on earth
and kept her there with the grip of a wrestler who is used
to pinning huskies to the mat. At the age of twenty, she
had given birth to a legend. When the peasants speak of
her later, they will be unable to refrain from evoking the
creature whose face was all swathed—like the face of a
wounded aviator, the very face of Weidmann, except for
the mouth and eyes—in strips of gauze, so as to shield the
thick coatings of a special beauty cream that protected
her skin from sunburn and hay when she came in summer-
time to do the haying at her father's place. But bitterness
had passed over her face like an acid, eating away the
sweetness. She now feared whatever could not be spoken
of in a simple and familiar way, with a smile. This fear
alone proved the danger of a relapse into the power of
the Greedy One (Beauty). Though the fastenings that
bound and delivered her over to powers whose contact or
merely whose approach upset her, were loose, nevertheless they were solid. They were art, religion, love, which
are enveloped in the sacred (for at the sacred, which is
called, alas, the spiritual,[1] one neither laughs nor smiles; it
is sad. If it is that which touches upon God, is God therefore sad? Is God therefore a painful idea? Is God therefore evil?) and which are always approached with a courtesy that guards them. Among the appurtenances of the

[1] The sense of this passage turns on the word *spirituel*, which has
the double meaning of spiritual and witty. (Translator's note.)

village were an old feudal castle surrounded by moats that rumbled with frogs, a cemetery, the house of the unwed mother and the unwed mother herself, a bridge with three stone arches above three arches of clear water, over which hung, every morning, a thick mist that finally lifted from the landscape. The sun would slash it to tatters, which would then go and, very briefly, dress up the scrawny black trees as gypsy children.

The sharp blue slates, the granite stones of the house, and the high window panes isolated Culafroy from the world. The games of the boys who lived beyond the river were unknown games, complicated by mathematics and geometry. They were played along the hedges, with the rams and colts of the fields as attentive spectators. The players themselves, actor-children away from school, away from the town, slipped back into their rustic personalities, again became cowherds, bird nesters, climbers, mowers of rye, and stealers of plums. If they were for Culafroy—without being able quite to fathom his feeling, though they suspected it, a race of fascinating demons—Culafroy, on the other hand, unwittingly had for them a certain glamor that he possessed by virtue of his isolation, of the refinement and legend of Ernestine, and of the slate roof of his house. Though they hated him, there was hardly a small boy who did not dream about him, envying the cut of his hair, the elegance of his leather schoolbag. The slate house was supposed to contain fabulous riches in the midst of which Culafroy had the glamor of walking about slowly and the privilege of venturing familiar gestures, such as drumming on some article of furniture or sliding on the parquet, in a setting that they judged to be regal, smiling like a crown prince, perhaps playing cards there. Culafroy seemed to secrete a royal mystery. King's sons are too common among children for the village schoolboys to be able to take this one seriously. But they regarded it as a crime

on his part to divulge so clearly an origin that every one
of them kept well hidden within himself, and that offended their Majesty. For the royal idea is of this world;
if man does not hold it by virtue of carnal transmissions,
he should acquire it and adorn himself with it in secret so
as not to be degraded in his own eyes. Since the dreams
and reveries of children interlace in the night, each possessed the other unknowingly, in a rapacious (they were
really rapes) and almost total way. The village, which
they re-created for their own use, and where, as we have
said, the children were sovereign, was entangled in practices that were without strangeness to those who lived in a
village of strange nights, where stillborn children were
buried toward evening, carried to the cemetery by their
sisters in pine boxes as narrow and varnished as violin
cases; where other children ran about in the glades and
pressed their naked bellies, though sheltered from the
moon, against the trunks of beeches and oaks that were
as sturdy as adult mountaineers whose short thighs bulged
beneath their buckskin breeches, at a spot stripped of its
bark, in such a way as to receive on the tender skin of
their little white bellies the discharge of sap in the spring;
where the Italian woman walked by, spying on the old,
sick, and paralytic, whose souls she culled from their eyes,
listening to them die (the old die the way children are
born), having them at her mercy, and her mercy was not
her grace; a village whose days were no less strange than
its nights, where, on Corpus Christi or Rogation Day,
corteges went through the blazing noonday countryside
in processions composed of little girls with porcelain
heads wearing white dresses and crowned with cloth
flowers, of choir boys swinging in the wind censers
covered with verdigris, of women stiff in their green or
black moire, of men gloved in black, holding up a canopy
of oriental cast that was plumed with ostrich feathers,

under which walked the priest carrying a monstrance. Beneath the sun, amidst the rye, pines, and clover, and inverted in the ponds, with their feet to the sky.

That was part of Divine's childhood. There were lots of other things that we shall mention later. We must come back to it.

Let us say now that her carnal pleasures never made her fear the wrath of God, the scorn of Jesus, or the candied disgust of the Holy Virgin, never until Gabriel spoke about them to her, for as soon as she recognized the presence within her of seeds of these fears (divine wrath, scorn, disgust), Divine made of her loves a god above God, Jesus, and the Holy Virgin, to whom they were submissive like everyone else, whereas Gabriel, despite his fiery temperament, which often makes his face turn red, feared Hell, for he did not love Divine.

And who still loved her, except Darling?

Our Lady of the Flowers smiled and sang. He sang like an Aeolian harp, a bluish breeze passing over the strings of his body; he sang with his body; he did not love. The police did not suspect him. He did not suspect the police. The child's indifference was such that he did not even buy the newspapers. He went his melody.

Divine thought Darling was at the movies and that Our Lady, who was a shoplifter, was in a department store, but . . . Wearing American shoes, a very soft hat, a gold chain on his wrist—in short, quite the pimp—Darling, toward evening, walked down the stairs from the garret, and . . . Came the inevitable soldier. Where does he come from? From the street, into the bar where Divine was sitting? When the revolving door turned, at each turn, like the mechanism of a Venetian belfry, it presented a sturdy archer, a supple page, an exemplar of High Faggotry, one of those pimps whose ancestors of the dens, when they pandered for Mademoiselle Adna, wore earrings, and between whose legs, when now they stroll along the boulevard, shrill whistles squirt and fizz.

Gabriel appeared. I also see him going down an almost vertical street, running, like the bewitched dog that went down to the village by the main street, and it is to be supposed that he collided with Divine as he came out of a neighborhood grocery where he had just bought a surprise package, just as the bell of the glass door rang twice. I should have liked to talk to you about encounters. I have a notion that the moment that provoked—or provokes—them is located outside time, that the shock spatters the surrounding time and space, but I may be wrong, for I want to talk about the encounters that I provoke and that I impose upon the lads in my book. Perhaps some of these moments that are set down on paper are like populous streets on whose throng my gaze happens to fall: a sweetness, a tenderness, situates them outside the moment; I am charmed and—I can't tell why—that mob of people is balm to my eyes. I turn away; then I look again, but I no longer find either sweetness or tenderness. The street becomes dismal, like a morning of insomnia; my lucidity returns, restoring within me the poetry that the following poem had driven out: some handsome adolescent face, that I had barely caught a glimpse of, had lit up the crowd; then it disappeared. The meaning of Heaven is no longer strange to me. So, Divine met Gabriel. He passed in front of her, and he spread his back like a wall, a cliff. This wall was not very wide, but it unfurled such majesty upon the world, that is, such serene force, that it seemed to Divine to be made of bronze, the wall of darkness out of which flies a black eagle with outspread wings.

Garbriel was a soldier.

The army is the red blood that flows from the artillery-man's ears; it is the little lightfoot soldier of the snows crucified on skis, a spahi on his horse of cloud that has pulled up at the edge of Eternity; it is masked princes and brotherly murderers in the Foreign Legion; it is, in the Mariners of the Fleet, the flap that replaces the fly on the pants of the horny sailors lest, so they say, finding an excuse for everything, they be caught in the tackle during maneuvers; lastly, it is the sailors themselves who charm the sirens as they twist about the masts like whores about pimps; as they wrap themselves in the sails, they toy with them like Spanish women with their fans, laughing aloud, or, with both hands in their pockets, balancing themselves upright on the bridge, they whistle the true waltz of the sailors.

"And the sirens fall for that?"

"They dream of that spot where the kinship between their bodies and those of the seamen ends. 'Where does the mystery start?' they ask each other. It is then that they sing."

Gabriel was in the infantry and wore sky-blue cloth, cloth that was thick and fleecy. Later on, when we have seen more of him and there is less question about him, we shall describe him more fully. Divine, of course, calls him Archangel. And also: "My Liqueur." He lets himself be worshiped without batting an eyelash. He doesn't mind. Out of fear of Darling, especially out of fear of hurting him, Divine has not dared take the soldier to the garret. She meets him in the evening on the promenade of the boulevard, where he tells her very sweetly the story of his life, for he knows nothing else. And Divine says:

"It's not your life story you're telling me, Archangel, but an underground passage of my own, which I was unaware of."

Divine also says:

"I love you as if you were in my belly," and also:

"You're not my sweetheart, you're myself. My heart or my sex. A branch of me."

And Gabriel, thrilled, though smiling with pride, replies:

"Oh, you little hussy!"

His smile whipped up at the corner of his mouth a few delicate balls of white foam.

Meeting them one night, Milord the Prince, with his fingers circled in the form of a ring like those of an abbé preaching, tosses off to Divine, as one tosses an eyelash, "You busy bee, you!" and whisks away, having united them.

All along the way from Blanche to Pigalle, others bless them in like manner and consecrate their union.

Aging Divine sweats with anxiety. She is a poor woman who wonders:

"Will he love me? Ah, to have discovered a new sweetheart! to worship him on my knees, and, in return, he forgives me, simply. Perhaps I can win his love by trickery."

I have heard it said that one wins the devotion of dogs by mixing a spoonful of their master's urine in their mash every day. Divine tries this. Every time she invites Archangel to dinner, she manages to put a little of her urine into his food.

Winning his love. Slowly leading the artless one toward that love, as toward a forbidden city, a mysterious area, a black and white Timbuktu, black and white and thrilling as the lover's face on whose cheek plays the shadow of the face of the other. Teaching Archangel, forcing him to learn, a dog's attachment. Finding the child inert, yet hot; then, by dint of caresses, feeling him get even hotter, swelling beneath my fingers, filling out, bounding like you know what. Divine being loved!

On the garret couch she writhes about, she curls like a shaving from a turning lathe. She twists her lithe white arms, rolls and unrolls them. They strangle shadows. She was bound to have Gabriel up sooner or later. As the curtains are drawn, he finds himself in a darkness the more massive for having been mildewed for years (as by a scent of chilled incense) by the subtle essence of the farts that had blossomed there.

Divine was lying on the sofa in a pair of blue silk pajamas with white trimming. Her hair was in her eyes; she was shaved; her mouth was pure and her face sleek with shaving lotion. Nevertheless, she looked as if she had just got up with a hangover.

"Sit down."

With one hand, she pointed to a place near her, at the edge of the sofa, and held out the fingertips of the other.

"How's it going?"

Gabriel was wearing his sky-blue uniform. His loosely buckled army belt was sagging at his belly.

The coarse wool and delicate blue got Divine hot. She will say later on: "His get-up got me hot." A fine and equally blue cloth would have excited her less than a heavy black one, for the latter is the cloth of the country clergy and of Ernestine, and heavy gray cloth is that of the children of the state orphanages.

"Doesn't that wool make you itch?"

"You're nuts. I've got a shirt on. Besides, I'm wearing underwear. The wool doesn't touch my skin."

Amazing, isn't it, Divine, that with a sky-blue outfit he dares have such black eyes and hair?

"Look, there's some cherry brandy. Take as much as you like. Let me have a glass too."

Gabriel smiles as he pours himself a glass of liqueur. He drinks. Again he is sitting at the edge of the sofa. A slight embarrassment between them.

"Say, it's stuffy in here. Mind if I take off my jacket?"

"Oh, take off whatever you like."

He unbuckles his belt and takes off his jacket. The swish of the belt fills the garret with a roomful of sweaty soldiers back from maneuvers. Divine, as I have said, is also wearing sky-blue, which is loosely draped about her body. She is blond, and under such straw her face looks a little wrinkled; as Mimosa says, it's rumpled (Mimosa says this maliciously, to hurt Divine), but Gabriel likes her face. Divine, who wants to know he does, trembles like the flame of a candle as she says:

"I'm getting old. I'll soon be thirty."

Gabriel has the unconscious delicacy not to flatter her by a lie that would say: "You don't look it." He replies:

"But that's the best age to be. You understand everything a lot better then."

He adds:

"That's the real age."

Divine's eyes and teeth are gleaming and make those of the soldier gleam too.

"Say, there's something wrong."

He's smiling, but I feel he's embarrassed.

She is happy. Gabriel is now limp, all pale blue against her; two angels, tired of flying, who had perched on a telegraph pole and whom the wind has blown into the hollow of a ditch of nettles, are not more chaste.

One night, the Archangel turned faun. He held Divine against him, face to face, and his member, suddenly more potent, tried to enter from below. When he had found, he bent a little and entered. Gabriel had acquired such virtuosity that he was able, though remaining motionless himself, to make his tool quiver like a shying horse. He forced with his usual fury and felt his potency so intensely that—with his nose and throat—he whinnied with victory, so impetuously that Divine thought he was penetrating her with his whole centaur body. She swooned with love like a nymph in a tree.

They played their games over and over. Divine's eyes became brilliant and her skin suppler. The Archangel took his role of fucker seriously. It made him sing the *Marseillaise*, for he was now proud of being a Frenchman and a Gallic cock, of which only males are proud. Then he died in the war. One evening he went to the boulevard to see Divine.

"I got a furlough. I asked for it on account of you. Come on, let's go eat. I've got some dough now."

Divine raised her eyes to his face.

"So you do love me, Archangel?"

Gabriel's shoulders twitched with annoyance.

"You deserve a good smack," he said, clenching his teeth. "You can't tell, I suppose?"

Divine closed her eyes. She smiled.

"Go away, Archangel," she said in a hollow voice. "Go away. I have seen thee enough. Thou givest me too much joy, Archangel."

She spoke as a somnambulist would speak, standing straight and rigid, with a set smile on her face.

"Go away, or I'll fall into your arms. Oh, Archangel!"

She murmured:

"Oh, Archangel!"

Smiling gently, Gabriel walked off with long slow strides, for he was wearing boots. He died in the French campaign, and the German soldiers buried him where he fell, at the gate of a castle in Touraine. Divine came and sat on his grave, smoked a Craven there with Jimmy.

We recognize her sitting there, with her long legs crossed and a cigarette in her hand, level with her mouth. She is smiling, almost happy.

As she entered Graff's Café, Divine caught sight of Mimosa, who saw her. They made a little sign to each other with their fingers, a trifling flick of the fingers.

"Hello! And how's that Our Lady of yours, sweetie?"

"Oh! don't talk to me about her. She's run off. The Lady's gone, flown. Carried off by the angels. She's been stolen from me. Mimo, behold me the Quite-Tearful. Make a novena, I'm going to take the veil."

"Your Lady has gone off? You mean Your Lady has wiggled away? But that's just awful! She's a harlot!"

"Let's, let's forget her."

Mimosa wanted Divine to sit at her table. She said that she was rid of clients for the whole evening.

"I'm having a little Sunday outing, so there! Have a glass of gin, child."

Divine was worried. She did not love Our Lady to the extent of suffering at the thought that someone might squeal on him, if he should happen to get mixed up in some shady business, but she remembered that Mimosa had swallowed a photo of him the way one swallows the Eucharist, and that she had acted very offended when Our Lady had said to her: "You're a real bitch." She smiled, however, and brought her smile up to Mimosa's face, as if to kiss it, and their faces were suddenly so close that it seemed to them as if they were present at their nuptials. Both queens were horrified at the idea. Still smiling divinely, Divine murmured:

"I detest you."

She didn't say it. The sentence took shape in her throat. Then, immediately, her face closed up like a clover at twilight. Mimosa didn't understand what was going on. Divine had always kept to herself the singular communion of Mimosa, for she feared that if Our Lady learned of it, he might change his mind and make coy advances to her rival. Our Lady was coyer than a queen. He was as whorish as a gigolo. To herself, Divine explained that she wanted to spare Our Lady the sin of pride, for, as we know, it was very hard for Divine to be im-

moral, and she managed to be so only at the cost of long
detours which made her suffer. Her personage is tram-
meled by a thousand feelings and their opposites, which
tangle and untangle, knot and unknot, creating a mad
jumble. She did violence to her feelings. Her first desire
was of the following order: "Mimosa mustn't know a
thing. She's a bitch and I hate her." It was a pure desire,
born directly of the fact. However, Divine did not experience it in quite this form, for the heavenly saints were
standing by and watching, the female saints too; they did
not frighten Divine because they are terrible, that is, because they are avengers of wicked thoughts, but because
they are made of plaster and their feet are set on lace, in
flowers, and because, in spite of this, they are omniscient.
She thought to herself: "Our Lady is so proud! And so
dumb!" This clearly implied the first proposition, which
followed as a natural conclusion. But its moral cast allowed it to be stated. It was by an effort, a swagger, that
she managed to say: "She won't know anything, that slut"
(Mimosa), but in this way too she was disguising her
hatred beneath a bit of playful tinsel, for she referred to
Mimosa as "She." Had she said "He," it would have been
more serious. This we shall see later on. Divine was not so
vain as to believe that Mimosa was offering her a seat so
as to enjoy her company. She was therefore wary. She said
aloud:

"I'm playing Sitting Bull."

"Playing what?" said Mimosa.

Divine burst out laughing.

"Oh, I'm such a camp!"

Roger, Mimosa's man, must have smelled something
fishy. He wanted an explanation. Divine had learned
through experience that she was no match for Mimosa II.
For though she might not recognize the moment when
her friend's shrewdness was in play, she had had many a

proof of her detective-like shrewdness. "That Mimo, the slightest detail is all she needs." None but she could distinguish this detail and make it speak.

"So you're going? And you're taking Our Lady? You're mean. And selfish!"

"Look, angel, I'll see you later. I'm in a hurry today."

Divine kissed the palm of her hand, blew toward Mimosa (despite her smile, Divine's face suddenly took on the seriousness of the lady on the Larousse covers who scatters dandelion seed to the winds), and she went off as on the arm of an invisible lover, that is, heavy, weary, and transported.

When she said that Our Lady was proud and, upon learning that Mimosa had swallowed his photo, that he would have been more kindly disposed toward her, Divine was mistaken. Our Lady is not proud. He would have shrugged his shoulders, without even smiling, and simply said:

"The chick works hard. Now she's gulping down paper."

Perhaps this indifference was due to the fact that Our Lady felt nothing the way Mimosa did and did not imagine that anyone could feel a thrill by literally incorporating into himself the picture of a desired human being, by drinking him down, and he would have been incapable of recognizing in this an act of homage to his virility or beauty. Let us conclude from this that he had no desire of this kind. Yet, as we shall see, he was veneration itself. As for Divine, remember that she once answered Mimosa: "Our Lady will never be too proud. I want to make of him a statue of pride," thinking: "I want him to be molded of pride," and further: "molded in pride." Our Lady's tender youth (for he had his moments of tenderness) did not satisfy Divine's need to be subjected to brutal domination. The ideas of pride and statue very rightly go hand in hand, and with them the idea of massive stiffness. But we can see that Our Lady's pride was only a pretext.

As I have said, Darling Daintyfoot no longer came to the garret, and had even stopped meeting Our Lady in the grove of the Tuileries. He did not suspect that Our Lady knew all about his cowardly doings. In her garret, Divine lived only on tea and grief. She ate her grief and drank it; this sour food had dried her body and corroded her mind. Nothing—neither her own personal care nor the beauty parlors—kept her from being thin and having the skin of a corpse. She wore a wig, which she set most artfully, but the net of the underside showed at the temples. Powder and cream did not quite conceal the juncture with the skin of the forehead. One might have thought that her head was artificial. In the days when he was still in the garret, Darling might have laughed at all these embellishments had he been an ordinary pimp, but he was a pimp who heard voices. He neither laughed nor smiled. He was handsome and prized his good looks, realizing that if he lost them he would lose everything. Though the difficult charms employed in making beauty hold fast did not excite him, they left him cold and drew no cruel smile. It was quite natural. So many former girl friends had made themselves up in his presence that he knew that the damages to beauty are repaired without mystery. In shady hotels, he had witnessed clever restorations, had watched women as they hesitated with a lipstick in mid-air. Many a time he had helped Divine fasten her wig on. His movements had been skillful and, if I may say so, natural. He had learned to love that kind of Divine. He had steeped himself in all the monstrosities of which she was composed. He had passed them in review: her very white dry skin, her thinness, the hollows of her eyes, her powdered wrinkles, her slicked down hair, her gold teeth. He noted every detail. He said to himself that that's how it was; continued to screw it. He knew ecstasy and was caught good and proper. Darling the sturdy, all and always hot muscle and bush, was smitten with an artificial queen. Divine's wiles had nothing to do with it. Darling plunged headlong into this sort of debauch. Then, little by little, he had grown weary. He neglected Divine and left her. In the garret, she then had terrible fits of despair. Her advancing age was moving her into a coffin. It got to the point where she no longer dared a gesture or manner; people who came to know her during this period said that she seemed retiring. She still clung to the pleasures of bed and hallway; she cruised the tea rooms, but now it was she who did the paying. When making love, she would experience the wildest terror, fearing, for example, lest an excited youngster rumple her hair while she was on her knees, or press his head against her too roughly and push off her wig. Her pleasure was encumbered with a host of petty worries. She would stay in the garret in order to jerk off. For days and nights on end she would remain lying in bed, with the curtains drawn over the window of the dead, the Bay Window of the Departed. She would drink tea and eat fruitcake. With her head beneath the sheets, she would devise complicated debauches, involving two, three, or four persons, in which all the partners would arrange to discharge in her, on her, and for her at the same time. She would recall the narrow but vigorous loins, the loins of steel that had perforated her. Without regard for their tastes, she would couple them. She was willing to be the single goal of all these lusts, and her mind strained in an effort to be conscious of them simultaneously as they drifted about in a voluptuousness poured in from all sides. Her body would tremble from head to foot. She felt personalities that were strange to her passing through her. Her body would cry out: "The god, behold the god!" She would sink back, all exhausted. The pleasure soon lost its edge. Divine then donned the body of a male. Suddenly strong and muscular, she saw herself hard as nails, with her hands in her pockets, whistling. She saw herself doing the act on herself. She felt her muscles growing, as when she had tried to play virile, and she felt herself getting hard around the thighs, shoulderblades, and arms, and it hurt her. This game, too, petered out. She was drying up. There were no longer even any circles under her eyes.

It was then she sought out the memory of Alberto and satisfied herself with him. He was a good-for-nothing. The whole village mistrusted him. He was thievish, brutal, and coarse. Girls frowned when his name was mentioned in their presence, but their nights and sudden escapes during the dreary hours of work were taken up with his vigorous thighs, with his heavy hands that were forever swelling his pockets and stroking his flanks, or that remained there motionless, or moved gently, stealthily, as they lifted the taut or distended cloth of his trousers. His hands were broad and thick, with short fingers, a splendid thumb, an imposing, massive mound of Venus, hands that hung from his arms like sods. It was on a summer evening that the children, who are the usual bearers of staggering news, informed the village that Alberto was fishing for snakes. "Snake fisher, that's just what he's fit for," thought the old women. This was one more reason for wishing him to the devil. Some scientists were offering an attractive premium for every reptile captured alive. While playing, Alberto caught one unintentionally, delivered it alive, and received the promised premium. Thus was born his new profession, which he liked, and which made him furious with himself. He was neither a superman nor an immoral faun. He was just a boy with simple thoughts, though embellished by voluptuousness. He seemed to be in a state of perpetual delight or perpetual intoxication. It was inevitable that Culafroy should meet him. It was the summer he spent wandering along the roads. As soon as he saw Alberto's figure in the distance, he realized that there was the purpose and goal of his walk. Alberto was standing motionless at the edge of the road, almost in the rye, as if waiting for someone, his two shapely legs spread in the stance of the Colossus of Rhodes, or the one shown us by the German sentries, so proud and solid beneath their helmets. Culafroy loved him. As he passed by, brave and indifferent, the lad blushed and lowered his head, while Alberto, with a smile on his lips, watched him walk. Let us say that he was eighteen years old, and yet Divine remembers him as a man.

He returned the following day. Alberto was standing there, a sentinel or statue, at the side of the road. "Hello!" he said, with a smile that twisted his mouth. (This smile was Alberto's particularity, was himself. Anyone could have had, or could have acquired, the same stiff hair, the color of his skin, his walk, but not his smile. Now when Divine seeks out the lost Alberto, she tries to portray him on herself and invents his smile with her own mouth. She puckers her muscles in what she thinks is the right way, the way—so she thinks when she feels her mouth twisting —that makes her resemble Alberto, until the day it occurs to her to do it in front of a mirror, and she realizes that her grimaces in no way resemble the smile we have already called starlike.) "Hello!" muttered Culafroy. That was all they said to each other, but from that day on Ernestine was to get used to seeing him desert the slate house. One day, Alberto asked:

"Want to see my pouch?"

He showed him a closely woven wicker basket buckled by a strap. The only thing in it that day was one elegant and angry snake.

"Shall I open it?"

"Oh! no, no, don't open it!" he said, for he has always felt that uncontrollable repulsion for reptiles.

Alberto did not lift the lid, but he put his hard, gentle, briar-scratched hand on the back of Culafroy's neck, just as the child was about to drop to his knees. Another day, three snakes were writhing about each other. Their heads were hooded in little hard leather cowls that were tightened about their necks by nooses.

"You can touch them. They won't hurt you."

Culafroy didn't move. Rooted with horror, he could no more have run away than at the apparition of a ghost or an angel from heaven. He was unable to turn his head. The snakes fascinated him; yet he felt that he was about to vomit.

"You scared? Come on, admit it. I used to be scared too."

That wasn't true, but he wanted to reassure the child. With sovereign superiority, Alberto calmly and deliberately put his hand into the tangle of reptiles and took one out, a long, thin one whose tail flattened like a whipcord, but without a sound, about his bare arm. "Touch it!" he said, and as he spoke, he took the child's hand and placed it on the cold, scaly body, but Culafroy tightened his fist and only the joints of his fingers came into contact with the snake. That wasn't touching. The coldness surprised him. It entered his vein, and the initiation proceeded. Veils were falling from large and solemn tableaux that Culafroy's eyes could not make out. Alberto took another snake and placed it on Culafroy's bare arm, about which it coiled just as the first had done.

"You see, she's harmless." (Alberto always referred to snakes in the feminine.)

Just as he felt his penis swelling between his fingers, so the sensitive Alberto felt in the child the mounting emotion that stiffened him and made him shudder. And the insidious friendship for snakes was born. And yet he had not yet touched any, that is, had not even grazed them with the organ of touch, the finger tips, the spot where the fingers are swollen with a tiny sensitive bump, by means of which the blind read. Alberto had to open the boy's hand and slip the icy, lugubrious body into it. That was the revelation. At that very moment, it seemed to him that a host of snakes might have invaded him, climbed over him, and wound themselves into him without his feeling anything but a friendly joy, a kind of tenderness, and meanwhile Alberto's sovereign hand had not left his, nor had one of his thighs left the child's, so that he was no longer quite himself. Culafroy and Divine, with their delicate tastes, will always be forced to love what they loathe, and this constitutes something of their saintliness, for that is renunciation.

Alberto taught him culling. You must wait until noon, when the snakes are asleep on the rocks, in the sun. You sneak up on them and then, crooking the index and middle finger, you grab them by the neck, close to the head, so that they can't slip away or bite; then, while the snake is hissing with despair, you quickly slip the hood over its head, tighten the noose, and put it into the box. Alberto wore a pair of corduroy trousers, leggings, and a gray shirt, the sleeves of which were rolled up to the elbows. He was good-looking—as are all the males in this book, powerful and lithe, and unaware of their grace. His hard, stubborn hair, which fell down over his eyes to his mouth, would have been enough to endow him with the glamor of a crown in the eyes of the frail, curly-haired child.

They generally met in the morning, around ten o'clock, near a granite cross. They would chat for a while about girls and then leave. The harvesting had not yet been done. As the metallic rye and wheat were inviolable by all others, they found sure shelter there. They entered obliquely, crept along and suddenly found themselves in the middle of the field. They stretched out on the ground and waited for noon. At first, Culafroy played with Alberto's arms, the next day with his legs, the day after with the rest of him, and this memory thrilled Divine, who could see herself hollowing her cheeks the way a boy does when he whistles. Alberto violated the child everywhere until he himself collapsed with weariness.

One day Culafroy said:

"I'm going home, Berto."

"Going home? Well, see you this evening, Lou."

Why "See you this evening?" The phrase came out of Alberto's mouth so spontaneously that Culafroy took it for granted and replied:

"See you this evening, Berto."

Yet the day was over, they would not see each other until the following day, and Alberto knew it. He smiled foolishly at the thought that he had let slip a phrase that he had not meant. As for Culafroy, the meaning of this farewell remained hazy. The phrase had thrilled him, as do certain artless poems, the logic and grammar of which become apparent only after we have enjoyed their charm. Culafroy was thoroughly bewitched. It was washday at the slate house. On the drier in the garden, the hanging sheets formed a labyrinth where specters hovered. That would be the natural place for Alberto to wait. But at what time? He had mentioned no specific time. The wind shook the white sheets as the arm of an actress shakes a backdrop of painted canvas. Night thickened with its usual quietness and constructed a rigid architecture of broad planes, packed with shadows. Culafroy's stroll began just as the spherical, steaming moon rose in the sky. This was to be the scene of the drama. Would Alberto come to rob? He needed money, he said, "for his chick." He had a chick; hence he was a true cock. As for stealing, it was possible. He had once inquired about the furnishings in the slate house. Culafroy liked the idea. He hoped that Alberto would come for that too. The moon was rising into the sky with a solemnity calculated to impress sleepless humans. A thousand sounds that make up the silence of night pressed in about the child, like a tragic chorus, with the intensity of the music of brasses and the strangeness of houses of crime, and of prisons, too, where—oh, the horror of it—one never hears the rattle of a bunch of keys. Culafroy walked about barefoot, among the sheets. He was experiencing minutes as light as minuets, minutes composed of anxiety and tenderness. He even ventured a toe dance, but the sheets, which formed hanging partitions and corridors, the sheets, quiet and crafty as corpses, might have drawn together and imprisoned and smothered him, as the branches of certain trees in hot countries sometimes smother careless savages who lie down to rest in their shade. If he ceased to touch the ground, save by an illogical movement of his taut instep, this movement might have made him take off, leave the earth, might have launched him into worlds from which he would never return, for in space nothing could stop him. He placed the soles of his feet squarely on the ground so that they would hold him there more firmly. For he knew how to dance. He had plucked the following theme from a copy of *Screen Weekly:* "A little ballerina photographed in her ballet skirt, her arms curved gracefully above her head, her toe rooted to the floor, like a spearhead." And below the picture, the following caption: "Graceful Kitty Ruphlay, twelve years old." With an amazing sense of divination, this child, who had never seen a dancer, who had never seen a stage or any actor, understood the page-long article dealing with such matters as figures, entrechats, jetés-battus, tutus, toe-shoes, drops, footlights, and ballet. From the aspect of the word

Nijinsky (the rise of the N, the drop of the loop of the j, the leap of the hook on the k and the fall of the y, graphic form of a name that seems to be drawing the artist's élan, with its bounds and rebounds on the boards, of the jumper who doesn't know which leg to come down on), he sensed the dancer's lightness, just as he will one day realize that Verlaine can only be the name of a poet-musician. He learned to dance by himself, just as he had learned to play the violin by himself. So he danced as he played. His every act was served by gestures necessitated not by the act itself, but by a choreography that transformed his life into a perpetual ballet. He quickly succeeded in dancing on his toes, and he did it everywhere: in the shed while gathering sticks of wood, in the little barn, under the cherry tree. . . . He would put aside his sabots and dance on the grass in black wool slippers, with his hands clinging to the low branches. He filled the countryside with a host of figurines who thought they were dancers in white tulle tutus, but who nonetheless remained a pale schoolboy in a black smock looking for mushrooms or dandelions. He was very much afraid of being discovered, especially by Alberto. "What would I say to him?" He thought of the form of suicide that might save him, and he decided upon hanging. Let us go back to that night. He was surprised and startled by the slightest movement of the branches, the slightest breath that was a bit dry. The moon struck ten. Then came aching anxiety. In his heart and throat the child discovered jealousy. He was now sure that Alberto would not come, that he would go and get drunk; and the idea of Alberto's betrayal was so acute that it established itself despotically in Culafroy's mind, to such a degree that he declared: "My despair is immense." Generally, when he was alone, he felt no need to utter his thoughts aloud, but today an inner sense of the tragic bade him observe an extraordinary protocol, and so he declared: "My despair is immense." He sniffled, but he did not cry. About him, the setting had ceased to appear marvelously unreal. Everything was exactly as it had been before: there were still the same white sheets hanging on wire lines which sagged beneath the weight, the same star-spangled sky, but their meaning had changed. The drama that was being enacted there had reached its phase of high pathos, the dénouement: all that remained for the actor was to die. When I write that the meaning of the setting was no longer the same, I do not mean that for Culafroy—and later for Divine—the setting was ever any different from what it would have been for anyone else, namely, wash drying on wire lines. He was well aware that he was a prisoner of sheets, but I beg of you to see the marvelous in this: a prisoner of familiar, though stiff sheets in the moonlight—unlike Ernestine, whom they would have reminded of brocade hangings or the halls of a marble palace, she who could not mount one step of a stairway without thinking of the word tier, and in the same circumstances, she would not have failed to feel profound despair and make the setting change attribution, to transform it into a white marble tomb, to magnify it, as it were, with her own sorrow, which was as lovely as a tomb, whereas for Culafroy nothing had moved, and this indifference of the setting better signified its hostility. Each thing, each object, was the result of a miracle, the accomplishing of which filled him with wonder. Likewise each gesture. He did not understand his room, nor the garden, nor the village. He understood nothing, not even that a stone was a stone, and this amazement in the face of what *is*—a setting which, by dint of being, ends by no longer being—left him the writhing prey of primitive, simple emotions: grief, joy, pride, shame. . . .

He fell asleep, like a drunken harlequin on the stage who sinks into his baggy sleeves and collapses on the grass beneath the violent light of the moon. The following day, he said nothing to Alberto. The fishing and the lolling in the rye at noon were what they were every day. That evening, the idea had crossed Alberto's mind of prowling about the slate house, with his hands in his pockets, whistling as he walked (He had a remarkable way of whistling with metallic stridency, and his virtuosity was not the least of his charms. This whistling was magical. It bewitched the girls. The boys, aware of his power, envied him. Perhaps he charmed the snakes.), but he did not come, for the town was hostile to him, especially if, like an evil angel, he went there at night. He slept.

They continued making love in the midst of the snakes. Divine remembers this. She thinks it was the loveliest period of her life.

One night on the boulevard she met Seck Gorgui. The big sunny Negro—though he was only the shadow of the Archangel Gabriel—was on the make.

He was wearing a gray worsted suit that clung to his shoulders and thighs, and his jacket was more immodest than the form-fitting tights in which Jean Borlin garbed his round balls. He was wearing a pink tie, a cream-colored silk shirt, gold rings with fake or real diamonds (what does it matter!); he had extraordinary fingernails, long and dark, and, at the base, as light as sound, year-old hazelnuts. In a trice, Divine was again the Divine of eighteen, for she thought naïvely, though vaguely, that, being black and a native of a warm country, Gorgui would be unable to tell her age or perceive her wrinkles or wig. She said:

"My, my! So here you are! Oh! I'm delighted."

Seck laughed:

"Pretty good," he said, "and you?"

Divine stuck close to him. He stood firm and straight,

though leaning slightly back, motionless and solid, in the position of a kid who braces himself on his nervous knees to piss against nothing at all, or in the pose in which, you will recall, Lou discovered Alberto (Colossus of Rhodes), the most virile pose of sentinels: thighs spread, and their bayonet-guns, which they grip with both hands, planted smack between their boots, right up to their mouths.

"What have you been doing? Playing the sax?"

"No, I'm through with that. I'm divorced. I dropped Banjo!" he said.

"Really? Why? Banjo was rather nice."

Here Divine got the better of her good nature. She added:

"A teenchy bit plump, a trifle round, but really, she had such a good disposition. What about now?"

Gorgui was free that evening. In fact, he was looking for customers. He needed money. Divine took the blow without flinching.

"How much, Gorgui?"

"Five louis."

It was precise. He got his hundred francs and followed Divine to the garret. Negroes have no age. Mlle. Adeline could explain to us that when they try to count they get all mixed up in their calculations, for they are quite aware that they were born at the time of a famine, of the death of three jaguars, of the flowering of the almond trees, and these circumstances, mingled with the figures, make it easy for them to go astray. Gorgui, our Negro, was vital and vigorous. A movement of his back shook the room, the way Village, the Negro murderer, shook his prison cell. I have tried to recapture, in the cell where I am now writing, the odor of carrion spread by the proud-scented Negro, and thanks to him I am better able to give life to Seck Gorgui. I have already spoken of my fondness for odors, the strong odors of the earth, of latrines, of the loins of

Arabs and, above all, the odor of my farts, which is not the odor of my shit, a loathsome odor, so much so that here again I bury myself beneath the covers and gather in my cupped hands my crushed farts, which I carry to my nose. They open to me hidden treasures of happiness. I inhale, I suck in. I feel them, almost solid, going down through my nostrils. But only the odor of my own farts delights me, and those of the handsomest boy repel me. Even the faintest doubt as to whether an odor comes from me or someone else is enough for me to stop relishing it. So, when I knew him, Clément Village filled the cell with an odor stronger than death. Solitude is sweet. It is bitter. One might think that the head should be emptied there of all past entries (precursory practice of purification), but you are well aware, while reading me, that this is not the case. I was exasperated. The Negro cured me to some extent. It seemed that his extraordinary sexual potency was sufficient to calm me. He was as strong as the sea. His radiance was more restful than a remedy. His presence was conjuratory. I would sleep.

Between his fingers he would roll a soldier whose eyes are no more than two musical pauses drawn by my pen on his smooth pink face; I can no longer meet a sky-blue soldier without seeing him lying on the Negro's chest, and immediately being irritated by the smell of turpentine that, mixed with his, used to befoul the cell. It was in another French prison, where the corridors and their straight lines, which were as long as those in a king's palace, wove and constructed geometrical patterns on which the gnarled prisoners, tiny in proportion to the scale of the corridors, glided by on felt slippers. As I passed each door, I would read a label indicating the category of the occupant. The first labels read: "Solitary confinement"; the next: "Transportation"; others: "Hard labor." Here I received a shock. The penal colony materialized before my eyes. Ceased to be word and became flesh. I was never at the end of the corridor, for it seemed to me to be at the end of the world, at the end of all, and yet it made signs to me, it emitted appeals that touched me, and I too shall probably go to the end of the corridor. I believe, though I know it to be false, that on the doors can be read the word "Death" or perhaps, what is graver still, the words "Capital Punishment."

In that prison, which I shall not name, every convict had a little yard, where every brick of the wall bore a message to a friend: "B.A.A. of Sébasto—Jacquot of Topol, known as V.L.F., to Lucien of La Chapelle," an exhortation, a votive offering to the mother, or a scathing: "Polo of Gyp's Bar is a stool pigeon." It was also in that prison that the chief guard used to give each of us a gift of a small packet of coarse salt on New Year's Day.

When I entered my cell, the big Negro was putting blue paint on his little lead soldiers, the biggest of which was littler than his littlest finger. He would seize them by the thigh, the way Lou-Divine used to grab frogs, and slap a coat of light blue over the whole body. Then he would put them down to dry on the floor, where they lay in great disorder, a tiny, irritating confusion, which the Negro heightened by coupling them lasciviously, for the solitude also sharpened his lasciviousness. He greeted me with a smile and a puckering of the brow. He was back from the Clairvaux State Prison, where he had put in five years, and had been here for a year while waiting to be sent to the penal colony. He had killed his girl; then, having sat her down on a yellow silk cushion with little green tufts, had walled her up, arranging the masonry in the form of a bench. He was annoyed that I didn't remember the story, which you must have read about in the papers. Since this misfortune had shattered his life, may it serve his glory, for it is a misfortune worse than being Hamlet and not being a prince.

"I am Clément," he said, "Clément Village."

I used to think that his big hands with their pink palms tortured the lead soldiers. His round forehead, which was as free of wrinkles as a child's (Gall would have called it a muliebral forehead), would bend over them. "I'm making buck privates."

I learned to paint them too. The cell was full of them. The table, shelves, and floor were covered with these tiny warriors, who were as hard and cold as corpses, whose number and inhuman smallness created for them a peculiar kind of soul. At night, I would kick them aside, lay out my straw mattress, and fall asleep in their midst. Like the inhabitants of Lilliput, they tied me down, and to get loose I offered Divine to the Archangel Gabriel.

During the day, the Negro and I would work in silence. However, I was sure that one day he would tell me his story. I don't like stories of that kind. Despite myself, I can't keep from thinking how often the narrator must have told it, and I feel as if it reaches me like a dress that has been handed down until . . . And besides, I have my own stories. Those which spring from my eyes. Prisons have their silent stories, and so do the guards, and even the lead soldiers, which are hollow. Hollow! The foot of one of the lead soldiers broke, and the stump revealed a hole. This certainty of their inner emptiness delighted and distressed me. At home, there used to be a plaster bust of Queen Marie-Antoinette. I lived right next to it for five or six years without noticing it, until the day when its chignon miraculously broke, and I saw the bust was hollow. I had had to leap into the void in order to see it. So what do I care about stories of Negro murderers, when mysteries of this kind, the mystery of the nothing and the no, signal to me and reveal themselves, as they revealed themselves in the village to Lou-Divine? The church played its role of Jack-in-the-box. The services had accustomed Lou to magnificence, and each religious holiday made him uneasy because he would see emerging from some hiding place the gilded candelabra, the white enameled lilies, the silver-embroidered cloths; from the sacristy came the green, violet, white, and black chasubles, some of moire and some of velvet, the albs, the stiff surplices, the new hosts. Unexpected and astounding hymns rang out, among them the most disturbing of all, the *Veni Creator*, which is sung at marriage ceremonies. The charm of the *Veni Creator* was that of sugared almonds and wax orange blossoms, the charm of the white tulle (to which is added still another charm, more peculiarly possessed by glaciers —we shall speak of this later), of the fringed armbands of children taking first communion, of the white socks; it was what I am obliged to call the nuptial charm. It is important to speak of it, for it is the one that transported the child Culafroy to seventh heaven. And I cannot tell why.

Over the gold ring lying on a white linen cloth on the tray which he bears before the bride and groom, the priest makes the sign of the cross with four little shocks of his sprinkler that leave four little drops on the ring.

The sprinkler is always moist with a tiny droplet, like Alberto's prick which is stiff in the morning and which has just pissed.

The vaults and walls of the chapel of the Virgin are whitewashed, and the Virgin has an apron as blue as a sailor's collar.

Facing the faithful, the altar is neatly arranged; facing God, it is a jumble of wood in the dust and spider webs.

The purses of the usherette who takes up the collection are made of a pink silk left-over of the dress of Alberto's sister. But the objects in the church became more familiar to Culafroy. Before long, only the church in the neighboring town could provide new spectacles for him. Little by little it was abandoned by its gods, who fled at the child's approach. The last question he asked them received a reply as sharp as a slap. One day, about noon, the mason was repairing the porch of the chapel. Perched at the top of a double ladder, he did not seem to Culafroy to be an archangel, for the child could never take seriously the wonderland of the image makers. The mason was the mason. A good-looking fellow, too. His corduroy pants set off his buttocks and hung loosely about his legs. At his open-necked shirt collar, his neck emerged from a bush of stiff hairs, as a tree trunk emerges from the fine grass of the undergrowth. The door of the church was open. Lou passed beneath the rungs of the ladder, lowered his head and eyes beneath a sky inhabited by a pair of corduroy pants and slipped into the choir. The mason, who had seen him, said nothing. He was hoping that the kid would play some trick on the priest. Culafroy's sabots rattled over the flagstones until he reached the spot where the floor was covered with a rug. He stopped beneath the chandelier and kneeled very ceremoniously on a tapestried prayer stool. His genuflections and gestures were a faithful copy of those made by Alberto's sister on this same prayer stool every Sunday. He adorned himself with their beauty. Thus, acts have esthetic and moral value only insofar as those who perform them are endowed with power. I still wonder what is the significance of the emotion that rises up within me when I hear some silly song just as it does when I am in the presence of a recognized masterpiece. This power is delegated to us sufficiently for us to feel it within us, and this is what enables us to bear our having

to lower our head in order to step into a car, because when
we lower it an imperceptible memory turns us into a
movie star, or a king, or a vagrant (but he's another king)
who lowered his head the same way (we saw him in the
street or on the screen). Rising on the toes of my right
foot and raising my right arm to take down my little mirror from the wall, or to grab my mess tin from the shelf, is
a gesture that transforms me into the Princess of T . . . ,
whom I once saw make this movement in order to put
back a drawing she had shown me. Priests who repeat
symbolic gestures feel themselves imbued with the virtue
not of the symbol but of the first executant; the priest who,
at Divine's funeral mass, imitated the sly gestures of
burglary and theft, was adorning himself, with the gestures, *spolia opima*, of a guillotined second-story man.

So, no sooner had Culafroy taken a few drops from the
basin of holy water at the entrance than Germaine's hard
breasts and buttocks were grafted on to him, as muscles
were grafted on at a later time, and he had to carry them
in the current fashion. Then he prayed, in pose and mutter, accentuating the bowing of his head and the noble
slowness of the sign of the cross. Shadowy calls rang out
from all corners of the choir, from all the stalls of the altar.
The little lamp was gleaming; at noon, it was seeking a
man. The mason whistling under the porch belonged to
the world, to Life, and Lou, alone there, felt himself
master of the whole works. He must answer the clarion
calls, must enter the shadow, which was as dense as a
solid. . . . He stood up silently. His sabots moved forward
and bore him with infinite caution over the tufted wool of
the rug, and the smell of the old incense, poisonous as that
of old tobacco in a seasoned pipe, as a lover's breath, de-
sensitized the fears that were born thick and fast with
each of his gestures. He moved slowly, with tired muscles,
soft as those of a deep-sea diver, numbed by the odor

which pushed back the moment so artfully that Culafroy seemed to be neither here nor now. The altar was suddenly within arm's reach, as if Lou had unwittingly taken a giant stride, and he felt himself sacrilegious. The Epistles had fallen down on the stone table. The silence was a peculiar silence, a silence that was present, which sounds from the outside could not penetrate. They squashed against the thick walls of the church like rotten fruit thrown by children. Though they were audible, they in no way disturbed the silence.

"Cula!"

The mason was calling.

"Sh! Don't shout in church."

The two cries made a huge crevice in the edifice of the silence, the silence of cottages that are being robbed. The double curtains of the tabernacle did not quite come together, and from the slit, as obscene as an unbuttoned fly, protruded the little key that keeps the door shut. Culafroy's hand was on the key when he regained consciousness, only to lose it again immediately. The miracle! Blood will flow from the hosts if I take one! Idle stories about Jews, about Jews biting into the Holy Species, stories of prodigies, in which hosts falling from the mouths of children stain the floor and cloths with blood, stories about simoniacal brigands, had all prepared this agonizing moment. It cannot be said that Lou's heart beat faster—on the contrary, a kind of foxglove (foxglove is known as Virgin's finger in those parts) slowed down its rhythm and force—nor that his ears buzzed—silence emerged from them. A wild silence. He had risen on his toes and found the key. He had stopped breathing. The miracle. He expected to see the plaster statues come tumbling down from their niches and crush him; he was certain they would. As far as he was concerned, it was already done before being done. He awaited damnation with the resignation of a man con-

demned to death; knowing it was imminent, he awaited it
in peace. Thus, he acted only after the act had virtually been
performed. The silence (it was squared, cubed) was on
the point of blowing up the church, of turning the things
of God into fireworks. The ciborium was there. He had
opened it. The act seemed to him so outlandish that he was
curious enough to watch himself do it. The dream almost
collapsed. Lou-Culafroy seized the three hosts and let
them fall to the carpet. They descended hesitantly, drifting like leaves that fall in calm weather. The silence
rushed at the child, bowled him over like a team of boxers,
pinned his shoulders to the floor. He let go of the ciborium,
which made a hollow sound as it fell on the wool.

And the miracle occurred. There was no miracle. God
had been debunked. God was hollow. Just a hole with any
old thing around it. A pretty shape, like the plaster head
of Marie-Antoinette and the little soldiers, which were
holes with a bit of thin lead around them.

Thus I lived in the midst of an infinity of holes in the
form of men. I slept on a mattress that lay on the floor, as
there was only one bed, in which Clément slept. I would
watch him from below, stretched out, as on a bench, on
the stone of the altar. He would move only once during
the entire night, to go to the latrine. He performed this
ceremony with the greatest mystery. In secret, in silence.
Here is his story as he told it to me. He was from Guade-
loupe and had been a nude dancer at the *Viennese Dream-
land*. He lived with his Dutch girlfriend, whose name was
Sonia, in a little flat in Montmartre. They lived there the
way Divine and Darling lived, that is, a splendid and casual life, a life that a breath might shatter—so think the
bourgeois, who sense the poetry of the lives of creators of
poetry—dancers, Negroes, boxers, prostitutes, soldiers—
but who do not see that these lives have an earthly tie,

since they are big with terror. Early in May, 1939, there took place between them one of those typical scenes between whores and pimps, for the take had been insufficient. Sonia spoke of leaving. He slapped her. She screamed. She insulted him in German, but as the tenants of the building were very tactful folk, no one heard. Then she decided to get her valise, which was hidden under the bed, and she quietly began to gather her underthings which were scattered about. The big Negro went over to her. His hands were in his pockets.

"Stop that, Sonia," he said.

Perhaps he had a cigarette in his mouth. She continued stuffing her valise with silk stockings, dresses, pajamas, towels.

"Stop it, Sonia."

She stuffed away. The valise was lying on the bed. Clément pushed her on to it. She lost her balance, and as she fell back, her feet, which were still wearing silver shoes, flew up to his nose. The girl uttered a tiny cry. The Negro grabbed her by the ankles, and, lifting her up like a tailor's dummy, with a dazzling gesture, a sunlike gesture, swinging rapidly on his heel, he broke her head on the post of the little brass bed. Clément told me the story in his soft Creole speech, in which the r's are dropped and the ends of phrases are drawled out softly.

"You und'stand, Missie Jean. Ah hit huh head theah. Huh head theah smacked on the brass bed."

He was holding in his fingers a little soldier whose symmetrical face expressed only foolishness and caused that feeling of malaise which we also get from primitive drawings, from the same drawings that prisoners carve on prison walls and scribble in library books, and on their chests which they are going to tattoo, and which show the profiles with an eye in full-face. Clément finally told me of the anguish into which he had been thrown by the rest of the episode: the sun, he said, was coming through the window of the little apartment, and never before had he noticed a certain quality of the sun, namely, malevolence. It was the only living thing. It was more than an accessory —it was a triumphal, insidious witness, important as a witness (witnesses are almost always for the prosecution), jealous as actors at not having top billing. Clément opened the window, but then it seemed to him that he had just publicly confessed his crime; the street came crowding into the room, upsetting the order and disorder of the drama so that it could take part in it too. The fabulous atmosphere lasted quite a while. The Negro leaned out the window; at the far end of the street he saw the sea. I do not know whether, in attempting to reconstitute the state of mind of the criminal who surmounts the disastrous horror of his act, I am not secretly trying to ascertain what the best method will be (the one most in keeping with my nature) in order not to succumb likewise to horror when the time comes. Then, all the possible ways of getting rid of Sonia occurred to him at once, grouped, interlaced, crowding each other, offering themselves to his choice as on a street stand. He did not remember ever having heard about walling up a corpse, and yet this was the means he felt had been singled out before he chose it.

"So Ah locked the do'. Ah put key in m'pocket. Ah took the valise f'm off the bed, ah pulled back the blankets. Ah put Sonia in bed. Funny thing, Missie Jean, held Sonia theah. Blood stuck on huh cheek."

And then there began that long life of heroism which lasted an entire day. By a powerful effort of will, he escaped banality—maintaining his mind in a superhuman region, where he was a god, creating at one stroke a private universe where his acts escaped moral control. He sublimated himself. He made himself general, priest, sacrificer, officiant. He had commanded, avenged, sacrificed, offered. He had not killed Sonia. With a baffling instinct, he made use of this artifice to justify his act. Men endowed with a wild imagination should have, in addition, the great poetic faculty of denying our universe and its values so that they may act upon it with sovereign ease. Like someone who overcomes his fear of water and the void which he is about to enter for the first time, he breathed deeply, and, bringing himself to a point of icy determination, he became insensible and remote. Having gone through with the irremediable, he resigned himself to it and came to terms with it. Then he tackled the remediable. As of a cloak, he divested himself of his Christian soul. He sanctified his acts with a grace that owed nothing to a God Who condemns murder. He stopped up the eyes of his spirit. For a whole day, as if automatically, his body was at the mercy of orders that did not come from here below. It was not so much the horror of the murder that terrified him: he was afraid of the corpse. The white corpse disconcerted him, whereas a black corpse would have disturbed him less. So, he left the apartment, which he locked with extreme care, and went off at daybreak to a construction yard to get twenty pounds of cement. Twenty pounds was enough. In a distant neighborhood, around the Boulevard Sebastopol, he bought a trowel. In the street, he had regained his man's soul; he acted like a man, giving his activity a commonplace meaning: that of making a little wall. He bought fifty bricks and had them hauled to a street near his own, where they were left in a hired wheelbarrow. It was already noon. Getting the bricks into the apartment was quite a job. He made ten trips from the wheelbarrow to his home, carrying five or six each time and concealing them under a coat that he carried on his arm. And when all the materials were ready in the room, he returned to his empyrean. He uncovered the corpse; then he was alone. He set the body against the

wall, near the fireplace. His plan was to immure it standing up, but it had already curled; he tried to straighten the
legs, but they had the hardness of wood and had assumed
their final form. The bones snapped like a bunch of fire-
crackers. So he left it squatting there at the foot of the
wall, and he set to work. Works of genius owe a great deal
to the collaboration of circumstances and workman. When
his job was done, Clément saw that he had given it, with
marvelous exactness, the form of a bench. That suited
him. He worked like a sleepwalker, preoccupied and determined; he refused to see the gulf in order to escape
from dizzying madness, the same dizziness which, later, a
hundred pages later, Our Lady of the Flowers did not resist. He knew that if he flinched, that is, if he relaxed that
attitude, an attitude as severe as a bar of steel, he would
have sunk. Sunk, that is, run to the police station and
melted into tears. He understood this and kept repeating
it to himself as he workèd, mixing exhortations with invo-
cations. As he told the tale, the little lead soldiers ran rapidly between his big light fingers. I paid close attention.
Clément was handsome. You know from *Paris-Soir* that he
was killed during the jailbreak at Cayenne. But he was
handsome. He was perhaps the handsomest Negro I have
ever seen. How lovingly I shall caress, with the memory
of him, the image I shall compose, thanks to it, of Seck
Gorgui. I want him too to be handsome, nervous, and vulgar. Perhaps his destiny heightened his beauty, like those
silly songs to which I listen here in the evening and which
grow poignant because they reach me across cells and
cells of guilty convicts. His faraway birth, his dancing at
night, his crime, were elements which enveloped him in
poetry. His forehead, as I have said, was round and
smooth; he had laughing eyes, with long curved lashes. He
was gentle and proud. In a eunuch's voice, he would hum

old songs of the islands. Finally the police got him, though
I don't know how.

The little soldiers continued their work of invasion, and
one day the foreman brought the soldier that was one too
many. Village whimpered to me:

"Ah've had enough, Missie Jean. Look, anotha so'dja."

From that day on, he grew more taciturn. I knew that
he hated me, though without my being able to understand
why and also without our comradely relations suffering
thereby. He began, however, to manifest his hatred and
irritation by all kinds of acts of petty meanness, about
which I could do nothing, for he was invulnerable. One
morning, after waking up, he sat down on his bed, looked
around the room, and saw it full of stupid-looking figurines
that were lying about everywhere, as mindless and mock-
ing as a race of fetuses, as Chinese torturers. The troops
rose up in sickening waves to attack the giant. He felt himself capsizing. He was sinking into an absurd sea, and the
eddies of his despair were sucking me into the shipwreck.
I grabbed hold of a soldier. They were all over the floor,
everywhere, a thousand, ten thousand, a hundred thousand! And though I was holding the one I had picked up
in the warm hollow of my palm, it remained icy, without
breath. There was blue everywhere in the room, blue mud
in a pot, blue spots on the walls, on my nails. Blue as the
apron of the Immaculate Conception, blue as enamels,
blue as a standard. The little soldiers whipped up a swell
that made the room pitch.

"Jes' look at me."

Clément was sitting on the bed and uttering sharp little
cries. His long arms would rise and drop heavily on his
knees (women carry on like that). He was weeping. His
lovely eyes were swollen with tears that ran down to his
mouth. "Oh! Oh!" But I, here, all alone, remember only
the elastic muscle he dug into me without using his hand.

I remember that live tool to which I would like to raise a temple. Others were taken by it. And Divine by Seck Gorgui, and others by Diop, by N'golo, by Smaïl, by Diagne.

With Gorgui, Divine was very quickly all at sea. He played with her like a cat with a mouse. He was ferocious.

As she lies with her cheek on his black chest (her wig is on firmly), Divine thinks about that tongue of his which is so strong while hers is so soft. Everything about Divine is soft. Softness or firmness is only a matter of tissues in which the blood is more or less abundant, and Divine is not anemic. Divine is she-who-is-soft. That is, whose character is soft, whose cheeks are soft, whose tongue is soft, whose tool is supple. With Gorgui, all is hard. Divine is amazed that there can be any relationship among these various soft things. Since hardness is equivalent to virility . . . If Gorgui had only one hard thing . . . and since it is a matter of tissue. The explanation eludes Divine, who has stopped thinking anything except: "I'm the Quite-Soft."

So Gorgui lived in the garret, flying over the rows of graves, the columns of tombs. He brought his linen, guitar, and saxophone. He would spend hours playing homely melodies from memory. At the window, the cypresses were attentive. Divine felt no special tenderness toward him. She prepared his tea without love, but as her savings were running out, she went back to working the streets, and that kept her from being bored. She would sing. To her lips came unformed melodies in which tenderness blended with pompousness, as in primitive songs which are the only kind that can stir emotion, as do certain orisons and psalms, as do sober and solemn attitudes dictated by a code of primitive liturgy from which pure and blaspheming laughter is banished, although they are still all soiled with the desires of the divinities: Blood, Fear, Love. Darling used to drink inexpensive pernods, but Gorgui drinks cocktails composed of costly liquors; on the other hand, he eats little. One morning, it might have been eight o'clock, Our Lady knocked at the door of the garret. Divine was curled up in the shadow (as fragrant perhaps as a savanna) of the Negro who was sleeping candidly on his back. The knocking awoke her. We know that for some time she had been wearing pajamas at night. Gorgui continued napping. She crawled over his hot naked belly, hitting against his moist but firm thighs as she climbed over him, and asked:

"Who is it?"

"It's me."

"But who?"

"Oh, shit! Don't you recognize me? Let me in, Divine."

She opened the door. The odor, even more than the sight of the Negro, informed Our Lady.

"What a stink! You got a tenant. Not bad. Say, I've got to get some sleep. I'm pooped. Got room for me?"

Gorgui had awakened. He was embarrassed at finding himself with a hard-on, the kind one has in the morning. He was naturally modest, but the whites had taught him immodesty, and in his zeal to be like them, he outdid them. Fearing lest his gesture seem ridiculous, he did not draw back the covers. He simply offered his hand to Our Lady, whom he did not know. Divine introduced them.

"Would you like a cup of tea?"

"All right."

Our Lady was sitting on the bed. He was getting used to the odor. While Divine prepared the tea, he unlaced his shoes. The laces were knotted. One might think that he put his shoes on and took them off without any light. He took off his jacket and tossed it on the rug. The water was about to boil. He tried to take off his shoes and socks with the same movement, for his feet were sweating and he was afraid they might smell in the room. He didn't quite manage it, but his feet didn't smell. He refrained from glancing at the Negro, and he thought: "Am I going to have to snooze next to Snowball? I hope he's going to beat it." Divine was not very sure about Gorgui. She did not know whether or not he was one of the many stool pigeons of the vice squad. She did not question Our Lady. All in all, Our Lady was his usual self. Neither his eyes nor the corners of his mouth were tired; only his hair was a little mussed. A few strands over his eyes. All the same, a bit of a hangover look. He was waiting on the edge of the bed with his elbows on his knees and was scratching his head.

"Your water cooking?"

"Yes, it's boiling."

On the little electric stove the water was boiling away. Divine poured it over the tea. She prepared three cups. Gorgui had sat up. He was being gradually impregnated with objects and beings, and first of all with himself. He felt himself being. He emitted a few timid ideas: heat, an unfamiliar fellow, I got a hard-on, tea, spots on his nails (the face of the American girl who did not want to shake hands with one of his friends), ten after eight. He did not remember Divine's having spoken to him about this unfamiliar fellow. Whenever she introduces him, Divine says: "A friend," for the murderer has strongly advised her never to call him Our Lady of the Flowers in front of a stranger. As things turn out, this has no importance. Gorgui looks at him again. He sees his slightly turned profile and the back of his head. It's the very same head that's pinned to the wall with a safety pin. But he looks better in the flesh, and Our Lady, turning slightly toward him, says:

"Say, pal, going to make room for me? I didn't sleep a wink all night."

"Oh! go right ahead, my boy. I'm getting up."

We know that Our Lady never excused himself. It seemed, not that everything was due him, but that everything was bound to happen (and happened in due course), nothing was addressed to him, no special attention, no mark of esteem, that, in short, everything occurred according to an order with only one possibility.

"Say, Divine, will you hand me my shirt?" said the Negro.

"Wait, you're going to have tea."

Divine handed one cup to him and one to Our Lady. So once again begins the three-cornered life in the garret which looks out over the dead, the cut flowers, the drunken gravediggers, the sly ghosts torn by the sun. Ghosts are composed of neither smoke nor opaque or translucent fluid: they are as clear as air. We pass through them during the day, particularly during the day. Sometimes they are outlined in pen strokes on our features, on one of our legs, crossing their thighs on ours, in one of our gestures. Divine spent several days with the airy Marchetti who ran off with Our Lady, and led him astray— and almost murdered him—and whose ghost Our Lady did not always pass through without carrying off in his movement sparkling shreds, invisible to Darling and his great friend (perhaps he wanted to say "my good pal" and one day he said "my pretty pal"). He takes a cigarette. But it is Marchetti who, with a roguish flick, shoots it from the pack. Shreds of the Marchetti ghost cling all over Our Lady. They disguise him beyond recognition. These ghostly tatters do not become him. He really looks disguised, but only like poor little peasant lads at Carnival time, with petticoats, shawls, wristlets, button boots with Louis XV heels, sunbonnets, fichus stolen from the closets of grandmothers and sisters. Little by little, petal by petal, Our Lady of the Flowers plucks off his adventure. True or false? Both. With Marchetti, he robbed a safe that was hidden in an antique cabinet. As he cut the electric wire connecting it with a bell in the watchman's quarters, Marchetti (a thirty-year-old, handsome blond Corsican, a Greco-Roman wrestling champion) put a finger to his lips and said:

"Now it's quiet."

Squatting, probably on a rug, they sought the number and found it after having entangled themselves to the point of despair in combinations which jumbled up their age, their hair, the smooth faces of their love, with multiples and sub-multiples. Finally, this diabolic tangle was organized into a rosette and the door of the cabinet opened. They pocketed three hundred thousand francs and a treasure in fake jewels. In the car, on the way to Marseilles (for even if one isn't thinking of leaving, after that kind of job, one always goes to a port. Ports are at the end of the world), Marchetti, for no other reason than nervousness, struck Our Lady on the temple. His gold signet ring drew blood. Finally (Our Lady learned of it later, through Marchetti's confessing it to a pal), Marchetti thought of bumping him off. In Marseilles, after dividing the swag, Our Lady entrusted him with all of it, and Marchetti beat it, abandoning the child.

"He's a son of a bitch, Divine, ain't he?"

"You were crazy about him," said Divine.

"Aw, go on, you're nuts."

But Marchetti was handsome. (Our Lady talks about the sweater that shows his figure, like velvet. He feels that it envelops the charm that subjugates, the iron hand in the velvet glove.) Blond Corsican with eyes . . . of blue. The wrestling was . . . Greco-Roman. The signet ring . . . of gold. On Our Lady's temple, the blood flowed. In short, he owed his life to the one who, having just murdered him, resurrected him. Marchetti, by his grace, restored him to the world. Then, in the garret, Our Lady became

sad and joyous. One might think he was singing a song of
death to the air of a minuet. Divine listens. He is saying
that, if caught, Marchetti will be transported. He will be
shipped off. Our Lady does not exactly know what transportation is, for all he has ever heard of it is what a youngster once said to him, in speaking of the courts: "Transportation's a rough deal," but he suspects that it will be
frightful. For Divine, who is familiar with prisons and
their pensive hosts, Marchetti is going to prepare himself
in accordance with the rites, as she explains to Our Lady,
perhaps as was done by a man condemned to death who
in one night, from twilight to dawn, sang all the songs he
knew. Marchetti will sing songs with the voice of Tino
Rossi. He will pack up. Will pick the photos of his prettiest
girl friends. Also his mother's. Will kiss his mother in the
visitors' room. Will leave. Afterwards, it will be the sea,
that is, the devil's isle, Negroes, rum distilleries, coconuts,
colonials wearing Panamas. The Beauty! Marchetti will
play the Beauty! He will *be* the Beauty! I am touched at
the thought of it and could weep with tenderness over his
handsome muscles, submissive to the muscles of other
brutes. The pimp, the lady killer, the hangman of hearts,
will be queen of the labor gang. Of what use will his Greek
muscles be? And he will be called "Flash" until a younger
hoodlum arrives. But no. And does God take pity on him?
A decree no longer allows the departure for Cayenne. The
hardened offenders remain to the end of their days in the
huge state prisons. The Beauty's chance, his hope, has
been abolished. They will die nostalgic for the homeland
that is their true homeland, which they have never seen,
and which is denied them. He is thirty. Marchetti will remain between four white walls to the end of ends, and so
as not to waste away with boredom, it will be his turn to
elaborate these imaginary lives, never realized and without hope of ever being realized. It will be the death of

Hope. Well-to-do captives of a dice-shaped cell. I am very glad of it. Let this arrogant and handsome pimp in turn know the torments reserved for the weakly. We occupy our minds with giving ourselves splendid roles through luxurious lives; we invent so many that we remain enfeebled for a life of action, and if one of them came, by chance, to be realized, we would be unable to be happy in it, for we have exhausted the dry delights (and many a time recalled the memory of their illusion) of the thousand possibilities of glory and wealth. We are blasé. We are forty, fifty, sixty years old; we know only petty, vegetative misery, we are blasé. Your turn, Marchetti. Don't invent ways of making a fortune, don't buy knowledge of a sure way of smuggling, don't look for a new trick (they're all used up, more than used up) to fool jewelers, to rob whores, to bamboozle priests, to distribute phony identity cards, for if you don't have the heart to try to escape, resign yourself to the possibility of suddenly getting the right break (without specifying to yourself exactly what it may be): the one that gets you out of trouble forever, and enjoy it as you can, deep in your cell. For I hate you lovingly.

DIVINARIANA (*continued*)

Despite the abjection in which you may hold her, Divine still reigns on the boulevard. To a newcomer (perhaps fifteen years old) in shabby linen, who winks mockingly, a pimp says, shoving her aside:

"Her, she's Divine. You, you're a slob."

Divine has been seen at the market at about eight in the morning. Shopping bag in hand, she was discussing the price of vegetables, violets, eggs.

The afternoon of the same day, five friends at tea: "Behold, my darlings, behold Divine wedded to God. She rises at cock's crow to go to communion, the Quite-Repentant."

The chorus of friends:

"Pitah, pitah, for Divine!"

The following day:

"My dear, they made Divine strip at the police station. She was all bruised. She'd been biffed. Her Darling's been beating her."

The chorus of friends:

"Woo, woo, woo, Divine's getting licked!"

Now, the fact is that Divine wore next to her skin a clinging hair shirt, unsuspected by Darling and the clients.

Someone is talking to Divine (it's a soldier who wants to re-enlist):

"What can I do to get along? I have no money."

Divine:

"Work."

"You can't find work right away."

He tries to tempt Divine and persists:

"So?"

He hopes she will answer, or think: "Steal." But Divine dared not reply, because, musing on what she would have done in such a case, she saw herself holding out to the birds her crumbs of hunger, and she thought: "Beg."

Divine:

"We have seen cyclists, wrapped in the garlands of the song they whistled, going dizzily down the celestial slope of the hills. We awaited them in the valley, where they arrived in the form of little pats of mud."

Divine's cyclists awake in me an ancient terror.

It is absolutely essential that I come back to myself, that I confide in a more direct way. I wanted to make this book out of the transposed, sublimated elements of my life as a convict. I am afraid that it says nothing about the things that haunt me. Although I am striving for a lean style, one that shows the bone, I should like to address to you from my prison a book laden with flowers, with snow-white petticoats and blue ribbons. There is no better pastime.

The world of the living is never too remote from me. I remove it as far as I can with all the means at my disposal. The world withdraws until it is only a golden point in so somber a sky that the abyss between our world and the other is such that the only real thing that remains is our grave. So I am beginning here a really dead man's existence. More and more I prune that existence, I trim it of all facts, especially the more petty ones, those which might readily remind me that the real world is spread out twenty yards away, right at the foot of the walls. Among my concerns, I rule out those most apt to remind me that they were necessitated by an established social practice: for example, tying my shoelaces with a double bow would remind me too sharply that, in the world, I used to do that to keep them from coming undone during the miles of walking I did. I don't button my fly. To do so would oblige me to check on myself again in the mirror or when I leave the can. I sing what I would never have sung out there, for example, that frightful: "We're the ones who are mopey and lousy and tough . . . ," which, ever since I sang it at La Roquette when I was fifteen, comes to mind every time I go back to prison. I read things I would never read elsewhere (and I believe in them): the novels of Paul Féval. I believe in the world of prisons, in its reprehended practices. I accept living there as I would accept, were I dead, living in a cemetery, provided that I lived there as if I were really dead. But the diversion must be based not on the difference be-

tween the occupations, but on their essence. I must do
nothing clean or hygienic: cleanliness and hygiene are of
the earthly world. I must feed on the gossip of the law
courts. Must feed on dreams. Must not be dandyish and
bedeck myself with new adornments, other than a tie and
gloves, but must give up being smart and trim. Must not
want to be good-looking: must want something else. Must
use another kind of speech. And must think that I've been
imprisoned once and for all, and for eternity. That's what
is meant by "building a life": giving up Sundays, holidays,
concern about the weather. I was not surprised when I
discovered the practices of prisoners, the practices that
make of them men on the margin of the living: cutting up
matches lengthwise, making cigarette lighters, smoking
ten to a butt, walking round and round the cell, and so on.
I think that hitherto I bore that life within me secretly and
that all I needed was to be put into contact with it for it
to be revealed to me, from without, in its reality.

But now I am afraid. The signs pursue me and I pursue
them patiently. They are bent on destroying me. Didn't I
see, on my way to court, seven sailors on the terrace of a
café, questioning the stars through seven mugs of light
beer as they sat around a table that perhaps turned; then,
a messenger boy on a bicycle who was carrying a message
from god to god, holding between his teeth, by the metal
handle, a round, lighted lantern, the flame of which, as it
reddened his face, also heated it? So pure a marvel that he
was unaware of being a marvel. Circles and globes haunt
me: oranges, Japanese billiard balls, Venetian lanterns,
jugglers' hoops, the round ball of the goalkeeper who
wears a jersey. I shall have to establish, to regulate, a
whole internal astronomy.

Fear? And what worse can happen to me than what will
happen? Apart from physical suffering, I fear nothing.
Morality clings to me only by a thread. Yet, I am afraid.

Did I not suddenly realize, on the eve of the trial, that I had been awaiting that moment for eight months, during which time I never gave it a thought? Few are the moments when I escape from horror, few the moments when I do not have a vision, or some horrifying perception of human beings and events. Even, and especially, of those commonly judged to be the most beautiful. Yesterday, in one of those narrow cells in the "Mousetrap" where you wait until it's time to go up to the chambers of the examining magistrate, there were twelve of us, standing, crowded together. I was at the back, by the latrines, near a young Italian who was laughing and relating some trivial experiences. But owing to his voice and his accent and his French, these adventures vibrated with pathos. I took him for an animal that had been metamorphosed into a man. I felt that, in the presence of this privilege which I thought he possessed, he could, at any given moment, turn me, by his simple wish, even unexpressed, into a jackal, a fox, a guinea hen. Perhaps I was hypnotizing myself in the presence of this privilege which I thought he possessed. At one point, he exchanged a few naïve and mortal remarks with a child-pimp. He said, among other things: "I skinned the gal," and in the narrow cell he was suddenly so close to me that I thought he wanted to love me, and so fierce that I thought he meant: "I skinned the woman" in the sense that one says of a rabbit: "I skinned it," that is, carved it up. He also said: "The warden says to me straight off: 'You're a funny egg,' and I answer back: 'Let me tell you, eggs like me are worth just as much as eggs like you.'" I think of the word "egg" in the mouths of babies. It's horrible. The marvelous horror was such that when I remember those moments (it had to do with crap games), it seems to me that the two kids were suspended in air, without support, their feet off the floor, and that they were shooting remarks at each other in silence. I am so certain of remembering that they were in the air that in spite of myself my intelligence tries to figure out whether they didn't have some gadget that enabled them to lift themselves up, a hidden mechanism, an invisible spring, under the floor, some kind of plausible device. But as nothing of the sort was possible, my memory strays into the sacred horror of the dream. Frightful moments— which I seek out—when you cannot contemplate either your body or heart without disgust. I encounter every-where a trivial incident, seemingly innocuous, which plunges me into the foulest horror: as if I were a corpse being pursued by the corpse that I am. It's the odor of the latrines. It's the hand of the man condemned to death, the hand with its wedding ring, which I see when he puts it outside the grating of his cell to take the soup tin from the assistant: since he himself remains invisible to me, the hand is like the hand of the god of a trick temple, and that cell, in which the light is kept on day and night, is the Space-Time amalgam of the anteroom of death—a vigil of arms which will last for forty-five times twenty-four hours. It's Darling with his trousers down, sitting on the white enamel toilet seat. His face is contracted. When the hot lumps, suspended for a moment, drop from him, a whiff apprises me that this blond hero was stuffed with shit. And the dream swallows me with one gulp. It's the fleas biting me, and I know they're malicious and that they're biting me with an intelligence that at first is human, and then more than human.

Do you know some poison-poem that would burst my cell into a spray of forget-me-nots? A weapon that would kill the perfect young man who inhabits me and makes me give asylum to a whole agglomeration of animals?

Swallows nest beneath his arms. They have masoned a nest there of dry earth. Snuff-colored velvet caterpillars mingle with the curls of his hair. Beneath his feet, a hive

of bees, and broods of asps behind his eyes. Nothing
moves him. Nothing disturbs him, save little girls taking
first communion who stick out their tongues at the priest
as they clasp their hands and lower their eyes. He is cold
as snow. I know he's sly. Gold makes him smile faintly, but
if he does smile, he has the grace of angels. What gypsy
would be quick enough to rid me of him with an inevitable dagger? It takes promptness, a good eye, and a fine
indifference. And . . . the murderer would take his place.
He got back this morning from a round of the dives. He
saw sailors and whores, and one of the girls has left the
trace of a bloody hand on his cheek. He may go far away,
but he is as faithful as a pigeon. The other night, an old
actress left her camellia in his button hole. I wanted to
crumple it; the petals fell on the rug (but what rug? my
cell is paved with flat stones) in big, warm, transparent
drops of water. I hardly dare look at him now, for my eyes
go through his crystal flesh, and all those hard angles make
so many rainbows there that that is why I cry. The end.

It may not seem like much to you, yet this poem has
relieved me. I have shat it out.

Divine:
"By dint of saying that I'm not alive, I accept the fact
that people stop thinking about me."

Though Darling's personal relations had dwindled as a
result of his betrayals, Divine's had increased. In her date
book, famous for its oddness, where every other page was
strewn with a jumble of penciled spirals, which intrigued
Darling until Divine once confessed that these were the
pages of cocaine days, where she noted her accounts, fees,
and appointments, we already read the names of the three
Mimosas (a Mimosa dynasty had been reigning over
Montmartre since the triumphs of Mimosa the Great,

the fluffy-wuffy of high thievery), of Queen Oriane, First Communion, Duckbill, Sonia, Clairette, Fatty, the Baroness, Queen of Rumania (why was she called Queen of Rumania? We were once told that she had loved a king, that she was secretly in love with the King of Rumania, because his mustache and black hair gave him a gypsy look. That in being sodomized by one male who represented ten million, she felt the spunk of ten million men flowing into her, while one tool lifted her like a mast to the midst of the suns), of Sulphurous, Monique, Sweet Leo. At night they haunted narrow bars which had not the fresh gaiety and candor of even the shadiest dancehalls. They loved each other there, but in fear, in the kind of horror we experience in the most charming dream. There is a sad gaiety in our love, and though we have more wit than Sunday lovers by the water's edge, our wit attracts misfortune. Here laughter springs only from trouble. It is a cry of pain. At one of these bars: as she does every evening, Divine has placed on her head a little coronet of false pearls. She resembles the crowned eagle of the heraldists, with the sinews of her neck visible beneath the feathers of her boa. Darling is facing her. Sitting about at other tables are the Mimosas, Antinea, First Communion. They are talking about dear absent friends. Judith enters and, in front of Divine, bows to the ground:

"Good evening, Madame!"

"What an ass!" exclaims Divine.

"Die Puppe hat gesprochen," says a young German.

Divine bursts out laughing. The crown of pearls falls to the floor and breaks. Condolences, to which malicious joy gives rich tonalities: "The Divine is uncrowned! . . . She's the great Fallen One! . . . The poor Exile!" The little pearls roll about the sawdust-covered floor, and they are like the glass pearls that peddlers sell to children for a penny or two, and these are like the glass pearls that we thread every day on miles of brass wire, with which, in other cells, they weave funeral wreaths like those that bestrewed the cemetery of my childhood, rusted, broken, weathered by wind and rain, with just a tiny little pink blue-winged porcelain angel, attached to a thin blackened wire. In the cabaret, all the faggots are suddenly on their knees. Only the men stand upright. Then, Divine lets out a burst of strident laughter. Everyone pricks up his ears: it's her signal. She tears her bridge out of her open mouth, puts it on her skull and, with her heart in her throat, but victorious, she cries out in a changed voice, with her lips drawn back into her mouth:

"Dammit all, Ladies, I'll be queen anyhow!"

When I said that Divine was composed of a pure water, I ought to have made clear that she was hewn of tears. But making her gesture was a slight thing compared to the grandeur of soul required for the other: taking the bridge from her head, putting it back into her mouth, and fastening it on.

And it was no slight matter for her to parody a royal coronation. When she was living with Ernestine in the slate house:

Nobility is glamorous. The most equalitarian of men, though he may not care to admit it, experiences this glamor and submits to it. There are two possible attitudes toward it: humility or arrogance, both of which are explicit recognition of its power. Titles are sacred. The sacred surrounds and enslaves us. It is the submission of flesh to flesh. The Church is sacred. Its slow rites, weighed down with gold like Spanish galleons, ancient in meaning, remote from spirtuality, give it an empire as earthly as that of beauty and that of nobility. Culafroy of the light body, unable to escape this potency, abandoned himself to it voluptuously, as he would have done to Art had he known it. The nobility has names as heavy and strange as the names of snakes (already as difficult as the names of old, lost divinities), strange as signs and escutcheons or venerated animals, totems of old families, war cries, titles, furs, enamels—escutcheons that closed the family with a secret, as a signet seals a parchment, an epitaph, a tomb. It charmed the child. Its procession in time, indistinct and yet certain, and present, a procession of rough warriors, of whom he was, so he thought, the final issue, therefore they themselves—a procession whose sole reason for being had been to arrive at the following result: a pale child, prisoner of a village of thatched cottages—moved him more than an actual and visible procession of weather-beaten soldiers, of whom he might have been chief. But he was not noble. Nobody in the village was noble, at any rate nobody bore the traces of nobility. But one day, among the rubbish in the attic, he found an old history book by Capefigue. In it were recorded a thousand names of barons and knights-at-arms, but he saw only one: Picquigny. Ernestine's maiden name was Picquigny. No doubt about it, she was noble. We quote the passage from Monsieur Capefigue's *Constitutional and Administrative History of France* (page 447):

". . . a preliminary and secret meeting of the Estates, which was organized by Marcel and the municipal magistrates of Paris. It was carried out as follows. Jean de Picquigny and several other men-at-arms went to the castle where the King of Navarre was held captive. Jean de Picquigny was governor of Artois. The men-at-arms, who were burghers of Amiens, set up ladders under the walls and took the guards by surprise, but they did not harm them . . ."

In order to get precise information about this family, he read all through Capefigue's history. Had they been available, he would have ransacked libraries, worked his way through books of gramarye, and that is how scholarly vocations are born, but all he discovered was that islet

emerging from a sea of glamorous names. But then why
didn't Ernestine have a nobiliary particle in her name?
Where was her coat of arms? Indeed, what was her coat
of arms? Did Ernestine know of this passage in the book
and of her own nobility? Had he been less young and
dreamy, Culafroy would have noticed that the corner of
page 447 had been worn away by the sweat of fingers.
Ernestine's father had known the book. The same miracle
had opened it at the same place and had shown him the
name. It pleased Culafroy that the nobility belonged to
Ernestine rather than to himself, and in this trait we may
already see a sign of his destiny. To be able to approach
her, to enjoy her intimacy, her special favors, was agreeable to him, just as many persons are more pleased to be
the favorite of a prince than the prince himself, or a priest
of a god than the god, for in this way they can receive
Grace. Culafroy could not keep from telling about his discovery, and, not knowing how to raise the question with
Ernestine, he blurted out to her:

"You're noble. I saw your name in an old history of
France."

He was smiling ironically, so as to give the impression
of scorning the aristocracy, the vanity of which our school-
master spoke of sumptuously whenever reference was
made in class to the night of August 4th. Culafroy thought
that scorn indicates indifference. Children, and particularly her own child, intimidated Ernestine almost as much
as a servant intimidates me. She blushed and thought she
had been found out, or thought she had been found out
and blushed, I don't know which. She too wanted to be
noble. She had put the same question to her father, who
had blushed in the same way. This *History* must have
been in the family for a long time, playing as best it could
the role of title of nobility, and perhaps it was Ernestine
who, exhausted by a lavish imagination that made of her

an impoverished countess, a marquise, or even several, all of them laden with blazons and crowns, had relegated it to the attic, out of her sight, in order to escape its magic; but she did not realize that in placing it above her head she would never be able to free herself from it, the only effective means being to bury it in loamy earth, or to drown it, or burn it. She did not reply, but, could Culafroy have read within her, he would have seen the ravages wrought there merely by that unrecognized nobility, of which she was uncertain and which, in her eyes, put her above the villagers and the tourists from the cities. She described the blazon. For she was now familiar with heraldry. She had gone all the way to Paris to ferret in d'Hozier's *Genealogy*. She had learned history from it. As we have said, scholars hardly act otherwise or from other motives. The philologist does not admit (besides, he doesn't realize it) that his taste for etymology comes from the poetry (so he thinks, or might think, for it is a carnal potency that incites him) contained in the word *esclave* (slave), in which are found, if he likes, the word *clé* (key), and the word *genou* (knee). It is because a young man one day learns that the female scorpion devours her male that he becomes an entomologist, and another becomes a historian when he happens to read that Frederick the Second of Germany made children be brought up in solitude. Ernestine tried to avoid the shame of this confession (her lust for nobility) by the quick confession of a less infamous sin. This is an old trick, the trick of partial confessions. Spontaneously I confess a little, the better to keep more serious things hidden. The examining magistrate told my lawyer that if I were putting on an act, I was giving a great performance; but I didn't put it on throughout the investigation. I multiplied errors of defense, and it was lucky I did. The court clerk looked as though he thought I was simulating ingenuousness, which is the mother of blunders. The judge seemed rather inclined to accept my sincerity. They were both wrong. It is true that I drew attention to compromising details that they had been unaware of. (A number of times I had said: ("It was at night," a circumstance that aggravated my case, as the judge told me, though he also thought that a crafty delinquent would not have confessed this; I therefore must have been a novice. It was in the judge's chambers that it occurred to me to say that "it was at night," for there were things about that night that I had to keep hidden. I had already thought of parrying the accusation with a new offense, namely nighttime, but since I had left no trace, I attached no importance to it. Then the importance shot up and grew—I don't know why—and I said mechanically: "At night," mechanically, but insistently. But during a second interrogation I suddenly realized that I was not confusing facts and dates sufficiently. I was calculating and foreseeing with a rigor that disconcerted the judge. It was all too clever. I had only my own case to think about; but he had twenty. So he questioned me, not about things he ought to have examined and would have, had he been shrewder or had more time, and about which I had planned my answers, but about rather obvious details to which I hadn't given a thought because it hadn't occurred to me that a judge might think of them.) Ernestine did not have time enough to invent a crime; she described the coat of arms: "It's argent and azure of ten pieces, over all a lion gules membered and langued. On the crest, Melusina." It was the arms of the Lusignans. Culafroy listened to this splendid poem. Ernestine had at her finger tips the history of this family, which numbered kings of Jerusalem and princes of Cyprus. Their castle in Brittany was supposed to have been built by Melusina, but Ernestine did not dwell on this; it was in the legend, and her mind, in order to build the unreal, wanted solid materials. Legend is twaddle. She did not believe in fairies, who are creatures fabricated for the purpose of diverting dreamers of bold allegories from their straight path, but she had her great thrills when she came across a historic phrase: "The overseas branch . . . The singing arms . . ."

She knew she was lying. In trying to make herself illustrious through an ancient lineage, she was succumbing to the call of darkness, of the earth, of the flesh. She was seeking roots. She wanted to feel, trailing at her feet, the dynastic force, which was brutal, muscular, fecundating. In effect, the heraldic figures illustrated it.

The sitting posture of Michelangelo's *Moses* is said to have been necessitated by the compact form of the block of marble he had to work with. Divine is always being presented with odd-shaped marbles that make her achieve masterpieces. Culafroy, in the public park, the time he ran away, had had the same good luck. He had been strolling through the lanes; when he reached the end of one of them, he saw that he would have to turn around so as not to walk on the lawn. As he watched himself moving, he thought: "He spun about," and the word "spun," immediately caught on the wing, made him about-face smartly. He was about to begin a dance with restrained, barely indicated gesticulations, everything to be merely suggested, but the sole of his yawning shoe dragged over the sand and made such a shamefully vulgar sound (for this also should be noted: that Culafroy or Divine, they of the delicate, that is, finical, in short, civil tastes—for in imagination our heroes are attracted, as girls are, by monsters—have always found themselves in situations that repel them). He heard the sound of the sole. This reminder made him lower his head. He assumed with utter naturalness a meditative posture and sauntered back slowly. The strollers in the park watched him go by. Culafroy saw that they noticed his paleness, his thinness, his

lowered eyelids, which were as round and heavy as
marbles. He bowed his head more deeply, his pace grew
even slower, so much so that all of him was the very image
of vocative fervor and that he—not thought—but whispered aloud a cry:

"Lord, I am among Thy elect."

For a few steps, God carried him off toward His throne.

Divine—let us get back to her—was leaning against a
tree on the boulevard. All the youngsters knew her. Three
of these hooligans approached her. First, they came up
laughing about something or other, perhaps about Divine;
then they said hello and asked how the grind was going.
Divine was holding a pencil, the pencil played mechanically over her fingernails and drew an irregular piece of lace
and then, more consciously, a diamond shape, a rosette,
a holly leaf. The little tramps started teasing her. They
said that pricks must hurt, that old men . . . that women
had more charm . . . that they themselves were pimps . . .
and other things, which they no doubt say without meaning any harm but which hurt Divine. She feels more and
more uncomfortable. They're just young little hoodlums,
whereas she's thirty. She could shut them up with the back
of her hand. But *they* are males. Still very young, but
tough-looking and with tough muscles. And all three of
them there, dreadfully inflexible, like the Fates. Divine's
cheeks are burning. She pretends to be seriously occupied
with the drawings on her nails and occupied with that
only. "Here's what I might say," she thought, "to make
them think I'm not upset." And holding out her hands to
the children, with the nails up, she smiles and says:

"I'm going to start a fashion. Yes, yes, a new fashion.
You see, it's pretty. The we-women and the they-women
will have lace drawn on their nails. We'll send for artists
from Persia. They'll paint miniatures that you'll have to
look at with a magnifying glass! Oh God!"

The three hoodlums felt foolish, and one of them, speaking for the others as well, said:

"Jesus, she's the limit."

They left.

The fashion of decorating fingernails with Persian miniatures dates from this episode.

Divine thought that Darling was at the movies and that Our Lady, who was a prospector of display cases, was in a department store. Wearing American-style shoes, a very soft hat and a gold chain-bracelet on his wrist, Darling, toward evening, went down the stairs. As soon as he was outside, his face lost its steel-blue glints, its statue-like hardness. His eyes grew softer and softer, until there was no gaze left, until they were merely two holes through which the sky passed. But he still walked with a sway. He went to the Tuileries and sat down in an iron chair.

Coming from God knows where, whistling in the wind, with a lock of hair standing straight up, Our Lady arrived and installed himself in a second chair. It began:

"Where are you up to?"

"I won the battle, naturally. So I'm at a big party. You understand, the officers are giving a big party in my honor, and I deserve it. So I'm handing out decorations. What about you?"

"All right . . . I'm still only the King of Hungary, but you're fixing it to get me elected Emperor of the West. Get it? It'll be great, Darling. And Yours Truly stays with you."

"Sure thing, mug."

Darling put his arm around Our Lady's neck. He was going to kiss him. Suddenly eight savage young men leaped forth from Our Lady; they seemed to be detaching themselves from him in flat layers as if they had formed his thickness, his very structure, and they jumped on Darling as if to cut his throat. It was a signal. He disengaged

Our Lady's neck, and the garden was so calm that it let
bygones be bygones and forgave. The conversion continued on its royal and imperial way. Our Lady and Darling
were winding their two imaginations into one another;
they were entwining like two violins unreeling their melodies, as Divine wound her lies into those of her clients, to
the point of creating a jumble denser than a thicket of
creepers in the Brazilian forest, where neither of them
was sure that he was pursuing his own theme rather than
that of the other. These games were carried on consciously,
not for the purpose of deceiving, but of enchanting. Begun
in the shadow of the boulevard promenade, or as they
sat with cups of coffee that had grown lukewarm, they
were continued up to the desk of the shady hotel.
There one utters one's name discreetly and shows one's
papers, discreetly; but the clients always drowned in that
pure and perfidious water which was Divine. Without
trying to, she would undo the lie with a word or a shrug,
with a blink of her eye; she would thereby cause a delightful agitation, something like the emotion I feel when I
read a thrilling phrase or see a painting or hear a musical
motif, in short, when I detect a poetic state. It is the elegant and sudden, the luminous and clear solution of a conflict in my depths. I have proof of it in the peace that follows my discovery. But this conflict is like the kind of knot
that sailors call the whore's knot.

How are we to explain that Divine is now thirty and
more? For she really must be my age so that I can appease
my need to talk about myself, simply. I feel such a need
to complain and to try to win a reader's love! There was a
period, from the age of twenty to twenty-seven, when Divine, though appearing among us at irregular intervals,
pursued the complicated, sinuous, looped existence of a
kept woman. She cruised the Mediterranean, then went
even farther, to the Sunda Isles, in a white yacht. She was

always forging ahead of herself and of her lover, a young American, modestly proud of his gold. When she returned, the yacht touched at Venice, where a film director took a fancy to her. They lived for a few months through the huge rooms, fit for giant guards and horsemen astride their mounts, of a dilapidated palace.

Then it was Vienna, in a gilded hotel, nestling beneath the wings of a black eagle. Sleeping there in the arms of an English lord, deep in a canopied and curtained bed. Then there were rides in a heavy limousine. Back to Paris. Montmartre and the sisters of the neighborhood. And off again to an elegant Renaissance castle, in the company of Guy de Roburant. She was thus a noble chatelaine. She thought of her mother and of Darling. Darling received money orders from her, sometimes jewels, which he would wear for one evening and quickly resell so that he could treat his pals to dinner. Then back to Paris, and off again, and all in a warm, gilded luxury, all in such comfort that I need merely evoke it from time to time in its snug details for the vexations of my poor life as prisoner to disappear, for me to console myself, console myself with the idea that such luxury exists. And, though it is denied me, I evoke it with such desperate fervor that at times (more than once) I have really believed that a trifle would be enough—a slight, imperceptible displacement of the plane on which I live—for this luxury to surround me, to be real, and really mine; that a slight effort of thought would be enough for me to discover the magic formulas opening the flood gates.

And I invent for Divine the cosiest apartments where I myself wallow.

When she returns, she mingles more in the faggots' life. She is to be found in all the tiny bars. She preens herself, ruffles her feathers, and, in the midst of all our gestures, thinks she is tossing, strewing them about her, petals of roses, rhododendra, and peonies, as, in the village, little girls strew them along the paths of the Corpus Christi. Her great friendly enemy is Mimosa II. In order to understand her, here are some "Mimosariana."

To Divine:
"I like my lovers to be bow-legged, like jockies, so they can grab me around the thighs better when they ride me."

At *The Tabernacle,* the queens:
One, Marquis de? . . . :
"Mimosa II has had the coat-of-arms of the Count of A . . . painted on he buttocks. Thirty-six quarters of nobility on her ass, with colored inks."

Divine has introduced Our Lady to her. Some days later, showed her, decent girl that she was, a little "photo-matic" photo of the murderer.
Mimosa takes the photo, puts it on her outstretched tongue, and swallows it.
"I simply adore that Our Lady of yours. I'm communioning her."

About Divine, to First Communion.
"Just imagine, Divine's carrying on like a great actress. She knows how to play her cards. If the façade collapses, she shows her profile. If that goes, then she turns her back. Like Mary Garden, she makes her bit of noise in the wings."

All the queens of *The Tabernacle* and the neighboring bars, about Mimosa:
"She's a plague."
"The Evil One."
"A tart, my dears, a tart."

"A she-devil."

"Venenosa."

Divine lightly accepts this moth's life. She gets tipsy on alcohol and neon light, but especially on the headiness of their Quite-Quite gestures and their dazzling remarks. "This life in a whirl is driving me mad," and she said "in a whirl" as one says hair "in bangs," a beauty patch "à la Pompadour," tea "Russian style." But, Darling's absences from the garret were growing more and more frequent. He would remain away for nights on end. A whole street of women, the Rue de la Charbonnière, had recaptured him, then, afterward; one woman alone. His bulky prick was working wonders, and his lacy-fingered hands were emptying the bawd's bag. He had stopped robbing show cases; he was being kept. Then it was Our Lady's turn to disappear, but him we shall soon find again.

What would the destiny of the splendid Marchettis matter to Divine and me if it did not call to mind what I suffered upon returning from my adventures, in which I magnified myself, and if it did not remind Divine of her impotence? To begin with, the tale of Our Lady of the Flowers lulls present time, for the very words the murderer uses are the magic words that equally handsome hoodlums spat out like so many stars, like those extraordinary hoodlums who pronounce the word "dollar" with the right accent. But what is to be said of one of the strangest of poetic phenomena: that the whole world— and the most terribly dismal part of it, the blackest, most charred, dry to the point of Jansenism, the severe, naked world of factory workers—is entwined with marvels, the popular songs lost in the wind, by profoundly rich voices, gilded and set with diamonds, spangled or silky; and these songs have phrases which I cannot think of without shame if I know they are sung by the grave mouths of workers

which utter such words as: succumb . . . tenderness . . .
ravishing . . . garden of roses . . . cottage . . . marble steps
. . . sweethearts . . . dear . . . love . . . jewels . . . crown
. . . oh my queen . . . dear stranger . . . gilded room . . .
lovely lady . . . flowered basket . . . treasure of flesh . . .
golden waning . . . my heart adores you . . . laden with flowers . . . color of the evening . . . exquisite and pink . . . in
short, those fiercely luxurious words, words which must
slash their flesh like a ruby-crested dagger. They sing
them, perhaps without giving them much thought. They
whistle them too, with their hands in their pockets. And
poor, shameful me, I shudder at the thought that the
toughest of workers is crowned at all times of the day with
one or another of these garlands of flowers: mignonette,
and roses which have bloomed among the rich, gilded,
jeweled voices, maidens all, simple or sumptuous, shep-
herdesses or princesses. See how beautiful they are! All
of them, their bodies busked by machines, like a loco-
motive being inaugurated, are adorned, as the solid body
of the hundred thousand hoodlums one meets is also
adorned with moving expressions, for a popular literature,
light because unwritten, light and flitting from mouth to
mouth, in the wind, says of them: "My little monkey-face,"
"little tramp," "cute little bastard," "little louse" (note
that the word "little," if applied to me or to some object
dear to my heart, overwhelms me; even if someone says to
me, "Jean, your *little* hairs" or "your *little* finger," it turns
me inside out). These expressions certainly have a melodic
relationship with young men, the glamor of whose superhuman beauty derives from the uncleanness of dreams, a
beauty so potent that we penetrate it in one swoop, and so
spontaneously that we have the feeling of "possessing" it
(in both senses of the word: of being full of it and of tran-
scending it in an external vision), of possessing it so absolutely that there is no room, in this absolute possession,

for the slightest question. In like manner, certain animals, by their gaze, make us possess at one swoop their absolute being: snakes, dogs, in the twinkling of an eye we "know them" and to such a degree that we think it is they who know, and we therefore feel a certain uneasiness mixed with horror. These expressions sing. And the little tramps, cute bastards, little bastards, sweet monkey-faces, are sensitive, as is crystal to the finger, to those musical inflections (they should be noted here to be well rendered), which, I think when I see them coming in the song of the streets, are going to pass unperceived by them. But on seeing their bodies undulate or contract, I recognize that they have quite caught the inflection and that their entire being shows their relationship.

It was this dreadful part of Lou-Divine's childhood that was destined to soothe her bitterness. For we see her in prison the time she ran away from the slate house. There is no point in going into the details of her arrest. A simple policeman was enough to throw her into a state of terror worthy of a condemned man, the kind of terror every man has been through, just as every man has also known in his life the exaltation of a royal coronation. Children who run away from home all give the excuse of being mistreated. One might not believe them, but they are so clever about embellishing this excuse with circumstances that are so new, so adapted to themselves, to their names, and even to their faces, in short, circumstances that are so individual, that all our recollections of novels and stories in newspapers about children who have been kidnapped, confined, defiled, sold, abandoned, raped, beaten, and tortured come back in a rush, and the most suspicious people, such as judges, priests, and policemen, think, though without saying so: "One never knows," and the fumes of sulphur that rise slowly from the charged pages of cheap novels lull them, praise them, and caress them. Culafroy invented a cruel-stepmother story. He was therefore put into jail, not out of unkindness, of hardness of heart, but out of habit. His cell was gloomy, narrow, and inhabited. In a patch of shadow, a heap of covers wiggled and disengaged a dirty, kinky, laughing little brown head.

"Well, pal?"

Culafroy had never seen anything so dirty as this cell, nor anything so sordid as that head. He did not answer. He was choking. Only evening, with the sluggishness it induces, could loosen his tongue, and open his heart.

"Did you beat it from home?"

Silence.

"Oh come on, man, you can talk. You don't have to worry with me. We're among men."

He laughed and squinted his narrow eyes. He turned about in his pack of brown rags, which rattled like scrap iron. What was it all about? It was nighttime. Through the closed skylight shone the icy sky with its free and mobile stars. And the miracle, that catastrophic horror, horrifying as an angel, blazed forth, though radiant as the solution of a mathematical problem, frighteningly exact. The little hoodlum pulled back the covers daintily and asked:

"Will you help me off with my leg?"

He had a wooden leg which was fastened to a stump below the knee by a system of straps and buckles. Culafroy felt the same repulsion for all infirmities as he did for reptiles. He was assailed by the horror that kept him away from snakes, but Alberto was no longer there to charge him, by his presence, his gaze, and the laying on of his broad hands, with the faith that moves mountains. The other kid had undone the buckles and freed the rest of the thigh. With a sublime effort, Lou triumphed. He put his hand to the wood as if to a fire, tugged and found himself with the apparatus suddenly clasped to his chest. It was now a live limb, an individual, like an arm or leg detached from the trunk by a surgical operation. The peg spent the night standing up, a night of vigil, leaning in a corner against the wall. The little cripple also asked Lou to sing, but, thinking of Alberto, Lou answered that he was in mourning, and this reason did not surprise either of them. Culafroy had also given it so that it might be an adornment, so that black muslins might protect him from the cold and forlornness.

"Sometimes I feel like beating it for Brazil, but with my trick paw it's not so easy."

To the cripple, Brazil was an island beyond the sun and seas, where men with rugged faces and the builds of athletes squatted in the evening around huge fires like the bonfires of Midsummer Night, peeling in fine curling strips enormous oranges, with the fruit in one hand and a broad-bladed knife in the other, as, in old pictures, emperors hold the scepter and the golden globe. This vision so obsessed him that he said: ". . . suns." It was the word-poem that fell from the vision and began to petrify it; the night-cube of the cell, where the oranges attracted by the word "Brazil" whirled about like suns (which mingled with the legs of an acrobat in light blue tights executing the giant circle on the horizontal bar). Then, releasing a fragment of thought that had been working its way through him for some time, Lou declared: "What is the people's wish?" It was a phrase he had murmured mentally one evening when he foresaw himself in his prison. But did he actually foresee himself in the mahogany of the dressing table, or was it not rather that an unconscious perception associated the place (his room) and the past moment with the word and the present moment (but then what was it that brought back this memory of the room?),

superimposing the two ideas so far as to make him think
he had had a prevision?

The children slept. Later they were committed to a
home—or colony—for Child Correction. The very day that
Lou-Divine arrived at the reformatory, he was put into a
cell. He remained there, crouching, for an entire day. He
was alive to what he suspected to be the mystery of child
outcasts (they have their arms tattooed with the words
"Child of Misfortune"). In the courtyard, little feet, dusty
no doubt, were lifting heavy sabots in a very slow rhythm.
He guessed that punished youngsters, forbidden to open
their mouths, were walking round and round in circles.

During a pause, he heard the following:

". . . through the window of the locksmith shop . . ."

"   "
  . . .

"It's Germain."

"   "
  . . .

"All right, if I see him this evening."

"   "
  . . .

"Boy, that's some job."

The voice he heard was muffled—like the lanterns of
prowlers of old—was directed toward a single point by a
cupped hand framing the serious mouth of a child. It was
addressed from the yard to a friend in a cell whom Culafroy did not hear answer. They might have been whispering
about a convict who had escaped from the state prison,
which was not far from the reformatory. Thus, the reformatory lived in the shadow of all those suns blazing
away in their gray cells—the men—and the kids were
waiting to be old enough to be with the big fellows whom
they revered, whom they imagined swaggering in front
of the guards, insolent and haughty. So the kids were
waiting to be able to commit real crimes, as an excuse for
going to hell.

At the home, the other little tramps performed very

skillfully their role of telltale imps. Their vocabulary was shrouded with magic formulas, their gestures were faun-like, woodland, and at the same time suggested alleys, patches of shadow, walls, scaled enclosures. Amidst this little world, regulating it just enough so that all that could be heard from it was an indecent snicker, there moved, borne up like ballerinas on their puffed skirts, the nuns. Immediately, Culafroy composed for them a grotesque ballet. According to the scenario, they all went out into the cloistered yard, and, as if they had—Gray Sisters, guardians of the hyperborean nights—got drunk on champagne, they squatted, raised their arms, and wagged their heads. In silence. Then they formed a circle, turned about like schoolgirls dancing a round and finally, like whirling dervishes, whirled around and around until they fell, dying with laughter, while the chaplain, with great dignity, walked through their midst carrying the monstrance. The sacrilegiousness of the dance—the sacrilege of having imagined it—disturbed Culafroy, just as he would have been disturbed, had he been a man, by the rape of a Jewess.

Very quickly, despite his tendency to daydream, or perhaps because of this daydreaming, he became, in appearance, very much like the others. If his schoolmates had kept him out of their games, it had been owing to the slate house, which had made of him a prince. But here he was, in the eyes of the other kids only a vagabond who had been picked up just as they had been, a delinquent with no other oddity, though it was an impressive one, than his having come from somewhat far away. His finely cruel air, his exaggeratedly obscene and vulgar gestures, created such an image of him that the cynical and candid children recognized him as one of their own, and he, eager to be conscientious, to be the supposed character to the very end of the adventure, conformed to it. He did not want to disappoint. He joined in the

rough stuff. With a few others of a small band that was as
tightly knit as a gang, he helped commit a petty theft inside the home. The Mother Superior was said to be of an
illustrious family. Anyone trying to get a favor from her
would invariably be told: "I am only the servant of the
servant of the Lord." So vainglorious a pedestal abashes
one. She asked Lou why he had stolen. All he could
answer was:

"Because the others thought I was a thief."

The Mother Superior could make nothing of this juve-
nile nicety. He was called a hypocrite. Besides, Culafroy
had an aversion to this nun which had come about in a
strange way: the day of his arrival, she had taken him
aside in her small reception room, which was very smartly
set up, and had spoken to him about the Christian life.
Lou listened to her quietly; he was about to answer with a
sentence beginning: "The day of my first communion . . . ,"
but a slip of the tongue made him say: "The day of my
marriage . . ." Out of embarrassment, he lost his footing. He had the acute feeling of having committed an
incongruity. He blushed, stammered, made efforts to rise
to the surface; they were vain. The Mother Superior
looked at him with what she called her smile of mercy.
Culafroy, frightened at having stirred up within himself a
whirlpool over a muddy bottom from which he rose up
in a dress with a white satin train, wearing a crown of
artificial orange blossoms, hated the old woman for having
been the cause and witness of that artful and loveliest of
adventures. "Of my marriage!"

Here is what the nights in the home—or colony—were
like. The heads disappear under the covers in the motionless hammocks of the dormitory. The custodian has
reached his cubbyhole, which is at the far end. Silence
is imperative for half an hour, the silence of the jungle,
full of its pestilence, of its stone monsters, and as if atten-

tive to the repressed sighs of tigers. In accordance with
the rite, the children are reborn from the dead. Heads
cautious as those of snakes, intelligent too, wily, venomous
and poisonous, rise up; then, whole bodies emerge from
the hammocks, without the hooks creaking. The general
aspect—seen from above—of the dormitory remains un-
changed. The colonists are crafty and know how to draw
up and fill out the covers so that they seem to be wrapped
around sleeping bodies. Everything goes on underneath.
The lads quickly crawl together. The suspended city is
deserted. Flint strikes steel, and with the burning wicks
they light cigarettes as thin as straws. They smoke.
Stretched out under the hammocks, in little groups, they
draw up rigorous plans for escape, all doomed to fail. The
colonists are living. They know they are free and masters
of the darkness, and they form a kingdom which is ad-
ministered very strictly, with its despot, peers, and com-
moners. Above them lie the white abandoned swings. The
great nocturnal occupation, admirably suited for enchanting the darkness, is tattooing. Thousands and thousands
of little jabs with a fine needle prick the skin and draw
blood, and figures that *you* would regard as most extravagant are flaunted in the most unexpected places.
When the rabbi slowly unrolls the Torah, a mystery sends
a shudder through the whole epidermis, as when one sees
a colonist undressing. The grimacing of all that blue on
a white skin imparts an obscure but potent glamor to the
child who is covered with it, as a neutral, pure column
becomes sacred under the notches of the hieroglyphs.
Like a totem pole. Sometimes the eyelids are marked, the
armpits, the hollow of the groin, the buttocks, the penis,
and even the soles of the feet. The signs were barbaric
and as meaningful as the most barbaric signs: pansies,
bows and arrows, hearts pierced and dripping blood, over-
lapping faces, stars, quarter-moons, lines, swallows, snakes,

boats, triangular daggers and inscriptions, mottoes, warnings, a whole fearful and prophetic literature.

Under the hammocks, amidst the magic of these occupations, loves were born, flared up, and died, with all the
usual trappings of love: hatred, cupidity, tenderness, consolation, revenge.

What made the colony a realm distinct from the realm
of the living was the change of symbols and, in certain
cases, of values. The colonists had their own dialect, which
was closely related to that of the prisons, and hence a
particular ethics and politics. The form of government,
which was involved with the religion, was the regime of
force, protector of Beauty. Their laws are seriously observed. The colonists are enemies of laughter, which might
unsettle them. They show a rare aptitude for the tragic
attitude. Crime begins with a carelessly worn beret. These
laws are not the products of abstract decrees: they were
taught by some hero who had come from a heaven of force
and Beauty and whose spiritual and temporal power
existed truly by divine right. Besides, they do not escape
the destinies of heroes, and they can be met every day
in the colony yard, in the midst of mortals, bearing the
features of a journeyman baker or locksmith. The trousers
of the colonists have only one pocket: this is something
else that isolates them from the world. A single pocket, on
the left side. A whole social system is upset by this simple
detail of dress. Their trousers have only one pocket, as
the skin-tight breeches of the devil have none, as those
of sailors have no fly, and there is no doubt but that they are
humiliated by this, as if someone had amputated a male
sexual attribute—which is really what is involved. Pockets,
which play so important a role in childhood, are to us a
sign of superiority over girls. In the colony, as in the navy,
it's the trousers that count, and if you want to be a man,
"you defend your pants." I am amazed that adults have

been so bold as to set up seminaries for children who are preparing for the role of dream characters, and that they have been shrewd enough to recognize the details that would make of children these little monsters, whether malicious or gracious, or light or sparkling or uneasy or sneaky or simple.

It was the sisters' clothes that gave Culafroy the idea of running away. All he had to do was put into action a plan that the clothes conceived by themselves. The nuns would leave their linen hanging in a drying room for nights on end, and they locked their stockings and coifs in a workroom. He quickly learned which was the right door and the way it opened. With spylike prudence, he spoke of his plan to a wide-awake youngster.

"If a guy wanted to . . ."

"Well, shall we clear out?"

"Right!"

"You think we'll be able to go far?"

"Sure, farther than this way (pointing to his ridiculous uniform), and besides we'll be able to beg."

Don't complain about improbability. What's going to follow is false, and no one has to accept it as gospel truth. Truth is not my strong point. But "one must lie in order to be true." And even go beyond. What truth do I want to talk about? If it is really true that I am a prisoner who plays (who plays for himself) scenes of the inner life, you will require nothing other than a game.

So our children waited for a night well-disposed to their nerves in order to steal a skirt, jacket, and coif; but finding only shoes that were too narrow, they kept their sabots. Through the window of the washroom they went out into the dark street. It must have been midnight. It took them only a second to get dressed under a porch. They helped each other and put the coifs on with great care. For a moment, the darkness was disturbed by the rustlings of woolens, the click of pins between teeth, by such whisperings as: "Tighten my string. . . . Move over." In an alley, sighs were tossed from a window. This taking of the veil made of the town a dark cloister, the dead city, the valley of Desolation.

In the home, they were probably slow to notice the theft of the clothes, for nothing was done during the day "to stop the fugitives." They walked fast. The peasants were hardly surprised; rather, they were amazed to see these two serious-looking little nuns, one in sabots and the other limping, hurrying along the roads with dainty gestures: two delicate fingers lifting up three pleats of a heavy gray skirt. Then hunger gripped their stomachs. They dared not ask anyone for a bite of bread, and, as they were on the road leading to Culafroy's village, they would probably have got there very soon, were it not that, in the late afternoon, a shepherd's dog came up and sniffed at Pierre. The shepherd, who was young and had been brought up in the fear of God, whistled to his dog, who did not obey. Pierre thought he had been discovered. He rushed off with jittery agility. He ran limping to a lone umbrella pine at the edge of the road and he climbed up. Culafroy ha the presence of mind to climb up another tree nearer by. Seeing which, the dog got down on its knees beneath the blue sky, in the evening air, and uttered the following prayer: "Since the sisters, like magpies, make their nests in umbrella pines, Lord, grant me remission for my sins." Then, having crossed himself, he got up and rejoined the flock. To his master the shepherd he related the miracle of the pines, and all the villages around were informed of it that very evening.

I shall speak again about Divine, but Divine in her garret, between Our Lady, the marble-hearted, and Gorgui. If Divine were a woman, she would not be jealous. She

would be perfectly willing to go out alone in the evening
to pick up customers between the trees on the boulevard.
What would it matter to her that her two males spent their
evenings together? On the contrary, a family atmosphere,
the light of a lamp shade, would utterly delight her; but
Divine is *also* a man. She is, to begin with, jealous of Our
Lady, who is young and handsome and without guile. He
is in danger of obeying the sympathies of his name. Our
Lady, without guile and wily as an Englishwoman. He
may arouse Gorgui. It would be easy. Let us imagine
them at the movies one afternoon, side by side in the
artificial darkness.

"Got your snotrag, Seck?"

No sooner said than done, his hand is on the Negro's
pocket. Oh! fatal movement. Divine is jealous of Gorgui.
The Negro is her man, and that little tramp of an Our
Lady is young and pretty. Beneath the trees of the
boulevard, Divine is looking for old geezers, and she is
being torn apart by the anguish of a double jealousy.
Then, as Divine is a man, she thinks: "I have to feed them
both *together*. I'm the slave." She is becoming bitter. At
the movies, well-behaved as schoolboys (but, as around
schoolboys, who—and that's enough—lower their heads
together behind the desk, there prowls, ready to leap, a
mad little act), Our Lady and Gorgui smoke and see only
the film. In a little while they will go for a glass of beer,
unsuspecting, and they will return to the garret, but not
without Our Lady's having strewn on the sidewalk little
pistol caps with which Gorgui amuses himself by exploding them beneath his steel-tipped shoes; thus, like the
whistle blasts between those of pimps, sparks blazed forth
between his calves.

The three of them are about to leave the garret. They're
ready. Gorgui is holding the key. Each has a cigarette in

his mouth. Divine strikes a kitchen match (she sets fire to her own stake each time), lights her cigarette, then Our Lady's, and holds out the flame to Gorgui.

"No," he says, "not three on a match. That's bad luck."

Divine:

"Don't play around with that, you never know what it can lead to."

She seems weary and drops the match, now all black and skinny as a grasshopper. She adds:

"One starts with a little superstition and then falls into the arms of God."

Our Lady thinks:

"That's right, into the priest's bed."

At the top of the Rue Lepic is the little cabaret of which I have already spoken, *The Tabernacle,* where the habitués practice sorcery, concoct mixtures, consult the cards, question the bottoms of teacups, decipher the lines of the left hand (when questioned, fate tends to answer the truth, Divine used to say), where good looking butcherboys are sometimes metamorphosed into princesses in flowing gowns. The cabaret is small and low-ceilinged. Milord the Prince governs. Assembled there are: All of them, but especially First Communion, Banjo, the Queen of Rumania, Ginette, Sonia, Persifanny, Clorinda, the Abbess, Agnes, Mimosa, Divine. And their Gentlemen. Every Thursday the little latch door is closed to the curious and excited bourgeois visitors. The cabaret is given over to the "pure few." Milord the Prince (she who said, "I make one cry every night," speaking of the safes he cracked which the jimmy made creak) sent out the invitations. We were at home. A phonograph. Three waiters were on duty, their eyes full of mischief, lewd with a joyous lewdness. Our men are at the bar playing poker dice for drinks. And we are dancing. It is customary to come in drag, dressed as ourselves. Nothing but cos-

tumed queens rubbing shoulders with child-pimps. In
short, not a single adult. The make-up and the lights
distort sufficiently, but often we wear black masks or
carry fans for the pleasure of guessing who's who from
the carriage of a leg, from the expression, the voice, the
pleasure of fooling each other, of making identities over-
lap. It would be an ideal spot for committing a murder,
which would remain so secret that the fluttering queens,
in a state of panic (though quickly one of them, startled
into maternal severity, would be able to transform herself
into a rapid and precise detective), and the little pimps,
their faces tense with terror, their bellies drawn in, hud-
dling against the ladies, would try in vain to know who
was the victim and who the murderer. A crime at a
masked ball.

Divine has dug out for this evening her two 1890 silk
dresses, which she keeps, souvenirs of former carnivals.
One of them is black, embroidered with jet; she puts it on
and offers the other to Our Lady.

"You're nuts. What'll the guys say?"

But Gorgui insists, and Our Lady knows that all his
pals will have a laugh, that not a single one will snicker;
they esteem him. The dress drapes Our Lady's body,
which is naked under the silk. He rather likes the way he
looks. His legs, with their downy, even slightly hairy skin,
brush against each other. He bends down, turns around,
looks at himself in the mirror. The dress, which has a
bustle, makes his rump stick out, suggesting a pair of
cellos. Let us put a velvet flower into his tousled hair. He
is wearing Divine's tan shoes, the ones with ankle straps
and high heels, but they are completely concealed by the
flounces of the skirt. They dressed very quickly that evening because they were going out for real fun. Divine puts
on her black silk dress and over it a pink jacket, and takes
a spangled tulle fan. Gorgui is wearing tails and a white

tie. Occurred the scene of the match being blown out.
They went down the stairs. Taxi. *The Tabernacle*. The
doorman, quite young and ever so good looking, leers three
times. Our Lady dazzles him. They enter the brilliant
fireworks of silk and muslin flounces which cannot fight
clear of the smoke. They dance the smoke. They smoke the
music. They drink from mouth to mouth. Our Lady is
acclaimed by his pals. He had not realized that his firm
buttocks would draw the cloth so tight. He doesn't give
a damn that they see he has a hard-on, but not to such a
point, in front of the fellows. He would like to hide. He
turns to Gorgui and, slightly pink, shows him his bulging
dress, muttering:

"Say, Seck, let me ditch that."

He barely snickers. His eyes seem moist, and Gorgui
does not know whether he is kidding or annoyed; then, the
Negro takes the murderer by the shoulders, hugs him,
clasps him, locks between his mighty thighs the jutting horn
that is raising the silk, and carries him on his heart in
waltzes and tangoes which will last till dawn. Divine
would like to weep with rage, to tear cambric handkerchiefs with her nails and teeth. Then, a former state resembling the present one suddenly recalled the following:
"She was in Spain, I believe. Kids were chasing her and
screaming 'Maricona' and throwing stones at her. She ran
to a sidetrack and climbed into an empty train. The kids
continued from below to insult her and pepper the doors
of the train with stones. Divine crouched under a seat,
cursing the horde of children with all her might, hating
them until she rattled with hatred. Her chest swelled out;
she longed for a sigh so as not to choke with hatred. Then
she realized it was impossible to devour the kids, to rip
them to pieces with her teeth and nails, as she would
have liked, so she loved them. The pardon gushed forth
from her excess of rage, of hatred, and she was thereby

appeased." She consents, out of love, to the Negro's and Our Lady's loving each other. Around her is the room of Milord the Prince. She is sitting in a chair; on a carpet, masks are strewn about. They are all dancing downstairs. Divine has just slit everyone's throat, and in the mirror of the wardrobe she sees her fingers contracting into criminal hooks, like those of the Düsseldorf vampire on the covers of novels. But the waltzes ended. Our Lady, Seck, and Divine were among the last to leave the ball. It was Divine who opened the door, and quite naturally Our Lady took Gorgui's arm. The union, destroyed for a moment in the leave-taking, had been so abruptly reconstructed, unknotting the tricks of hesitation, that Divine felt a bite in her side, the bite of contempt with which someone dispatches us. She was a good loser; so she remained behind pretending to fasten a garter. At five A.M. the Rue Lepic went straight down to the sea, that is, to the promenade of the Boulevard de Clichy. The dawn was tight, a little tight, not very sure of itself, on the point of falling and vomiting. The dawn was nauseous when the trio was still at the top of the street. They went down. Gorgui had placed his top hat very properly on his kinky head, at a slight angle. His white shirt-front was still rigid. A big chrysanthemum was drooping in his buttonhole. His face was laughing. Our Lady was holding him by the arm. They descended between two rows of garbage cans full of ashes and comb-scrapings—those garbage cans which every morning receive the first shifty glances of the merrymakers, those garbage cans which zigzag down the street.

If I were to put on a play in which women had roles, I would insist that these roles be performed by adolescent boys, and I would so inform the audience by means of a placard which would remain nailed to the right or left of the sets throughout the performance. Our Lady, in his pale-blue faille dress, edged with white Valenciennes lace,

was more than himself. He was himself and his comple-
ment. I'm mad about fancy dress. The imaginary lovers of
my prison nights are sometimes a prince—but I make him
wear a tramp's castoffs—and sometimes a hoodlum to
whom I lend royal robes. I shall perhaps experience my
greatest delight when I play at imagining myself the heir
of an old Italian family, but the impostor-heir, for my real
ancestor would be a handsome vagabond, walking barefoot under the starry sky, who, by his audacity, would
have taken the place of this Prince Aldini. I love imposture. So, Our Lady walked down the street as only the
great, the very great ladies of the court knew how to walk,
that is, without too much stiffness and without too much
swaying, without kicking aside his train, which casually
swept the gray cobblestones, dragged along straw and
bits of wood, a broken comb, and a leaf of yellowed arum.
The dawn was purging itself. Divine followed from some
distance. She was furious. The costumed Negro and murderer staggered a bit and leaned against each other. Our
Lady was singing:

> *Taraboom ti-ay!*
> *Taraboom ti-ay! Taraboom ti-ay!*

He laughed as he sang. His smooth bright face, the lines
and masses of which had been knocked awry by a night of
dancing and laughter, of tumult and wine and love (the
silk of the dress was spotted), offered itself to the dawn-
ing day as to the icy kiss of a corpse. Though the roses
in his hair were only of cloth, they had wilted on the brass,
but they still held up, a flower basket in which the water
had not been changed. The cloth roses were quite dead.
To freshen them up a bit, Our Lady raised his bare arm,
and the murderer made almost the very gesture, though
perhaps a trifle more rough, that Emilienne d'Alençon
would certainly have made in rumpling her chignon. In

fact, he resembled Emilienne d'Alençon. The big proud
Negro was so moved by the bustle of Our Lady's blue
dress (what was called a false bottom) that he drooled
slightly. Divine watched them tripping down to the beach.
Our Lady was singing among the garbage cans. Imagine
a blond Eugénie Buffet, in a silk dress, singing in court-
yards one early morning, clinging to the arm of a Negro
in evening dress. We're surprised that none of the windows on the street opened on the sleepy face of a dairy-
woman or her mate. Such people never know what goes
on beneath their windows, and that's as it should be. They
would die of grief if they knew. Our Lady's white hand
(his nails were in mourning) was lying flat on Seck Gorgui's forearm. The two arms grazed each other so delicately (they had probably seen this kind of thing in the
movies) that had you watched them you would certainly
have been reminded of the madonnas of Raphael, who
perhaps is so chaste only because of the purity that his
name implies, for he lit up the gaze of little Tobias. The
Rue Lepic descended perpendicularly. The Negro in full
dress was smiling as champagne can make one smile, with
that festive, that is vacant air. Our Lady was singing:

> *Taraboom ti-ay!*
> *Taraboom ti-ay!*

The air was cool. The coldness of the Paris morning
froze his shoulders and fluttered his dress from top to
bottom.

"You're cold," said Gorgui looking at him.

"And how!"

Without anyone's taking notice, Seck's arm went around
Our Lady's shoulders. Behind them, Divine arranged her
face and gestures so that, upon turning around, they both
thought her preoccupied with a very practical inventory.
But neither of the two seemed to care whether Divine

was absent or present. They heard the morning angelus, the rattle of a milk can. Three workmen went by on bicycles along the boulevard, their lamps lit, though it was day. A policeman on his way home, where perhaps he would find an empty bed (Divine hoped so, for he was young), passed without looking at them. The garbage cans smelled of sink and cleaning women. Their odor clung to the white Valenciennes lace of Our Lady's dress and to the festoons on the flounces of Divine's pink jacket. Our Lady continued to sing and the Negro to smile. Suddenly they were at the brink of despair, all three of them. The marvelous road was traveled. Now it was the flat and banal asphalt boulevard, the boulevard of everybody, so different from the secret path they had just cleared in the drunken dawn of a day, with their perfumes, silks, laughter, songs, across houses whose guts were hanging out, houses cleft down the front, where, continuing their naps, suspended in sleep, were old people, children, pimps—pimple-dimple-girly-flowers—barmen, so different, I repeat, from that out-of-the-way path that the three children approached a taxi in order to escape the vexation of a commonplace return. The taxi anticipated them. The driver opened the door and Our Lady stepped in first. Gorgui, because of his position in the group, ought to have got in first, but he moved aside, leaving the opening free for Our Lady. Bear in mind that a pimp never effaces himself before a woman, still less before a faggot (which, however, with respect to him, Our Lady had that night become); Gorgui must have placed him quite high. Divine blushed when he said:

"Get in, Danie."

Then, instantly, in order to think more nimbly, Divine again became the Divine she had left behind while going down the Rue Lepic. For, though she felt as a "woman," she thought as a "man." One might think that, in thus re-

verting spontaneously to her true nature, Divine was a
male wearing make-up, disheveled with make-believe
gestures; but this is not a case of the phenomenon of re-
course to the mother tongue in times of stress. In order to
think with precision, Divine must never formulate her
thoughts aloud, for herself. Doubtless there had been
times when she had said to herself aloud: "I'm just a foolish girl," but having felt this, she felt it no longer, and, in
saying it, she no longer thought it. In Mimosa's presence,
for example, she managed to think "woman" with regard
to serious but never essential things. Her femininity was not
only a masquerade. But as for thinking "woman" completely, her organs hindered her. To think is to perform
an act. In order to act, you have to discard frivolity and set
your idea on a solid base. So she was aided by the idea of
solidity, which she associated with the idea of virility, and
it was in grammar that she found it near at hand. For if,
to define a state of mind that she felt, Divine dared use
the feminine, she was unable to do so in defining an action
which she performed. And all the "woman" judgments she
made were, in reality, poetic conclusions. Hence, only
then was Divine true. It would be curious to know what
women corresponded to in Divine's mind, and particularly
in her life. No doubt, she herself was not a woman (that is,
a female in a skirt); she was womanly only through her
submission to the imperious male; nor, for her, was Ernestine, who was her mother, a woman. But all of woman was in
a little girl whom Culafroy had known when he was a kid,
in the village. Her name was Solange. On broiling days
they would sit curled up on a white stone bench, in a delicate little patch of shade, narrow as a hem, with their feet
tucked under their smocks so as not to wet them with sun;
they felt and thought in common in the shelter of the snowball tree. Culafroy was in love, since, when Solange was
sent to a convent, he made pilgrimages. He visited the

Grotto Rock. Mothers used that granite rock as a bogy, peopling its cavities, to terrify us, with evil creatures, sandmen, and vendors of shoelaces, pins, and charms. Most of the children paid no heed to the stories dictated by the mothers' prudence. Only Solange and Culafroy, when they made their way there—as often as possible—had the sacred terror in their souls. One summer evening, which was heavy with gathering storm, they approached it. The rock advanced like a prow through a sea of golden crops with glints of blue. The sky descended upon earth like a blue powder in a glass of water. The sky was visiting the earth. A mysterious and mystic air (imitated from temples) which only a landscape set off from the village could preserve in all seasons: a pond inhabited by salamanders and framed by little groves of firs which were idealized in the green water. Firs are amazing trees which I have often seen in Italian paintings. They are meant for Christmas mangers and are thus involved in the charm of winter nights, of the magi, of gypsy musicians and vendors of postcards, of hymns and of kisses given and received at night, barefooted on the rug. Culafroy always expected to find in their branches a miraculous virgin, who, so that the miracle might be total, would be made of colored plaster. He had to have this hope in order to tolerate nature. Hateful nature, anti-poetic, ogress swallowing up all spirituality. As ogrish as beauty is greedy. Poetry is a vision of the world obtained by an effort, sometimes exhausting, of the taut, buttressed will. Poetry is willful. It is not an abandonment, a free and gratuitous entry by the senses; it is not to be confused with sensuality, but rather, opposing it, was born, for example, on Saturdays, when, to clean the rooms, housewives put the red velvet chairs, gilded mirrors, and mahogany tables outside, in the nearby meadow.

Solange was standing at the top of the rock. She leaned

back very slightly, as if she were inhaling. She opened her mouth to speak and remained silent. She was waiting for a thunderclap or for inspiration, which were not forthcoming. A few seconds passed in a tangle thick with fright and joy. Then, she uttered, in a pale voice:

"In a year, a man will throw himself from the rock."

"Why in a year? What man?"

"You're an idiot."

She described the man. He was stout, wore gray trousers and a hunting jacket. Culafroy was as upset as if he had been told that a suicide had just been committed there and that a body still warm was lying in the brambles under the rock. The emotion entered him in light, short waves, invading him, and escaped through his feet, hands, hair and eyes, gradually drifting throughout nature as Solange went on to relate the phases of the drama, which was as complicated and cunning as I imagine a Japanese drama must be. Solange took great pains with it, and she had chosen the tone of tragic recitative, in which the voice never joins the tonic.

"He's a man who comes from afar, no one knows why. He's probably a pig dealer returning from the fair."

"But the road's far away. Why does he come here?"

"To die, you innocent. You can't kill yourself on the road."

She shrugged her shoulders and tossed her head. Her lovely curls struck her cheeks like leaded whips. The little pythoness had crouched. Seeking on the rock the carved words of the prophecy, she resembled a mother hen scratching around in the sand to find the grain that she will show to her chicks. Thereafter, the rock became a place that is visited, haunted. They went there as one goes to a grave. That piety for one of the future dead hollowed out in them a kind of hunger or one of those weaknesses which resist fever.

One day Culafroy thought to himself: "That was nine months ago, and Solange is returning in June. So, in July she'll be here to see the climax of the tragedy of which she's the author." She returned. At once he realized that she belonged to a world different from his. She was no longer part of him. She had won her independence; this little girl was now like those works that have long since dropped away from their author: no longer being directly flesh of his flesh, they no longer benefit from his maternal tenderness. Solange had become like one of those chilled excrements which Culafroy used to deposit at the foot of the garden wall among the currant bushes. When they were still warm, he took a tender delight in their odor, but he spurned them with indifference—at times with horror —when they had too long since ceased to be part of himself. And if Solange was no longer the chaste little girl taken from his rib, the little girl who used to pull her hair into her mouth to nibble at it, he himself had been charred by living near Alberto. A chemical operation had taken place within him, giving birth to new compounds. The past of both youngsters was already as old as the hills. Neither Solange nor Culafroy found the games and words of the year before. One day they walked to the hazel trees, which the summer before had been the scene of their wedding, of a baptism of dolls and a banquet of hazelnuts. Upon once again seeing the spot, which the goats always kept in the same condition, Culafroy remembered the prophecy of the Grotto. He wanted to speak of it to Solange, but she had forgotten. To be exact, it was thirteen months since she had announced the violent death of the pig dealer, and nothing had happened. Culafroy saw another supernatural function fade away. A measure of despair was added to the despair which was to accompany him until his death. He did not yet know that the importance of any event in our life lies only in the resonance it sets up within us, only in the degree to which it makes us move toward asceticism. As for him, who receives only shocks, Solange on her rock had not been more inspired than he. In order to show off, she had played a role; but then, though one mystery was thereby disposed of, another and denser one rose up: "I'm not the only one," he thinks, "who can play at not being what they are. So I'm not an exceptional creature." Then, finally, he suddenly detected one of the facets of feminine glitter. He was disappointed, but above all he was filled with another love and with a certain pity for the too pale, delicate, and distant little girl. Alberto had attracted to him, like a fork of lightning, all the marvelousness of the external. Culafroy told Solange a little about snake fishing, and he knew, like a knowing artist, how to confess and suppress. She was sweeping the ground with a hazel branch. Certain children have in their hands, without anyone's suspecting it, inherent powers of sorcery, and people who are naïve are astonished at the perturbations in the laws of animals and families. Solange had formerly been the fairy of the morning spiders—Grief, says the chronicle. I interrupt myself here to observe, "this morning," a spider that is weaving in the darkest corner of my cell. Destiny has artfully directed my gaze to it and its web. The oracle manifests itself. I can only bow without cursing: "You are your own fate, you have woven your own spell." Only one misfortune can befall me, that is, the most terrible. Here am I, reconciled with the gods. The arts of divination do not make me set myself questions, since they are divine. I should like to come back to Solange, to Divine, to Culafroy, to the sad, drab creatures I sometimes desert for handsome dancers and hoodlums; but even the former (especially the former) have been far away from me since I received the shock of the oracle. Solange? She listened like a woman to Culafroy's confidences. For a moment she was embarrassed and laughed, and her laugh was such that a skeleton seemed to be frisking about on her close-set teeth and hammering them with sharp blows. In the heart of the countryside she felt herself a prisoner. She had just been bound. Jealous, the girl. She had difficulty finding enough saliva to ask: "You like him?" and her swallowing was painful, as if she were swallowing a package of pins. Culafroy hesitated to answer. The fairy ran the danger of oblivion. At the moment when it had to be done, when the answer was a "yes" suspended whole and visible, ready to explode, Solange dropped the hazelwand and in order to pick it up bent down, in a ridiculous position, just as the fatal cry fell, the nuptial "yes," with the result that it was mingled with the sound of the sand which she scraped; it was thereby stifled, and the shock to Solange was absorbed. Divine never had any other experience with woman.

Near the taxi, no longer obliged to think, she became Divine again. Instead of getting in (she had already grasped between two fingers the ruffle of her black dress and lifted her left foot), as Gorgui, already settled, was inviting her in, she let out a burst of strident laughter, festive or mad, turned to the driver and, laughing in his face, said:

"No, no. With the driver. I always get in with the driver, so there."

And she became kittenish.

"Does the driver mind?"

The driver was a regular fellow who knew his business (all taxi drivers are procurers and traffic in snow). The fan in Divine's fingers did not unfold. Besides, Divine did not take the fan to throw people off the track; she would have been mortified at seeing herself mistaken for those horrible titty females. "Oh! those women," she would say, "those wicked, wicked things, those vile sailors' tarts, those tramps, those dirty nasties. Oh! those women, how I hate them!" The driver opened the door of his own seat and, smiling pleasantly, said to Divine:

"Come, get in, baby."

"Oh, that driver, he's he's . . . "

Cracklings of taffeta riddled the driver's splendid thigh.

The day was wide-awake when they reached the garret, but the darkness made by the drawn curtains, the odor of tea and, even more, the odor of Gorgui, engulfed them in a night of magic. As was her wont, Divine slipped behind the screen to take off her mourning dress and put on a pair of pajamas. Our Lady sat down on the bed and lit a cigarette (at his feet, the mossy mass of the lace of his dress made for him a kind of rustling base), and, with his elbows on his knees, watched—chance having accepted and instantly organized them—Gorgui's evening jacket, white satin vest, and pumps assume before him on the rug the form of the evidence that a ruined gentleman leaves on the banks of the Seine at three in the morning; Gorgui went to bed naked. Divine reappeared in green pajamas, because, for the room, the green of the cloth was becoming to her ocher-powdered face. Our Lady had not yet finished his cigarette.

"You coming to bed, Danie?"

"I am, just wait till I finish this."

As always, he answered as one answers from the depths of thought. Our Lady never thought of anything, and that was what gave him the air of knowing everything straight away, as by a kind of grace. Was he the favorite of the Creator? Perhaps God had let him in on things. His gaze was purer (emptier) than du Barry's after an explanation by her lover the King. (Like du Barry, at that moment he did not realize that he was moving in a straight line toward the scaffold; but, since men of letters explain that

the eyes of little Jesuses are sad unto death at the anticipa-
tion of Christ's Passion, I have every right to request you
to see, in the depths of Our Lady's pupils, the microsopic
image, invisible to your naked eye, of a guillotine.) He
seemed numbed. Divine ran her hand through the blond
hair of Our Lady of the Flowers.

"You want me to help you?"

She meant: help him undo his dress and take it off.

"O.K., grab hold, go on."

Our Lady dropped his butt and crushed it on the rug;
standing on the toes of one foot, he took off one shoe, then
the other. Divine unlaced the back of the dress. She
stripped Our Lady of the Flowers of one part, the prettiest
part, of his name. Our Lady was a little tight. The last
cigarette had made him woozy. His head rolled and suddenly fell on his chest, like those of the plaster shepherds
kneeling on the tree trunks in the Christmas mangers
when you put a coin into the slot. He hiccupped with sleep
and ill-digested wine. He let his dress be taken off without
the slightest movement to help himself, and, when he was
naked, Divine lifted up his feet and toppled him on the
bed, where he rolled against Seck. Usually Divine slept between them. She saw that today she would have to content
herself with remaining on the outer edge, and the jealousy
which had gripped her at *The Tabernacle* revived her bitterness. She turned off the lamp. The ill-drawn curtains
admitted a very thin ray of light which was diluted into
blond dust. The room was filled with the chiaroscuro of
poetic mornings. Divine lay down. At once she drew Our
Lady to her; his body seemed boneless, nerveless, with
milk-fed muscles. He was smiling vacantly. He smiled in
this complacent way when he was mildly amused, but Divine did not see the smile until she took his head in her
hands and turned toward herself the face that at first had
been turned toward Gorgui. Gorgui was lying on his back.

The wine and liquor had dulled him, as they had dulled Our Lady. He was not sleeping. Divine took Our Lady's closed lips into her mouth. We know that his breath was fetid. Divine therefore wanted to shorten her kiss on the mouth. She slid down to the foot of the bed, licking as she went the downy body of Our Lady, who awoke to desire. Divine buried her head in the hollow of the murderer's legs and belly, and waited. Every morning it was the same scene, once with Our Lady and the next time with Gorgui. She did not wait long. Our Lady suddenly turned over on his belly and, holding his still supple tool, roughly thrust it with his hand into Divine's open mouth. She drew back her head and pursed her lips. The violent member turned to stone (go to it, condottieri, knights, pages, ruffians, gangsters, under your satins go stiff against Divine's cheek) and tried to force open the closed mouth, but it knocked against the eyes, the nose, the chin, slid along the cheek. That was their game. Finally, it found the lips. Gorgui wasn't sleeping. He sensed the movements by their echo on Our Lady's naked rump.

"What a fine pair! You're getting me all hot. I want to get in on this!"

He stirred. Divine was playing at offering herself and withdrawing. Our Lady was panting. Divine's arms encircled his solemn flanks, her hands caressed them, smoothed them, though lightly, so as to feel them quiver, with her finger tips, as when one tries to feel the eyeball rolling under the lids. She ran her hands over Our Lady's buttocks, and behold! Divine understood. Gorgui mounted the blond murderer and tried to penetrate him. Despair— terrible, profound, unparalleled—detached her from the game of the two men. Our Lady was still seeking Divine's mouth and found the eyelids, the hair, and in a voice broken with panting, but moist with smiling, he said:

"Ready, Seck?"

"Right," said the Negro.

His breath must have been blowing through Our Lady's blond hair. A furious movement started above Divine.

"That's life," Divine had time to think. There was a pause, a kind of oscillation. The scaffolding of bodies collapsed into regret. Divine's head climbed back to the pillow. She had remained alone, abandoned. She was no longer excited, and for the first time she did not feel the need to go to the toilet to finish off with her hand.

Divine might have got over Seck's and Our Lady's offense had it not been committed in her home. She would have forgotten it. But the insult was likely to become chronic, since all three seemed to be settled in the garret permanently. She hated Seck and Our Lady equally, and she felt quite clearly that this hatred would have blown over had they left each other. She would keep them in the garret no longer. "I'm not going to fatten up those two sloths." Our Lady was becoming hateful to her, like a rival. In the evening, when they had all got up, Gorgui grabbed Our Lady by the shoulders and, with a laugh, kissed him on the back of the neck. Divine, who was preparing tea, acted as if her thoughts were elsewhere, but she could not refrain from glancing at Our Lady's fly. A new fit of rage seized her: he had a hard-on. She thought she had stolen this glance without being seen, but she lifted up her head and eyes just in time to catch the quizzical glance of Our Lady who was pointing at her for the Negro's benefit.

"You might at least be decent," she said.

"We're not doing any harm," said Our Lady.

"Ah! you think so!"

But she did not want to seem to be expressing disapproval of an amorous understanding, nor even to seem to have discovered it. She added:

"You can't stay a minute without roughhousing."

"We're not roughhousing, eh, baby? Here, take a look."

He was showing, clutching it in his fist, the bump under the throbbing cloth.

"That's a serious matter," he said with a laugh.

Gorgui had let go of Our Lady. He was brushing his shoes. They drank their tea. Never had Divine had the occasion—never had she dreamed of being jealous of the physique of Our Lady of the Flowers. There is every reason to believe, however, that this jealousy existed, that it was veiled, hidden. Let us recall a few small facts that we have merely noted in passing: Divine once refusing Our Lady her mascara; her joy (quickly concealed) at discovering the horror of his foul breath; and, without realizing it herself, she pinned to the wall Our Lady's ugliest photo. This time, the physical jealousy (we know how bitter it is) was obvious to her. She planned and carried out in thought acts of frightful revenge. She scratched, slashed, amputated, lacerated, flayed, vitriolized. "May he be *odiously* mutilated," she thought. As she wiped the tea cups, she carried out appalling executions. After laying aside the dish cloth, she was pure again, but, however, returned among humans only by a skillful gradation. Her acts bore the marks of it. Had she taken vengeance upon a faggot, Divine would doubtless have achieved a miracle of the martyrdom of Saint Sebastian. She would have shot a few arrows—but with the grace she had while saying: "I toss you an eyelash," or "I toss you a bus." A few scattered shafts. Then a salvo. Would have defined the faggot's contours with arrows. Would have imprisoned her in a cage of arrows and finally nailed her outright. She wanted to make use of that method against Our Lady. But this method has to be carried out in public. Though he allowed anything in the garret, Our Lady would not tolerate being kidded in front of the gang. He was ticklish. Divine's arrows hit against granite. She looked for arguments and, naturally, she found them. One day she caught him red-handed in an act worse than selfish. They were in the garret. Divine was still in bed. The evening before, Our Lady had bought a pack of Cravens. When he awoke he looked for the pack: there were only two cigarettes left. He handed one to Gorgui, took the other and lit them. Divine was not sleeping, but she kept her eyes closed and tried to look as if she were still asleep. "It's to see what they're going to do," she said to herself. The liar knew perfectly well that it was a pretext to keep herself from seeming annoyed if they forgot her in the distribution, and to enable her to retain her dignity. Now that she was nearing thirty, Divine began to feel the need of dignity. Trifles shocked her; she who, when young, had been of a boldness that had made barmen blush, herself blushed and felt herself blushing at the least little thing which, by the very subtlety of that symbol, recalled states in which she had really been able to feel herself humiliated. A slight shock—and terrible because the slighter—brought her back to her periods of wretchedness. You will be surprised to see Divine growing in age and sensitivity, whereas the common notion is that the older one gets, the thicker one's skin becomes. She was no longer ashamed, obviously, of being a queen for hire. If need be, she would have boasted of being one who lets jissom flow through her nine holes. It was all the same to her if men and women insulted her. (Until when?) But she lost control of herself, became crimson, and almost failed to pull herself together without a scandal. She clung to dignity. With her eyes closed, she imagined Seck and Our Lady scowling in order to excuse each other for having reckoned without her, when Our Lady made the blunder of uttering aloud the following remark (which grieved Divine, entrenched in her night of closed eyes), a remark that emphasized, indeed proved the fact that a long and complicated exchange of signs concerning her had just taken place: "There're only two cigarettes left." She herself knew that. She heard the match being struck. "After all, they're not going to cut one of them in half." She answered herself: "Well, he should have cut it (the *he* was Our Lady), or even have done without it and left it for me." So, from this scene dated the period when she refused what Seck and Our Lady offered her. One day Our Lady came home with a box of candy. The scene was as follows. Our Lady to Divine:

"You want a candy?" (But, Divine noticed, he was already closing the box.)

She said:

"No, thanks."

A few seconds later, Divine added:

"You never give me anything in a generous way."

"I *am* generous. If I didn't feel like giving it to you, I wouldn't offer it to you. I never ask you twice when I don't feel like giving."

Divine thought with additional shame: "Never has he offered me anything twice." Now when she went out, she always wanted to be alone. This practice had only one effect: of drawing the Negro and the murderer closer together. The phase that followed was one of violent reproaches. Divine could no longer contain herself. Fury, like speed, sharpened her insight. She exposed intentions everywhere. Or was Our Lady obeying, without realizing it, the game she was directing, and which she was directing to lead her toward solitude and, still more, toward despair? She overwhelmed Our Lady with invective. Like fools who do not know how to lie, he was a dissembler. Caught in the trap, he sometimes blushed; his face lengthened, literally, for the two wrinkles along his mouth strained it, drew it downward. He was pitiable. He did not know what to answer and could only smile. This smile, constipated though it was, relaxed his features, unwrinkled his morale. In a way, like a sunbeam traversing a

thorn bush, he had gone through a thicket of invective,
and yet he knew how to seem to emerge unscathed, with
no blood on his fingers. Then Divine, in a rage, tore into
him. She became pitiless, as she could be when she went
after someone. But Our Lady hardly felt her arrows (we
have told why), and if at times, finding a tenderer spot,
the point entered, Divine buried the shaft up to the
feathers, which she had smeared with a healing balm. She
feared at the same time that if Our Lady were wounded
he would get violent, and she was angry with herself for
having shown too much bitterness, for she thought, quite
wrongly, that Our Lady would be quite happy about that.
To each of her poisoned remarks she added a touching re-
storative. As Our Lady never noticed anything except the
good that one seemed to wish him (that's why he was said
to be trusting and without guile), or perhaps also because
he caught only the ends of her sentences, it was only these
ends that struck him and he thought that she was finishing
a long compliment. Our Lady cast a spell on the pains
Divine took to wound him, but, without his knowing it, he
was shot through with evil arrows. Our Lady was happy
in spite of Divine and thanks to her. When Our Lady one
day admitted to the thing that humiliated him (having
been robbed and abandoned by Marchetti), Divine held
Our Lady's hands. Though she was overwhelmed and her
throat grew tense, she smiled gently so that both of them
would not be moved to the point of despair, which would
probably have lasted only a few minutes but would have
marked them for life, and so that Our Lady would not
dissolve in that humiliation. This was exquisitely sweet
to her, like the feeling that melted me to tears when:

"What's your name?" the butler asked me.

"Jean."

and when he called me to the servants' hall for the first
time, he cried: "Jean." It was so good to hear my first

name. I thought I had found a family through the tenderness of the servants and masters. I now confess to you: that I have never felt anything but the appearance of warm caresses, something like a look full of a deep tenderness which, directed to some handsome young creature standing behind me, passed through me and overwhelmed me. Gorgui hardly ever thought, or did not show that he might be thinking. He walked about through Divine's tirades, concerned only with his linens. One day, however, this intimacy with Our Lady, which Divine's jealousy had begotten, caused the Negro to say:

"We're going to the movies, I've got tickets."

Then he caught himself: "Am I an ass! I always think there're only two of us."

This was too much for Divine; she resolved to put an end to it. With whom? She knew that Seck enjoyed that happy life; it gave him shelter, food, and friendship, and the timorous Divine feared his anger: he would surely not have abandoned the garret without a Negro's revenge. Finally, she again found herself—after a period of pause— preferring exaggerated virility, and in this respect Seck more than satisfied her. Should she sacrifice Our Lady? What would Gorgui say? She was helped by Mimosa, whom she met in the street. Mimosa, old lady:

"I've seen her! Ba, Be, By, Bo, Boo, I love that Our Lady of yours. Always just as fresh, always just as Divine. She's the one who's Divine."

"You like her?" (Among themselves, the queens always spoke of their sweethearts in the feminine.) "You want her?"

"My, my, so she doesn't want you any more, my poor dear?"

"Our Lady gives me a pain in the ass. First of all, she's stupid, and I find her lifeless."

"You don't even give her a hard-on any more."

Divine thought: "You bitch, I'll fix you."

"Well, you're really letting me have her?"

"All you've got to do is take her. If you can."

At the same time, she hoped that Our Lady would not let himself be taken.

"You know she detests you."

"Right right right. First they hate me, and then they adore me. But look, Divine, we can be good pals. I'd like to get hold of Our Lady. Let me have her. One good turn deserves another, my sweet. You can count on me."

"Oh! Mimo, of course I know you. You have my confidence, my Quite."

"The way you say that! But look, I assure you, at heart I'm a good girl. Bring her over some evening."

"And what about your man Roger?"

"She's leaving for military service. Don't you worry, down there with those cute officers she's going to forget me. Ah! I'll really be the Quite-Widowed! So, I'll take Our Lady and keep her with me. Why, you've got two sweeties. You've got them all!"

"All right, fine, I'll talk to her about it. Come and have tea with us around five o'clock."

"What a nice girl you are, Divine, let me kiss you. You're still pretty, you know. A bit rumpled, nicely rumpled, and so kind."

It was in the afternoon. It was perhaps two o'clock. As they walked, they held each other by their two pinkies, curved in the form of hooks. A little later, Divine found Gorgui and Our Lady together. She had to wait until the Negro, who no longer left Our Lady, went to the toilet. Divine prepared Our Lady as follows:

"Look, Danie, do you want to make a hundred francs?"

"What's up?"

"It's like this: Mimosa would like to sleep with you for

an hour or two. Roger's going into the army. She's being left alone."

"Oh! a hundred, hell, that's not enough. If you're the one who made the price, you didn't knock yourself out."

He sneered. And Divine:

"I didn't make any price. Look, go with her and you'll work it out. Mimosa's not stingy with guys she likes. Of course, you can do whatever you please. I'm just telling you, you can do as you like. At any rate, she's coming to the garret at five o'clock. Only, we'll have to get Gorgui out of the way, you understand, so we can be freer."

"We going to fuck in the garret with you?"

"Oh, don't be silly, no, you'll go to her place. You'll have time to talk the matter over. But don't swipe anything, please, don't swipe anything, or there'll be trouble."

"Ah! there's something to swipe? But don't worry, I don't rob pals."

"Try to make it last, be a nice little pimp."

Divine had very intentionally and very cleverly suggested theft. It was a sure way to manage Danie. And what about Gorgui? When he returned, Our Lady told him what was up.

"You ought to do it, Danie."

All the Negro saw was the hundred francs. But then a suspicion occurred to him; up to now he had thought that the money that Our Lady had in his pockets came from his clients, but the scruple he observed in him today made him think that there was something else. He wanted to know what, but the murderer was suppler than a snake. Our Lady had resumed his cocaine business. In a little cell-shaped bar on the Rue de l'Elysée-des-Beaux-Arts, every four days he met Marchetti, back in Paris, and broke, who supplied him. The dope was contained in little tissue-paper bags, gram by gram, and these bags were themselves in a bigger one of brown cloth. He had devised the following system: he kept his left hand in the torn pocket of his trousers in order to be able to soothe or stroke his violent member. In this left hand he held a long string from which there swung, inside the trouser leg, the dark bag.

"If the dicks come along, I let go of the string and the packet falls to the ground without making a riot. Like that, everything's all right."

He clung by a string to a secret organization. Every time Marchetti gave him the dope, he would say: "All right, kid" and accompanied the remark by a look that Our Lady recognized among Corsicans who make use of it among themselves when they brush against one another on the sidewalk and mutter: "Ciao Rico."

Marchetti asking Our Lady whether he had guts:

"It's coming out of my ears!"

"Brother Bullshit," someone answered.

Here I cannot refrain from coming back to those words of argot which stream from pimps' lips as his farts (pearls) stream from Darling's downy behind. The reason is that one of them, which, more perhaps than all the others, turns me inside out—or, as Darling always says, gnaws at me, for he is cruel—was uttered in one of the cells in the Mousetrap that we call "Thirty-six Tiles," a cell so narrow that it is the alleyway of a ship. About a husky guard, I heard someone mutter: "the lock-sucker"; then, a moment later: "the yard-on." Now, it so happened that the man who said that had told us that he had been at sea for seven years. The magnificence of such an achievement—impalement by a boom—made me tremble from head to foot. And the same man said a little later: "Or, if you're a fairy, you let down your pants and the judge gets it in the bull's eye. . . ." But this expression was already rather Rabelaisian; it was an unhappy expression and destroyed the charm of the other one, and I regain my footing on the solid basis of joking, whereas poetry always pulls the ground away from under your feet and sucks you into the bosom of a wonderful night. He also said: "Cockassuckeroo!" but it was no better. At times, during my most harrowing moments, when I'm pestered by the guards, I sing within me that poem "The Yard-on!" that I apply to no one in particular but which comforts me and dries unwelled tears as I sail across becalmed seas, a member of the crew we saw around 1700 on the frigate Culafroy.

Darling wandered from one department store to another. They were the only luxury he could approach at close range, in which he could wallow. He was attracted by the elevator, the mirrors, the carpets (especially the carpets, which muted all the inner workings of the organs of his body; silence entered him through his feet, padded the whole play of his mechanism—in short, he no longer felt himself); he was hardly at all attracted by the salesgirls, for inadvertently certain gestures, though very restrained, certain mannerisms of Divine escaped him. At first, he had dared a few just for the fun of it, but slyly, little by little, they were conquering the stronghold, and Darling did not even notice that he was shedding his skin. It was at a later time—and we shall tell how—that he realized the falseness of what he had blurted out one evening: "A male that fucks another male is a double male!" Before going into Lafayette's Department Store, he unhooked the gold chain that was beating against his fly. As long as he was alone on the sidewalk, struggle was still possible, but in the meshes of all the low lanes that the counters and showcases wove into a shifting net, he was lost. He was at the mercy of the will of "another," who stuffed his pockets with objects which, when he got to his room and put them on the table, he did not recognize, for the sign which made him choose them at the moment of theft was hardly common to the Divinity and Darling. At the moment of this taking possession by the Other, from Darling's eyes, his ears, his slightly open and even closed mouth, there would flutter out, with a flapping of tiny wings, little gray or red Mercurys with wings on their ankles. Darling the tough, the cold, the irrefragable, Darling the pimp would come to life, like a steep rock from which, at each wet and mossy hollow, a brisk sparrow emerges, flitting about it like a flight of winged pricks. Sooner or later he was bound to take a crack at it, that is at stealing. He had, on several occasions, already engaged in the following game: on a showcase, among the objects on display and in the most inaccessible spot, he would place, as if inadvertently, some trifling object that had been bought and duly paid for at a distant counter. He would let it lie there for a few minutes, ignoring its existence, and examine the surrounding displays. When the object had melted sufficiently into the rest of the display, he would steal it. Twice a store detective had caught him, and twice the management had been obliged to excuse itself, since Darling had the sales' slip.

Stealing from showcases is done in several ways, and perhaps each mode of display requires the use of one rather than another. For example, with one hand you can take hold of two small objects (wallets) at the same time, hold them as if there were only one, examine them leisurely, slip one into your sleeve and finally put the other back as if it were not quite what you wanted. In front of piles of silk remnants, you casually put one hand into the pocket (which is slit) of your overcoat. You approach the counter until your stomach touches it and, while your free hand is fingering the cloth, moving it about and throwing the silks into disorder, the hand which is in the pocket goes up to the top of the counter (still on a level with the navel), draws in the cutting at the bottom of the pile and thus slides it, for it is supple, under the overcoat, which hides it. But I am giving recipes that all housewives and purchasers are familiar with. Darling preferred to seize, to make the object describe a prompt parabola from the display case to his pocket. It was bold, but more beautiful. Like falling stars, bottles of perfume, pipes, lighters streamed in a pure, brief curve and swelled out his thighs. It was a dangerous game. Whether it was worth the effort, only Darling could tell. The game was a science that required training, preparation, like military science. You first had to study the layout of the mirrors and their bevels, and also the oblique ones hooked to the ceiling, which reflect you in an upside-down world, but which the detectives, by a stage trick that functions in their brain, quickly turn right side up and orient correctly. You had to watch for the moment when the salesgirl's eyes were elsewhere and when the customers, always traitors, were not looking. Finally, you had to find, like a lost object—or better, like one of those picture-puzzle figures, the lines of which on dessert plates are also those of trees and clouds—the detective. Find the detective. It's a woman. The movies —among other games—teach the natural, a natural made up completely of artifices and a thousand times more deceptive than the real. By dint of succeeding in resembling a delegate to a convention or a midwife, the movie detective has given to the faces of real delegates and real midwives the faces of detectives, and the real detectives, haggard amidst this disorder which mixes up faces, unable to put up with this any longer, have chosen to look like detectives, which simplifies nothing. . . . "A spy who looked like a spy would be a bad spy," a dancer said to me one day. (One usually says: "a dancer, one evening.") I don't believe it.

Darling was about to leave the store. Having nothing

better to do, and in order to seem natural, and also because it's hard to shake off that turbulence, a Brownian
movement, as dense and mobile, and moving as morning
torpor—he lingered, as he passed, to look at the displays,
where one sees shirts, bottles of glue, hammers, toy lambs,
rubber sponges. In his pockets were two silver lighters
and a cigarette case. He was being followed. When he
was near the door, which was guarded by a uniformed
colossus, a little old woman said to him quietly:

"What have you stolen, young man?"

It was the "young man" that charmed Darling. Otherwise he would have made a dash for it. The most innocent words are the most pernicious, they're the ones you
have to watch out for. Almost immediately, the colossus
was upon him and grabbed his wrist. He charged like a
tremendous wave upon the bather asleep on the beach.
Through the old woman's words and the man's gesture, a
new universe instantaneously presented itself to Darling:
the universe of the irremediable. It is the same as the
one we were in, with one peculiar difference: instead of
acting and knowing we are acting, we know we are acted
upon. A gaze—and it may be of your own eyes—has the
sudden, precise keenness of the extra-lucid, and the order
of this world—seen inside out—appears so perfect in its
inevitability that this world has only to disappear. That's
what it does in the twinkling of an eye. The world is
turned inside out like a glove. It happens that I am the
glove, and that I finally realize that on Judgment Day
it will be with my own voice that God will call me:
"Jean, Jean!"

Darling had known too many—as many as I had—of
these world's ends for him to lament in rebellion against
this one when he regained his footing. A rebellion would
have merely made him flip-flop like a carp on a carpet
and would have made him ridiculous. Submissively, as

on a leash and in a dream, he let himself be taken by the doorman and the female detective to the office of the store's special police superintendent in the basement. He was done for, nabbed. That very evening a police wagon took him to the station, where he spent the night with numerous tramps, beggars, thieves, pickpockets, pimps, forgers, people who had emerged from between the ill-joined stones of houses set up against each other in the darkest blind alleys. The following day Darling and his companions were taken to Fresnes Prison. He then had to tell his name, his mother's name, and the given name, hitherto secret, of his father (he invented: Romuald!). He also gave his age and occupation.

"Your occupation?" asked the court clerk.

"Mine?"

"Of course, yours."

Darling was on the point of seeing issue from between his blossoming lips: "Barmaid," but he answered:

"No occupation. I don't work."

However, these words had for Darling the meaning and value of "barmaid."

Finally, he was undressed and his clothes were searched, including the hems. The guard made him open his mouth, inspected it, ran his hands through Darling's thick hair and furtively, after having mussed it over his forehead, grazed the back of his neck, which was still hollow and warm and vibrant, sensitive and ready, at the slightest caress, to cause frightful damage. It is by the back of his neck that we see that Darling can still make a delicious trooper. Finally the guard said to him:

"Bend down."

He bent. The guard looked at his anus and saw a black spot.

". . . eeze," he cried. Darling sneezed. But he had misunderstood. It was "squeeze" that the guard had cried.

The black spot was a rather big lump of dung, which
got bigger every day and which Darling had already
several times tried to pull away, but he would have had
to pull the hairs out with it, or take a hot bath.

"You've sure been shitting," said the guard. (Now, to
be shitting also means to be scared, and the guard did not
know this.)

Darling of the noble bearing, of the swaying hips, of the
motionless shoulders! At the reformatory, an inspector (he
was twenty-five years old and wore fawn-colored leather
boots up to his thighs which were no doubt hairy) had
noticed that the youngsters' shirttails were stained with
shit. Every Sunday morning, when we changed linen,
he therefore made us hold out our dirty shirts by the outspread sleeves. With the thin end of his whip he would
lash the face, already tortured by humiliation, of the boy
whose shirttail was doubtful. We no longer dared to go to
the toilet, but, when we were driven to it by a case of
the gripes, after wiping our fingers on the whitewashed
wall (there was no paper) which was already yellow with
piss, we took good care to lift up our shirttails (I now
say "we," but at the time each kid thought he was the
only one who did it), and it was the seat of the white
pants that was solied. On Sunday mornings we felt the
hypocritical purity of virgins. Larochedieu was the only
one who, toward the end of the week, got tangled up in
his shirttails and dirtied them. Though the matter was not
serious, the three years that he spent in the penitentiary
were poisoned by the preoccupation with those Sunday
mornings—which I now see decorated with garlands of
little shirts flowered with light touches of yellow shit, before mass—with the result that on Saturday evenings he
would rub the corner of his shirt on the whitewash of
the wall to try to whiten it. Passing in front of him—the
boy drawn and quartered, already in the pillory, cruci-

fied at fifteen—the leather-booted inspector, his eyes
tawny and gleaming, remained motionless. Without any
preconceived cleverness on his part, there passed over his
harsh features (the feelings which we shall say were
painted there, because of that harshness, like a charge)
disgust, contempt, and horror. With his body erect, he
spat right in Larochedieu's marble face, which awaited
only this spit. We who read this can imagine that the
inspector's shirttails and the seat of his underpants were
shitty. Thus, Darling Daintyfoot could divine the soul
of a bum like Larochedieu on whose behind one spits.
But he paid little attention to these momentary exchanges
of souls. He never knew why, after certain shocks, he
was surprised to find himself back in his skin. He did not
say a word. The guard and he were alone in the locker
room. His chest was bursting with fury. Shame and fury.
He left the room, trailing after him that noble behind—
and it was by his behind that one could tell that he would
have made a brilliant bullfighter. He was locked in a
cell, and finally, under lock and key, he felt free and
washed; with his fragments glued together again, he was
once more Darling, gentle Darling. His cell might be anywhere. The walls are white, the ceiling is white, but the
filthy black floor sets it down on the floor and situates it
there, precisely, that is, between a thousand cells which
crush it, though they are light, on the fourth floor of the
Fresnes Prison. We are now there. The longest detours finally lead me back to my prison, to my cell. Now, almost
without trimmings, without transposition, without any intermediary, I could tell of my life here. My present life.

In front of all the cells runs an inner balcony onto
which each door opens. We stand behind our door waiting
for the guard and fall into poses that identify us; for in-
stance, a certain bum indicates, by standing with his cap

in his extended hand, that he usually begs in front of churches. When he returns from the walk and waits for the guard, each prisoner, if he leans forward, cannot help hearing some guitar serenade, or feel, at this rail, that the big vessel is lurching wildly beneath the moon and is about to go down. My cell is an exactly cubic box. In the evening, as soon as Darling stretches out in bed, the window carries the cell off toward the west, detaches it from the masoned block and flies off with it, hauling it like the basket of a balloon. In the morning, if a door opens—they're all closed at that time and this is a deep mystery, deep as the mystery of number in Mozart or the use of the chorus in tragedy—(in prison, more doors are opened than closed) an elastic draws it back from the space in which it had been hovering and sets it in place again; that is when the prisoner has to get up. He pisses, straight and solid as an elm, into the bowl of the latrine, then gives his limp tool a shake or two; the relief that comes from the flowing urine restores him to active life, places him on earth, though delicately, carefully, unties the bonds of night, and he gets dressed. With the whisk broom he sweeps up ashes and dust. The guard comes by, opening the doors for five seconds to give the men time to put out the sweepings. Then he shuts them again. The prisoner is not quite over the nausea that comes from waking with a start. His mouth is full of pebbles. The bed is still warm. But he does not lie down again. He must grapple with the daily mystery. The iron bed fastened to the wall, the shelf fastened to the wall, the wooden chair fastened to the wall by a chain—this chain, residue of a very ancient order, in which prisons were called keeps and dungeons, in which prisoners, like sailors, were galley slaves, dims the modern cell with a romantic Brest or Toulon fog, carries it back through time and makes Darling shudder subtly at the suspicion that he is in the

Bastille (the chain is a symbol of a monstrous power; weighted with a ball, it used to shackle the numb feet of His Majesty's Galley Slaves)—the dry kelp mattress, narrow as the bier of an Oriental queen, the bare hanging bulb, are as rigid as a precept, as bones and exposed teeth. When he returns home, to the attic, Darling will never again, if he sits or lies down, or has tea, be able to forget that he is resting or sleeping on the framework of an armchair or sofa. The iron hand in the velvet glove is a reminder. Let the veil be lifted. Alone in the cell, in almost breastlike rhythm (it beats like a mouth), the white tile latrine gives its comforting breath. It alone is human.

The Darling-Block walks with little swaying steps. He is alone in his cell. From his nostrils he plucks acacia and violet petals. With his back to the door, where an anonymous eye is always spying, he eats them, and with the back of his thumb, where he has let the nail grow long, like that of a scholar, he hunts for others. Darling is a fake pimp. The schemes he devises suddenly peter out in poetical meanderings. Almost always he walks with a regular and casual step: he is haunted by a memory. Today he is pacing to and fro in his cell. He is unoccupied, which is very rare, for he is almost constantly at work, in secret, but with fidelity to his curse. He goes to the shelf and raises his hand to the level where, in the garret, on a piece of furniture, the revolver lies. The door opens with a great rattling, as of locks being forged, and the guard yells out:

"Quick, the towels."

Darling stands rooted there, holding in his hands the clean towels he has been given for the dirty ones. Then he continues by fits and starts the gestures of the drama which he is unaware he is acting out. He sits down on his bed; he rubs his hand over his forehead. He hesitates to . . . Finally he gets up and, in front of the little two-penny mirror nailed to the wall, he pushes aside his blond hair and, without realizing what he is doing, looks for a bullet wound at his temple.

Night unlooses Darling from his tough rind of determined pimp. In his sleep he grows tender, but all he can do is clutch at the pillow, cling to it, lay his cheek tenderly on the rough cloth—the cheek of a kid about to burst into tears—and say: "Stay. Please, my love, stay." In the hearts of all the "men" is enacted a five-second tragedy in verse. Conflicts, cries, daggers, or prison which resolves; the liberated man has just been the witness and matter of a poetic work. For a long time I thought that the poetic work posed conflicts: it cancels them.

At the foot of the prison walls, the wind is kneeling. The prison draws along all the cells where the prisoners are asleep; grows lighter and slips away. Run, censors, the thieves are far. The second-story men are mounting. By stairwell or elevator. Subtly they spirit away. They steal. And steal away. On the landing, the midnight bourgeois, overwhelmed by the dread of the mystery of a child who steals, of an adolescent jimmying doors, the robbed bourgeois dares not cry out, "Stop thief!" He hardly turns his head. The thief makes heads turn, houses pitch, castles dance, prisons fly.

Darling is asleep at the foot of the wall. Sleep, Darling, stealer of nothing, stealer of books, of bell ropes, of horses' manes and tails, of bikes, of fancy dogs. Darling, tricky Darling, who can rob women of their compacts; and, with a limed stick, priests of the money in the collection box; the devout taking communion at low mass of the bags they leave on the prayer stool; the pimps of their beat; the police of their inside tips; concierges of their sons or daughters; sleep, sleep, hardly has the day dawned when a ray, on your blond hair, of the oncoming sun locks you in your prison. And the days that follow make your life longer than broad.

When it is time to get up, a prisoner runs all the way around the balcony and bangs once on each door. One after the other, with the same gestures, three thousand prisoners disturb the heavy atmosphere, get up, and do the little morning jobs. Later a guard will open the grate of cell 329 to hand out the soup. He looks and doesn't say a word. In this story, the guards also have their job. They are not all fools, but they are all purely indifferent to the game they play. They haven't the slightest notion of the beauty of their function. Recently they have been wearing a dark blue uniform which is an exact copy of aviators' outfits, and I think, if they are high-minded, that they are ashamed of being caricatures of heroes. They are aviators fallen from the sky, smashing the glass of the ceiling. They have escaped into prison. On their collars there still cling stars which, from close up, seem white and embroidered, because it is daytime when we can see them. One imagines that they threw themselves from their planes in terror (the wounded child Guynemer fell curled with fear; he fell with his wing shattered by the hard air it had to cleave, his body bleeding a benzine rainbow, and that is what is meant by falling into a heaven of glory); they are at last in a world which does not surprise them. They have the right to walk by all the cells without opening them, to look at the humble, gentle-hearted hoodlums. No. They do not think of doing so because they have no desire to. They fly in the air: they have no desire to open the gates and, through the diamond-shaped opening, take by surprise the familiar gestures of murderers and thieves, take them by surprise when they are washing their linen, tucking in their bedclothes for the night, sealing their windows, as a matter of good housekeeping, with their big fingers and a pin slitting matches

in two or in four, and to make a trivial—hence human—
remark to them to see whether they are not transformed
at once into lynxes or foxes. They are guardians of tombs.
They open the doors and shut them again, unconcerned
about the treasures they protect. Their honest (beware of
the word "noble" and the word "honest" which I have just
used), their honest faces, pulled downward, smoothed
by the vertical fall without parachutes, are not altered by
rubbing shoulders with racketeers, crooks, pimps, fences,
forgers, killers, and counterfeiters. Not a flower bespatters
their uniform, not a crease of dubious elegance, and if I
could say of one of them that he walked on velvet feet,
it was because a few days later he was to betray, to go
over to the opposite camp, which is the thieving camp,
to go straight back up into the sky, with the cash box
under his armpit. I had noticed him at mass, in the
chapel. At the moment of communion, the chaplain left
the altar and went up to one of the first cells (for the
chapel is also divided into five hundred cells, standing
coffins), carrying the host to a prisoner who was supposed
to wait for it on bended knees. Hence, this turnkey—
who, wearing his cap, was in a corner of the altar platform, with his hands in his pockets, his legs spread, in
short, assuming the posture in which I so enjoyed seeing
Alberto again—smiled, but in a pleasantly amused way,
which I would never have thought possible in a turnkey.
His smile accompanied the Eucharist and the return of
the empty ciborium, and I thought that, while rubbing his
balls with his left hand, he was jeering at the worshiper.
I had already wondered what would come of the meeting
of a handsome young guard and a handsome young
criminal. I took delight in the following two images: a
bloody and mortal shock, or a sparkling embrace in a
riot of spunk and panting; but I had never taken special
notice of any guard, until finally I saw him. From my cell,

which was in the last row, I could hardly make out his features and so I was able to give him those of a young, cowardly Mexican half-breed whose face I had cut out of the cover of an adventure novel. I thought: "You little rat, I'll give you a communion all right." My hatred and horror of that breed must have given me a still stiffer hard-on, for I felt my tool swelling under my fingers— and I shook it until finally . . . —without taking my eyes off the guard, who was still smiling pleasantly. I can tell myself now that he was smiling at another guard or at a murderer and that, since I was between them, his luminous smile passed through me and decomposed me. I could believe the turnkey was vanquished and grateful.

In the presence of the guards, Darling felt like a little boy. He hated and respected them. All day long he smokes until he rocks on his bed. In his nausea, light spots form islands: the gesture of a mistress; the face, smooth and beardless as a boxer's, of a girl. He flings his butts away for the pleasure of the gesture. (One can expect anything of a pimp who rolls his cigarettes because this gives his fingers a certain elegance, who wears crepe-soled shoes so as to take the people he passes by surprise, people who will look at him with more astonishment, will see his tie, will envy his hips, his shoulders, the back of his neck, who, without knowing him, will create for him, despite his incognito, from one passerby to the next, a procession strewn and interrupted with homage, will accord a discontinuous and momentary sovereignty to this stranger, and the result of all these moments of sovereignty will be that, all the same, he will, at the end of his days, have gone through life like a sovereign.) In the evening, he gathers up the scattered tobacco and smokes it. Lying in bed on his back, with his legs spread, he flicks the cigarette ash with his right hand. His left hand is under his head. It is a moment of happiness, made up of Darling's delightful aptitude for being that which, by virtue of his pose, is profoundly that, and which this essential quality makes live again there with its true life. Lying on a hard bed and smoking, what could he be? Darling will never suffer, or will always be able to get out of a tight spot by his ease in taking on the gestures of some fellow he admires who happens to be in the same situation, and, if books or anecdotes do not provide him with any, in creating them —thus, his desires (but he realized it too late, when there was no longer time to recede) were neither the desire to be a smuggler, king, juggler, explorer, or slave trader, but the desire to be one of the smugglers, one of the kings, jugglers, etc., that is, as if . . . In the most woeful of postures, Darling will be able to remember it was also that of one of his gods (and if they never assumed it, he'll force them to have assumed it), and his own posture will be sacred and thereby even better than merely bearable. (In this way, he is like me who create those men—Weidmann, Pilorge, Socaly—in my desire to be them; but he is quite unlike me in his faithfulness to his characters, for I have long since resigned myself to being myself. But the fact is that my longing for a splendid imaginary destiny has, as it were, condensed the tragic, purple elements of my actual life into a kind of extremely compact, solid, and scintillating reduction, and I sometimes have the complex face of Divine, who is herself, first and at times simultaneously, in her features and gestures, the imaginary and yet so real creatures of election with whom, in strict privacy, she has contentions, who torture and exalt her but who allow her no rest and give her, by subtle contractions of wrinkles and the quiverings of her fingers, that disquieting air of being multiple, for she remains silent, as shut as a tomb and, like a tomb, peopled by the unclean.) Lying on a hard bed and smoking, what could he be? "That which, by virtue of his pose, is most profoundly that, that is, a jailed pimp smoking a cigarette, that is, himself." You will therefore understand to what degree Divine's inner life was different from Darling's inner life.

Darling has written Divine a letter, on the envelope of which he is obliged to put "Monsieur," and has also written one to Our Lady of the Flowers. Divine is in the hospital. She sends a money order of five hundred francs. We shall read his letter later on. Our Lady has not answered.

A guard opens the door and pushes a newcomer into the cell. Is it I or Darling who will receive him? He brings with him his blankets, mess tin, cup, wooden spoon, and his story. At his first words I stop him. He keeps on talking, but I am no longer there.

"What's your name?"

"Jean."

That's enough. Like me and like the dead child for whom I am writing, his name is Jean. Besides, what would it matter if he were less handsome, but I have a run of bad luck. Jean there. Jean here. When I tell one of them that I love him, I wonder whether I am not telling it to myself. I am no longer here, because I am again trying to relive the few times he let me caress him. I dared all and, in order to tame him, I allowed him to have the superiority of the male over me; his member was as solid as a man's, and his adolescent's face was gentleness itself, so that when, lying on my bed, in my room, straight and motionless, he discharged into my mouth, he lost nothing of his virginal chastity. It is another Jean, here, who is telling me his story. I am no longer alone, but I am thereby more alone than ever. I mean that the solitude of prison gave me the freedom to be with the hundred Jean Genets glimpsed in a hundred passers-by, for I am quite like Darling, who also stole the Darlings whom a thoughtless gesture let escape from all the

strangers he had brushed against; but the new Jean brings
into me—as a folding fan draws in the designs on the
gauze—brings in I know not what. Yet, he is far from un-
likable. He is even stupid enough for me to feel a certain
tenderness for him. His narrow black eyes, brown skin,
bushy hair, and that wide-awake look . . . Something like
a Greek hooligan whom one pictures crouching at the
foot of the invisible statue of Mercury, playing the game
of goose, but keeping an eye on the god in order to steal
his sandals.

"What are you in for?"

"Pimping. They call me the Pigalle Weasel."

"Don't hand me that. You're not dressed for it. At
Pigalle there's only fairies. Let's hear it."

The Greek child tells that he was caught in the act
just as he was removing his hand, which was stuffed with
bills, from the cash drawer of a bar.

"But I'll get even. When I get out, I'm gonna bust all
his windows with stones, at night. But I'm gonna put
on gloves to pick up the stones with. Because of the finger-
prints. Can't muck around with me."

I continue my reading of cheap novels. It satisfies my
love of hoodlums dressed up as gentlemen. Also my taste
for imposture, my taste for the sham, which could very
well make me write on my visiting cards: "Jean Genet,
bogus Count of Tillancourt." Amidst the pages of these
thick books, in flattened type, marvels appeared. Like
straight lilies there surge up young men, who are, thanks
in part to me, both princes and beggars. If from myself
I make Divine, from them I make her lovers: Our Lady,
Darling, Gabriel, Alberto, lads who whistle through their
teeth and on whose heads you can, if you look closely,
see, in the form of an aureole, a royal crown. I cannot prevent them from having the nostalgic quality of cheap
novels with paper as gray as the skies of Venice and

London, all marked up with the drawings and fierce signs of convicts: profiles with eyes in full-face, bleeding hearts. I read these works which are idiotic to the sense of reason, but my reason is not concerned with a book from which poisoned, feathered phrases swoop down on me. The hand that launches them sketches, as it nails them somewhere, the dim outline of a Jean who recognizes himself, dares not move, awaiting the one that, aimed at his heart in earnest, will leave him panting. I am madly in love (as I love prison) with that close print, compact as a pile of rubbish, crammed with acts as bloody as linens, as the fetuses of dead cats, and I do not know whether it is stiffly erect pricks which are transformed into tough knights or knights into vertical pricks.

And after all, is it necessary for me to talk about myself so directly? I much prefer to describe myself in the caresses I reserve for my lovers. The new Jean came very close to becoming Darling. What did he lack? When he farts, with a sharp noise, he makes that gesture of bending on his thighs while keeping his hands in his pockets and turning his torso a little, as though he were screwing it on. It is the movement of a pilot at the helm, and he is the image of Darling, about whom I liked, among other things, the following: when he hummed a java tune, he would do a dance step and place both hands in front of him as if they were holding the waist of a partner (depending on his mood, he made the waist more or less narrow, drawing his always mobile hands apart or together); he therefore seemed also to be holding the sensitive steering wheel of a Delage on an almost straight road; he also seemed to be a nervous boxer protecting his liver with flat, agile hands; thus, the same gesture was common to a number of heroes, whom Darling suddenly became, and it always so happened that this gesture was the one that symbolized most forcefully the most graceful of males.

He would make those marvelous gestures which bring us
to their knees. Tough gestures that spur us on and make
us whimper, like that city whose flanks I saw bleeding
streams of statues on the march, advancing to a rhythm of
statues borne up by sleep. The battalions advance in their
dreams through the streets like a flying carpet or like a
tire which falls and rebounds with a slow, heavy rhythm.
Their feet stumble in the clouds: then they awake. But
an officer says a word: they close their eyes and go on in
their sleep, on their boots, which are as heavy as pedestals,
the dust being a cloud. Like the Darlings who have passed
through us, far away on their clouds. The one thing that
makes them different is their steely hips, which can never
make crooked, flexible pimps of them. It amazes me that
Horst Wessel, the pander, which he was said to be, gave
birth to a legend and a ballad.

Mindless, fecundating as a golden powder, they fell on
Paris, which for one whole night repressed the beating of
its heart.

As for us, we shudder in our cells, which sing or complain with forced voluptuousness, for, merely suspecting
that debauch of males, we are as excited as if we saw a
giant standing with his legs spread and with a hard-on.

Darling had been in the jug about three months when
(at the time I met the minors whose faces seemed to
me so willful, so hard, though so young, making my poor
white flesh—in which I no longer see anything of the fierce
colonist of Mettray—appear flabby, but I do recognize
them and fear them) he went downstairs for a medical
examination. There a youngster spoke to him about Our
Lady of the Flowers. Everything that I tell you here in
straightforward fashion, Darling learned in bits and scraps,
through words whispered behind a hand spread fanwise,
in the course of a number of medical examinations.
Throughout his astounding life, Darling, who is up on

everything, will never know anything. Just as he will always be ignorant of the fact that Our Lady is his son, so he will not know that, in the story the kid tells him, Pierrot the Corsican is Our Lady under a nickname he used for peddling dope. So, Our Lady was at the home of the kid who is going to talk, when the elevator of the building stopped at the landing. The sound of its stopping marked the moment from which the inevitable must be assumed. An elevator that stops quickens the heartbeat of the one who hears it, like the sound of nails being hammered in the distance. It makes life as brittle as glass. Someone rang. The sound of the bell was less fatal than that of the elevator. It restored a bit of certainty, of the accepted. If the kid and Our Lady had heard nothing more after the sound of the elevator, they would have died of fright. It was the kid who opened the door.

"Police!" said one of the men, making the familiar gesture of turning back his lapel.

At present, the image of fatality is, for me, the triangle formed by three men too ordinary-looking not to be dangerous. Imagine that I am walking up a street. All three of them are on the left-hand sidewalk, where I have not yet noticed them. But *they* have seen me. One of them crosses over to the right side of the street, the second stays on the left, and the last slackens his pace and forms the apex of the triangle in which I am about to be enclosed: it's the Police.

"Police."

They stepped into the anteroom. The whole floor was covered with a rug. Anyone who is willing to mix detective-story adventures into his daily life—a life of shoes to be laced, buttons to sew on, blackheads to remove—has to be a bit fey himself. The detectives walked with one hand on the cocked revolvers in their jacket pockets. At

the other end of the kid's studio apartment, the mantelpiece was topped by a huge mirror framed in rocaille
crystal, with complicated facets; a few chairs upholstered
in yellow silk were scattered about. The curtains were
drawn. The artificial light came from a small chandelier;
it was noon. The detectives smelled crime, and they were
right, for the studio reproduced the stuffy atmosphere in
which Our panting Lady, his gestures caught in a form
stiff with courtesy and fear, had strangled the old man.
There were roses and arum on the mantelpiece, in front of
them. As in the old man's apartment, the varnished furniture was all curves, from which the light seemed to well
up rather than settle, as on the globes of grapes. The detectives moved forward, and Our Lady watched them
move forward in a silence as fearful as the eternal silence of unknown space. They were moving forward, as
was he himself then, in eternity.

They came at just the right moment. In the middle of
the studio, on a big table, a big naked body lay flat on the
red velvet cover. Our Lady of the Flowers, who was standing attentively beside the table, watched the detectives
approach. At the same time that the ominous idea of a
murder occurred to them, the idea that this murder was
sham destroyed the murder; the awkwardness of such a
proposition, the awkwardness of its being both absurd and
possible, of its being a sham murder, made the detectives
feel uneasy. It was quite obvious that they could not have
been in the presence of the dismembering of a murdered man or woman. The detectives were wearing signet
rings of real gold, and their neckties had genuine knots.
As soon as—and before—they got to the edge of the table,
they saw clearly that the corpse was a tailor's wax dummy.
Nevertheless, the idea of murder clouded the simple data
of the problem. "You there, I don't like your looks." The
eldest of the detectives said this to Our Lady because the

face of Our Lady of the Flowers is so radiantly pure that
the idea immediately occurred to everyone that it was
false, that this angel must be two-faced, with flames and
smoke, for everyone has had occasion to say at least once
in his life: "You'd have thought he was a true saint," and
wants at all costs to be foxier than destiny.

So a sham murder dominated the scene. The two detectives were merely after the cocaine that one of their
stool pigeons had tracked down to the kid's place.

"Hand over the coke, and make it snappy."

"We don't have any coke, chief."

"Come on, kids, make it snappy. Otherwise, we'll take
you in and search the premises. That won't help you any."

The kid hesitated a second, three seconds. He knew the
ways of detectives, and he knew he was caught. He made
up his mind.

"Here, that's all we have."

He held out a tiny packet, folded like a packet of
pharmaceutical powder, which he removed from the
case of his wristwatch. The detective pocketed it (his
vest pocket).

"What about him?"

"He don't have any. Honest, chief, you can search."

"And what about that? Where does it come from?"

The dummy. Here we must perhaps recognize Divine's
influence. She is present wherever the inexplicable arises.
She, the Giddy One, strews traps in her wake, artful pit-
falls, deep dungeon cells, even at the risk of being caught
in them herself if she does an about-face, and because of
her the minds of Darling, Our Lady, and their cronies
bristle with ridiculous gestures. With their heads high,
they take falls that doom them to the worst of fates. Our
Lady's young friend was also a crook, and one night he
and Our Lady of the Flowers stole a cardboard box from
a parked car. When they opened it, they found it full of

the frightful pieces of a wax dummy that had been dis-
assembled.

The cops were putting on their overcoats. They didn't
answer. The roses on the mantelpiece were lovely, heavy,
and excessively fragrant. This further unsteadied the detectives. The murder was fake or unfinished. They had
come looking for dope. Dope . . . laboratories set up in
garret rooms . . . which explode . . . wreckage . . . Does
that mean cocaine is dangerous? They took the two young
men to the Vice Squad, and that same evening they went
back with the Commissioner to make a search that yielded
three hundred grams of cocaine. Which did not mean they
left the kid and Our Lady in peace. The detectives did all
they could to get as much information out of them as
possible. They fired questions at them, searched through
the darkness to unravel a few threads that might lead to
other seizures. They subjected them to modern torture:
kicks in the belly, slaps, rulers in the ribs, and various
other games, first one· and then the other.

"Confess!" they screamed.

Finally, Our Lady rolled under a table. Wild with rage,
a detective dashed at him, but a second detective held
him back by the arm, mumbled something to him, and
then said aloud:

"Let him go, come on, Gaubert. After all, he hasn't
committed a crime."

"Him, with that baby-doll mug of his? He's capable of
it, all right."

Trembling with fear, Our Lady came out from under
the table. They made him sit down on a chair. After all,
it was only a cocaine offense, and in the adjoining room
the other kid was being treated less roughly. The officer
who had stopped the game of massacre remained alone
with Our Lady. He sat down and offered him a cigarette.

"Tell me what you know. No great harm done. Just a

couple of grams of dope. You're not going to get the guillotine."

It will be very difficult for me to explain precisely and describe minutely what took place inside Our Lady of the Flowers. It is hardly possible to speak in this connection of gratitude toward the more soft-spoken of the detectives. The easing of the strain that Our Lady felt as a result of the phrase "There's not much harm done"—no, it's not quite that. The detective said:

"The thing that got him sore was your dummy."

He laughed and inhaled a mouthful of smoke. Gargled it. Did Our Lady *fear* a lesser punishment? First, there came from his liver, right up against his teeth, the confession of the old man's murder. He didn't make the confession. But the confession was rising, rising. If he opens his mouth, he'll blurt it all out. He felt he was lost. Suddenly he gets dizzy. He sees himself on the pediment of a not very high temple. "I'm eighteen. I can be sentenced to death," he thinks very quickly. If he loosens his fingers, he falls. Come, he pulls himself together. No, he won't say anything. It would be magnificent to say it, it would be glorious. No, no, no! Lord, no!

Ah! he's saved. The confession withdraws, withdraws without having crossed.

"I killed an old man."

Our Lady has fallen from the pediment of the temple, and instantly slack despair lulls him to sleep. He is rested The detective has hardly moved.

"Who, what old man?"

Our Lady comes back to life. He laughs.

"No, I'm kidding. I was joking."

With dizzying speed he concocts the following alibi: a murderer confesses spontaneously and in a idiotic way, with impossible details, to a murder so that they'll think he's crazy and stop suspecting him. Wasted effort. They start torturing him again. There's no use screaming that he was only joking. The detectives want to know. Our Lady knows that they will know, and because he's young, he thrashes about. He is a drowning man who is struggling against his gestures and upon whom, nevertheless, peace —you know, the peace of the drowned—slowly descends. The detectives are now mentioning the names of all men murdered during the last five or ten years whose murderers have not been caught. The list lengthens. Our Lady has the needless revelation of the extraordinary ignorance of the police. The violent deaths unroll before his eyes. The detectives mention names, more names, and whack him. Finally, they're on the verge of saying to Our Lady: "Maybe you don't know his name?" Not yet. They mention names and stare at the child's red face. It's a game. The guessing game. Am I getting warm? Ragon? . . . His face is too upset to be able to express anything comprehensible. It's all in disorder. Our Lady screams:

"Yes, yes, it's him. Leave me alone."

His hair is in his eyes. He tosses it back with a jerk of his head, and this simple gesture, which was his rarest precosity, signifies to him the vanity of the world. He wipes away some of the drool that is flowing from his mouth. Everything grows so calm that no one knows what to do.

Overnight, the name of Our Lady of the Flowers was known throughout France, and France is used to confusion. Those who merely skim the newspapers did not linger over Our Lady of the Flowers. Those who go all the way to the end of the articles, scenting the unusual and tracking it down there every time, brought to light a miraculous haul; these readers were school-children and the little old women who, out in the provinces, have remained like Ernestine, who was born old, like Jewish children who at the age of four have the faces and gestures they will have at fifty. It was indeed for her, to enchant her twilight, that Our Lady had killed an old man. Ever since she had started making up fatal tales, or stories that seemed flat and trivial, but in which certain explosive words ripped the canvas, showing, through these gashes, a bit of what went on, as it were, behind the scenes, people were staggered when they realized why she had talked that way. Her mouth was full of stories, and people wondered how they could be born of her, who every evening read only a dull newspaper: the stories were born of the newspaper, as mine are born of cheap novels. She used to stand behind the window, waiting for the postman. As the time for the mail approached, her anguish would heighten, and when finally she touched the gray, porous pages that oozed with the blood of tragedies (the blood whose smell she confused with the smell of the ink and paper), when she unfolded them on her knees like a napkin, she would sink back exhausted, utterly exhausted, in an old red armchair.

A village priest, hearing the name of Our Lady of the Flowers float about him, without having received a pastoral letter concerning the matter, one Sunday, from the pulpit, ordered prayers and recommended this new cult to the particular devotion of the faithful. The faithful, sitting in their pews, quite startled, said not a word, thought not a thought.

In a hamlet, the name of the flower known as "queen of the fields" made a little girl who was thinking of Our Lady of the Flowers ask:

"Mommy, is she someone who had a miracle?"

There were other miracles that I haven't time to report.

The taciturn and feverish traveler who arrives in a city does not fail to go straight to the dives, the red-light districts, the brothels. He is guided by a mysterious sense that alerts him to the call of hidden love, or perhaps by the bearing of, the direction taken by, certain habitués, whom he recognizes by sympathetic signs, by passwords exchanged between their subconscious minds, and whom he follows on trust. In like manner, Ernestine went straight to the tiny lines of the short crime items, which are—the murders, robberies, rapes, armed assaults—the "Barrios Chinos" of the newspapers. She dreamed about them. Their concise violence, their precision left the dream neither time nor space to filter in: they floored her. They broke upon her brutally, in vivid, resounding colors: red hands placed on a dancer's face, green faces, blue eyelids. When this tidal wave subsided, she would read all the titles of the musical selections listed in the radio column, but she would never have allowed a musical air to enter her room, for the slightest melody corrodes poetry. Thus, the newspapers were disturbing, as if they had been filled only with columns of crime news, columns as bloody and mutilated as torture stakes. And though the press has very parsimoniously given to the trial, which we shall read about tomorrow, only ten lines, widely enough spaced to let the air circulate between the overviolent words, these ten lines—more hypnotic than the fly of a hanged man, than the words "hempen collar," than the word "Zouave" —these ten lines quickened the hearts of the old women and jealous children. Paris did not sleep. She hoped that the following day Our Lady would be sentenced to death; she desired it.

In the morning, the sweepers, impervious to the sweet, sad absences of those sentenced to death, whether dead or not, to whom the Criminal Court gives asylum, stirred up acrid dust, watered the floor, spat, blasphemed, and joked with the court clerks who were setting out the files. The hearing was to begin at exactly twelve forty-five, and at noon the porter opened the doors wide.

The courtroom is not majestic, but it is very high, so that it gives a general impression of vertical lines, like lines of quiet rain. Upon entering, one sees on the wall a big painting with a figure of justice, who is a woman, wearing big red drapings. She is leaning with all her weight upon a saber, here called a "glaive," which does not bend. Below are the platform and table where the jurors and the presiding judge, in ermine and red robe, will come to sit in judgment on the child. The name of the presiding judge is "Mr. Presiding Judge Vase de Sainte-Marie." Once again, to attain its ends, destiny resorts to a low method. The twelve jurors are twelve decent men suddenly become sovereign judges. So, the courtroom had been filling up since noon. A banquet hall. The table was set. I should like to speak sympathetically about the courtroom crowd, not because it was not hostile to Our Lady of the Flowers—I don't mind that—but because it is sparkling with a thousand poetic gestures. It is as shuddering as taffeta. At the edge of a gulf bristling with bayonets, Our Lady is dancing a perilous dance. The crowd is not gay; its soul is sad unto death. It huddled together on the benches, drew its knees and buttocks together, wiped its collective nose, and attended to the hundred needs of a courtroom crowd that is going to be weighed down by so much majesty. The public comes here only insofar as a word may result in a beheading and as it may return, like Saint Denis, carrying its severed head in its hands. It is sometimes said that death hovers over a people. Do you remember the skinny, consumptive Italian woman that it was for Culafroy, and what it will later be for Divine? Here death is only a black wing without a body, a wing made with some remnants of black bunting and supported by a thin framework of umbrella ribs, a pirate banner without a staff. This wing of bunting floated over the Court, which you are not to confuse with any other, for it is the Court of Law. The wing enveloped it in its folds and had detailed a green crepe de Chine tie to represent It in the courtroom. The tie, which lay on the Judge's table, was the only piece of evidence. Death, visible here, was a tie, and this fact pleases me: it was a light Death.

The crowd was ashamed of not being the murderer. The robed lawyers were carrying briefs under their arms and smiled as they greeted each other. They occasionally approached the Little Death quite closely and most pluckily.

The newspapermen were with the lawyers. The delegates of the Church Youth Centers were speaking in whispers among themselves. They were disputing a soul. Was it necessary to throw dice for it in order to send it to the Vosges? The lawyers, who, despite their long silken robes, do not have the gentle and death-driven bearing of ecclesiastics, kept coming together in little groups and then breaking up. They were very near the platform, and the crowd could hear them tuning up their instruments for the funeral march. The crowd was ashamed of not dying. The religion of the hour was to await and envy a young murderer. The murderer entered. All one could see was strapping Republican Guards. The child emerged from the flanks of one of them, and the other unchained his wrists. Reporters have described the movements of the crowd when a famous criminal enters. I therefore refer the reader, if I may, to their articles, as my role and my art do not lie in describing mob behavior. Nevertheless, I shall make so bold as to say that all eyes could read, graven in the aura of Our Lady of the Flowers, the following words: "I am the Immaculate Conception." The lack of light and air in his cell had made him neither too pale nor too puffy; the lines of his closed lips were the lines of a sober smile; his clear eyes knew nothing of Hell; his entire face (but perhaps he stood before you like the prison, which, as that woman walked by singing in the darkness, remained for her an evil wall, whereas all the cells were secretly taking flight, flown by the hands, which were beating like wings, of the convicts who were electrified by the singing), his image and his gestures released captive demons or, with several turns ot a key, locked in angels of light. He was wearing a very youthful, gray flannel suit, and the collar of his blue shirt was open. His blond hair kept falling over his eyes, you recall the toss of the head with which he drove it back. Thus, when he had everyone in front of him, Our Lady, the murderer, who in a little while would be dead, murdered in turn, tossed his head slightly, while blinking his eyes, which made his curly lock, that fell close to his nose, bound back to his head. This simple scene transports us, that is, it lifts up the moment, as the fakir's oblivion to the world lifts him up and holds him suspended. The moment was no longer of the earth, but of the sky. Everything gave grounds for fear that the hearing might be chopped up into those cruel moments that would pull away trap doors from under the feet of the judges, lawyers, Our Lady, and the guards, and, for an eternity, would leave them lifted up as fakirs, until the moment when slightly too deep a breath would restore the suspended life.

The guard of honor (members of the colonial troops) entered noisily with their hobnailed boots and rattling bayonets. Our Lady thought it was the firing squad.

Have I mentioned the fact that the audience was made up mostly of men? But all of them, darkly dressed, with umbrellas on their arms and newspapers in their pockets, were shakier than a bower of wisteria, than the lace curtain of a crib. Our Lady of the Flowers was the reason why the courtroom, all invaded by a grotesque, dressed-up crowd, was a May hedgerow. The murderer was sitting on the criminal's bench. The removal of the chains enabled him to put his hands deep into his pockets. Thus he seemed to be anywhere, that is, rather in the waiting room of an employment bureau, or on a park bench, watching from afar a Punch and Judy show in a kiosk, or perhaps even in church, at Thursday catechism. I swear he was waiting for anything. At a certain moment, he took one hand out of his pocket and, as a while before, flicked back, with, at the same time, a toss of his pretty little head, the blond curly lock. The crowd stopped breathing. He completed his gesture by smoothing back his hair, down to the nape of the neck, and I am thereby reminded of a strange impression: when, in a person who has been dehumanized by glory, we discern a familiar gesture, a vulgar feature (there you have it: tossing back a lock of hair with a jerk of the head) that breaks the hardened crust, and through the crevice, which is as lovely as a smile or an error, we glimpse a patch of sky. I had once noted this in the case of one of Our Lady's thousand forerunners, an annunciatory angel of this virgin, a blond young boy ("Girls blond as boys . . . " I shall, indeed, never weary of this phrase, which has the charm of the expression: "a French guardswoman") whom I used to watch in gymnasium groups. He depended upon the figures that he helped to form and, thus, was only a sign. But whenever he had to place one knee on the floor and, like a knight at a coronation, extend his arms at the word of command, his hair would fall over his eyes and he would break the harmony of the gymnastic figure by pushing it back, against his temples, and then behind his ears, which were small, with a gesture that described a curve with both his hands, which, for an instant, enclosed, and pressed like a diadem, his oblong skull. It would have been the gesture of a nun pushing aside her veil, if at the same time he had not shaken his head like a bird preening itself after drinking.

It was also this discovery of the man in the god that once made Culafroy love Alberto for his cowardice. Alberto's left eye had been gouged out. In a village, an event of this kind is no small matter. After the poem (or fable) that was born of it (recurring miracle of Anne Boleyn: from the steaming blood sprang a bush of roses, that might have been white, but were certainly fragrant), the necessary sifting was done in order to disengage the truth scattered beneath the marble. It then became apparent that Alberto had been unable to avoid a quarrel with his rival over his girl friend. He had been cowardly, as always, as the whole village knew him to be, and this had given victorious promptness to his opponent. With a stab of his knife, he had put out Alberto's eye. All Culafroy's love swelled up, as it were, when he learned of the accident. It swelled with grief, with heroism, and with maternal tenderness. He loved Alberto for his cowardice. Compared to this monstrous vice, the others were pale and inoffensive and could be counterbalanced by any other virtue, particularly by the most beautiful. I use the popular word in the popular sense, which is so becoming to it and which implies the fullest recognition of the bodily powers: guts. For we may say of a man who is full of vices: All is not lost so long as he doesn't have "that one." But Alberto did have *that* one. So it made no difference whether he had all the others; the infamy would have been none the greater. All is not lost so long as valor remains, and it was valor that Alberto had just lacked. As for suppressing this vice— for example, by pure and simple negation—that was out of the question, but it was easy to destroy its belittling effect by loving Alberto for his cowardice. Though his downfall, which was certain, did not embellish him, it poetized him. Perhaps Culafroy drew closer to him because of it. Alberto's courage would not have surprised him, nor left him indifferent, but now, instead, he was discovering another Alberto, one who was more man than god. He was discovering the flesh. The statue was crying. Here, the word "cowardice" cannot have the moral—or immoral—

sense usually ascribed to it, and Culafroy's taste for a
handsome, strong, and cowardly young man is not a fault
or aberration. Culafroy now saw Alberto prostrate, with a
dagger stuck into his eye. Would he die of the wound?
This idea made him think of the decorative role of widows,
who wear long crepe trains and dab their eyes with little
white handkerchiefs rolled up as tight as snowballs. He
no longer thought of anything but observing the external
signs of his grief, but as he could not make it visible to
people's eyes, he had to transport it into himself, as Saint
Catherine of Siena transported her cell. The country folk
were confronted with the spectacle of a child who trailed
behind him a display of ceremonial mourning weeds; they
did not recognize it. They did not understand the meaning of the slowness of his walk, the bowing of his forehead, and the emptiness of his gaze. To them it was all
simply a matter of poses dictated by the pride of being
the child of the slate house.

Alberto was taken to the hospital, where he died; the
village was exorcised.

Our Lady of the Flowers. His mouth was slightly open.
Occasionally he would shift his eyes to his feet, which the
crowd hoped were wearing selvaged slippers. At the drop
of a hat they expected to see him make a dance movement. The court clerks were still fussing with the records.
On the table, the lithe little Death lay inert and looked
quite dead. The bayonets and the heels were sparkling.

"The Court!"

The Court entered by a door that was cut out of the
wallpaper behind the jurors' table. Our Lady, however,
having heard in prison of the ceremoniousness of the
Court, imagined that today, by a kind of grandiose error,
it would enter by the great public door which opened in
the middle, just as, on Palm Sunday, the clergy, who usually leave the sacristy by a side door near the choir, sur-

prise the faithful by appearing from behind them. The Court entered, with the familiar majesty of princes, by a service door. Our Lady had a foreboding that the whole session would be faked and that at the end of the performance his head would be cut off by means of a mirror trick. One of the guards shook his arm and said:

"Stand up."

He had wanted to say: "Please, stand up," but he didn't dare. The audience was standing in silence. It sat down again noisily. M. Vase de Sainte-Marie was wearing a monocle. He looked shiftily at the tie and, with both hands, fumbled about in the file. The file was as crammed with details as the chamber of the examining magistrate was crammed with files. Facing Our Lady, the prosecuting attorney did not let out a peep. He felt that a word from him, a too commonplace gesture, would transform him into the devil's advocate and would justify canonization of the murderer. It was a difficult moment to endure; he was risking his reputation. Our Lady was seated. A slight movement of M. Vase de Sainte-Marie's fine hand brought him to his feet.

The questioning began:

"Your name is Adrien Baillon?"

"Yes, sir."

"You were born on December 19, 1920?"

"Yes, sir."

"In . . . ?"

"In Paris."

"Very well. Which district?"

"The eighteenth, sir."

"Very well. Your . . . er-acquaintances gave you a nickname . . . (He hesitated; then:) Would you mind telling it to the Court?"

The murderer made no answer, but the name, without being uttered, emerged through the forehead, all winged, from the brain of the crowd. It floated over the courtroom, invisible, fragrant, secret, mysterious.

The judge replied aloud:

"Yes, that's right. And you are the son of . . . ?"

"Lucie Baillon."

"And an unknown father. Yes. The accusation . . ." (Here the jurors—there were twelve of them—took a comfortable position, which, though suiting each of them individually because it favored a certain propensity, was consistent with each one's dignity. Our Lady was still standing, with his arms dangling at his sides, like those of that bored and delighted little king who from the stairway of the royal palace witnesses a military parade.)

The judge continued:

". . . on the night of July 7 to 8, 1937, entered, and no trace has been found of forced entry, into the apartment situated on the fifth floor of the building located at number 12 Rue de Vaugirard and occupied by M. Paul Ragon, sixty-seven years of age."

He raised his head and looked at Our Lady:

"Do you acknowledge the facts?"

"Yes, sir."

"The investigation specifies that it was M. Ragon himself who opened the door for you. At least, that is what you have stated without being able to prove it. Do you still maintain it?"

"Yes, sir."

"Then, it appears that M. Ragon, who knew you, seemed delighted with your visit and offered you liquor. Then, without his expecting it, with the help . . . (he hesitated) . . . of this tie, you strangled him."

The judge took the tie.

"Do you recognize this tie as belonging to you and as being the instrument of the crime?"

"Yes, sir."

The judge had the soft tie in his fingers, a tie like a piece of ectoplasm, a tie that had to be looked at while there was still time, for it might disappear at any moment or stiffen in the dry hand of the judge, who felt that if it did actually become erect or disappear, he would be covered with ridicule. He therefore hastened to pass the instrument of the crime to the first juror, who passed it to his neighbor, and so on, without anyone's daring to linger over recognizing it, for each of them seemed to be running the risk of being metamorphosed before his own eyes into a Spanish dancer. But the precautions of these gentlemen were futile, and though they were not aware of it, they were thoroughly changed. The guilty gestures of the jurors, seemingly in connivance with the destiny that governed the murder of the old man, and the murderer, who was as motionless as a mediumistic subject who is being questioned, and who, by virtue of such immobility, is absent, and the place of this absence, all these darkened the courtroom where the crowd wanted to see clearly. The judge droned on and on. He had reached the following point:

"And who gave you the idea of this method of committing murder?"

"Him."

The entire world understood that Him was the dead man, who was now replaying a role, he who had been buried and devoured by worms and larvae.

"The victim?"

The judge started shouting frightfully:

"It was the victim himself who showed you how you were to go about getting rid of him? Come, come now, explain what you mean."

Our Lady seemed embarrassed. A gentle modesty prevented him from speaking. Shyness too.

"Yes. You see . . . M. Ragon was wearing a tie that was too tight. He was all red. So he took it off."

And the murderer very gently, as if he were consenting to an infamous deal or a charitable action, admitted:

"So I thought that if I tightened it, it'd be worse."

And a little lower still, barely loud enough for the guards and the judge (but it was lost on the crowd):

" 'Cause I got good arms."

The judge, overwhelmed, lowered his head:

"You wretch!" he cried. "Why?"

"I was fabulously broke."

Since the word "fabulous" is used to qualify a fortune, it did not seem impossible to apply it to destitution. And this fabulous impecuniousness made for Our Lady a pedestal of cloud; he was as prodigiously glorious as the body of Christ rising aloft, to dwell there alone and fixed, in the sunny noonday sky. The judge was twisting his beautiful hands. The crowd was twisting its faces. The clerks were crumpling sheets of carbon paper. The eyes of the lawyers suddenly looked like those of extra-lucid chickens. The guards were officiating. Poetry was kneading its matter. Alone, Our Lady was alone and kept his dignity, that is, he still belonged to a primitive mythology and was unaware of his divinity and his divinization. The rest of the world knew not what to think and made superhuman efforts not to be carried off from the shore. Their hands, the nails of which had been ripped away, clung to any safety plank: crossing and uncrossing their legs, staring at stains on their jackets, thinking of the family of the strangled man, picking their teeth.

"Now explain to the court how you proceeded."

It was awful. Our Lady had to explain. The police had demanded details, so had the examining magistrate, and now it was the court's turn. Our Lady was ashamed, not of his deed (that was impossible), but of continually repeating the same old story. He was so tired of ending his account with the words: "Until he was done for," that he boldly thought of giving a new version. He decided to relate something else. Yet, at the same time, he related exactly the story he had told in the very same words to the detectives, the judge, the lawyer, and the psychiatrists. For, to Our Lady, a gesture is a poem and can be expressed only with the help of a symbol which is always, always the same. And all that remained with him of his two-year-old act was the bare expression. He was rereading his crime as a chronicle is reread, but it was no longer really about the crime that he was talking. Meanwhile, the clock on the wall opposite him was behaving in orderly fashion, but time was out of order, with the result that, every second, the clock ticked off long periods and short ones.

Of the twelve good old men and true of the jury, four were wearing spectacles. These four were cut off from communion with the courtroom, glass being a bad conductor—it insulates—and they followed, elsewhere, other adventures. In fact, none of them seemed interested in this murder case. One of the old men kept sleeking his beard; he was the only one who appeared to be attentive, but, looking at him more closely, we see that his eyes are hollow, like those of statues. Another was made of cloth. Another was drawing circles and stars on the green table cover; in daily life he was a painter, and his sense of humor led him at times to color pert little sparrows perched on a garden scarecrow. Another was spitting all his teeth into his pale blue—France blue—handkerchief. They stood up and followed the judge through the small hidden door. The deliberations are as secret as the election of a chief of masked bandits, as the execution of a traitor within a confraternity. The crowd relieved itself by yawn-

ing, stretching, and belching. Our Lady's lawyer left his
bench and walked over to his client.

"Keep your chin up, my boy," he said, squeezing Our
Lady's hands. "You answered very well. You were frank. I
think the jury is with us."

As he spoke, he squeezed Our Lady's hands, supported
him or clung to him. Our Lady smiled. It was a smile that
was enough to damn his judges, a smile so azure that the
guards themselves had an intuition of the existence of God
and of the great principles of geometry. Think of the
moonlight tinkling of the toad; at night it is so pure that
the vagabond on the highway stops and does not go on
until he has heard it again.

"They putting up a fight?" he asked, winking.

"Yes, yes, it's all right," said the lawyer.

The guard of honor presented arms, and the unhooded
Court emerged from the wall. M. Vase de Sainte-Marie sat
down in silence; then everyone sat down very noisily. The
judge placed his head between his beautiful white hands
and said:

"We shall now hear the witnesses. Oh! first let's look at
the police report. Are the inspectors here?"

It is extraordinary that a presiding judge should be so
absentminded as to forget so serious a thing. Our Lady
was shocked by his mistake, just as he would have been
shocked by a spelling mistake (had he known how to
spell) in the prison regulations. A clerk ushered in the two
detectives who had arrested Our Lady. The one who had
formerly carried on the now two-year-old investigation
was dead. They therefore gave a succinct report of the
facts: an astounding story in which a fake murder led to
the discovery of a real one. This discovery is impossible,
I'm dreaming. "All because of a trifle!" But, after all, I admit this amusing discovery, which leads to death, a little
more readily ever since the guard took away the manu-

script I had in my pocket during recreation. I have a feeling of catastrophe; then I dare not believe that a catastrophe of this kind can be the logical outcome of such slight carelessness. Then I think of the fact that criminals lose their heads because of such slight carelessness, so slight that one should have the right to repair it by backing up, that it's so trifling that if one asked the judge, he would consent, and that one cannot. Despite their training, which they say is Cartesian, the members of the jury will be unable, when, in a few hours, they condemn Our Lady to death, to figure out whether they did so because he strangled a doll or because he cut up a little old man into pieces. The detectives, instigators of anarchism, withdrew with a pretty kowtow to the judge. Outside, snow was falling. This could be guessed from the movement of the hands in the courtroom, which were turning up coat collars. The weather was overcast. Death was advancing stealthily over the snow. A clerk called the witnesses. They were waiting in a little side room, the door of which opened opposite the prisoner's box. The door opened, each time, just enough to let them edge through sideways, and one by one, drop by drop, they were infused into the trial. They went straight to the bar, where each raised his right hand and replied "I so swear" to a question no one asked. Our Lady saw Mimosa II enter. The clerk, however, had called out, "René Hirsch." When he called "Antoine Berthollet," First Communion appeared; at "Eugène Marceau," Lady-apple appeared. Thus, in the eyes of Our bewildered Lady, the little faggots from Pigalle to Place Blanche lost their loveliest adornment, their names lost their corolla, like the paper flower that the dancer holds at his finger tips and which, when the ballet is over, is a mere wire stem. Would it not have been better to have danced the entire dance with a simple wire? The question is worth examining. The faggots showed the framework that

Darling discerned behind the silk and velvet of every armchair. They were reduced to nothing, and that's the best thing that's been done so far. They entered aggressively or shyly, perfumed, made up, expressed themselves with studied care. They were no longer the grove of crinkly paper that flowered on the terraces of cafés. They were misery in motley. (Where do the faggots get their *noms de guerre?* But first it should be noted that none of them were chosen by those who bore them. This, however, does not hold for me. I can hardly give the exact reasons why I chose such and such a name. Divine, First Communion, Mimosa, Our Lady of the Flowers and Milord the Prince did not occur to me by chance. There is a kinship among them, an odor of incense and melting taper, and I sometimes feel as if I had gathered them among the artificial or natural flowers in the chapel of the Virgin Mary, in the month of May, under and about the greedy plaster statue that Alberto was in love with and behind which, as a child, I used to hide the phial containing my spunk.) Some of them uttered a few words that were terrifyingly precise, such as: "He lived at 8 Rue Berthe," or "I met him for the first time on October 17. It was at Graff's Café." A raised pinkie, lifted as if the thumb and forefinger were holding a teacup, disturbed the gravity of the session, and by means of this stray straw could be sensed the tragic nature of its mass. The clerk called out: "M. Louis Culafroy." Supported by Ernestine, who was wearing black and stood bolt upright, the only real woman to be seen at the trial, Divine entered. What remained of her beauty fled in confusion. The lines and shadows deserted their posts; it was a debacle. Her lovely face was uttering heart-rending appeals, howls as tragic as the cries of a dying woman. Divine was wearing a brown, silky camel-hair coat. She too said:

"I so swear."

"What do you know about the accused?" asked the judge.

"I've known him for a long time, your Honor, but nevertheless I can say that I think he's very naïve, very childlike. I've always regarded him as being very sweet. He could be my son."

She went on to tell, with a great deal of tact, how they had lived together for a long time. There was no mention of Darling. Divine was at last the grown-up she had not been allowed to be anywhere else. By God! here he is again, the witness, who has finally emerged from the child Culafroy whom he had never ceased to be. If he never performs any simple act, it is because only a few old men can be simple, that is, pure, purged, simplified as a diagram, which is perhaps the state of being of which Jesus said: ". . . like unto little children" (though no child is ever like that), which a life-long withering labor does not always achieve. Nothing about him was simple, not even his smile, which he liked to draw out with the right corner of his mouth or spread across his face, with his teeth clenched.

The greatness of a man is not only a function of his faculties, of his intelligence, of whatever gifts he may have; it is also made up of the circumstances that have elected him to serve them as support. A man is great if he has a great destiny; but this greatness is of the order of visible, measurable greatness. It is magnificence seen from without. Though it may be wretched when seen from within, it is then poetic, if you are willing to agree that poetry is the break (or rather the meeting at the breaking point) between the visible and the invisible. Culafroy had a wretched destiny, and it is because of this that his life was composed of those secret acts, each of which is in essence a poem, as the infinitesimal movement of the finger of a Balinese dancer is a sign that can set a world in motion because it issues from a world whose multifarious meaning is unavowable. Culafroy became Divine; he was thus a poem written only for himself, hermetic to whoever did not have the key to it. In short, this is his secret glory, like the one I have decreed upon myself so as to obtain peace at last. And I have it, for a fortuneteller in a fair-booth assured me that some day I would be famous. With what sort of fame? I tremble at the thought. But this prophecy is enough to calm my old need for thinking I have genius. I carry within me, preciously, the words of the augury: "Some day you will be famous." I live with it in secret, like families, in the evening, by the lamp, and always, if they have one, with the shining memory of their kinsman who was sentenced to death. It illuminates and horrifies me. This quite virtual fame ennobles me, like a parchment that no one can decipher, an illustrious birth kept secret, a royal bar sinister, a mask or perhaps a divine filiation, the kind of thing Josephine must have felt, she who never forgot that she had given birth to the child who was to become the prettiest woman in the village, Marie, the mother of Solange—the goddess born in a hovel who had more blazons on her body than Mimosa had on her buttocks and in her gestures, and more nobility than a Chambure. This kind of consecration had kept the other women of her age (the others, mothers of men) away from Josephine. In the village, her situation was akin to that of the Mother of Jesus among the women of the Galilean village. Marie's beauty made the town illustrious. To be the human mother of a divinity is a more disturbing state than that of divinity. The Mother of Jesus must have had incomparable emotions while carrying her son, and later, while living and sleeping side by side with a son who was God—that is, everything and herself as well—who could make the world not be, His Mother, Himself not be, a God for whom she had to prepare, as Josephine did for Marie, the yellow corn mush.

Moreover, it was not that Culafroy, as child and Divine, was of exceptional finesse. But exceptionally strange circumstances had chosen him as their place of election, without informing him, had adorned him with a mysterious text. He served a poem in accordance with the whims of a rhyme without rhyme or reason. It was later, at the hour of his death, that, in a single wonder-struck glance, he was able to reread, with his eyes closed, the life he had written upon his flesh. And now Divine emerges from her inner drama, from that core of the tragic which she bears within her, and for the first time in her life is taken seriously in the parade of humans. The prosecuting attorney stopped the parade. The witnesses had left by the open door. Each having appeared for but a second, they burned up as they passed; the unknown whisked them away. The true centers of life were the witness room —a Court of Miracles—and the chamber of the jury. It was there that the room of the foul crime, with all its accessories, was reconstructed. The amazing thing was that the necktie was still there, crouching on the green table, paler than usual, soft, but ready to dart forth, as a slouching hoodlum on the bench in a police station might dart forth. The crowd was as restless as a dog. Someone announced that Death had been delayed by a derailment. It grew dark all at once. Finally, the judge called upon the expert alienist. It was he who, really and truly, sprang up through an invisible trap door of an invisible box. He had been sitting among the audience, which had not suspected him. He stood up and walked to the bar. He read his report to the members of the jury. From the winged report dropped such words as the following: "Unbalanced . . . psychopathy . . . inter-relation . . . splanchnic system . . . schizophrenia . . . unbalanced, unbalanced, unbalanced, unbalanced . . . equilibrist," and all at once, poignant, bleeding, "the sympathetic nerve." He did not pause: ". . . Unbalanced . . . semi-responsibility . . . secretion . . . Freud . . . Jung . . . Adler . . . secretion . . ." But the perfidious voice was caressing certain syllables, and the man's gestures were struggling against enemies: "Father, watch out on the left, on the right." Certain words finally ricocheted on the perfidious voice (as in pig Latin words where you have to unscramble other words that may be naïve or nasty: edbay, oorday). One understood the following: "What is a malefactor? A tie dancing in the moonlight, an epileptic rug, a stairway going up flat on its belly, a dagger on the march since the beginning of the world, a panicky phial of poison, gloved hands in the darkness, a sailor's blue collar, an open succession, a series of benign and simple gestures, a silent hasp." The great psychiatrist finally read his conclusions: "That he (Our Lady of the Flowers) is psychically unbalanced, non-affective, amoral. Yet, that in any criminal act, as in any act, there is an element of volition which is not due to the irritating complicity of things. In short, Baillon is partly responsible for the murder."

Snow was falling. About the courtroom, all was silence. The Criminal Court was abandoned in infinite space, all alone. It had already ceased to obey the laws of the earth. Swiftly it flew across stars and planets. It was, in the air, the stone house of the Holy Virgin. The passengers no longer expected help from the outside world. The moorings had been cut. It was at that moment that the frightened part of the courtroom (the crowd, the jurymen, the lawyers, the guards) should have dropped to their knees and broken out into hymns of praise, when the other part (Our Lady), freed from the weight of carnal labors (to put someone to death is a carnal labor), had organized itself as a couple and sung: "Life is a dream . . . a charming dream . . ." But the crowd does not have the sense of grandeur. It does not obey this dramatic injunction, and nothing was less serious than what followed. Our Lady himself felt his pride softening. He looked at Judge Vase de Sainte-Marie for the first time with the eyes of a man. It is so sweet to love that he could not keep from dissolving into a feeling of sweet, trusting tenderness for the judge. "Maybe he ain't a louse!" he thought, and at once his sweet insensitivity collapsed, and the relief it afforded him was like the release of urine from the penis after a night of continence. Remember that when Darling used to wake up, he would find himself on earth after he had pissed. Our Lady loved his executioner, his first executioner. He was already granting a kind of wavering, premature pardon to the icy monocle, the metallic hair, the earthly mouth, the future sentence delivered according to frightful Scriptures. Exactly what is an executioner? A child dressed as a Fatal Sister, an innocent isolated by the splendor of his purple rags, a poor, a humble fellow. Someone lit the chandeliers and wall lights. The prosecuting attorney took the floor. Against the adolescent murderer, who had been cut out of a block of clear water, he said only things that were very fair, within the scope of the judge and jurors. That is, it was necessary to protect rentiers, who sometimes live all the way upstairs, beneath the roof, and to put to death children who slaughter them. . . . It was all very reasonable, spoken in a very sagacious and at times noble tone. With an accompaniment of his head:

". . . It is regrettable (in a minor key; then, continuing in the major) . . . it is regrettable . . ."

His arm, pointing at the murderer, was obscene.

"Strike hard!" he cried. "Strike hard!"

The prisoners referred to him as "The Blowhard." At that formal session, he illustrated very accurately a poster nailed to a huge door. An old marquise, lost in the darkness of the crowd, thought to herself: "The Republic has already guillotined five of us. . . ." But her thought went no deeper. The tie was still on the table. The jurors still had not got over their fear. It was just about then that the clock struck five. During the indictment, Our Lady had sat down. The courthouse seemed to him to be situated between apartment buildings, at the rear of the kind of well-shaped inner courtyard on which all the kitchen and toilet windows look out, where uncombed housemaids lean forward and, with their hands cupped over their ears, listen and try to miss nothing of the proceedings. Five stories and four faces. The maids are toothless and spy on each other behind them. Through the gloom of the kitchen, one can make out the gold or plush spangles in the mystery of the opulent apartments where ivory-headed old gentlemen watch with tranquil eyes the approach of murderers in slippers. For Our Lady, the courthouse is at the bottom of this well. It is small and light, like the Greek temple that Minerva carries in her open hand. The guard at his left made him stand up, for the judge was questioning him: "What do you have to say in your defense?" The old tramp who was his cellmate in the Santé Prison had prepared a few suitable words for him to say to the Court. He looked for them but was unable to find them. The phrase "I didn't do it on purpose" took shape on his lips. Had he said it, nobody would have been surprised. Everyone expected the worst. All the answers that occurred to him came forward in slang, and a feeling for the proprieties suggested to him that he speak French, but everyone knows that in trying moments it is the mother tongue that prevails. He had to be natural. To be natural, at that moment, was to be theatrical, but his maladroitness saved him from ridicule and lopped off his head. He was truly great. He said:

"The old guy was washed up. He couldn't even get a hard-on."

The last word did not pass his jaunty little lips. Nevertheless, the twelve old men, all together, very quickly put their hands over their ears to prevent the entry of the word that was as big as an organ, which, finding no other orifice, entered all stiff and hot into their gaping mouths. The virility of the twelve old men and of the judge was flouted by the youngster's glorious immodesty. Everything was changed. Those who were Spanish dancers, with castanets on the fingers, became jurors again, the sensitive painter became a juror again, the old man of cloth became a juror again, so did the old grouch, so did the one who was pope and the one who was Vestris. You don't believe me? The audience heaved a sigh of rage. With his beautiful hands the judge made the gesture that tragic actresses make with their lovely arms. Three subtle shudders ruffled his red robe as if it were a theater curtain, as if there clung to the flap, at the calf, the desperate claws of a dying kitten, the muscles of whose paws had been contracted by three little death throes. He nervously ordered Our Lady to behave with decorum, and the lawyer for the defense took the floor. With mincing little steps under his robe (which were really like little farts), he came to the bar and addressed the Court. The Court smiled, that is, with the smile imparted to the face by the austere choice (already made) between the just and the unjust, the royal rigor of the brow that knows the dividing line— that has seen clear and judged—and that condemns. The Court was smiling. The faces were relaxing from the tension; the flesh was softening up again; little pouts were ventured, but, quickly startled, withdrew into their shells. The Court was pleased, quite pleased. The lawyer was doing his utmost. He spoke volubly, his sentences went on and on. One felt that they had been born of lightning

and would peter out in tails of comets. He was mingling
what he said were his childhood memories (of his
own childhood, in which he himself had been tempted by
the devil) with notions of pure law. Despite such contact,
pure law remained pure and, in the gray drool, retained
its hard, crystal brilliance. The lawyer spoke first of being
brought up in the gutter, the example of the street, of
hunger, of thirst (my God, was he going to make of the
child a Father de Foucauld or a Michel Vieuchange?); he
spoke also of the almost carnal temptation of the neck,
which is made the way it is in order to be squeezed. In
short, he was off the track. Our Lady esteemed this elo-
quence. He did not yet believe what the lawyer was saying,
but he was ready to undertake anything, to assume anything. Yet, a feeling of uneasiness, the meaning of which
he understood only later, indicated to him, by obscure
means, that the lawyer was undoing him. The Court was
cursing so mediocre a lawyer, who was not even according
it the satisfaction of overcoming the pity it should normally
have felt while following the speech for the defense. What
game was this idiotic lawyer playing? If only he would
say a word, a trifling or crude word, that would make the
jurors, for at least the space and time of a murderous
leer, be smitten with an adolescent corpse and, thus aveng-
ing the strangled old man, feel that they, in turn, had the
soul of a murderer (sitting comfortably in the warm room,
without any risks, except merely the little Eternal Damnation). Their pleasure was disappearing. Would they have
to acquit because the lawyer was a blockhead? But did
anyone think that this might have been the supreme foxi-
ness of a poet-lawyer? Napoleon is said to have lost Water-
loo because Wellington committed a blunder. The Court
felt that it had to sanctify this young man. The lawyer
was drooling. He was speaking, at the moment, of possible
re-education—in their reserved stall, the four representa-

tives of the Church Youth Centers then played poker dice
to settle the fate of the soul of Our Lady of the Flowers.
The lawyer was asking for an acquittal. He was imploring.
They no longer understood him. Finally, as with a promptness for sensing the one moment in a thousand for saying
the crucial word, Our Lady, gently as always, screwed up
his face and said, though without thinking it:

"Ah no, not the Corrida, it ain't worth it. I'd rather
croak right away."

The lawyer stood there dumbfounded; then quickly,
with a cluck of his tongue, he gathered his scattered wits
and stammered:

"Child, see here, child! Let me defend you."

"Gentlemen," he said to the Court (he might, without
any harm, as to a queen, have said "Madame"), "he's a
child."

At the same time, the judge was saying to Our Lady:

"See here, see here, what are you saying? Let's not rush
matters."

The cruelty of the word stripped the judges and left
them with no other robe than their splendor. The crowd
cleared its throat. The presiding judge did not know that
in slang the Corrida is the reformatory. Sitting motionless
on his wooden bench, squarely and solidly, between his
guards in their yellow leather girths and their boots and
helmets, Our Lady of the Flowers felt himself dancing a
light jig. Despair had shot through him like an arrow,
like a clown through the tissue paper of a hoop; despair
had gone beyond him, and all that remained was the
laceration, which left him there in white rags. Though he
was not intact, he held his ground. The world was no
longer in the room. That's how it should be. It all has to
end. The Court was re-entering. The rapping of the rifle
butts of the guard of honor gave the alarm. Standing bareheaded, the monocle read the verdict. It uttered for the

first time, following the name Baillon, the words: "Known as Our Lady of the Flowers." Our Lady was given the death penalty. The jury was standing. It was the apotheosis. It's all over. When Our Lady of the Flowers was given back to the guards, he seemed to them invested with a sacred character, like the kind that expiatory victims, whether goat, ox, or child, had in olden times and which kings and Jews still have today. The guards spoke to him and served him as if, knowing he was laden with the weight of the sins of the world, they had wanted to bring down upon themselves the benediction of the Redeemer. Forty days later, on a spring evening, the machine was set up in the prison yard. At dawn, it was ready to cut. Our Lady of the Flowers had his head cut off by a real knife. And nothing happened. What would be the point? There is no need for the veil of the temple to be ripped from top to bottom because a god gives up the ghost. All that this can prove is the bad quality of the cloth and its deterioration. Though it behooves me to be indifferent, still I would not mind if an irreverent scapegrace kicked through it and ran off shouting, "A miracle!" Its flashy and would make a very good framework for the Legend.

I have reread the earlier chapters. They are now closed, rigorously, and I note that I have given no smile to Culafroy, Divine, Ernestine, or the others. The sight of a little boy in the visitor's room makes me aware of this and makes me think of my childhood, of the ribbons on my mother's white petticoats. In each child I see—but I see so few—I try to find the child I was, to love him for what I was. But when I saw the minors during the medical examination, I looked at those two little mugs, and I left feeling deeply moved, for that was not what I had been like, too white a child, like an underbaked loaf of bread; it is for the men they will be that I love them. When they passed before me, rolling their hips and with their shoulders erect, I already saw at their shoulder blades the hump of the muscles covering the roots of their wings.

All the same, I would like to think that I was like that one. I saw myself again in his face, especially in his forehead and eyes, and I was about to recognize myself completely when, bang, he smiled. It was no longer I, for in my childhood I could no more laugh, or even smile, than in any other period of my life. When the child laughed, I crumbled, so to speak, before my very eyes.

Like all children, adolescents, or mature men, I smiled readily, I even laughed heartily, but as my life rounded out a cycle, I dramatized it. Eliminating the elements of mischievousness, levity, and prankishness, I have retained only those which are properly tragic: Fear, Despair, unhappy Love . . . and I free myself from them only by declaiming those poems which are as convulsed as the faces of sybils. They leave my soul clarified. But if the child in whom I think I see myself laughs or smiles, he breaks up the drama which had been constructed and which is my past life when I think back to it; he destroys it, falsifies it, at least because he manifests an attitude which the character could not have had; he tears to bits the memory of a harmonious (though painful) life, forces me to see myself becoming another, and on the first drama grafts a second.

DIVINARIANA *(conclusion)*

So here are the last Divinariana. I'm in a hurry to get rid of Divine. I toss off helter-skelter, at random, the following notes, in which you, by unscrambling them, will try to find the essential form of the Saint.

Divine, in thought, pushes mimicry to the point of assuming the exact posture that Darling had assumed in that very spot. Thus, her head is in place of Darling's head, her mouth in place of his mouth, her member in place of his, etc., then she repeats, as exactly as possible—hesitantly, for it must be done with studied refinement (refinement alone, by its difficulty, makes one aware of the game)—the gestures that were Darling's gestures. She occupies, successively, all the space he occupied. She follows him, fills continually all that contained him.

Divine:
"My life? I'm desolate, I'm a Valley of Desolation."
And it is a valley similar—with pines black beneath the storm—to the landscapes I have discovered during my imaginary adventures beneath the brown, lice-infested blankets of prisons everywhere and which I called Valley of Desolation, of Consolation, Vale of Angels.

She (Divine) did not act, perhaps, in accordance with Christ. She was reproached for this. But she: "Does Lifar dance home from the Opera?"

Her detachment from the world is such that she says: "What does it matter to me what X... thinks of the Divine I was? What do I care about the memory he has of me? I am another. Each time I will be another." Thus, she fought against vanity. Thus, she was always ready for some new infamy, without feeling the fear of opprobrium.

She cut off her lashes so as to be even more repulsive. Thinking she is thus burning her boats.
She lost her mannerisms. She managed to attract attention by dint of discretion. Freezing her face. Formerly, when insulted, she could not keep from twitching her

muscles. Anguish drove her to that so that it might be slightly beguiled; the puckering of her face produced a grimace in the form of a smile. Frozen, her face.

Divine, of herself: "Lady of High Pansiness."

Divine could not bear hearing on the radio, the *March from the Zauberflöte*. She kisses her fingers, and then, unable to bear it any longer, she turns the dial.

Her pale, celestial voice (a voice I would like to imagine being that of movie actors, a voice of an image, a flat voice) telling me, as she pointed to my ear:

"But Jean, you've got another hole there."

She strolls in the street. She is spectral. A young cyclist walks by, holding his machine by the handlebar.

Quite near, Divine makes an airy gesture (with arm rounded) of enlacing him about the waist. The cyclist suddenly turns to Divine, who finds herself actually enlacing him. He looks at her for a fraction of a second, astounded, says not a word, jumps on his bike, and flees.

Divine retreats into her shell and regains her inner heaven.

In the presence of another handsome young man, a brief desire:

"It's the Again that has clutched me by the throat."

She will go on living only to hasten toward Death.

The swan, borne up by its mass of white feathers, *cannot* go to the bottom of the water to find mud, nor *can* Jesus sin.

For Divine, to commit a crime in order to free oneself from the yoke of the moral powers is still to be tied up with the moral. She will have nothing to do with a fine crime. She sings that she is buggered out of taste.

She robs and betrays her friends.

Everything concurs to establish about her—despite her —solitude. She lives simply in the privacy of her glory, of the glory she has made tiny and precious.

"I am," she says, "Bernadette Soubiroux in the Convent of Charity long after her vision. Like me, she lived an ordinary life with the memory of having spoken familiarly with the Holy Virgin."

At times a regiment goes into the desert and—for purposes of tactics—a small column of men detaches itself and goes off in a different direction. The fragment may advance thus for some time, quite near the regiment, for an hour or more. The men of the two sections could speak together, see one another, and they do not speak together, they do not see one another: no sooner did the detachment take a step in the new direction than it felt a personality being born to it. It knew that it was alone and that its actions were its action.

Divine has repeated a hundred times that little gesture for detaching herself from the world. But, however far she may depart from it, the world calls her back.

She has spent her life hurling herself from the top of a rock.

Now that she no longer has a body (or she has so little left, a little that is whitish, pale, bony, and at the same time very flabby), she slips off to heaven.

Divine, of herself:
"Madame née Secret."

The saintliness of Divine.
Unlike most saints, Divine had knowledge of it. There

is nothing surprising in this, since saintliness was her vision
of God and, higher still, her union with Him. This union
did not occur without difficulty (pain) on both sides. On
Divine's side, the difficulty was due to her having to give
up a stable, familiar, and comfortable situation for too
wondrous a glory. To retain her position, she did what
she thought fitting: she made gestures. Her whole body
was then seized with a frenzy to remain behind. She made
some gestures of frightful despair, other gestures of hesitation, of timid attempts to find the right way, to cling to
earth and not rise to heaven. This last sentence seems to
imply that Divine made an ascension. That is not so. Rising to heaven here means: without moving, to leave Divine for the Divinity. The miracle, occurring in privacy,
would have been ferocious in its horror. She had to stand
her ground, whatever the cost. Had to hold her own
against God, Who was summoning her in silence. Had to
keep from answering. But had to attempt the gestures that
will keep her on earth, that would replant her firmly in
matter. In space, she kept devising new and barbaric
forms for herself, for she sensed intuitively that immobility makes it too easy for God to get you in a good
wrestling hold and carry you off. So she danced. While
walking. Everywhere. Her body was always manifesting
itself. Manifesting a thousand bodies. Nobody was aware
of what was going on and of Divine's tragic moments as
she struggled against God. She assumed poses as astounding as those of certain Japanese acrobats. You might have
taken her for some mad tragic actress who, unable to re-
enter her own personality, keeps trying, trying. . . . Finally,
one day, when she wasn't expecting it, as she lay still in
bed, God took her and made her a saint. Let us mention,
however, a characteristic event. She wanted to kill herself.
To kill herself. To kill my kindness. The following brilliant
idea therefore occurred to her, and she carried it out: her

balcony, which was on the ninth floor of an apartment house, looked down on a paved court. The iron railing was latticed, but across it was stretched a wire netting. One of her neighbors had a two-year-old baby girl to whom Divine used to give candy and who occasionally came to visit her. The child would run to the balcony and look at the street through the netting. One day, Divine made up her mind: she detached the netting and left it leaning against the railing. When the little girl came to see her, she locked her in and ran downstairs. When she got to the yard, she waited for the child to go and play on the balcony and lean against the railing. The weight of her body made her fall into the void. From below, Divine watched. None of the child's pirouettes was lost on her. She was superhuman, to the point of—without tears or cries or shudders—gathering with her gloved fingers what remained of the child. She was given three months of preventive custody for involuntary manslaughter, but her goodness was dead. For: "What good would it do me to be a thousand times good now? How could this inexpiable crime ever be redeemed? So, let us be bad."

Indifferent, so it seemed, to the rest of the world, Divine was dying.

For a long time, Ernestine did not know what had become of her son, whom she had lost sight of when he ran away a second time. When she finally did hear from him, he was a soldier. She received a somewhat sheepish letter asking her for a little money. But she did not see her son, who had become Divine, until quite some time later, in Paris, where she had gone for an operation, as do all women from the provinces. Divine was then living in rather grand style. Ernestine, who knew nothing about her vice, guessed it almost instantly and thought to herself, "Lou's got an El Dorado between his buttocks." She made no comment to him. It hardly affected her opinion of her-

self to know that she had brought forth a monstrous creature, neither male nor female, scion or scioness of the
Picquignys, ambiguous issue of a great family, of which
the siren Melusina was mother. Mother and son were as
remote as if they had been at a distance, looking into
emptiness: a grazing of insensitive skins. Ernestine never
said to herself, "He is flesh of my flesh." Divine never said
to herself, "All the same, she's the one who spawned me."
But Divine was, for her mother, a pretext for theatrical
gestures, as we showed at the beginning. Divine, out of
hatred of that bitch of a Mimosa, who detested her
mother, pretended to herself to love and respect her own.
This respect pleased Darling, who, like a good pimp, like
a real bad boy, had, deep down in his heart, as they say,
"a little spot of purity dedicated to an old mama" whom
he did not know. He obeyed the earthly injunctions that
govern pimps. He loved his mother, just as he was a pa-
triot and a Catholic. Ernestine came to see Divine die. She
brought some sweets, but, by signs that country women
recognize—signs that tell more surely than crape—she
had known that Divine was leaving.

"He's going away," she said to herself.

The priest—the same one we saw officiating so oddly—
brought the Holy Sacrament. A candle was burning on the
little tea table, near a black crucifix and a bowl of holy
water in which a dry, dusty little branch of box holly was
soaking.

Usually, Ernestine accepted in religion only what was
most *purely* marvelous in it (not the mystery that is added
to the mystery and conceals it); the marvelous that she
found in it was as sound as sterling. Judge from the following: knowing that lightning has a fancy for entering
by the chimney and leaving by the window, she, from her
armchair, would watch herself go through the window-
panes, retaining—including her bust, neck, legs, and skirts

—the stiffness, the coagulation of a starched cloth, and falling on the lawn or rising to the sky, with her heels together, as if she were a statue. Thus, she would fall downward or upward, the way we see saints and angels flying in old paintings, the way Jesus goes straight to heaven, without being carried by clouds.

That was her religion. As at other times, the days of big flush and gush, days of mystic debauch, she would say to herself: "Suppose I played at believing in God?" She would do it until she trembled.

At the hour of Divine's death, she played so well at believing in God that she couldn't help having a bit of a transport.

She saw God gulping down an egg. "To see" is here a casual way of speaking. Regarding revelation, there is not much I can say, for all I know of it is what was granted me to know, thanks to God, in a Yugoslav prison. I had been taken from town to town, depending on where the police van stopped. I would stay a day or two, sometimes longer, in each of the town prisons. Finally I arrived and was locked up in a rather large room with about twenty other prisoners. Three gypsies had organized a school for pickpockets there. It worked as follows: while one of the prisoners lay sleeping on his bunk, each of us, in turn, had to remove from his pockets—and put back without waking him—the objects that were already there. It was delicate work, for we often had to tickle the sleeper in a certain way so that he would turn in his sleep and free the pocket on which he was lying with the full weight of his thighs.

When it was my turn to operate, the head gypsy called me and ordered me to go to work. Beneath the cloth of the jacket, I felt my heart beating, and I fainted. I was carried to my bunk and was left there until I came to. I still have a very exact memory of the arrangement of the theater. The cell was a kind of passageway that left just enough room for the sloping wooden bunks that lined the walls. At one of the ends, opposite the door, was a slightly arched skylight which was fortified with bars. The yellow light that filtered in from a sky invisible to us was falling obliquely, exactly the way it is shown in prints and novels.

When I regained consciousness, I was in the corner near the window. I squatted, the way Berbers and little children do, with my feet wrapped in a blanket. In the other corner, standing in a bunch, were the other men.

They looked at me and burst out laughing. As I did not know their language, one of them pointed at me and made the following gesture: he scratched his hair and, as if he had pulled out a louse, made a show of eating it, with the mimetic gestures characteristic of monkeys.

I do not remember whether I had lice. In any case, I have never devoured any. My head was covered with dandruff that formed a crust which I would scrape off with my nail and then knock from my nail with my teeth, and which I sometimes swallowed.

It was at that moment that I understood the room. I realized—for a fraction of a second—its essence. It remained a room, though a prison of the world. I was, through my monstrous horror, exiled to the confines of the obscene (which is the off-scene of the world), facing the graceful pupils of the school of light-fingered theft. I saw clearly ("see," as in the case of Ernestine) what that room and those men were, what role they were *playing*: it was a major role in the march of the world. This role was the origin of the world and at the origin of the world. It seemed to me suddenly, thanks to a kind of extraordinary lucidity, that I understood the system. The world dwindled, and its mystery too, as soon as I was cut off from it. It was a truly supernatural moment, similar, in respect to this detachment from the human, to the one I experienced

when Chief Warrant Officer Cesari, at the Cherche-Midi
Prison, had to write a report on my sexual practices. He
said to me, "That word" (he didn't dare utter the word
"homosexual"), "is it written as two words?" And he
pointed to it on the sheet with his forefinger extended . . .
but not touching the word.

I was ravished.

Like me, Ernestine was ravished by God's Angels, who
are details, meetings, coincidences of the following order:
the toe step or perhaps the meeting place of the thighs of
the ballerina which the smile of a beloved soldier makes
blossom in the hollow of my chest. She held the world between her fingers for a moment and looked at it with the
severity of a schoolmistress.

During the preparation for the last sacrament, Divine
emerged from her coma. On seeing the taper, beacon of
her own end, she quailed. She realized that death had always been present in life, though its symbolic face had
been hidden by a kind of mustache which adjusted its
ghastly reality to current taste—that Frankish mustache
which, once soldierly, now falling from the scissors, made
it look as sheepish as a castrato, for its face at once grew
gentle and delicate, pale, with a tiny chin and rounded
forehead, like the face of a female saint on Romanesque
stained glass or a Byzantine empress, a face we are accustomed to seeing capped with a veiled hennin. Death was
so close that it could touch Divine, could tap at her with
its lean forefinger, as at a door. She clenched her rigid
fingers, tugged at the sheets, which also stiffened, froze.

"But," she said to the priest, "I'm not dead yet. I've
heard the angels farting on the ceiling."

". . . dead yet," she repeated to herself, and in voluptuously swinging, nauseating and, in effect, paradisial
clouds, Divine again sees the dead woman—and the death

of the dead woman—old Adeline of the village, who used to tell him—and Solange—stories about Negroes.

When the old woman (his cousin) died, he was unable to weep, and in order, nevertheless, to make people think that he was deeply grieved, it occurred to him to moisten his dry eyes with saliva. A ball of smoke is rolling in the heart of Divine's belly. Then she feels herself being invaded, as if by seasickness, by the soul of old Adeline, whose high-heeled button shoes Ernestine made her wear to school after the old lady's death.

On the night of the wake, moved by curiosity, Culafroy got up. As he started to tiptoe out of his room, there surged forth from every corner a throng of souls which formed a barrier that he had to cross. He entered into their midst, strong in his hieratic delegation, frightened, thrilled, more dead than alive. The souls, the shades, formed an immense, a numerous cortege, rose up from the beginnings of the world; generations of shades trailed behind him to the deathbed. It was fear. He was walking barefoot, as unsolemnly as possible.

He was advancing as a thief in the night is supposed to advance, perhaps as many a night he had stolen to the closet to steal sugared almonds, almonds that had been given to Ernestine at some baptism or wedding and which he munched with respect, not as a trivial tidbit, but as a sacred food, a symbol of purity, regarding them in the same way he did white wax orange blossoms that lay under a glass globe: a musty smell of incense, a vision of white veils. And that air: the *Veni Creator*.

"What if the woman keeping vigil is at her post? What will she say?" But she was in the kitchen, drinking coffee.

The room was empty. Emptied. Death creates a vacuum otherwise and better than does an air pump. The bed sheets outlined the face in relief, like clay that has barely been touched by the sculptor.

With outstretched hand and rigid arm, Culafroy lifts
the sheets. The corpse was still there. He drew near so as
to be less frightened. He dared touch the face and even
kiss the eyelids, which were as round and icy as agate
marbles. The body seemed fecundated by reality. It was
uttering the truth.

At that moment, the child was invaded, as it were, by a
disorderly troop of memories of readings and stories he
had heard: for example, that the room of Bernadette Soubiroux, at the hour of her death, was full of the scent of invisible violets. He therefore instinctively sniffed, but did
not recognize the odor that is said to be the odor of sancity.
God was forgetting His servant. And a good thing too. In
the first place, you shouldn't waste the scent of flowers on
the bed of a dead old maid; and furthermore, you should
fear to sow panic in the souls of children.

But that moment seems to have been the starting point
of the thread that was to lead Culafroy-Divine, in accordance with a superlatively devised fatality, to death. The
tentative groping had begun long before. The preliminary
investigation, which had been carried on at first in the
wonderment arising at the first replies, dated from remote,
misty, opaque ages, when he belonged to the people of
the gods, exactly like the primitives, who have not yet
been unswaddled of their urine-scented wrappings and
who possess the dignity—which they share with children
and certain animals—the gravity, and the nobility that are
rightly called ancient. Now—and increasingly so, until the
attainment of the exactly poetic vision of the world—
knowledge having been acquired, the swaddling clothes
were thrust aside. As each questioning, each sounding,
rendered a more and more hollow sound, it indicated
death, which is the only reality that satisfies us wholly.

Gone was the joyous rebound upon contact with objects. At each touch, his blindly scrutinizing little finger

plunged into emptiness. Doors turned by themselves and revealed nothing. He kissed the old lady on the eyes, and the snakelike iciness froze him. He was about to reel, perhaps fall, when the Memory came to his rescue: the memory of Alberto's corduroy pants. As a man who, through some unexpected privilege, has caught a glimpse of the very heart of the mysteries, quickly looks away so as to regain his footing on earth, so the terror-stricken Culafroy flung himself, burying his head, into the warm, enveloping memory of Alberto's trousers, where he thought to find, to his relief, comforting broods of titmice.

Then, borne by Alberto, who had come down from heaven, he went back to his room and to bed, where he wept. But—and don't let this surprise you—he wept at being unable to weep.

Here is how our Great Divine died.

Having looked for her little gold watch, she found it between her thighs and, with her fist closed over it, handed it to Ernestine, who was sitting at her bedside. Their two hands met in the form of a shell with the watch in the middle. A vast physical peace relaxed Divine. Filth, an almost liquid shit, spread out beneath her like a warm little lake, into which she gently, very gently—as the vessel of a hopeless emperor sinks, still warm, into the waters of Lake Nemi—was engulfed, and with this relief she heaved another sigh, which rose to her mouth with blood, then another sigh, the last.

Thus did she pass away, one might also say drowned.

Ernestine was waiting. Suddenly, by some miracle, she realized that the throbbing of their joined hands was the ticking of the watch.

Because she lived among omens and signs, she was not superstitious. She therefore laid out the corpse all by herself and dressed Divine in a very modest blue cheviot suit of English cut.

So here she is dead. The Quite-Dead. Her body is caught in the sheets. It is, from head to foot, forever a ship in the breaking-up of ice-floes, motionless and rigid, drifting toward infinity: you, Jean, dear heart, motionless and rigid, as I have already said, drifting on my bed to a happy Eternity.

And with Divine dead, what is left for me to do? To say?

This evening, the poplars, of which I see only the tops, are being cruelly dashed together by an angry wind. My cell, lulled by that kindly death, is so sweet today!

What if I were free tomorrow?

(Tomorrow is the day of the hearing.)

Free, in other words, exiled among the living. I have made myself a soul to fit my dwelling. My cell is so sweet. Free: to drink wine, to smoke, to see ordinary people. And tomorrow, what will the jury be like? I have anticipated the stiffest possible sentence it can inflict. I have prepared myself for it with great care, for I have chosen my horoscope (according to what I can read of it from past events) as a figure of fatality. Now that I can obey it, my grief is less great. It is annihilated in the face of the irremediable. It is my hopelessness, and what will be, will be. I have given up my desires. I too am "already far beyond that" (Weidmann). Let me therefore live between these walls for a man's lifetime. Who will be judged tomorrow? Some stranger bearing a name that was once my name. I can continue to die, until my death, amidst all these widowers. Lamp, washbasin, regulations, broom. And the straw mattress, my spouse.

I do not feel like going to sleep. Tomorrow's hearing is a solemnity that requires a vigil. It is this evening that I should like to weep—as one who stays behind—for my farewells. But my lucidity is like a nakedness. The wind outside is getting wilder and wilder and is being joined

by the rain. The elements are thus a prelude to tomorrow's
ceremonies. Today is the 12th, isn't it? What shall I decide? Warnings are said to come from God. They don't
interest me. I already feel that I no longer belong to the
prison. Broken is the exhausting fraternity that bound me
to the men of the tomb. Perhaps I shall live. . . .

At times I am shaken with a burst of brutal and unac-
countable laughter. It resounds within me like a joyous
cry in the fog, which it seems to be trying to dissipate, but
it leaves no trace other than a wistful longing for sun and
gaiety.

What if I am condemned? I shall don homespun again,
and this rust-colored garment will immediately entail the
monastic gesture: hiding my hands in my sleeves; and the
equivalent attitude of mind will follow: I shall feel myself
becoming humble and glorious; then, snug under my
blankets—it is in *Don Juan* that the characters come back
to life on the stage and kiss each other—I shall, for the enchantment of my cell, refashion lovely new lives for Darling, Divine, Our Lady and Gabriel.

I have read moving letters, full of wonderful touches, of
despair, of hopes, of songs; and others more severe. I am
choosing from among them one which will be the letter
Darling wrote to Divine from prison:

"Dearest,
I'm writing a few lines to give you the news, which isn't
good. I've been arrested for stealing. So try to get a lawyer
to handle my case. Arrange to pay him. And also arrange
to send me a money order, because you know how lousy
things are here. Also try to get permission to come and see
me and bring me some linens. Put in the blue and white
silk pajamas. And some undershirts. Dearest, I'm awfully
sorry about what's happened to me. Let's face it, I'm plain

unlucky. So I'm counting on you to help me out. I only wish I could have you in my arms so I could hold you and squeeze you tight. Remember the things we used to do together. Try to recognize the dotted lines. And kiss it. A thousand big kisses, sweetheart, from

Your Darling."

The dotted line that Darling refers to is the outline of his prick. I once saw a pimp who had a hard-on while writing to his girl place his heavy cock on the paper and trace its contours. I would like that line to portray Darling.

Fresnes Prison, 1942

Made in the USA
Lexington, KY
24 October 2012